THE WITCHFINDER

THE
WITCH
FINDER

A DEIPARIAN SAGA NOVEL

J. TODD KINGREA

bhc
press™

Livonia, Michigan

Editor: Chelsea Cambeis
Proofreader: Hannah Ryder

THE WITCHFINDER

Published by BHC Press

Library of Congress Control Number: 2020937787

ISBN: 978-1-64397-236-7 (Hardcover)
ISBN: 978-1-64397-237-4 (Softcover)
ISBN: 978-1-64397-238-1 (Ebook)

For information, write:
BHC Press
885 Penniman #5505
Plymouth, MI 48170

Visit the publisher:
www.bhcpress.com

To my sons, Brett and Matthew

I am proud to be your dad.

THE WITCHFINDER

1
TEKOYA

A beautiful day for the salvation of souls dawned. The sun blazed bright but not unduly hot—unusual for this time of year—and a soft breeze whispered like a new mother's prayer. The miserable summer winds would soon arrive, humid and prickly. But today's promised comfort, a welcome change from winter's frigid gusts. The birds took advantage of it, wheeling and gliding across a sky that would soon be blackened with the smoke of burning bodies.

Witchfinder Imperator Malachi Thorne sat beneath the awning of the grandstand and looked out over the crowd in Talnat's main square. Congregants jostled one another for better views, some with small children perched on their shoulders. Others gossiped, shared bawdy jokes or purchased gingerbread and custard cups from the vendors around the square. An acrobat on stilts entertained giggling children. Clots of men hooted and jeered at the prisoners lined up before the grandstand, commonly known as the Judgment Seat, on the northern end of the square.

The wealthy filled the balconies that jutted from buildings like crooked teeth, where they could enjoy the tekoya without having to mix with the sweaty crowds below. Handsome sums exchanged hands to be waited on by servants and savor the spectacle from the luxury of padded couches and leather chairs. They placed bets on how long it would take a heretic to scream once the fire took hold or before a hanged man stopped jerking.

Thorne smiled as he absorbed the perfect day—his favorite day: a viridian-streaked sky, the succulent aroma of kebobs over coals, the colorful banners of the Four Orders undulating in the breeze, the infectious tune of a minstrel band.

And four souls that would find eternal release from the corruption that had lured them from the Church's embrace. Four crimson stakes, like the bloodied talons of a demon from the Twelve Planes, stood in a diamond pattern in the center of the square. Men piled wood and straw around each one.

Behind him, Talnat city officials talked softly about the tekoya—the epitome of the Church's order and law. Its formality was reassuring, the purpose unquestionable.

"Good morning, Malachi," Constable Thurl Cabbott said as he approached the cathedra. He wore wine-colored leather armor and a matching cape, held in place by the diamond-shaped pin worn by all ranking Church servants. His black breeches fit snugly into worn black boots. Sharp blue eyes lined with wrinkles looked up at Thorne. "So how many does this make for you?" He gestured toward the prisoners.

"Dario tells me two hundred."

Cabbott whistled. "That's a lot of heretics in only three years' time."

Thorne traced his raven-black mustache and goatee with thumb and forefinger. "Souls, Thurl," he corrected. "Their words and deeds may have turned them into heretics, but the Church released them from that. Their souls have been purified."

"How many of those were involved in the Communion?"

He shook his head, ponytail swaying. "That I don't know. You'd have to ask Dario."

"You should be proud, Malachi. That's quite a feat for the youngest Imperator in history." Cabbott scratched at his gray-streaked beard. "Merrick would've been proud of you."

The familiar pang of guilt and grief pricked Thorne's chest at the mention of his mentor's name. He tried to keep it from showing on his face.

The two men watched the square in silence for a moment. Acrobats and jesters cavorted to the applause of children. Behind the grandstand, a dog barked.

"Beautiful day," Thorne said, awkwardly changing the subject.

"That it is. Wish I'd had one like this on my last day off."

"Am I still giving you days off?" Thorne glanced at the constable with a lighthearted gleam in his eyes.

"Not enough. I'm getting to be an old man. I should have more free time."

"You're not getting old." Though Cabbott's widening circle of visible scalp begged to differ.

"I'm nearly a quarter century older than you."

Thorne smiled. "And still able to run circles around your two deputies."

"Yeah, but all that running makes me tired. I should have more free time—you know, to rest."

In the square, the preparations were complete. Deputies maintained a clean perimeter around the edge of the crowd. As the sun climbed higher, it glinted off the twisted steel towers of Old Talnat. Gaping holes revealed rows of vacant floors and debris. Structural beams poked out like the broken ribs of an animal carcass.

Talnat—or Atlanta as some claimed it was once named—like most major towns, still possessed these crumbling relics of its former life. Before the Great Cataclysm, they had been called "skyscrapers." To Thorne, they represented tombstones more than towers—symbols of humanity's frailty and hubris. Extremely unsafe and suffused with a nagging sense of dread, few birds chose to nest among the ruins. Even wild dogs shunned them. They testified to a lost and dead world where the Church said too much personal choice had led to destruction.

"We're ready to begin, Your Grace," the Bishop of Talnat said as he stepped into Thorne's line of sight. He wore the traditional blue cassock and white cope of the Kyrian Order. His face seemed too small beneath the upturned brim of his domed hat.

Thorne nodded and sat up straighter on the worn cushion. The unforgiving wood pressed against his back like half an iron maiden.

A sleepy-looking clerk with spidery fingers, dressed in the white-and-gold robes of the Cartulian Order, sat to Thorne's left. He laid out several quills and a stack of parchment, uncorked a bottle of ink and nodded at Thorne, who gestured for the bishop to proceed.

In front of the grandstand, two trumpeters played a fanfare that echoed off the surrounding buildings. Laughter and conversation stopped. Vendors finalized their sales. The band put down their instruments. Only the tattle of birds along the rooftops defied the silence.

"By the will of Heiromonarch Dobrin Kristur," the bishop said in a strong, mellifluous voice, "according to the laws by which we live and in the name of the Divine Church in whom we have our being, let it be recorded that the Talnat tekoya of May 22nd, 999, Apocalypse Era hereby begins."

The trumpeters replayed the fanfare. Whooping and hollering and a smattering of applause rippled through the crowd.

Tang Tien Qui, the short and officious Witchfinder of Talnat, tugged at his scarlet surcoat as he stepped to the front. His cape, capotain hat, tunic and breeches—all black—were identical to Thorne's. He made a show of adjusting his rank pin, and Thorne rolled his eyes.

"Congregants of Talnat." Qui's voice was higher than the bishop's but bore the same authority and ceremony. "We are gathered here today because the laws of the Divine Church—as defined by the sacred Testament—have been broken.

The offenders must be punished, or else chaos and darkness will swallow us as it did our forebears over a thousand years ago, when the moon fell to Earth and the land turned against us.

"Out of that time of lawlessness and barbarism, our ancestors forged the order and society we enjoy today. They established and maintained the foundation of law. We must likewise maintain that which has been entrusted to us, for the sake of future generations who will love and serve the Church."

Qui paused before proclaiming, "The Church is generous."

The crowd responded, "The Church is generous."

"The Church is compassionate."

A single voice of unified hundreds repeated the phrase.

"The Church is God."

Again the repetition.

"Let us now declare the Four Tenants of the Church," Qui said, gesturing toward the banners of each Order.

The single word embroidered in bold letters on each was stated in unison: "Faith. Wisdom. Obedience. Loyalty."

"This tekoya is carried out by the authority of the Church through its official representative—His Grace, Master Malachi Thorne, Witchfinder Imperator of the Paracletian Order. Let all that transpires here today be recorded for the salvation of our souls, according to the grace of the Church. Amen."

"Amen," the crowd repeated. They signed themselves with the symbol of the Church—the fingertips of one hand to the forehead, down to the left shoulder, to the middle of the chest and up to the right shoulder—in one smooth motion. Some jokingly referred to it as "quartering" oneself, but only when no Churchmen were within earshot.

Qui and the bishop sat down behind the cathedra.

Thorne walked to the edge of the grandstand. The square smelled of freshly cut wood, warm bread and unwashed bodies. Somewhere among the crowd, a dog barked twice. Placing his hands on the railing, he looked into the variegated cyan sky. His gaze lowered to take in the brooding stone buildings, the silent sentinels of untold tekoyas. He wondered if the prisoners realized what a blessing it was for their souls to be saved on such a beautiful day as this. Finally, he scanned the sea of faces.

"Before us today," Thorne said, his sonorous voice in sharp contrast to that of Qui and the bishop, "stand four who have been found guilty of crimes against the community and our God, the Divine Church. Because they have committed the capital offenses of witchcraft and heresy, their four bentanni will be hung in the Talnat Cathedral as a reminder of their shame and guilt. These bentanni will remain on display until the family of each prisoner has passed the fourth generation, beginning today."

He fixed his gaze on the four prisoners lined up before the Judgment Seat. "May the Church have mercy on your souls. Bring forth the heretic Barnabas Kordell."

Two deputies ushered a stout black man toward the dock before the grandstand. He limped, and his shaved head gleamed in the sunlight as he climbed the four narrow stairs to the platform.

Like all heretics, he wore the bentanni, a yellow shift with red and orange cloth flames sewn around the hem. The flames rose to the waistline, and above them, encircling the torso, gruesomely painted demons and devils cavorted. But unlike most heretics, who by this point were reduced to fits of wailing or pleading, Kordell stood tall in the dock. He rested his manacled hands on the railing that encompassed three sides of the platform.

"Barnabas Kordell, the courts of the Paracletian Order have found you guilty of heresy. Evidence has been brought against you and verified. You have confessed to this crime while in the presence of a cleric and a lawyer. Do you have anything to say before sentence is carried out?"

Kordell stared coldly up at him with his remaining eye and squared his shoulders. He'd displayed a profound tolerance for pain and had endured much at the hands of the torturer but refused to recant his treasonous teachings or divulge his associates. It was surprising Kordell could stand at all, much less walk. Harsh imprisonment and torture made him look nearly twice his forty-four years, yet he displayed no contrition or meekness.

"You wish me to admit that I've undermined the authority of the Church with unorthodox teaching. You want me to grovel and say there's no path other than that offered by the Church. You want a faithful penitent, cowed by threats and fear, broken by your system—"

"That's enough!"

"—convinced there is no freedom outside the Church." Kordell's voice grew louder. "But I will not!"

"Silence!" Thorne slammed his hands on the railing and leaned forward. "Deputies!"

Kordell pivoted so he faced the crowded square. "Friends! There *is* a better way! And Traugott knows. He speaks of it—and *many* are listening!"

Two deputies neared the dock.

"Listen to Traugott!" he bellowed. "It's not heresy he speaks, but *freedom* and *choice*!"

Somewhere in the crowd, a dog barked three times.

Kordell collapsed as if he were a child's marionette whose strings had been cut.

The deputies paused as they reached the steps, eyes widening, confusion etched across their faces. They looked down. An arrow shaft protruded from each of their chests. Blood seeped onto their wine-colored leather armor. Realization dawned, and they lurched against each other before toppling to the ground where they lay unmoving.

From somewhere in the crowd, a flaming torch arced through the air. Several others followed from different locations.

Thorne gripped the railing. "What in the Twelve Planes—"

The torches plummeted into the crowd. People screamed and shoved as bits of clothing caught fire. A few tried to extinguish the flames, but the majority scattered in a maelstrom of colliding bodies and flailing limbs. The performer on stilts collapsed into a cart of jellied candies. Children snatched and grabbed as parents yanked them to safety.

Deputies tried to maintain order but were too few in number. They bobbed among the people like corks in boiling water.

The pounding of horse's hooves sounded above the din.

"Constables, secure this crowd!" Thorne roared. That they probably didn't hear him—couldn't hear him through the chaos—only enraged him further.

In the dock, Kordell leapt to his feet and descended the stairs as quickly as his manacled ankles allowed.

A vendor's stand erupted in flame, scattering those nearby in all directions.

"Damn it! He's getting away!" Thorne said through clenched teeth.

Qui and Cabbott sprinted toward the dock.

Three horses burst through the crowd on the eastern side of the square. They appeared to be panicked by the noise and confusion.

The overtaxed deputies attempted to restore order but clearly didn't know whether to put out the fires or keep people from trampling each other. Meanwhile, looters scampered away with their hands full.

Two of the horses raced into the center of the square. The third veered toward a wagon loaded with wood and straw parked just south of the stakes. Smoke plumed from several locations.

Below, Kordell stumbled as his feet hit the ground but maintained his balance. The two horses bore down on him. Qui closed in on the prisoner but then collided with a pair of looters. All three crashed to the ground as pies and sausages flew into the air.

The bishop leaned over the grandstand railing, taking in the pandemonium with bulging eyes. "Horses don't run *toward* fire…"

"What?" Thorne yelled, shooting him a sideways glance.

"Those horses." The older man pointed. "Something's not right about them."
Both horses slowed as they reached the dock.

The truth hit Thorne like a punch.

Each horse carried a bareback rider hanging low and snug to the horse's far side. A black roan halted in front of the dock, a brown one behind it. Both riders wore garments that matched their mount's coloring. The brown horse's rider hauled himself upright by the mane. With his other hand, he hoisted Kordell up behind him. The prisoner flopped on his stomach, feet kicking the air like a beached fish.

The horseman in front of the dock righted himself and leveled a crossbow at the grandstand.

Qui was on his feet again. More deputies converged on the square, halberds and sabers clattering.

The black horse's rider fired the crossbow toward Thorne.

"Bolt!" Thorne yanked the bishop down with him. The projectile zipped over their heads and gashed a hole through the canvas behind them.

Both horses galloped toward the southern end of the square as townspeople scampered out of the way. Thorne peered over the railing, then leapt to his feet. He grabbed a crossbow from the corner of the grandstand. "Damn, damn, damn!"

Kordell bounced like a sack of wheat as the horses raced past the fuel wagon. The third rider threw a torch into the wagon. Flames caught the wood and straw. Smoke blanketed the square with a grimy haze. Deputies chased on foot, while others grabbed horses of their own.

"Son of a—" Thorne cursed under his breath as he sighted down the length of the crossbow. He exhaled, squeezed the trigger, felt the crossbow kick. The bolt sailed into the smoke and flames. He watched through the shimmering heat as the escapees disappeared down a side street. He ground his teeth together and flung the crossbow into the square.

"Damn it!" He twisted around and shoved the cathedra aside. The clerk recoiled. City officials cowered. Thorne bared his teeth and glared at the bishop, who was picking himself off the floor. "Find me the Chief Constable—*now!*" He stomped through the grandstand. "And have that runt, Qui, up here by the time I get back." He took the stairs two at a time.

A few congregants lingered, waiting for what might happen next. For a moment, Thorne thought he heard laughter and cheering from somewhere. The sound turned his stomach.

He'd heard of dissention in other places. Reports came to the Church with troublesome and increasing frequency, telling of congregants who spouted dangerous ideas and created disturbances. But Thorne hadn't heard of any that were so brazen as to attack a tekoya. Until now. He snarled—face flushed, fists clenched—as he stormed into the square, shouting instructions to the deputies. People drifted back to the perimeter of the square. All of the fires were extinguished except for the fuel wagon, which was now a bonfire on wheels.

"Find those archers!" Thorne demanded, pointing at the two corpses lying by the dock. "Arrest whoever threw those torches! And secure this area *immediately!*"

Deputies scattered from the Witchfinder's intimidating six-and-a-half-foot presence. Thorne put his hands on his hips and glared around at the results of the bedlam.

A deputy hauled the remaining prisoners off the ground. They had attempted to flee but forgot they were manacled together. They didn't bother to hide their pleasure as the guard led them away.

Cabbott approached, breathing hard, his face streaked with soot and perspiration.

"Well?" Thorne snapped.

The constable shook his head and exhaled. "Qui's got men...after them."

"I want to know who shot those deputies."

"I'll pull a team together. We'll go through...every building. We'll also check witnesses. Maybe somebody saw someone with a bow."

"I want statements from every person on those balconies." Thorne gestured around the square. "Get these buildings closed down. Search every room and roof overlooking this square."

"Like a whore checking for disease. I get it."

Two mounted deputies barreled up and reined to a halt before Thorne and Cabbott, adding more dust to the cloudy air. Both looked as if they would rather be doing most anything else.

"No luck, m'Lord," one said. "Those streets are a maze—"

"But we still got men looking for 'em," the other added quickly upon seeing Thorne's eyes narrow into slits of emerald fire.

"It might be a maze," Thorne growled, "but those riders obviously know their way through it. And you work here, do you not? You know these streets."

"Aye, we do," the first one replied. He pointed behind him. "But in that part of town, the streets turn all over the place, and they got dead ends aplenty."

The second one nodded. "That's what we're trying to tell you, my Lord. It's such a warren of alleys an' dead ends, only someone familiar with 'em—"

"Local help," Cabbott spat.

"Yes, sir," the deputy replied. "At least one of them riders—maybe all of 'em—must be from Talnat."

Thorne nodded. At least it was a start. "How many roads lead out of there?"

The deputies glanced at each other. "Probably fifteen or twenty, at least," the second offered.

Thorne nodded again and folded his arms. "Get back to your search. Cover as many exits as you can. Report to me directly when you have something."

Both turned and galloped away.

Cabbott studied the buildings. Thorne knew the constable's mind was working feverishly, estimating an arrow's flight distance, trajectories and where potential clues or evidence might be found.

"Have someone remove the bodies." Thorne ran a hand over his hair. It was warm, verging on hot, from the bright sun.

Cabbott motioned several men to join him but turned briefly to acknowledge Thorne's command.

Thorne looked around as he retied his ponytail. Order slowly returned to the square. "I'm going back to wait for Qui and Constable Kefflen," he said. "See that some of the other constables get this area cordoned off. It's a crime scene, and it's already been ruined. We'll probably come across a purple bull with wings in this mess quicker than we'll find a decent clue."

Cabbott nodded and went back to giving orders.

2

MISTAKE

FRIDAY, MAY 22, 999 AE

Night settled upon Talnat like a lover slipping into bed. In the common room of the Cup & Swords, Thorne took another drink of wine and rubbed his temples. The headache had started earlier in the day as he'd dashed from one interrogation to other.

What's wrong with people? he wondered. Why did they rebel against the benevolence of the Church? Why risk their immortal souls for false teaching and witchcraft?

He ate the last potato on his plate and tore off a piece of bread. It was the first food he'd had since breakfast.

It had to be the millennium. People were naturally anxious about it. They didn't know what to expect. There was more spiritual fervor of late, but not all of it would draw people closer to the Church. Some of it—as the past few months of work had shown him—sent people into ecstasy, madness and blatant rebellion. He shook his head and emptied his wine glass. *They're afraid of another Great Cataclysm.*

According to the Storicos, the erudite historians of the Church, humanity had barely survived when chunks of the moon smashed into Earth. Those impacts set off a chain reaction of natural disasters. The Storicos claimed that "the folly of humanity"—weapons of unimaginable scope and power—were then triggered and laid waste to much of the world. Whether those weapons had been triggered intentionally or by accident was a question lost to history.

The tavern door opened to admit Dario Darien, a middle-aged man wearing a white tunic that contrasted with his charcoal skin. A gold sash hung over his left shoulder, and a wide belt encircled his waist.

"How are you, Dario?"

"Tired, like you," he replied with a weak smile, "and more than ready to get out of this damnable town." He sat down, pulling a pipe and tobacco bag from one of the many pouches on his belt. As he filled the pipe, the mellow aroma mixed with the earthy goodness of the room. He struck a match and puffed.

Thorne chewed his last piece of bread. "Did you get to see your sister yesterday?"

Darien nodded. "We had dinner together."

"Anything new with Jairus's case?"

A look of disdain crossed Darien's face. "Nothing, Malachi. She said the *authorities*"—he pronounced the word contemptuously—"still claim it was a bandit attack. An ordinary robbery. They think Jairus tried to fight them off and was killed in the process."

Thorne leaned forward, elbows on the table. "What about his broken back?"

Darien shook his head, causing the dim light to wink off the silver rings in both his ears. "They think it happened during the fight. Either that or maybe he got stepped on by a horse…"

"Except that his body had no hoof prints on it. Did any known bandits work the area he traveled through?"

Darien puffed on his pipe, the smoke creating ethereal dancers who gave a single performance before vanishing above his stiff black hair. "No, they're going with the theory that it was a nomadic group passing through. But that's nonsense. Jairus still had his stonecutting tools, his wagon and horse—hells, even his belt pouch—on him." He sent another stream of smoke into the air. "The authorities in this place couldn't find a cowhide in a tanner's shop."

"How's your sister doing?"

Darien shook his head again. "Demerra's still numb even though it's been two months. Though she did seem, well…*paranoid* is the word I'd use. She says she feels as if someone is watching her—following her."

Thorne raised his eyebrows. "Does she suspect anyone? Did you see anything?"

"No, no. I kept a close eye on everything while we were together. I didn't see anyone or anything that made me the least bit concerned. I think her grief may be manifesting that way."

Thorne sat back in his chair. "Well, as soon as we find Kordell and see him executed, you and I are going to get to the bottom of this."

Darien was about to reply when the door opened again. Thurl Cabbott tromped in, followed by Tycho Hawkes and Solomon Warner, the two deputies assigned to apprentice under him. They were dressed in the standard issue leather armor, breeches and boots. Sabers hung at their sides. Their faces drooped, and they all went straight to the bar.

At a table by the front window, four men stopped their quiet conversation and stared at the newcomers before returning to their drinks.

The sullen barkeep pulled three tankards of ale and thumped them down, sloshing foam down the sides. Cabbott sat down with Thorne and Darien. Hawkes and Warner pulled chairs from neighboring tables and joined them.

"What's with him?" Hawkes asked, jabbing a thumb at the bartender. "Looks like he could shit a horseshoe."

"I'm afraid he's not very happy with me," Thorne replied.

Cabbott smirked. "In this town tonight, he's not the only one."

"The place was full when I arrived. I barely sat down before it cleared out." He gestured toward the table by the window. "They're the only ones who stayed."

"Boss, you done screwed up a Friday night at the tavern!" Warner squinted his one good eye—the other was covered with a black leather patch—and laughed, clear and musical. He was the shortest man at the table but stout as an anvil, with skin black as midnight.

"Well, I'm going to screw it up even more." Thorne stood up and motioned toward the window. "You men at the table—"

Once more, the four faces turned toward the center of the room, their exasperation beginning to show.

"I need you to leave the tavern. Now. Church business." Thorne pointed toward the door.

They stared at him for a moment before getting up and tossing coins on the table. The bartender grumbled under his breath.

"You too, barkeep."

Still complaining to himself, he followed his customers outside.

"Tycho, make sure there's no one else in the kitchen," Cabbott said.

"Yes, sir." The thin-framed deputy moved fluidly around the bar and disappeared into the back room.

"Solomon, check upstairs. If you find anyone, escort them outside."

"You got it, Boss." The deputy took the worn wooden stairs beside the bar two at a time. His footsteps thudded overhead.

Hawkes returned. "All clear."

Thorne held up a hand to him. "Tycho, stay there, behind the bar—"

"No complaints from me." Hawkes shot him a wide grin.

"—and make sure no one comes in through the back."

The deputy leaned against a kitchen doorframe festooned with dangling strands of dried herbs. His red hair hung loosely around his shoulders—his off-duty look.

"Dario, did you send the messages?" Thorne asked.

Darien nodded. "I arranged for a redvalk to fly south to Colobos with your orders to send out search parties to intercept Kordell. I also sent a 'valk to Attagon, informing the Paracletian Council about today's events."

Cabbott emptied his mug of ale as Warner returned.

"Solomon, stay by the door," Thorne said, then turned to Cabbott. "What've you found out?"

The constable leaned back in his chair and crossed his arms. Narrow, squinty eyes hinted at a lifetime spent scrutinizing people and evidence. "Well, the locals are interviewing every witness we've got. The jail's overflowing with them."

"I don't care if every man in this city has to work all night long."

"Speaking of 'every man'—extra deputies have also been recruited from some of the outlying villages."

"What of the escapees?" Thorne asked.

"Qui's got several parties scouring the southern roads. They've been at it ever since the escape. Might well be the biggest manhunt in Talnat history."

"But no news." Darien finished his pipe and cleaned the bowl with a penknife.

Thorne ran his finger along a groove in the tabletop. "And the arrows?"

Cabbott and Darien shook their heads.

"Nothing unusual," Darien replied, tucking the knife and pipe into his belt.

"Standard longbow arrows. Could've been made or bought anywhere. Nothing special about the fletching or the heads, no craftsman's mark," Cabbott said. "And no, we didn't find the bows either. I know that's your next question."

"There were about two dozen vantage points where the archers could've been," Hawkes said, leaning on the bar now to be closer to the conversation.

"So unless they disposed of the bows extremely well," Darien added, "we have to assume they took them."

Thorne gritted his teeth. "Does anybody have anything useful to report? What about witnesses?"

"Nothin', Boss," Warner said. "All anybody could remember was people runnin' and yellin'. Just confusion and craziness. I mean, people saw the riders, but in all that mess…well, nobody got a good enough look to be able to identify anybody."

Thorne shook his head in exasperation. "Two deputies assassinated," he said, more to himself than his companions. "When was the last time a Church official was murdered during a tekoya?"

Darien shrugged his narrow shoulders. "I honestly have no idea, Malachi. A very long time ago, I'm sure. I'd have to check Church records in Attagon to know for certain."

Rarely did Dario Darien fail to have the correct facts or data available. Many times, he'd produced the exact testimony or piece of information Thorne needed at a critical moment. Darien was conscientious and loyal, with a love of history, a quick hand and quicker mind.

"I'd focus on those riders. They were skilled horsemen. Trick riders." Cabbott ran his tongue across his upper teeth. "Maybe there's a carnival nearby?"

Hawkes interrupted: "I saw plenty of trick riders like that growing up in the traveling fairs."

"That's not a bad idea," Darien said.

"There probably aren't a lot of trained equestrians like that around," Thorne said. "Remind me to ask Qui about that."

Someone rapped on the tavern door.

"Who's there?" Warner shouted through the wood. If an answer came, the other men didn't hear the reply.

"Well, well," Warner said before opening the door.

Tang Tien Qui stepped inside.

The Talnat Witchfinder was Ahzin, a tribe of people from before the Great Cataclysm—or so the Storicos claimed. Some said the Ahzin came from the other side of the world, but most serious-minded folks knew that nothing lay beyond the Eastern Ocean or the Devouring Lands to the west. Qui carried himself proudly despite being even shorter than Warner. His black hair lay flat but thick against his scalp and was nearly shaven on the sides. He wore no facial hair at all.

"Come, join us, Qui," Thorne said with more congeniality than he felt. The wine had done nothing to help his headache.

Darien stood up and drew another chair to the already overcrowded table.

Qui's shoulders slumped as he moved toward the table. His almond-shaped dark brown eyes were weak and watery. The confident, even pompous quality that Thorne had come to know vanished.

"Master Thorne," Qui began as he sat down, "I have to—"

"Tell me something," Thorne interrupted. "Do you know of any trained equestrians in the area? We've been discussing the horsemen and… Qui, what's wrong, man?"

Qui stared at the tabletop as if it weren't there. "Equestrians…?" He looked up as if coming out of a trance. "Yes, yes. There are a few people in this region who teach riding." His voice sounded like his eyes looked.

"Any carnivals or fairs nearby?" Hawkes asked.

Qui shook his head.

"Something's troubling you," Darien said.

Cabbott grunted. "This morning—that's what's bothering him. Hells, the whole day, in fact!"

Qui ignored Cabbott's bait. "We found one…" His gaze dropped to the table once more.

"What?" Thorne asked, leaning forward.

"We found one. We have one."

"One what?" Cabbott pressed.

Qui cleared his throat. "We found one of the accomplices from this morning's…events. One of the torch-throwers. He was part of the distraction so that the escape attempt would have a better chance of success."

"Excellent!" A wolfish grin spread across Thorne's face. "Finally something we can use! Now we are getting somewhere."

"No, wait." Qui raised a thin-fingered hand. He sighed miserably. "There's no easy way to say this, and I take full responsibility…" He reached into the pocket of his surcoat and pulled out the heavy, diamond-shaped rank pin.

"Responsibility for what?" Darien asked, sounding curious but gentle.

Qui laid the pin on the table and slid it toward Thorne, then straightened his shoulders and raised his head to face Thorne's gaze and rapidly disappearing smile.

"Explain," Thorne demanded.

"Master Malachi Thorne," Qui said, his accustomed formality reasserting itself. "It's my duty as Witchfinder of Talnat—"

"Get on with it, man!"

Qui licked his thin lips. "The man we captured, his name is Dugart Newman. During his interrogation today, he revealed the identity of Traugott's second-in-command."

"That's good," Thorne said, brightening at the news. "Very good!" He placed his elbows on the table and tapped his fingertips together in front of him. Perhaps he could salvage this mess after all. "What does he know about this second-in-command?"

"He knows…that he escaped."

Thorne frowned. "What do you mean by that?"

Cabbott bit his lip. "Oh damn…"

Qui looked at him and nodded. Ice formed in Thorne's stomach.

Qui closed his eyes. "Traugott's second-in-command is…Barnabas Kordell."

Cabbott exhaled loudly. The room fell silent. Warner shattered it with a low, prolonged whistle of surprise.

"Let me make sure I understand this clearly," Thorne said. "You are saying that the man who escaped from my tekoya today—Barnabas Kordell—is Traugott's right-hand man?" Calm and measured, the Witchfinder snapped each word into bite-sized pieces.

Darien and Cabbott exchanged glances.

The three had been together for so long—Darien with him for ten years, Cabbott for eight of those—that they understood the nuances of each other's speech and mannerisms. They knew this meant Thorne was barely holding his anger in check.

"That is correct, Master Thorne. As I said, I take full—"

Thorne shot out of his chair, fists clenched. "How could you have him in custody, under torture, and not discover his identity?"

Qui sat like a statue, looking at the far side of the room and the blackened fireplace there. A muscle in his cheek twitched.

"Damn it!" Thorne paced the floor. In mid-stride, he turned, bolted to the table and slammed his fist down. Cups and plates jumped and rattled. Qui flinched but didn't say anything. "You tell me," Thorne snarled through bared teeth, "how this happened." His headache raged behind his temples.

Qui swallowed and tried to sound unfazed, but his voice betrayed him. "As you know, Your Grace, Kordell was subjected to the Ordeal as required. He endured up to and through the Fourth Degree. At that point, the attending physician, the lawyer and I determined that Kordell could go no further without severe risk to his life. And I would point out"—Qui hesitated—"that you were present for several of the sessions. I don't recall *you* discerning any more than anyone else did."

Hawkes drew in a breath, and Warner shook his head and looked at the floor to avoid whatever came next.

Thorne's lips peeled back from his clenched teeth. He glared at Qui. He knew his failure all too well, and he'd be damned if this pretentious jackass would hang Kordell's interrogations around his neck, too. The urge to throttle Qui intensified.

"Gentlemen…" Darien interjected in a clear attempt to diffuse the boiling tension. He looked from Thorne to Qui. "Master Qui, in all the time Kordell was in custody, did he ever admit to being in league with Traugott?"

"No. He confessed to heretical beliefs against the Church but never mentioned Traugott," Qui replied, a bit more composed now.

"Did you *ask* the damn fool if he was working with Traugott? Or if he *knew* Traugott?" Cabbott asked.

Qui shook his head. "We convicted him based on his confession of seeking to undermine the Church. We had the evidence and the confession. We didn't—*I didn't*—look beyond that. As I said, the error and responsibility are mine alone."

Thorne slammed his fist against the tabletop again. His cheeks flushed with anger, Qui's with shame. Then he picked up the heavy silver pin and flung it against Qui's chest.

"You're not getting off that easily, Qui," he said with the same barely controlled, clipped tone. "You are going to get out there and find Kordell. And you aren't going to rest until you do. I don't care if you have to call in help from Last Chapel on the other side of the realm. You are going to fix this."

"What—what if I can't find him?" Qui asked.

Thorne couldn't imagine a stupider thing to ask. He leaned closer, a predator intimidating its prey. "Oh, you *will* find him. Because if you don't, I will personally throw you into the Wheel and crank it until you're nothing but meat scraps fit for the dogs. Now get out of here." Thorne turned his back on the table and stomped to the fireplace. He stared at the two rusty, pitted swords that hung above the mantle as Qui hurried from the room like a scolded dog.

A moment later, Darien broke the silence. "What do we do now?" It was a question for no one in particular, and it hung in the air too long.

Thorne crossed his arms, his eyes now glued to a point above Darien's head. Hawkes shuffled around behind the bar before approaching the table with a tray carrying three wooden cups and a pitcher. He sat it down, returned to the bar and delivered a cup to Warner.

"You ever think about becomin' a tavern wench?" Warner asked him.

"Shut up, Sol."

"I'm jus' sayin', the way you carried that tray…"

"Solomon, I swear by the Church—"

"Get you some boobs—ya already got the long hair—and you could make some money on the side." Warner grinned into his cup.

Hawkes punched him in the shoulder and walked back to the bar.

Thorne returned to the table but remained standing with his arms crossed.

"You okay, Malachi?" Cabbott asked.

"Fine," he said, although pain throbbed behind his eyes. He looked at his men. The day's events weighed heavily upon them, but their fatigue went beyond this debacle. They'd been on the road for—*how long has it been now?* When he concentrated, his head hurt worse. They needed rest. He sighed. "Unless Qui turns up something in the next few hours, we'll start for Attagon in the morning."

"We're going home?" Hawkes asked, surprise and hope filling his voice.

"Yes, but not for long. We'll stop over in Caloohn."

Darien stood up, stretched and rubbed his wide, flat nose. "You don't believe Kordell is going to Colobos, do you?"

Thorne curled his lip. "I believe he's going *toward* Colobos. But he's too smart to get trapped between search parties. He's going west. I'll stake my name on it."

"Couldn't he go east?" Warner asked.

Cabbott looked at the deputy. "Yes, he could. But why wouldn't he?"

The newest and youngest deputy thought for a moment. "The ocean."

Cabbott nodded. "If he goes east, he's trapped himself against the Eastern Ocean. Search parties could pick him up as easy as shooting rabbits in a pen."

"He'll go west," Thorne said. "Probably to meet up with Traugott." He spat out the name as if it were a turd on his tongue.

"So why Attagon? If you think he's headin' west, why not follow him?" Warner asked.

Thorne smiled. "Tomorrow morning, I'm sending 'valks out to every town and city west of here with a description of Kordell. I want every Church official between here and Baymouth to be on the lookout for him. He'll have to move slower and more cautiously. If the authorities don't spot him, our familiars most certainly will, especially since he'll have to stay low to the ground."

"I'd bet if we increased what we pay the familiars for their information, they'd find Kordell by midnight tonight."

"In the meantime, I need to speak to the Regent Sempect about all of this," Thorne added.

"Does anyone have any idea what *freedom* Kordell meant? What choice was he talking about?" Hawkes asked.

"Maybe freedom from payin' taxes?" Warner ventured.

"Probably freedom to do whatever he wants." Cabbott laughed and emptied his second tankard.

"Wait a minute..." Darien raised a brow. "Thurl may not be far off. What if this freedom that Traugott promotes is, well...freedom from the Church?"

Hawkes guffawed.

Cabbott stared at Darien as if his skin had suddenly changed color.

"Freedom from the Church..." Thorne mused.

"Think about it: What could be more treasonous than wanting to live free from Church rule? What could be more heretical than to believe the Church shouldn't be in control? It sounds crazy, but maybe Traugott wants to live in a world where no one is in charge."

Cabbott scoffed. "Now how in the Twelve Hells would that even be possible?"

"I don't know." Darien shrugged. "It's just a thought."

Thorne walked to the front window. Lamps in the street appeared as clouded halos of sickly yellow light through the whorled glass. He leaned on the windowsill. The ache in his temples seemed to be receding. "As outrageous as it is, who knows what madness Traugott is plotting, much less thinking. Solomon, tell the barkeep to come back in."

The tavern keeper slipped in like a frightened animal expecting a trap.

"Thank you for your patience, congregant." Thorne offered a placating smile. "There was important Church business to attend to."

The barkeep merely nodded. Eyes downcast, he crossed the room and cleared their table.

Thorne walked to the bar, counted out five silver coins and two gold ones from the purse on his belt and laid them down. "For your trouble."

The tavern keeper's eyes widened. "Th-Thank you, Your Grace. The blessing of the Church and the Heiromonarch be upon you."

Thorne retrieved his cloak from a hook on the wall. He threw it around his shoulders and fastened it in place with a rank pin that was more detailed than Qui's. Thorne's pin featured red, triangular stones set into each of the four points of the diamond, reflecting the rank of Witchfinder Imperator. Qui's pin had only two red stones—on the bottom and right-hand side—since he ranked lower than an Imperator and a Supreme. Cabbott's pin contained a single red triangular stone at the bottom. The deputies' pins had no stones in the points, only the small diamond-shaped inset in the center common to all pins that held the principal symbol of the Church's authority: a sliver of bone from the Ossaturan of Michael the First.

They stepped out into the street. The remains of the moon formed a glistening strand of icy debris across the sky. There was nothing substantial left up there to reflect the sun's light, resulting in nights as black as a witch's heart. They traversed the uneven streets, talking quietly and dodging the sewage that overflowed gutters and assaulted their nostrils. The distressed buildings leaned menacingly in upon them. When a dog barked a few streets away, Thorne froze. Then, shaking his head, he resumed walking.

3

PLOT

SATURDAY, MAY 23 – SUNDAY, MAY 24, 999 AE

East of Caloohn, on the outskirts of Sonor village, two men waited among the ruins of a stone farmhouse. Two crumbling walls formed an L that shielded them from the road. Weedy, rotted timber and weatherworn stone lay scattered across what was once the interior. A sagging fireplace remained where the wall around it had collapsed. Nocturnal insects chittered, and the warm air carried a faint hint of honeysuckle.

Over everything lay the invasive but useful kuzda vine. Nearly unkillable, its stem and roots were used for herbal remedies and basket-making. Vine and leaves supplied jelly, parchment, tea and livestock feed. It seemed to grow as fast as fire consumes straw and flourished everywhere across the southern half of Deiparia.

Kell Sampson raked a match across the wall and lit a tabák. The light wavered over his features, casting his squat, square face into sharp relief. The bridge of his nose was nearly straight where it connected to his forehead. Multiple scars crisscrossed his cheeks and brow. His beard and mustache needed a trim, as did his blond hair. He shook out the match, plunging them into darkness once again, and exhaled.

"Where the hells is he?"

"Give it a bloody rest, will ya?" the second man said over his shoulder as he urinated in the weeds. "That's the third time ya've asked that."

"He said Saturday midnight. It's past midnight." Sampson drew on the tabák and exhaled again. Dirty, silver smoke disappeared on the breeze.

"So what? It's not like ya bloody well got anything else to do." The second man turned around, wiping his hands on his pants, and looked down at Sampson. The shadows caused his gray teeth to appear black. "Gimme one of those."

Truth be told, Rennick Glave didn't mind being out here tonight. The card game in Sonor had gone well for him. He'd been on the verge of winning some bumpkin's cow when somebody caught him cheating. Everybody had jumped up, glaring and cursing. That's when he'd flipped the table onto two of them, kicked the third in the groin and punched the fourth in the throat. He'd been outside before any of them got off the floor. He didn't have any use for a bloody cow anyway.

Sampson surrendered the small box. There followed the scritch of match on stone, the snap of fire, the smell of smoke. Glave puffed and exhaled, the end of the tabák glowing softly in the night.

"Damn it!" Sampson swatted his hairy arm thick as cordwood. "These damn bugs are eatin' me up!"

"Yeah, me too."

"Lousy fuckin' place to meet up. Why couldn't we meet in Caloohn?" Sampson flicked ash and paced to the end of the wall closest to the road. He peered around the corner. Across what had once been the front yard and beyond the rutted track that passed for a road lay empty fields. The tree line behind them was a shapeless mass.

"What's it matter? Our contact said to meet here. We've got a job lined up. Who cares whether we meet here or in Caloohn or in the bloody Heiromonarch's palace? A job's a job."

"I care." Sampson paced back. "These damn bugs are eatin' me up." He swatted at the back of his neck, a meaty smack in the stillness.

Glave took a deep drag, then held up his hand. He whispered through exhaled smoke. "Listen. Did ya hear that?" His breath reeked of cheap tobacco and gamey sausage.

Sampson stood still. Amid the insect noise, he heard a horse approaching. Both men crushed out their tabáks and melted into the shadows. Glave eased a curved dagger off his hip. He knew that if anything happened, Sampson would rely on his quickness and size. He'd seen the man break necks as if they were rotted branches with his two hands. He was broad as a warhorse and just as mean. And he could move like a cat when he wanted. It wasn't the first time Glave appreciated having Sampson on his side instead of being against him.

Both men strained their eyes, trying to discern something recognizable in the inkiness around them. The soft creak of leather came closer.

The rider drew even with the ruined walls, edging the horse off the road and through the overgrown grass. Once out of direct sight of the road, the rider stopped.

The night remained still except for the insects and the horse's breathing.

"Let us rest here by the side of the road, horse," the rider said in a voice just above a whisper.

Glave waited before responding in his reedy voice, "Because the Church is ever watchful." He waited the span of several heartbeats before emerging into the open, sheathing his weapon. He didn't take his eyes off the rider.

Sampson, too, disengaged from the shadows. "It's about damned time."

"Sorry for the delay. It took longer to sneak out of Caloohn than I expected." The voice was muffled, obviously disguised.

Glave tipped another tabák out of the box and lit it. Harsh shadows flickered across his angular face and made his long beard, twisted into two braids, appear to move as if something wiggled beneath it. "So now yer finally here," he said. "Let's get on with it. What's the bloody job?"

The rider made no effort to dismount. "My…employer wants you to help with a murder." The voice from within the hood reminded Glave of an echo in a well.

Sampson took the box from Glave and fished for a tabák. "Who we killin'?"

"My employer is going to kill a Paracletian Deputy. Your services are needed to take care of those with him. Give me one of those."

Sampson pulled a second tabák from the box, lit them from the same match and handed one up to the rider. The horse shook his head, bridle rattling. The rider took the tabák with a gloved hand. "Little warm tonight to be wrapped up in a hood and cloak, don'tcha think?"

The rider ignored him.

"A deputy, huh? What's the story?" Glave asked. One thing he knew well: no matter who you were with, the longer you kept them talking, the more likely they'd give you something they didn't intend. It might be a word, a phrase or even the tone of voice. Usually, it was body language—the twitch of a cheek, the position of the arms, a tilt of the head. These said more to him than a full-blown speech. Tonight, however, he'd have to listen carefully since he couldn't see a thing.

"My employer's business with the deputy doesn't affect your task. Your job is to make sure my employer can finish their business uninterrupted."

"Who we killin'?" Sampson repeated. His voice sounded like distant thunder.

"The deputy's name is Solomon Warner. He rides in the service of Malachi Thorne. A constable by the name of Thurl Cabbott and another deputy ride with him."

The rider pulled on the tabák. As the tip brightened, neither man could see the face inside the hood, only a solid black oval. If it wasn't for the dusky red ponytail hanging from the side of the hood, they might've thought they were talking to a phantom.

"Malachi Thorne?" Sampson asked.

"Ya've heard of him," Glave said sideways. "Witchfinder Imperator. They call him the Hammer of the Heiromonarch."

"Oh yeah."

"Bloody big-time son of a bitch."

"I never killed a Witchfinder before." There was no apprehension in Sampson's tone, just curious interest.

"Well, with a target like that, the fee's gonna be higher," Glave said to the rider. "Draw a lot of attention hitting somebody that recognizable."

The rider shifted in the saddle, reached into a pocket and tossed a money bag into the weeds at their feet. "My employer assumed as much. That's double your standard fee."

"How do ya know what our fee is?" Suspicion crept into Glave's voice, and his hand trailed toward to the hilt of his dagger.

"My employer is quite thorough."

Sampson retrieved the money bag and tested its weight in his hand. He nodded at Glave.

"So when's this happening?"

"You'll meet my employer at noon on the first of June at the Hellhound Tavern in Talnat. You'll get all the details and begin the assignment then."

"What's to keep us from takin' the money and, you know, not showin' up?" Sampson cocked an eyebrow.

"Well, let's just say that you'd be extremely stupid sellswords if word got around that you broke your contracts and screwed people over," the rider said. "Plus, you'd also be pretty hungry from lack of work."

"What the fuck's to keep us from killin' you right here and now and takin' the money?" Sampson shot back, the thunder deepening in his throat.

The rider leaned forward in the saddle. "You can try."

"Shut the hells up, Kell. We're not bloody cutthroats or common bandits," Glave said. "We abide by our word and our contracts. Quit being an asshole."

"Fuck you, Rennick."

Glave ignored him and looked at the rider. "How will we know this person when we get to the tavern?"

The rider took a final drag on the tabák and flicked it into a pile of rocks. A column of smoke streamed from the hood. "Don't worry. My employer will find you. Just be sure you're there."

"Yeah, we'll be there." Glave spit into his palm and extended his hand toward the rider, who did the same in return. Then the rider turned the horse back toward the road and Caloohn.

Sampson and Glave waited until silence settled over them once more. They crept from the rubble and returned to their own mounts a quarter mile away.

"Good money, this," Sampson said, rattling the bag once he was in the saddle.

"It ought to be for tangling with a bloody Imperator. Plus a constable, at least one other deputy…and a clerk."

Sampson hooted. "Like a damned clerk's going to do anything!"

"So that makes it two against three—not counting the clerk," Glave said as they steered their horses toward the road.

"A clerk's about as useful in a fight as a pig is with a broom."

"Those're good odds for us. We've dealt with worse."

"Whatcha goin' to do with your share?" Sampson asked.

"I don't know… I need some new equipment. And I really want to go back to Kastoro Street in Baymouth."

"Oh, hells yeah!" Sampson grinned like a fool. "I don't mind helpin' them girls pay their taxes!"

Early in its existence, the Church attempted to outlaw some of humanity's more prevalent vices. However, it didn't take long to realize that it wasn't going to work. Jails and dungeons overflowed with brawlers, pimps and drunks. Paperwork for arrests and convictions created enormous logjams and resource problems. So Church leadership decided to legalize the three most popular vices: organized fighting, gambling and prostitution.

Prostitutes—whether an ordinary tramp in the alley or the refined professionals of Kastoro Street—were required by law to register with the Church. They paid an annual license fee and had to keep their license with them at all times. Four times a year, they were assessed a percentage on their earnings. The Church used these fees to help subsidize orphanages and provide medical care for children. It was a beneficial arrangement for all. Pimping in any form was considered theft from the Church and earned the perpetrator a felony charge.

"What about you, Kell?"

"Kastoro Street, for sure! Buy some equipment, same as you. Then probably spend a couple of months eatin' seafood and watchin' the sun set on a beach somewhere."

"Ha! Ya bloody romantic! I knew it."

Sampson waved him off. "Not me, pissbritches. I just want to get as far away from all this new millennium bullshit. The closer the end of the year gets, the crazier those bastards will be. Can you imagine how fuckin' hard they're goin' to clamp down on everythin'?" He spit into the darkness. "Hells, a man won't be able to pick his nose without interference from the Church."

"Speaking of interference—ya heard about this Traugott fellow?"

"Heard the name. What's his story?"

"Not sure. I've only caught bits and pieces. He's telling people that they can make their own decisions, like about who to marry and what kind of work to do. I've heard it's some new doctrine or something. Whatever it is, I know he's shoving a pole up the Church's ass. And anybody who does that is okay with me."

Sampson slapped his arm again. "At least next time we get to meet in a damned tavern where there ain't no bugs."

Glave chuckled. "We're meeting at the Hellhound, numbnuts. Don't forget they got bugs there, too. Some of them big enough to carry ya bloody drinks."

"Well, shit." Sampson huffed as they reached the outskirts of Sonor.

4

WARNING

The instruments and voices of the congregation faded away. From behind the pulpit, Bishop Gemmas Earl said, "Let us remain standing and recite the Deiparian Creed." The congregation signed themselves and said in unison:

"I believe in the Church of the Deiparous, the Giver of Life, the compassionate, the generous, the One true and supreme God.

I believe in the Heiromonarch as the Supreme Leader of the Church, the Avatar of all existence.

I believe in the Four Orders, the pillars upon which life is ordered and enjoyed, and the foundation upon which our society prospers.

I believe that the Church is Savior and Salvation of us all, from the days that followed the Great Cataclysm up to this present moment. Without the Church, I am lost, and my eternal soul is in jeopardy of the Twelve Planes of Hell.

With faith, wisdom, obedience and loyalty, I will one day dwell in the Heavenly Realms.

I herewith renew my pledge to serve and honor the Church, to work for its good and in all ways to acknowledge the Church as my God. As it was in the first days, and as it is in the Heavenly Realms, so let it be upon me this day. Amen."

The bishop motioned for the congregation to sit. He cleared his throat. "Today, we're honored to have with us a true son of the Church, a man who has visited us on previous occasions—Malachi Thorne, Witchfinder Imperator." He gestured toward the cathedra where Thorne sat on the right side of the pulpit. Thorne smiled and offered a slow nod of acknowledgement to the congregation.

Bishop Earl adjusted one sleeve of his blue cassock as he shifted his gaze back to the congregation. "Master Thorne has been hard at work rooting out the heresies and evil that would seek to afflict our beloved Church. We're honored and comforted to have a servant like him watching over us.

"My friends, we live in unsettled times. There is great fear and trepidation in our streets and in many hearts as our world moves toward the beginning of a new millennium. Heresy and violence beset us. Many have turned from the Church and rejected her teaching. At no time in my life can I remember such apostasy and rebellion as we see around us. Would you not agree, Master Thorne?"

Once more, Thorne nodded, his face solid as granite. He stared out over the sea of faces as the Bishop continued. The seats were filled all the way to the back. *Just as it should be on Worship Day.*

The morning light filtered through the windows on the east side of the building, suffusing the nave with a soft, golden glow. Bishop Earl continued speaking, a droning in the background of Thorne's mind. He let his gaze wander across the architecture. The skill and knowledge it took to raise these majestic structures never failed to impress him.

Cathedrals not only provided a place of worship; they reflected the orderliness of the Church. No aspect of their design was random or out of place. They testified to stability and the reassuring reminder that God was always with them.

Every cathedral adhered to the same architectural design: diamond-shaped, much like a child's kite, with the southward-facing front doors that opened into a narthex. Rows of pews stretched through the nave on either side of a central aisle. Smaller aisles ran underneath the galleries on the east and west sides. A transept ran parallel to the front doors and formed the crosspiece of the kite's structure. Smaller doors stood at each end.

Beyond the transept was the presbytery, where Thorne and the bishop sat. Behind imposing wooden doors on either side of the presbytery, the vestry and sacristy could be found. The northern end of the cathedral contained a massive stained glass window depicting scenes from Church history and former Heiromonarchs. Every cathedral also had four bell towers—two near the entrance, two flanking the northern window.

On a raised platform behind the presbytery stood the centerpiece of every cathedral: its relic. Some were little more than a lock of hair or piece of cloth, while others boasted bones, hands or possessions of former Heiromonarchs. Relics encouraged pilgrimages throughout the realm; congregants sought out the items for the spiritual or physical benefits they were said to convey.

The Arrow of Breshan the Right, twentieth Heiromonarch of the realm, lay in Caloohn Cathedral. Resting on an embroidered cushion, enclosed in a gold-and-glass case, were the fletching, arrowhead and two pieces of shaft from the weapon that killed Tandino Breshan in 413 AE. A gorgeously embroidered tapestry depicting scenes from Breshan's reign draped the case.

As with all Church relics, the Arrow was only displayed on special feast days or holidays. During times of civic crisis—such as drought or famine—it was carried reverently through the streets. To spend three hours in supplication and veneration of the exposed Arrow brought spiritual insight and discernment for decision-making. That the bishop charged pilgrims to view the exposed relic brought added financial benefit to the Church as well. But on normal Worship Days such as today, it remained covered.

Thorne studied the congregation as they bowed their heads in prayer.

Seating in a cathedral also reflected the Church's emphasis on order. The wealthy sat together in one section, their clothing and hairstyles testifying to their success. Widows had their own section, as did families. Congregants who'd been convicted of noncapital crimes sat together in one section. Every cathedral had at least one novitiate, whose responsibility was to keep a record of attendance for the transgressors' section. Failure to attend resulted in fines or additional punishment. Thorne had handed down both more times than he could count when those novitiate reports came across his desk before he had been appointed to the rank of Witchfinder. Back when...

No, I'm not going to think about that. What happened is over.

But you're still paying for it, aren't you?

I can't change what happened.

Of course you can't. But it's never going away, is it? Who needs the Twelve Planes when you've got your own private hell, right?

"...by the grace of the Church, our God, forever and ever. Amen."

The congregation repeated the amen and looked up.

Earl sat down on the left side of the platform. A novitiate stepped to the pulpit carrying a large book. He placed it on the lectern and opened it.

"Hear now this reading from the Testament of the Deiparous," he said in a youthful voice that sounded like crystal in the vaulted reaches of the cathedral. "The reading is taken from The Concordat, chapter two, sections one and two.

"And the terror wrought by the Great Cataclysm filled the hearts of every man, woman and child who remained. Desperate to survive, they gathered in tribes where resources could be shared. Resources were scarce in those bleak and savage days. A man would kill his brother for a piece of bread; a mother would abandon her child for a cup of water. Our world belonged to the ruthless, violent and cruel. Blood filled the streets so that the feet of those who walked upon it were permanently stained. Tribes battled one another for a better resource or a larger resource. The bodies of the dead lay scattered beneath the sky and soon became the source of the Death Scourge. Every man did whatsoever he decided in his own heart, for there was no rule or law."

The novitiate turned the page. The crackle of the aged parchment reminded Thorne of the library in the Church orphanage where he grew up. Musty. Ancient. Comforting.

"In the midst of this horror and depravation, the tribe of Deiparia was known for its compassion and generosity," the novitiate continued. "They took in refugees, ministered to the sick and dying, and fed the hungry. They provided employment, structure and greatest of all, hope, as humanity slowly recovered. People came to Deiparia in greater numbers, and no one was turned away. In time, Deiparia became larger and more successful than any of the other tribes. And on August 18th, 104 AE, the people chose from among themselves Michael Raymond as their leader, who became Heiromonarch Michael the First."

The youth closed the massive tome and slid it onto a shelf beneath the pulpit. As he returned to his seat, Thorne stood and stepped behind the pulpit.

Today, he wore his dress uniform. Beneath a sleeveless black vest that buttoned up the front was a red tunic with long sleeves and braided cuffs. A dress mantle, black bordered with red, hung from his shoulders. His rank pin, medals and awards decorated the right side of his chest, softly clinking with each movement. Black breeches with a red stripe down each leg were tucked neatly into black boots. A ceremonial rapier lay against his hip. His hair was pulled back in a ponytail, his black mustache and goatee perfectly trimmed.

"Congregants of Caloohn, on behalf of the Four Orders and in the name of Heiromonarch Dobrin Kristur, I greet you on this day of worship." His voice climbed the arches of the cathedral and ricocheted off the triforium. "I am indebted to my colleague, Bishop Earl, for this opportunity to speak to you this morning.

"As you are aware, two days ago, there was an incident in Talnat. A convicted heretic named Barnabas Kordell, scheduled for execution according to Church law, escaped with the aid of several well-trained riders and marksmen. The authorities captured one accomplice who agreed to assist the Church in its investigations."

He paused before continuing in a louder, more commanding tone.

"Barnabas Kordell *will* be captured, and all who have aided him in any way *will* be punished.

"I say this in the event that you might be tempted to offer asylum to this man." He narrowed his eyes as he scanned the upturned faces. "You know the law: anyone aiding or abetting a known heretic is considered a heretic. If you know anything about the events in Talnat two days ago, you are obligated to report your knowledge to the Church."

He straightened his arms as he gripped the sides of the pulpit.

"I asked for today's reading to be taken from The Concordat because we need to remember how we came to the grace of the Church."

He stepped from behind the pulpit, placed his hands behind his back, closed his eyes and quoted the text verbatim. He opened his eyes and studied the congregation before letting his gaze drift up to the windows in the clerestory. Shafts of amber light cascaded into the nave. Someone sneezed.

"None of us experienced those days," he said, his tone softer. "For nearly one thousand years, we have been kept secure in the arms of our beloved Church. Our God provides us with existence and purpose, and with the necessities of life. We are the recipients of all this"—he spread his arms to encompass the whole cathedral—"because the Deiparia tribe offered order, purpose and law to a turbulent, ruined land.

"The sacred text tells us that 'Every man did whatsoever he decided in his own heart, for there was no rule or law.'"

He let the words hang in the air like ghosts trapped in time as he walked back behind the pulpit. Every eye followed him.

"Is that what we want now? Do we want to return to the days when people traded their souls for a crust of bread?" He looked at a woman near the front who held a sleeping infant. "Good mother," he said, extending his hand, palm upturned, "do you want a world where your child is your neighbor's next meal?"

It took a moment, but the shock and horror settled on her young face. She shook her head and pulled her baby closer.

"Blessed grandmother," he said as he walked to the other side of the pulpit and made the same gesture toward an old woman in the widow's section, "would you see your sons and grandsons left bloody and gutted in the streets over a skin of milk?" Like the mother before her, the old woman shook her head. She signed herself, and Thorne smiled.

"Of course not. None of us would want such horrors for ourselves. But…"

He let the silence lengthen before continuing.

"If we allow every person to do whatever he decides in his own heart, then we *will* repeat those days. If even one person is allowed to destroy the order and law by which we live, others will soon follow. Left unchecked, the depravities of the human heart will dominate all.

"As Bishop Earl stated, we live in unstable spiritual times. Men such as Traugott and Kordell spout heresies that poison and deceive. The Enodia Communion targets women with false promises, turning them against family and community. And in many places, the most common observances of the Church are cast aside by those who flirt with their own damnation." He shook his head for dramatic effect.

"Salvation lies in your obedience to the Church. Do not be led astray. If you sow according to the desires of your own heart, you will reap a whirlwind of judgment. But if you sow according to the doctrine of the Church, you will reap life here, and life everlasting.

"As we approach a new millennium, I tell you that you must strengthen your connection with the Church. Recommit yourself anew to your God. Serve the Church joyfully and in complete obedience." He scanned the congregation once again.

"The Church is God," he said before returning to his seat.

The congregation replied quietly, "The Church is God."

"A sound message, Master Thorne, and an important one," Bishop Gemmas Earl said from behind his desk. Thorne finished his tea and stared out the window. A novitiate tended the garden in the courtyard below. The bergberry flowers were already in full bloom, their thin lemony petals bright against the nearly black stems and leaves.

"Thank you, Bishop," he replied, placing his teacup on the desk. He sighed.

Earl studied Thorne with sharp blue eyes. "Something troubles you. Something more than just Kordell."

Thorne looked down at the old man, whose scalp now held more age spots than it did hair. His beard was wiry and gray. On his long, narrow head, wrinkles pulled at his features.

"Yes," he replied at last. "I'm worried, Bishop. I'm worried for the people and for the Church."

"Worried in what way?"

"I've seen the reports from our western border. A great many people have fallen away from the Church." He walked across the room to a shelf that was thinly coated with dust opposite the bishop's desk. "Some accounts say that the Communion has increased their activity in Last Chapel by as much as thirty percent."

"By *that* much?" the bishop asked, his voice rising in surprise.

"Yes. And it's said there's ongoing conflict and violence as well."

"The western territory has always been—how shall we say?—undisciplined."

"That's putting it mildly." Thorne looked at the few books lying among the dust, then turned to face the bishop again. "The Church has received a request for reinforcements from the officials there, but they haven't acted on it." Thorne rubbed an eyebrow with his thumb. "I'm not sure why. That troubles me as well."

"Mysterious are the ways of God, as they say," Earl replied with a brief chuckle. "Do you suspect Traugott to be behind any of this?"

"Not all of it, no. We know that the Communion has been losing power for years, so it's not surprising they're trying to reclaim some of it. But I think the real reason is the approaching millennium. In my recent travels, I've seen an increase in zealots and freethinkers."

"People are indeed anxious about the year 1000. How do you feel about it?"

He walked back to the bishop's desk. "It's a different date, that's all. January 1st will be no different than December 31st. But I am worried for the people. Men like Traugott will lead them away from the Church, and the millennium will be an excellent backdrop and excuse for that. It's our responsibility to help people prepare for that transition, and it's becoming harder to do with the likes of Traugott and others advocating spiritual rebellion and damnation."

"This Kordell fellow in Talnat—was he connected to Traugott?"

Thorne hesitated and dropped his gaze to the floor.

"It's all right," Earl said with the soothing tone of a grandfather. "It wasn't your fault."

"I *will* find him, Gemmas." Thorne's voice turned hard. "He won't laugh in the face of the Church, not while I'm alive. If it takes a—" He stopped and stared at the bishop, who was smiling broadly. "What's so funny?"

"Not funny, just pleased. I can see once again why so many in the Church speak so highly of you."

He cocked his head and squinted. "What are you talking about?"

Earl stood up, cassock rustling. "Since you've been away on your recent trip, your popularity has increased. There are those who believe you're quite possibly the greatest Witchfinder the Church has ever known." He paused before adding, "Even greater than your mentor."

Thorne wasn't sure what to say. Certainly it was an honor to be regarded in such a way—

—*but it's an honor I don't deserve.*

The bishop laid a wrinkled hand on his shoulder. "Rumor has it that you may even become the youngest Heiromonarch in history." He offered Thorne a conspiratorial smile.

"You must be joking."

"Oh, no. I'm not joking. While you've been gone, there's been chatter in the Church's ranks. Your successes, Malachi, and your reputation—they've garnered no small amount of recognition. Your faith, your tireless commitment to the Church, your theology and ethics, the way you carry yourself—all that has impressed a growing number of higher-ups in the Church." He licked his lips. "The Church could use a leader like you at a time like this."

Thorne's eyes widened. He wasn't sure whether to laugh at the ridiculousness of the idea or be concerned for those who felt that way.

"Gemmas, I… Oh, come on! You know I have no desire to be a leader. I can't sit behind a desk and go to meetings all day. And I certainly don't want to get involved in all the political maneuvering and ecclesiastical pandering that goes on in the capital. My ambition extends only to assuring the doctrinal integrity and obedience of the people."

"And that, my friend, is precisely why you're garnering so much support among the Orders. You're not pursuing a higher rank for yourself. You're not jockeying for position or title. That's an unusual thing within the Church. You're committed to doing the best for the Church, not yourself. Don't underestimate how unusual that is these days."

"We both know there are hundreds of candidates waiting for every vacant seat of authority in my Order—in every Order, for that matter." He shook his head. "Even if I wanted a higher rank for myself—which I don't—do you know how long it would take to achieve something like that?"

"With your growing support, you'd be surprised how quickly things could change."

Thorne opened the door. "Don't fool yourself, Bishop. We both know the Church has long been corrupted by politics. Much of its mission has been compromised by too many political deals and self-preservation."

"True. But you could change that."

Thorne shrugged. "I will avoid politics at all costs. I certainly won't go looking for a leadership role."

Earl ushered him into the hallway. "You may have such a role thrust upon you, Your Grace, whether you wish it or not."

Thorne sighed as they clasped forearms and offered their goodbyes. He made the sign of the Church over Earl and walked off down the hall.

"Well, here he comes now," Hawkes said. He lounged against the stable door, flipping his dagger end over end and catching it by the handle each time.

"Are the horses ready?" Thorne asked him.

"You bet. We've been wondering where you were." He slid the dagger into its sheath and yawned as he retied his ponytail.

"Good, then let's go. I'm ready to see home again."

"Amen to that!" Hawkes disappeared into the stable, yelling for Warner.

People walked by in the street, chatting with one another. Those who passed closest to Thorne offered polite greetings and courteous deference. Most did their best to avoid being near him.

Warner emerged from the stable. "Hi, Boss. You ready to go?"

"That I am—assuming you're ready as well, *Jester*," he said with a needling smile.

Warner grinned, put his hands on his hips and shook his head in mock disbelief. He handed Thorne a pair of silver spurs. "You and Tycho ain't never gonna let me live this down, are you?" He pointed to the black patch over his left eye. "You *know* it was just a lucky shot."

"Oh, lucky shot, eh?" Thorne sat down and put on the spurs. "You're the only deputy in the entire Paracletian Order who's lost an eye—"

"He threw stuff at me."

"—because a clown in a play—"

"I tried dodgin' them props."

"—threw a fork at you." Thorne chuckled.

"Yeah, one of the things he threw was a fork."

"You could've ducked," he said, as he always did at this point in the story.

"I did duck!"

"Oh yes, that's right. You did duck. And that's when the fork hit you in the eye. When you ducked. Uh-huh."

"It *was* a lucky shot. And it was pretty dark."

"I know, I know." Thorne stood and took the reins of his horse, Gamaliel, from Hawkes. "*The jester was quick. He was an acrobat.* We've heard it all before." He mimed the exaggerated hand gestures that always accompanied this running joke.

"Laugh all you want," Warner said with an impish but regal demeanor. "But I was the one who recognized the escaped convict underneath his disguise. That clown might still be at large if it wasn't for my superior attention to detail."

Hawkes led his brown-and-tan mare out of the stable and secured his travel kit, made up of a bedroll, basic utensils, a change of clothes and personal items, to the saddle. "So now that you've lost the"—Hawkes motioned toward his own eye—"what do you have left? The 'superior' or the 'detail?'" His laugh turned into a yawn.

"I can see enough to know you're an idiot," Warner said. "You couldn't find a black cat in a white room. And why are you so tired today? Rough night?"

"I didn't get to sleep until late." Hawkes threw his leg over his horse's back. "I think my bed had bugs in it."

"Your brain has bugs in it…"

Thorne climbed into his saddle, and Cabbott rode his stallion out of the stable and joined them. The three cantered from the yard into the street.

"Hey!" Warner yelled. "Tycho, why didn't you bring my horse?"

The red-headed deputy turned in his saddle. A wide grin split his face. "Thought you could use the exercise."

"Man, I'm gonna exercise my foot right up your…" Warner grumbled as he disappeared inside the stable.

"And hurry up, Jester!" Cabbott yelled over his shoulder. "We may want some entertainment along the way!"

Warner caught up before they reached the outskirts of Caloohn. Dario Darien joined them there. They rode onto the buckled, crumbling gray stone of the 75 Road and turned northwest toward home.

5

ATTAGON

For the first time in six months, Thorne awoke in his own bed. He ate the breakfast prepared for him by Ames—his servant, cook and groom—on the balcony that overlooked the River Tense and the bustling city of Attagon. While he ate, he shuffled through the pile of documents that had greeted him upon his return. He pulled off a piece of bread and swirled it around the plate, gathering up the remaining gravy. He set the documents aside and looked out over the city.

The capital of Deiparia basked in the early light that broke over Mission Ridge and chased the night's shadows into hiding. Across the largest city in the realm, filaments of smoke from smithies and cooking fires curled into the sky. Often referred to as the Celestial Akropolis, it was the heart of the Church. It became the capital in the years following the Great Cataclysm.

The Storicos taught that when the lunar fragments made landfall, the ancient weapons of devastation erupted in searing clouds of heat and light, decimating everything for miles in every direction. Not long after the earth finished grinding and reforming, an illness took hold of the populace. The symptoms of the Devouring Sickness included nausea and fatigue, and after a period of time, the skin grew shiny and taut. Hair fell out in great clumps. Lesions covered the body. Victims wasted away to little more than skeletons. There were no skills or remedies to halt it.

As the death toll mounted, the survivors fled. Some migrated west, never to be heard from again. Others braved the extensive Great Appian Mountains to the east and over time reclaimed parts of them, as well as the coastal plains on the other side. Most people migrated south. The Deiparia tribe welcomed them in, and as the population grew, Attagon was founded along the river and between the surrounding mountains of a land once called Chattanooga. The Devouring

Sickness did not follow them, nor did it appear to have affected the animals or plants of the region. The rich soil had proven good for raising crops and feeding livestock.

It was in Attagon that the first Heiromonarch was crowned. Here, the Testament was compiled. From Attagon, God extended his beneficence, order and rule across the realm.

Almost everything in the city supported the Church. Every office, barracks, suite, chapel, training facility and library belonged to the Church. Businesses and tradesmen such as clothiers, masons, farriers, carpenters, cooks and smiths thrived.

Thorne rose, stretched and leaned on the scrolled metal railing. His living quarters enjoyed a corner balcony that extended across parts of the northern and western sides of the building. Three other residences occupied the remainder of the floor. Other buildings that also housed high-ranking Church officials perched atop the section of the city known as the Bluff, a promontory overlooking the south bank of the river.

Below him, the road from the Bluff sloped down into the alleys, shops, streets and stables that formed the central business district. The majority of Attagon's citizens worked for the Church in some capacity. Some farmed the land, raising tomatoes, corn, peaches, berries, potatoes and various types of greens. Others kept herds of cattle, sheep and pigs.

The Celestial Akropolis consisted of three main boroughs. One contained the dwellings for much of the population. One was the business district, which began at the river and crept south, ending at Elmking Road. Across this thoroughfare lay the biggest district: the seat of the Church. Rumor told of whole buildings hidden below ground, though Thorne knew of no evidence to corroborate such tales.

A thin, elderly man stepped out of the apartment and onto the balcony. Slightly bowlegged, he had a wan, beaky face with a semicircle of cottony gray hair that clung tenaciously to the back of his head.

"Master Thorne, Gamaliel is ready."

"Thank you, Ames."

"Do you wish anything else to eat, sir?"

"No, the breakfast was delicious. My compliments as usual."

"Thank you, sir." The old man grinned, his teeth still strong and, just as important, accounted for. "Your cloak and hat have been cleaned and are by the door as you requested. Will you be returning for lunch?"

Thorne thought for a moment. "No, I don't think so. But I will be back for dinner."

"Very good, sir." Ames retrieved the breakfast tray and went inside.

A moment later, Thorne followed. He donned the cloak and hat, descended the three flights of stairs and went out to the stable. He climbed into Gamaliel's saddle and rode down into the business district.

Closest to the river stood the shops of the fishmongers who bargained daily with the fishermen for the best catches and prices. Thorne rode past the shops of cordwainers and cobblers, bakers and wainwrights. Coin exchanged hands in return for services or supplies. From everywhere came the sounds of tapping hammers, grinding saws, hooves and voices. The air smelled of smoke, sawdust, fish and sewage. Pedestrians and carts moved aside for him. He scanned the avenues and faces, more alert than ever to any danger or disruption. The reason he had to be still left a sour taste in his mouth.

He'd find Kordell. And Traugott. They would not make a mockery of everything he'd dedicated his life to. If he had to carry their severed heads through every town and village in Deiparia, he'd do it to see that people stayed true to the faith.

He followed the road until it joined the widest and most recognizable street in the city—the Avenue of the Lord, which led directly to the Cathedral of the Heiromonarch. A median of trees nearly as old as the city itself divided the traffic flow north and south. Thorne guided Gamaliel to the right of them and turned south. Exclusive businesses offering the finest in spices, weaponry and fashion lined the street.

Thorne wiped sweat from his brow. Beneath his garments, his skin prickled. The temperature escalated as the sun climbed higher. He'd probably have to spend the summer on the road, tracking Kordell and Traugott in the miserable heat.

Something else to hate them for.

The Cathedral of the Heiromonarch loomed before him.

It was a magnificent structure and the only cathedral in the realm to use dual sets of flying buttresses. While this disseminated the weight of the 550-foot-tall building, it also had the unintended side effect of looking like jointed insect legs. Criminals had been known to refer to it as "the bughouse" until their tongues were removed for the dishonor.

Thorne steered Gamaliel to the right and into the cathedral's immense shadow. He turned onto a slightly smaller road that led to the offices of the Paracletian Order.

Each Order had its own campus. The Kyrian Order, located on the eastern side of the cathedral along Mission Ridge, oversaw all ecclesiastical matters. They maintained Church order and polity, created hymns, organized and led services, interpreted the Testament and established doctrine.

The Abthanian Order, located on the northern bank of the River Tense, served as the educational arm of the Church. All children received free education beginning at age five in Primary Catechism, where they learned the basics of reading, lettering and calculating. Next came Secondary and then Advanced Catechisms.

At eighteen, students completed public education and began pursuit of an apprenticeship or vocation. For men wanting to serve at higher levels in the Church, Seminary followed until age twenty-one and Abthanian Seminary until age twenty-five. Women were prohibited from any education beyond Advanced Catechism. The Enodia Communion had become adept at luring women away from the Church with promises of advanced learning.

The Cartulian Order occupied a sprawling conglomeration of buildings to the south of the cathedral, on the farthest edge of Attagon. They oversaw the day-to-day governance of the population through offices for labor and health, civic improvements, certificates and registrations, the minting of coins, taxation and dozens of other municipal departments. The Order also maintained, organized, cataloged and preserved all the records of the Church. Dozens of buildings were dedicated to everything from birth and death certificates to trial dockets and conviction sentences. Every meeting held, every license issued, every tax paid and every trade agreement signed were meticulously stored away, monitored by fussy librarians. Some ancient documents that had survived the Great Cataclysm lay in special archives accessible only to select Church officials.

Thorne had often wondered about those documents. His love of books and libraries fired his imagination. What secrets of the past did they contain? Were they harmless things, such as stories and poetry? Or did they hold dangerous philosophies and forbidden knowledge in long-dead languages? He'd never know, because even his rank of Witchfinder Imperator wasn't sufficient to access such ancient knowledge.

You could see them if you became the Heiromonarch, as Gemmas hinted. He shook his head as if to dislodge the thought, perplexed that it had come so freely.

If the Cartulian Order was the largest, then the Paracletian Order was the most feared. It represented all law enforcement and judiciary processes. Those wishing to serve in this capacity began at the introductory level of Paracletian Deputy. A promotion led to the office of Constable. Cities the size of Attagon or Talnat had dozens of constables, each assigned to specific districts. Small hamlets had only one. If a constable showed interest and aptitude, he could petition the Church for consideration to the rank of Witchfinder, which consisted of three levels: Witchfinder, Witchfinder Supreme and Witchfinder Imperator.

At the central offices, Thorne left Gamaliel with the stable hand and made his way into the building. Giant red banners—the word *OBEDIENCE* emblazoned in black—hung on both sides of the lobby. Hallways led off in different directions. People moved about their various tasks.

He climbed the staircase to the third floor, greeting those he passed along the way. He turned into another long corridor lined with cream-colored pilasters. The portraits of former Witchfinders stared solemnly down at him.

Gemmas probably had a spot picked out for his already.

The thought was even more incredulous as he passed the image of Valerian Merrick, Witchfinder Imperator. Every time he walked this way, he tried to avoid looking at it. And every time he failed. *"To dwell in the past robs us of the present moment and hinders the development of the future,"* Merrick used to say. Thorne tried to bear that in mind when he remembered his own failure.

And what had Gemmas said? *"There are those who believe you're quite possibly the greatest Witchfinder the Church has ever known. Even greater than your mentor."* He shook his head in disbelief as he reached a set of double doors. He entered and found Naomi Kestring sitting behind her desk. Along the back wall stood another set of closed double doors.

"Master Thorne!" she exclaimed with genuine warmth. "Good morning! It's so good to have you back." The smile lit up her young, round face.

He acknowledged her greeting as he removed his hat.

"How were your travels this time?"

"Too long," he said, "but nothing more than the usual difficulties of such a journey. Let me see… We wintered along the coast. Have you ever seen the Eastern Ocean in winter?"

She shook her head.

"It freezes for miles out from the shore, and on clear days, the sun makes it seem like a giant mirror for as far as the eye can see."

She continued smiling and watched him intently with her large brown eyes. "That sounds beautiful."

One of the doors behind her desk opened. An older, bearded man in a green frock limped out with the aid of a cane. He crossed the room, wheezing a perfunctory greeting in Thorne's direction as he departed.

"Just a moment, Master Thorne," Naomi said. "I'll let Master Lachlan know you're here."

The office of Regent Sempect was the second-highest rank in the Paracletian Order, just beneath the Paracletian Monarch, who answered only to the Heiromonarch himself. The Regent Sempect managed the descending ranks of Paracletian Patriarch, the Prime Exarch, the First Regent and the Second Regent. These functionaries had multiple responsibilities, and even though they outranked Thorne, he rarely dealt with them.

Naomi returned and motioned him inside.

It remained just as he remembered. Shelves lined the wall to his right, while windows occupied the one opposite. They faced the morning sun, and the room already felt sticky with trapped heat. A long wooden table littered with parchments sat in front of the bookshelves. More papers, scrolls and manuscripts sprawled along every shelf. It never failed to remind Thorne of the aftermath of a windstorm. Directly in front of him, three cushioned chairs sat before a chestnut-colored desk. The air smelled of tobacco and yellowed pages.

Behind the desk, a portly man stood up. He wore a dark gray cassock, the hood of which lay back on the black-and-red cope that hugged his shoulders. Two silver stripes ran from left shoulder to waist, which was encircled by a silver metal cincture. Medals and awards lay across his right breast, including his rank—two diamond-shaped pins, each identical to Thorne's.

"Regent Sempect Lachlan," he said, bowing to the sixty-one-year-old man. "The peace of the Heiromonarch and the benevolence of the Divine Church be upon you."

"And upon you, Malachi Thorne," Lachlan replied in a deep, warm voice. They clasped forearms, and he gestured for Thorne to take a seat. "It's good to have you back in the Celestial Akropolis."

He let out a long breath. "It's good to finally be back, Regent Sempect. This was the longest trip my men and I have ever been on."

Brior Lachlan laughed behind the brushy mustache that didn't quite reach his muttonchops, which were notable for having more hair than his head. "I'm sure your men were as anxious to get home as dogs in a thunderstorm."

"That they were, Regent Sem—"

Lachlan raised a pudgy hand covered in jeweled rings and waved it in front of him. "Have you been gone so long that you've forgotten you don't have to stand on ceremony with me?" He lifted a pipe from a stand on his desk and took a deep draw. He exhaled, and the smoke swirled in the humid air.

"No. No, sir." Thorne sat down and placed his hat on one of the empty seats. "I suppose I am—*I'm*—just accustomed to attending to the proper formalities since I've been dealing with so many congregants."

"Understandable, my boy, completely understandable. We must maintain decorum and dignity in our work for God." He took another draw from the pipe. "But in here, it's just you and me." He winked from beneath prickly eyebrows.

"Thank you, Master Lachlan." He stared at the top of the desk between them.

"Tell me about it," Lachlan said, not needing to be more specific.

With bared teeth, Thorne snarled through the chain of events that had marred his record and allowed a convicted heretic to escape. He all but chewed the names of Traugott and Kordell whenever he said them. With a face flushed with anger and a sigh that more closely resembled the growl of an enraged bear, he thrust himself out of the chair and began pacing.

Thorne had never laid eyes on Traugott, yet he had a mental image of the man: a frail, droopy-eyed freethinker; arrogant; blinded by his own sanctimonious heresies. The image swam in his mind so clearly, he could almost reach out and grab the scrawny throat. *A good, solid squeeze is all it would take.* He imagined the sharp crack as the windpipe gave way under the pressure of his thumbs.

"—thing to drink, Malachi?"

Thorne blinked and looked quizzically at the Regent Sempect.

"I asked if you wanted something to drink?"

He realized his hands were clasped together, fingers interlocked, as if praying. Or strangling someone. Thorne tried to act nonchalant as he lowered his arms.

"Yes. Yes, thank you."

Lachlan bobbed out of his chair and plodded over to an oaken sidebar. He filled two small glasses and handed one to Thorne before he resumed his seat. The chair protested loudly.

Thorne sat back down.

"Appian whiskey," Lachlan said. He held up his glass, nodded and tossed the dark liquid into his mouth.

Thorne did likewise. It burned his throat and warmth spread through his chest. He sat the empty glass on the edge of the desk. "Thank you."

"I seemed to lose you there for a moment, my boy."

"I apologize, Master Lachlan. I've had...difficulty...guarding my anger of late."

"Completely understandable, my boy. Can't say I'd react any differently."

Thorne shook his head. "I still can't believe Qui had Traugott's second-in-command and never even knew it." The anger in his voice softened to a dismal irritation.

"Did Qui get any additional information about Kordell or Traugott from the accomplice?"

"Not by the time we left Saturday morning. Have you heard anything? Have any redvalks or riders arrived?"

Lachlan shook his head, jowls wiggling. "Nothing more than the normal reports from our regular riders."

Thorne released an exasperated sigh and shook his head. "Damn it... Is there anything I can do?" He rarely felt helpless in his job or his life. Wherever he went, he issued the orders. He made things happen. But now, he felt trapped and impotent.

"Not in terms of tracking the escapee. *However*...the Council met yesterday afternoon in a called session to discuss these events. It was decided that the Church is going to increase pressure on our communities in order to ferret out Traugott, Kordell and anyone associated with them. The Paracletian Council believes we may've grown too...soft...in recent years."

Thorne smiled, nodded.

"We're increasing patrols in villages and towns, and our familiars are being ordered to quietly increase surveillance of their neighbors. Anyone suspected of heretical doings, of dabbling in witchcraft, or aiding rebels in any way whatsoever will receive the most ruthless punishments we have at our disposal." He drew on his pipe again, exhaled and placed it back on the stand.

"Malachi, we want you to strike as you've never done before. Since they call you the Hammer of the Heiromonarch out there, that's exactly what the Council wants you to be. Hit hard. The Council wishes to see the fear of God once more in people's eyes. You're our instrument for doing that."

"What of the Code?" Thorne traced his mustache and goatee with thumb and index finger.

Lachlan's eyes darkened beneath the overhanging shrubbery of eyebrows. He licked his lips. "The Code is rescinded until further notice."

Thorne nodded. "So *all* forms of interrogation are now acceptable?"

"Yes, absolutely, my boy—at your discretion. The Code's age limit restrictions are, of course, also lifted."

"And the First Degree of the Ordeal?"

"Simply showing the accused the instruments of torture? That's for you to decide on a case-by-case basis. You may get lucky with it; you never know," Lachlan said. "You'll be issued a decree before you depart that details the Council's decision. Have your clerk make copies and post it in every town you visit. Discipline them with fire and steel, Malachi. Show no mercy."

"It shall be as the Council decrees." He smiled like a wolf among sheep.

"Before this year is over, we want the realm cleansed of heretical filth so that our celebrations aren't just for a new millennium, but for the complete purification of our land. It'll be the beginning of an unparalleled one-thousand-year reign that'll be the glory of the Church," Lachlan said, his eyes sparkling at the idea.

"When do I begin?"

"You may leave whenever you and your men are provisioned and ready."

"Do I have a—"

An urgent knock sounded at the door.

"What is it?" Lachlan called across the room.

Naomi entered, handed Lachlan a rolled parchment and left.

He skimmed the document. "Well, well, *well*..."

"What is it?" Thorne asked.

Lachlan settled back in his ungrateful chair and read the note again. A smile lifted his muttonchops higher. "It's good news, my boy. Extremely good news. It looks like you're going to Colobos."

He frowned. "Colobos? Why?"

"Because according to this, which just arrived by 'valk, one of the riders who helped Kordell escape has been captured. They're holding him for you in Colobos."

6
MATRIARCH

MONDAY, MAY 25, 999 AE

I n the southern range of the Great Appian Mountains, where the massive Appian redvalks nested, Neris Ahlienor knelt on a circular rug in a cool stone cellar. A bowl of clear water sat in the center of the rug. Her eyes were closed, and she made rhythmic gestures with her hands over the bowl. She wore a silver-and-black gown, and golden hair hung in ringlets down her back. A thin, filigreed silver band rested upon her brow. In a barely audible voice, she intoned:

> *"O Gurov Matronis, Panivas Làcrime, seirbak pek'tà calah;*
> *chak'ái ngyn lumos ah'en bhenav chak'áe gurov phel'ast, kàkou gurov shalveta;*
>
> Guardian of the Way
> Thrice-Blessed Madonna,
>
> *Auxilimu'ahd, et vilbrimu'ahd, auxilimu'ahd,*
> *Ràmah làcrime, Be'lehham làcrime, selgra tuhmyrreh,*
>
> Keeper of the Keys,
> Kingdom without End
>
> *Vehr'fthagan, teh'abyihn seirbak pek'tà calah;*
> *nantuu a keia voda, làcrime tal'pyanteh, tehmyrrei vecummah,*
> *Auxilimu'ahd, et vilbrimu'ahd, et qevithu motika iyo."*

Beside the single wooden door, two torches crackled softly on the damp wall. The only furniture was a small table that supported a stone sculpture of a three-faced woman. The left face was that of a young girl, the middle one a matronly woman; the right resembled a gnarled crone. The air tasted of old smoke and mushrooms.

Rising gracefully, Neris moved to a different spot around the bowl. She knelt again, poured water from a small pitcher into the basin and repeated the phrase with her words and hands. She performed the ritual once more at a different point around the bowl, finally returning to where she started.

Breathing slowly and deeply, she let her mind meditate upon words known only to a select few. She remembered a time—how long had it been?—when she welcomed these meditations, warmly anticipating what to her had always been a spiritual experience. Her mind had opened to wisdom and knowledge, to immersion in something greater. Like a drop of water in an ocean. It had always left her calm and strengthened. She'd learned the ways of her craft and had communed with countless spirits. Sometimes, she'd spent hours in such meditative repose, her soul rising on the wings of tranquility.

But for months now, her meditations had been fragmented, unclear, elusive. Visions came too infrequently and lacked the spiritual comfort to which she was accustomed. Faces she didn't know and a world she didn't recognize intruded upon her, always leaving her with a clammy sense of foreboding. She couldn't find the power that she once did. She felt like a tree dying from the branches down. The unsettled condition of her spirit perfectly mirrored the state of the Enodia Communion.

Fewer brexia—the name they preferred to the Church's term *witch*—remained alive today than at any point in history. The brexia were scattered throughout Deiparia, and their powers weakened. The Church had done them great harm in the last several hundred years, executing those they could capture and forcing the rest into hiding.

Spirit restive and mind unfocused, Neris shook her head as if the motion might dispel her turmoil. Exhaling, she attempted to center herself and begin her meditations again.

After a moment, her arms tingled with gooseflesh. She opened her eyes. The dingy ochre light of the cellar transformed into a pale, arctic blue, like the inside of a chunk of ice. She watched the water in the bowl freeze over.

She shivered beneath her gown. She tucked her elbows to her sides, forearms extended, palms upward, as if offering an invisible tray. She reminded herself to breathe normally as she trembled in the plummeting temperature.

There was a slight disturbance of air behind her, and someone moved closer than they should. Neris didn't want or need to look behind her. She knew who was there.

"Priestess Ahlienor."

The voice spoke close enough that the hairs on the back of her neck moved with the breath. It sounded like icy teeth raking across stone and reeked of burnt flesh and misery.

"Thrice-Blessed Madonna," she said. Her teeth ached from the cold. "Welcome. You honor me with your presence." She watched her breath plume white in the air before her. "How may I s-serve you?" She couldn't stop shivering.

The air behind her shifted, sounding like sleet in a forest.

"Gather two others. Find a third to serve as a willing conduit. Summon the Elder Demon Rythok-An'hea."

"Preparations sh-shall be made. What are your w-wishes f-for it?" The hairs in her nostrils prickled. She quivered uncontrollably but did not lower her arms. She'd lost the feeling in her fingers and toes.

"The three of you will command him and unleash him to kill Malachi Thorne, Witchfinder Imperator. He is responsible for great damage to our sisterhood. I want him dead! Dead!"

"I understand, M-M-Matriarch. Your will shall be f-fulfilled."

"Do it before the summer solstice."

A moment passed, silent as new-fallen snow.

"Matriarch Trahnen?" Neris asked.

"Speak, Daughter of the Moon."

"Matriarch, my meditations remain…unsettled. I f-fear for the Communion. What is to b-become of us?"

"Peace, Child." The voice now came from above her, near the ceiling. "We are not so weak as many believe. There are brexia who bring the Communion new power."

"New power?"

"An innate power that is with them from birth. It is unrealized until they experience their first sanguinelle. We are gathering them, training them, to lead us into a new era."

Neris's gaze drifted down to the bowl. The frozen water captured part of the Matriarch's reflection—

The young priestess almost gasped aloud. What was she seeing?

The Matriarch's guttural voice drifted down from the aged ceiling beams. "The Church thinks we are dying. Let them. When the time is right, we shall reclaim our rightful place. We will be more powerful than ever before."

A crackling, rasping noise sounded overhead, as if a large spider were dragging the tips of its legs through ice. Reflected in the bowl, Neris saw an image of a distorted human form suspended from the ceiling.

Were those…multiple segmented legs?

The head above her turned. The face—it followed separately.

Neris clenched her eyes tight and heard sounds coming down the wall that she didn't want to think about.

"Remember," the bitter voice said from behind her once more, "before the summer solstice."

"It sh-shall be as the Witch of Tears h-has decreed."

She waited, feeling vulnerable and exposed.

Soon, the coldness dissipated. Warmth returned to her extremities. When she opened her eyes, the sickly torchlight had resumed its reddish-orange hue and the shadows of the cellar seemed normal.

Gathering up the hem of her gown, Neris hurried upstairs, knocking over the bowl of water in her haste. Something scuttled along behind her. She closed and locked the cellar door before the sound made it to the top.

7
REVENGE

MONDAY, JUNE 1, 999 AE

T he Hellhound Tavern crouched at the end of a cul-de-sac in the warren of streets and alleys where Kordell had made his escape a little over a week before. The building was constructed of ill-fitted stones and termite-infested timbers. It had originally been a three-story building, but after the roof collapsed, the sluggard owner recycled the debris to form a patchwork roof over the second floor. There weren't many souls brave enough to spend the night there. And this wasn't merely because of the rickety stairway and beleaguered rooms.

The place had a well-deserved reputation for violence and wickedness. Every vice that the Church prohibited could be bought, bartered or sold on the premises. The Paracletian Order had made numerous raids on the Hellhound. But no matter how many times the Church shut it down, it inevitably sprung up somewhere else. It was the kuzda vine of taverns.

Inside, hacked beams wrapped with bands of iron for stability supported the gummy, black ceiling. A fireplace dominated one end of the room. Tables and chairs stood in no apparent order, and puddles gathered on the sloping floor. A long bar stood directly opposite the front doors. Across the room from the fireplace, six booths sprouted from the wall like tumorous growths. The miasma of body odor, flatulence and something vaguely reptilian hung in the air.

Teska Vaun sat in the darkest booth. She wore her cloak hood up—a common enough appearance in the Hellhound—and turned the half-empty mug of ale on the table with her hand. She scanned the common room methodically, as she had done for the past two hours.

She'd watched Kell Sampson and Rennick Glave arrive for their appointed rendezvous. Both men fit the Hellhound the way a prisoner fit a gibbet. They'd taken a table, ordered food and drink, and talked quietly. On occasion, they looked in her direction—she held her breath each time—but they didn't seem to take notice of her. She waited until they had finished their meal, smoked several tabáks and grew visibly restless. Particularly Sampson, who drummed his heavy fingers on the tabletop. She could hear his impatient rumblings from where she sat.

She slid out of the booth just as Sampson looked in her direction. The startled look on his face assured her that her gift remained effective.

"What the fuck?"

Glave looked at him. "What now?" He followed Sampson's gaze to Teska as she walked toward them.

"Where the hells did she come from?" Sampson growled. "I swear on my mother's tits there wasn't nobody over there."

She stopped at their table. Without a word, she pulled a chair across the warped floorboards and sat down across from them. She put her left arm leisurely on the table, keeping the right one in her lap.

"Who're you?" Glave demanded, narrowing his eyes at her.

"And where'd you come from?" Sampson repeated.

She reached up and removed her hood. "My name is Teska Vaun. You're working for me."

Even with her hair braided like an innocent little girl's, she got the reaction she expected—the one she almost always got. Both men stared at her for a moment, dumbfounded. No matter the man, she always had the edge in the first moment. And it was all she ever needed.

Sampson lit a match. "You don't say." He clenched a fresh tabák between his teeth. His eyes roamed across her face.

She recognized his mounting disappointment when they drifted down but couldn't discern her breasts beneath the leather armor.

Glave smiled—a lecherous, greasy curve beneath his braided mustache.

Sampson licked his lips and exhaled a stream of smoke. "Well, this could get interestin' really fast."

She shifted in the chair, a tiny movement that neither man noticed, and pressed the toe of her left boot against the heel of the right. The soft click went unheard among the sounds of the tavern.

"I've paid you twice your normal fee. You'll work for me until the job is done or until I release you. Now let's get down to business."

Glave stroked one end of his mustache. "About bloody time."

"I know what business I'd like to get down to," Sampson said, his steely gaze still searching for a place to land. He reached across the table and put his hand over hers. Only the tips of her fingers were visible beneath the hairy bulk of his paw.

"I'll flip you to see who's first," Glave said, still smiling.

"Piss off, Rennick. I'm first."

"No, yer bloody not. I'm not going after you."

"Then you won't be going at all, jackass."

Teska batted her long eyelashes and made no effort to withdraw her hand from Sampson's sweaty palm. "Gentlemen…" she said, her voice satiny smooth.

Sampson barked out a laugh. "Hear that, Rennick! She called me a *gentleman*."

"…we really do have business to discuss." She looked at them demurely. A flick of her tongue across her lips caused Glave's eyes to widen and his grin to spread. It looked like it might split his head in half.

Sampson took the tabák out of his mouth and flicked ashes onto the floor. "We'll talk business later."

It was exactly what she'd been waiting for. Give men enough time, and they always did something stupid.

With one fluid motion, she yanked her hand from Sampson's, grabbed his wrist and forced his hand over. His knuckles thumped against the tabletop. Her right hand flew from her lap, a silver blur at the end of her arm.

"What the fu—"

Before either man could react, the point of her short dagger creased the flesh of Sampson's palm.

Teska's eyes burned into the mercenary as if she were trying to see through his skull. Her tone was like the edge of the blade, cold and precise. "You so much as twitch and I'll slice through every muscle in your hand. You won't be able to hold it to piss, much less use a weapon." She pressed down on the dagger to emphasize both her points.

"Hey, hey! Wait a second!"

She enjoyed watching the awareness of the situation cross his face, his bluster and bravado shriveling to nothing. Probably just like his balls.

"You bitch!" Glave yelled. He started to leap up but halted, surprise washing over his face. He crouched half in, half out of his chair.

Sampson moved to backhand Teska, but she leaned on the blade. He bellowed like a lost calf. "Rennick, do something, damn it!" The tabák dropped from his fingers and onto the table. "Why the hells are you just standin' there?"

"He can't do anything." Teska threw a quick glance at Glave. "Can you?"

"Uh…no, not exactly. Bloody hells…" He stared down at his crotch. The toe of her boot rested against the inside of his upper thigh, and a narrow blade was positioned against the femoral artery.

"Whaddaya mean? Disarm this bitch before she cuts my fuckin' hand off!"

Teska smiled, tiny dimples appearing on her cheeks.

"He can't help you right now. One twitch—from him or me—and he'll bleed to death in two minutes." She glanced at the thinner, taller man. "Right?"

His face ashen, Glave nodded stiffly. "Yeah." He eased back into the chair, the blade tracking each movement.

She looked back at Sampson. "So, are we going upstairs to rut around like animals…or staying here and discussing business? Will your cock make this decision or your brain? Answer carefully." She smiled as if she were at a tea party, conversing about dainty treats and proper etiquette, but dug both blades harder against their respective targets.

"Okay, okay! We're staying!" Glave raised his hands in surrender. The few patrons scattered throughout the room paid them no attention.

"Yeah, no problem, lady. Everythin's good." Sampson's hand quivered against the table.

She lowered her voice. "Do not mess with me—in *any* way." Madness danced at the edges of her eyes. "I'm not some tavern slut to be fondled. I'm your boss. You forget that, I'll slit your throat."

She applied additional pressure to the blades. Rennick stiffened, panic in his eyes. The tip of the dagger bit into Sampson's palm, drawing a bead of blood. He grunted.

"I'm Teska Vaun. I've paid for your services. You do what I say, when I say, until I say we're done. Clear?"

Both men nodded, swallowed.

The coquettish grin and dimples disappeared. Playtime was over. She withdrew the dagger from Sampson's palm but didn't sheath it until her hand was under the table. Glave's sigh of relief signaled the removal of the blade at his thigh.

"Damn, lady. We was just tryin' to have a little fun." Sampson moaned as he massaged his palm.

"Oh, we'll be having *lots* of fun." Her face was again as serious as when she sat down. "Just not like that."

Sampson picked up the tabák, took a final drag off what little remained and crushed it out on the tabletop. He reached into one of the pockets of his leather vest for another.

Glave sat and studied her, his frown deepening. "Teska…" he said under his breath. His brow furrowed like someone trying to remember where they put something.

Sampson opened the box. "Damn." He crushed the empty box and flicked it onto the table, then turned his attention to Teska. "So give us the details. Your lackey in Sonor said something about an Imperator and a deputy."

She relaxed a little but had yet to retract the blade into her boot. Always better to be prepared.

"That lackey was me. I intend to kill a deputy named Solomon Warner. He serves under a constable—Thurl Cabbott—who's attached to Malachi Thorne. He's the Imperator. You're going to keep everybody else busy while I kill Warner."

Sampson tapped a finger on the table and glanced at the crumpled tabák box. "So that's it? We just make sure everybody else plays nice until you get rid of the deputy?"

She nodded. "That's it. Nothing fancy. I made a vow to kill Warner, and I won't let anyone or anything get in my way—"

"Teska Vaun," Glave interjected. "*Teska* bloody *Vaun*…" Despite the gray teeth and rancid breath, her name sounded almost holy in his mouth. She and Sampson looked at him. Glave grinned. "Kell, I know who this is." The grin spread as if he'd just discovered a huge stash of gemstones. "This is Teska Vaun."

"Well, no shit, Rennick. She's already told us that."

"Hells, you're so bloody thick. Think, man! *Teska. Vaun.*" This time, her name sounded as if she were being called before the Judgment Seat at a tekoya. She suppressed a shudder.

"The Ghost," Glave stressed.

Sampson's scowl made it obvious that he was having trouble making the connection. He drummed four fingers on the table and glanced back and forth at them.

Glave sighed. "Unless I'm the next bloody Heiromonarch, this is the Teska Vaun that damn near ruled the Arkan coast a few years back. She's known from Skonmesto to Last Chapel." His tone assumed the reverential quality once more.

It took another moment, but awareness finally dawned on Sampson. He stared at her with a mixture of uncertainty, disbelief and respect.

"I'm right, ain't I?"

She nodded.

"Holy damn bloody fucking shit. I knew it! Kell, we've been hired by the Ghost herself."

"So you're the one who hit that Church caravan at Sen'Tobia? And the fair at Carthage?"

"And ya stole the bloody relic from the cathedral in Kestown, right?" Admiration beamed on Glave's scarred face. "What'd ya do with it?"

"How'd you pull it off?" Sampson asked.

She allowed herself a brief smile, just enough to flash the dimples again. "I threw it in the sea. Couldn't do much else with it. I sure as hells couldn't sell it."

Sampson's shoulders slumped. "Hey, I'm sorry that we—that I, uh—"

"Never mind," she said.

Sampson leaned back, his chair cracking loudly. "Why they call you the Ghost? And what happened to whatshisname—the guy you pulled all them jobs with?" He folded his arms across his shield-size chest but continued to drum the fingers of his right hand on his sleeve. Beads of sweat dotted his forehead.

She ignored the first question.

"Marco." A wistful look crossed her face, her smile and dimples evaporating like ice in fire. "Marco Bursey." Her eyes moistened at the edges, and she gritted her teeth. *Damn it. Not here, not in front of them.*

Both men watched her intently, the rhythm of Sampson's fingers the only movement either of them made. She swallowed as anger welled up inside her. When she spoke next, her voice was menacing, dark.

"Marco's the reason I'm going to kill Warner. We were going to get married. We'd decided to do one more job, then planned to get as far away from the Church as we could to live out the rest of our lives together."

"What happened?" Sampson asked.

"We were just outside of Nashton—a little place called Anlin that was having a fair. Since the job at Carthage had gone so well, we decided to use the same tactic. We'd hit the fair, head to Last Chapel and hide out there. We even talked about going farther west."

"Into the Devouring Lands?" Glave asked in surprise.

"We talked about it. Marco believed there had to be something else beyond the Devouring Lands. A good place, without the Church."

Sampson patted his belt and vest, likely feeling for another tabák box. "So obviously the job at the fair didn't go well."

She shook her head, the braids moving like serpents on her shoulder. "It started out well. We got in with a few of the performers and used the fair as cover, lying low in the exact place we planned to rob." She smiled at the irony.

"One night, Marco dressed up as a jester. He was just goofing around, having a good time. He really did like making people laugh, especially the kids… Anyway, we didn't know it, but there was a deputy in the audience that night."

"Solomon Warner?" Glave asked.

Her eyes smoldered. "That's him. He recognized Marco through the costume."

Sampson grunted. "I need a damn smoke."

"Ya can pick up a bloody box later. Shut up and listen."

"Warner rushed the stage. Marco grabbed some props and threw them to trip Warner up. Then he ran out the back, but a couple other deputies were around. They caught him."

"How come they didn't catch ya?" Glave asked. "Were ya there?"

She nodded. "I was there. Saw it all."

"And you didn't get caught?"

"No. I blended in with the crowd and got away."

"Wait a second," Sampson said. "If you're *the* Teska Vaun—*the Ghost*—then haven't I heard that you can walk through walls and shit? Hasn't the Church caught you before?"

"Yes, and I've escaped. Twice, in fact."

"Bullshit!"

Her eyes narrowed once again, pinning Sampson to his chair like a bug. "I'm sitting here right now, yes? You don't see any brands on me. I still have both my hands, don't I?"

"Yeah, but nobody can walk through walls and shit."

"You'd be surprised what a ghost can do."

Glave's frustration bubbled over. "Enough, Kell! Shit, let her finish the bloody story."

"Anyway, Warner arrested Marco—after he got a physician's help. Something Marco threw hit the bastard in the eye. He wears a patch now. Too bad it didn't kill him. I followed them as best I could, and I tried to bust Marco out of Church custody, but he was locked down tight."

Sampson chuckled. "Couldn't walk through the wall and get him out, huh?"

"I tried everything I could think of." She looked at Sampson, her voice a low growl. "And yes, dog, I tried walking through the walls." The growl disappeared as quickly as it came, replaced by a hollow softness. "But I couldn't save him. A week later, the Church executed him."

"I guess that makes you a wanted criminal too," Sampson said.

"The Church would love to hang me."

"Us, too." Glave glanced at his partner. "But that ain't going to happen. We always stay two steps ahead of those pompous psalm singers."

Seriousness creased her brow. "That's what Marco thought, too."

Sampson stood up. "What's your plan, then? I'm going to get some tabáks."

"We're in luck," she replied. "Warner and the others have been in Colobos the past few days. Get your equipment together and meet me back here in three hours. We'll make for Colobos. I'll figure out where they're going from there, and we'll ambush them. I kill Warner; you kill whoever you want who's with him."

"And how're you gonna find out where they're goin'?" Sampson spat. "You just gonna walk up and ask the Imperator for his travel schedule?"

She smirked. "No, Sampson. I'm going to walk through walls and shit and listen in on their conversation. I'm the Ghost, remember? I can come and go as I please. They'll never see me." She paused. "It worked on you."

The big man stopped and looked back at her, then huffed, mumbled something under his breath and stalked out of the tavern.

8

TORMENT

The city of Colobos sat at the northwestern tip of Blackshire Bay. It was renowned for its clean, organized market district—referred to as "Uptown" by the locals and as "Downtown" by everyone else—and like Attagon, was constantly expanding. The bay produced massive amounts of delicious salt-water fish that couldn't be found anywhere else, making Colobos a place of unique delicacies. It also laid claim to a burgeoning upper class of merchants and tradesmen.

This morning, Thorne and his men marched through the dungeon beneath the constabulary. Dozens of torches lined the hallway, but smoke did not pollute the air. It escaped through ventilation slits carved in the stone, rising naturally and dispersing in the streets above. The expulsions of the human body, however, lingered. Thorne could taste salty, metallic terror in the air. He imagined that if the look in a lamb's eyes before the slaughter could hold an aroma, this would be it.

"Ah, Master Thorne. I was afraid I'd be deprived of your company today," the prisoner said as they entered the room.

The battered man sat chained to a metal chair in an anteroom off the main torture chamber. A wooden counter along one wall held thumbscrews, hammers, knives of differing lengths and tongs. Torches guttered in sconces, filling the room with sanguineous light. Brown blood stains covered the floor. A closed door stood opposite where they'd entered.

Thorne positioned a chair in front of the prisoner and sat down. Darien settled into the desk in the corner and prepared his recording materials for the fourth day in a row. Cabbott and Warner sat in rickety chairs against the wall, while Hawkes stayed by the door.

"I see you still possess a glib tongue, Jarmarra Ravenwood," Thorne said. "A condition I can quickly remedy."

"Of course you can. Though if you remove my tongue, I cannot tell you that which you are so desperate to know."

Thorne stared at the prisoner, his voice cold as a winter's night. "You can write what I want to know."

The door opened, admitting a mountainous man in a soiled leather apron and greasy breeches. Thick gloves covered his hands, and his face was concealed behind a metal mask into which slits had been cut for the eyes. A series of vertical slits over the nose and mouth allowed for breathing. Thick leather straps buckled behind his scabrous head. In the flickering torchlight, his skin shone bronze. He ducked beneath the lintel and stepped aside to allow the man behind him to enter.

Nicoline Royse, a lawyer of the Paracletian Order, waddled in, already dabbing sweat from his forehead. He was a squat, obese man with waxy skin. As broad as the torturer was tall, standing side by side, they would've looked comical had the setting not been so grim.

"I'm sorry, Your Grace, but your bullish colleague"—Ravenwood nodded toward the torturer—"has already seen to it that I shall never write again." He gazed down at his shattered hand and wiggled his little finger at Thorne.

"Tell me the exact location of Traugott and Kordell, and your torment will cease, Jarmarra."

"I've already told you what I know."

"Then you leave me no choice. Torturer, prepare for the Fifth Degree." He watched Ravenwood's eyes but was disappointed to see no fear, only stoic resignation.

"The Fifth Degree?" Royse repeated in his phlegmatic voice. "Oh, no, Master Thorne. You'll do no such thing. I forbid it." He plodded across the stone floor and held his plump hand in front of Thorne.

"You *forbid*?"

Royse held Thorne's eyes like a vise. "I most certainly do. This man can endure no more torture without serious risk to his life."

"Get out of my way, Royse. This is my interrogation."

Cabbott flashed his deputies a here-we-go-again look.

Royse and Thorne had butted heads since arriving in Colobos. Thorne had elected to skip the First Degree of the Ordeal—stripping the prisoner and showing him the instruments of torture—and had moved straight to the Second Degree. Royse had challenged that decision as well.

"Under the circumstances, I believe it to be a waste of time," Thorne had replied.

"And why is that, sir?"

"First, because a man such as Jarmarra Ravenwood is unlikely to be moved to confession by the mere sight of thumbscrews, knives and bowls of salt. He will not spontaneously confess just because he looks at a pair of pinchers. Second, the Code has been temporarily rescinded. I have the prerogative of disposing of the First Degree if I deem it appropriate."

That had been Saturday. Royse grumbled but could do little as the torturer had started to work on Ravenwood. The Second Degree involved the infliction of pain, but only for brief periods of time—normally for as long as it took the lawyer or cleric present to recite the Four Tenants of the Church.

Thorne had shocked Royse again by moving to the Third Degree on Sunday. Normally, the Code forbade the use of torture on Worship Day. Royse had objected vehemently, and the two ended up in a visceral argument. In the end, Thorne won by sheer force of will. The torment upon Ravenwood had increased as the Third Degree allowed pain to be inflicted for the length of time it took to recite The Penitent's Prayer:

> "Have mercy on me, holy Church, for I have sinned and failed you.
>
> May the Heiromonarch look with favor upon me;
>
> May the Church look with favor upon me.
>
> Forgive my failings and restore my devotion to you, O God."

Yesterday, Thorne had advanced to the Fourth Degree, wherein the agony of specific tortures could be increased, such as yanking on a rope from which a prisoner was suspended. Once again, Royse had protested; another argument had ensued.

Ravenwood had passed out repeatedly, remaining unconscious longer each time. Time was running out, and Thorne needed more details. But by that point, Ravenwood had slipped into that place where the threat of additional pain held little incentive.

Now Thorne rose and faced the lawyer standing between him and Ravenwood. "I will not tell you again, Royse. Get the hells out of my way." He wanted to pillory the man, but he didn't have the time.

"Thorne, this man can't take any more. You're going to kill him before he surrenders what you want to know."

"He is going to die anyway. It might be today, in this room. It might be tomorrow in the one next door. It may be weeks from now at the next tekoya. He is a traitor and has aided and abetted a known heretic—"

"Be that as it may," Royse wagged a sausage-shaped finger in Thorne's face, "you are out of line."

Thorne gritted his teeth and did his best to control his tone. "You presume too much, Royse."

"I am here on behalf of this congregant."

"You," Thorne growled, "are under my direct authority. You have overstepped the bounds of rank and propriety. I am giving you a direct order: stand aside. *Now.*"

Everyone ogled the drama unfolding in the center of the room. Even Ravenwood watched with his one good eye, the other surrounded by swollen, purple flesh. Darien lit his pipe and added the aroma of tobacco to the stale sweat, blood and desperation that clung to the walls.

Lawyer and Witchfinder glared at each other. Thorne's fist clenched; Royse breathed heavily. Thorne towered over the corpulent lawyer, but their resolves seemed evenly matched.

"I will not say it again, Royse," he hissed between his teeth.

The lawyer stomped aside, his eyes never leaving Thorne's.

"Damn," Hawkes whispered to the torturer, "I was hoping for some action." The masked behemoth beside him stood silent and motionless, furry arms folded across his apron.

Seething, Thorne dropped back into his chair and leaned toward Ravenwood. "Last chance, Jarmarra. Tell me about Traugott and Kordell. Where are they? What is this 'freedom' that Traugott preaches?"

Darien resumed recording the interrogation.

Over the past three days, Thorne had gained more pieces to the puzzle of Traugott and Kordell. This torturer was exceptional in his work, and Ravenwood had broken several times.

After fleeing Talnat, the three riders had split up. One went east to Macon-On-Olugee; Ravenwood came south to Colobos. The third took Kordell west to High Pine and had lain low for a day or two. Someone else had escorted Kordell on to Rimlingham.

Thorne had learned that people were attentive to Traugott's ideology. He spoke to them everywhere he went, promoting his ideas and finding new support in every location. Groups of followers were kept small so as not to arouse suspicion.

Ravenwood didn't know where Kordell went after Rimlingham. Information in Traugott's network was dispersed only to those who needed it at the moment. Ravenwood's job had been to ride south and hide out in Colobos. He didn't know if the other riders had special orders or not.

Thorne continued to stare at Ravenwood, willing the prisoner to answer his questions. "The 'freedom,' Jarmarra—what is Traugott talking about?"

The prisoner looked at him with a mixture of pity and regret. "Something you wouldn't understand."

"Tell me and I will decide that."

Ravenwood remained silent.

"When we capture the other two riders, they will surrender their knowledge. You know this."

"Perhaps, perhaps not. We no longer fear your Church, Witchfinder."

"What? Are you so deranged as to forget that the Church holds your eternal destiny in its hands?"

Ravenwood managed a laugh that broke down into a coughing fit. "My soul is my own. It doesn't belong...to the Church. It never did."

Thorne jumped up, knocking over the chair. His fist slammed into Ravenwood's jaw, nearly toppling the prisoner.

Royse backpedaled and started to say something but stopped himself.

"You speak blasphemy!" Thorne exclaimed. "Does your soul mean so little to you?"

With great effort, Ravenwood spat a glob of bloody saliva on the floor. Fresh blood trickled from the corner of his mouth. "On the contrary, Witchfinder. *My soul* means everything to me. Would I endure all this if it didn't?"

"Your mind is broken. Traugott's lies have twisted your understanding. There is no salvation outside the Church. The Church is God."

"I assure you, while my body is certainly broken, my mind is perfectly clear. More clear than at any other time in my life."

"You have plotted against the Church and the Heiromonarch. You have poisoned the minds of those around you. You have sacrificed your immortal soul for the lies of a worthless traitor and heretic."

Ravenwood shook his head.

"You will die for your crimes." He lowered his voice, assuming a more paternal tone. "Traugott is not here to help you. He cares nothing for you. He has used you and discarded you like a goodwife casts aside corn husks."

"You know so little," Ravenwood replied. "And you prove it again and again...when you suppose that by silencing Traugott, you can silence his cause."

"What cause is that?" Thorne demanded, frustration ablaze in his emerald eyes. "The damnation of all those around him? His accession to power? Wealth?" He began to pace.

"Nothing so mundane and nothing so grand. It's the simplest and greatest of all human ideals."

"And that is?"

"You are truly blind, Witchfinder. I pity you. How can a man of such learning and experience not see what is all about you every day?"

"Enough of these riddles!" he roared. "Speak plainly!"

Ravenwood licked his lips. "Traugott's cause is freedom. It is superior to every doctrine you espouse and every coward who serves this travesty called a Church."

Thorne stopped in his tracks and stared at Ravenwood. Darien's quill fell silent. The only sounds were pitiful moans and entreaties from the main chamber.

Thorne locked his hands behind his back and walked to the wall with the closed door. He stared at it, as if reading something that only he could see.

When Thorne turned around his brow was furrowed, and he wore a sneering grin. The dim light from the torches created diabolical shadows across his face. Ravenwood spit again, the saliva slightly less bloody than before.

"Take him in there."

The torturer lumbered to the chair, released Ravenwood's chains and jerked him upright. Ravenwood hissed through his teeth and squeezed his eye tight. His left leg slid uselessly behind him. Thorne and Cabbott followed. Darien gathered his supplies and walked behind Royse.

The room was nearly identical to the previous one, only smaller. It had no windows, and torches lined the walls. Arches supported the ceiling. A decrepit wooden desk and chair awaited Darien, who curled his nose at the reek in the air. Three other chairs were scattered around the room. Empty manacles hung from hooks like metallic vines. A wooden wheel, slightly taller than a man, dominated the center of the room. It resembled a waterwheel encased in smooth planks. The wheel stood on a small platform into which a groove had been set so the wheel could revolve freely. A handle operated the gears that turned the foul-smelling mechanism. A narrow door stood open on the side of the wheel, showing only darkness within.

Darien took his place behind the desk and prepared his materials. Royse eased his bulk onto one of the chairs, but it cracked so loudly that he stood back up, cursing under his breath.

"Are you familiar with the Wheel, Jarmarra?" Thorne asked in a conversational manner.

The prisoner slouched like a lopsided puppet in the torturer's grasp but said nothing.

"It is an ingenious device. Not every dungeon has one, but we are fortunate here in Colobos." He plucked a torch from the wall and motioned the torturer toward the wheel.

The sweaty brute dragged Ravenwood onto the platform with him. Thorne thrust the torch into the doorway, and the torturer forced Ravenwood to lean inside. He attempted to recoil from the stench of urine, blood and excrement. Directly inside the door lay a bare section of flooring. However, on either side—and around the entire interior circumference—dozens of straight razor blades jutted horizontally out of the wood. The flickering light dulled the encrusted black gore. There was just enough height for a full-grown man to walk upright as the wheel turned.

The torturer hauled Ravenwood back.

Thorne grabbed the prisoner's chin and lifted his face so he could look down into Ravenwood's bleary eye. "That is what you are facing, Jarmarra. Tell me where Traugott is hiding. Tell me his plans." He paused. "I can help you, but you must answer me."

Ravenwood smiled. Several of his teeth were missing, his mouth bloody and bruised. He pulled his chin away from Thorne's hand and looked at the ground.

"If you do not tell me, you will be given three complete turns in The Wheel."

"Three turns!?" Royse exclaimed.

Ravenwood didn't respond.

"Very well." Thorne gestured to the Wheel. "Place him inside."

Royse shuffled up to the platform. "Master Thorne, what do you think you're doing? I thought you only planned to intimidate him with this—this vile contraption."

In a flash, everything from the past few days erupted inside Thorne. The interrogation sessions, the mind games, the riddles and vague responses, the lawyer with his piggy eyes and superior attitude, the frustration and failure he felt… He spun around with such force that Royse stepped back. Thorne flew off the platform and snatched the lawyer's frilly shirt in his fist. He stared down into Royse's hickory-colored, spooked eyes. The lawyer smelled of fancy powder and perspiration. "Did you hear the blasphemy that spews from this traitor's mouth?"

"Yes—yes, I did," Royse stammered. "But I—"

"And what did I say? Are we bound by the Code, Master Lawyer?" They were nearly nose to nose.

"N-No."

"Then shut the hells up and stay out of my way." He gripped the shirt tight and glared at Royse for a moment, then pushed him backward. "Get out of here."

Royse struggled to compose himself, his eyes searing holes in Thorne. For a moment, neither spoke.

"You'll regret this, Thorne." Royse stomped past Hawkes, face flushed with shame and rage. The door slammed shut behind him.

"The Wheel," Thorne repeated.

The torturer shoved Ravenwood through the doorway.

"Three complete turns, Jarmarra. Think about it. You will be slashed to ribbons. Save yourself such a fate. Tell me about Traugott."

Ravenwood shook his head almost imperceptibly. "No," he whispered.

Thorne cursed.

The torturer had almost closed the door when Ravenwood said, "Master Witchfinder."

Thorne looked at him.

"He's not what you think. He will not lift a finger against you, and yet you will fall before him." Ravenwood gave a sad smile and turned to face the blades.

With the door closed and secured by a small padlock, the torturer stepped behind the handle.

Thorne gave a frustrated, dismissive flick of the hand.

Our biggest lead yet and he'd rather die in there. Why? What sort of hold did Traugott have over these people? Was it magic?

The torturer gripped the handle, grunted and began to crank. The gears grated together, and the wheel creaked. Muscles bulging, the torturer put his weight behind his efforts, his breathing growing more pronounced behind his mask.

The wood groaned as the wheel began its first revolution. A dull thump issued from within, followed by a wail of agony. As the torturer found his rhythm, the wheel moved more smoothly. Ravenwood's screams, muffled by the wood, were punctuated by a persistent *thud—th-thump, thud—th-thump.*

After two revolutions, the suffering ceased. The muted thumping of the body continued until the torturer completed the third turn. Blood seeped from cracks between the boards.

The torturer released the padlock, pulled the door open and stepped aside. The heavy, coppery stench of blood boiled from the doorway. An unidentifiable chunk of meat landed in a rapidly expanding pool of blood. The torturer put his hands against the side of the wheel and gave it a firm shake. With a slow squelching sound, the remains of Jarmarra Ravenwood dropped from the top of the wheel. The body landed with a gelatinous splat, drenched in crimson and mutilated beyond recognition.

Thorne dismissed the torturer to gather servants to clean up the mess.

Cabbott stood up and stretched. "Did anything Ravenwood said make any sense to you?"

"No."

"Sounded to me like someone who's eaten too much crazy bread," Hawkes said.

Darien rolled up his documents and slipped them into a wooden cylinder. "I heard him say that Traugott is not what you think. What was the other thing he said to you? I didn't hear all of it."

Thorne frowned. "He said that Traugott won't fight me, and yet I'll fall beneath him."

"More riddles?"

"Of course. I suspect the manner of his impending death unhinged him at the end. But I'll tell you this: I would never bend my knee to such a man. No... the only one who will fall is Traugott."

"We done in Colobos?" Warner asked.

"It looks that way," Thorne replied. "There's nothing more to be learned here." He glanced back at the grisly pile of meat in the bottom of The Wheel. The air felt like warm lard against his skin.

"In that case, I'll get these documents filed with my Order here," Darien said as he crossed the room. He followed Cabbott, Hawkes and Warner out.

Thorne stood alone in the antechamber. What "freedom" had Traugott fed these people that would be worth dying for? There was only one thing Thorne would die for: the Church. What could be greater than to die in service to one's God?

He shook his head and walked out of the room.

9

ASSASSIN

Thorne passed doors leading to other chambers and cells. He reached the stairway just as his name was called. Nicoline Royse pursued him as rapidly as his bulk would allow. The lawyer's hair was plastered to his head, and sweat rolled down his face and stained his collar. He wheezed. "Master Thorne...I will speak with you."

"If you would care to walk with me. I have to be at the magistrate's house within the hour." Without waiting, he started up the stairs. Royse made a sound, but Thorne couldn't tell if it was a curse or a gasp of air. "What do you want?"

The lawyer did his best to keep pace. "I think you know...Master Thorne. Your conduct...these past few days...has been insufferable."

Out of the corner of his eye, he saw the man's cheeks puffing like a bellows. The stench of sweat was nearly tangible enough to plaster Thorne to the wall. "I am only carrying out the responsibilities of my job."

"And so am I. Except that...when I try to do my job...you overstep your boundaries."

"I overstep nothing, Royse. I am an Imperator. I outrank you significantly. Your job is to aid me in whatever ways I deem appropriate and not to question my decisions."

"Is this all just another step...in your career ambitions? I've heard about... your plans for higher ranks." Royse's ragged breathing sounded like a dying horse in the confines of the stairway.

Thorne spun around on the lawyer for the second time that morning. The advocate had fallen behind and struggled to close the gap, one waxy hand on the wall for balance. Sweat dripped off his nose. When he realized Thorne had stopped, pained relief swept across his face. A step below Thorne, he halted, mopping his face and brow.

"Master Royse, you would do well to shut your mouth. I do not know what rumors you have heard about me, but I have no ambition to reach higher ranks. And even if I did, it would be none of your concern. You tread perilously close to a formal reprimand and censure."

The lawyer's eyes searched Thorne's, and he wiped his forehead again. "Well, in my professional opinion...the way you've carried out this interrogation... has been problematic. You've rushed through the processes and procedures. You barely gave me...time to speak with the accused. Even your clerk had difficulty keeping up. I believe you have been too bloodthirsty in carrying out this assignment." He leaned against the cool stone wall like a felled ox. "Or are you just trying to live up to your nickname?"

"Is that it?" Thorne snapped, his jaw muscles tightening.

"I want you to know that I'll be filing a formal complaint with our Order citing your questionable conduct during this investigation."

"Do as you will," he said. "I, too, will file my report regarding your insubordination." He swung around and took the stairs two at a time.

"You see?" Royse blabbered as he attempted to follow. "That's part of what I'm talking about. Your rashness...makes it impossible..."

The lawyer's complaints were lost in the stairway as Thorne reached the landing and threw open the door. Walking toward him was Deputy Stefanis DeArmado, a look of concentration and purpose on his swarthy features.

"Master Thorne, sir," he said, "I was just coming ta find you."

"What is it now?"

Royse's labored breathing rolled from the stairway like smoke from a chimney.

"The woman that was brought in yesterday, Lucritia Barker—"

"What of her?"

"Well, sir, I think there's something a might wrong with 'er."

"She is the one accused of witchcraft, is she not?"

"That's right, sir."

"What is the problem, Deputy?" He didn't want to be trapped by Royse again.

DeArmado scratched the back of his head. "Well, sir, she ain't moved in over eighteen hours. Pretty much since the time she was brought in. She's jus' sitting in the middle of her cell. Jus' sitting there—"

Royse poured out of the doorway and gasped. "Master...Thorne. We need—"

"Quiet, Royse. She is just *sitting* there? Why the hells are you wasting my time, Deputy?"

"Well, sir, she seems ta be in some sort of deep sleep, even though she's sitting in the middle of her cell."

Thorne closed his eyes and pinched the bridge of his nose. "Is she *breathing*, Deputy DeArmado?"

"I'd say she is."

"You'd say? But you do not know for sure?" Thorne felt a stabbing pain in his temple.

"Well, sir, how could she not be? I mean, if she were dead…well, wouldn't she fall over?"

"Thorne," Royse said.

"Damnation's flames!" he roared, throwing his hands in the air. "I feel like I am surrounded by a bunch of Primary Catechism students! Very well, take me to her."

DeArmado spun around, and Thorne followed, gritting his teeth and rubbing his forehead. Royse cursed.

The deputy led Thorne into a connecting hallway, through a door and into a chamber with four holding cells along one wall. A row of arched windows near the ceiling stretched across the wall above the cells. The first cell held six women, the second four men, and the third four women. The last cell held a sole occupant, and just outside, a baby-faced deputy whom Thorne knew only as "Ward" looked curious and perplexed. Ward greeted him but kept his eyes on the prisoner.

The old woman sat on the stone floor facing the door. Her long gray hair was lusterless and flat. A mole lurked prominently above her right eyebrow, and age spots dotted her forehead, arms and hands. She was so aged and pale that she reminded Thorne of a crumpled piece of parchment. He scrutinized her for a moment. If she was breathing, it was extremely shallow.

"Lucritia Barker!" he shouted, voice booming in the enclosed chamber. The old woman didn't flinch. He yelled her name again, louder.

"She ain't a'moved since yeast'rdey," one of the women in the third cell volunteered. An audience of prisoners stared through the bars at the unfolding scene.

The door to the holding area opened, and Royse swayed in. He looked as if he'd been dunked in a river, his scarlet face drenched with sweat. "By…the… holy…Church…"

Once again, Thorne called the old lady's name as he rattled the cell door. Neither sound produced any result. "Royse! Come here."

The lawyer staggered toward the cell.

"Open it," Thorne told Ward.

The deputy unlocked the door. All four men stepped inside and gathered around the old woman. Thorne placed his index finger beneath her nose and held it there.

"She is breathing," he said.

"What…did you…need me for?" Royse asked.

Thorne looked at him. "Just in case she needs to say anything to a lawyer. We would not want to violate any processes or procedures, would we?"

The lawyer looked at him with disdain but had no breath with which to reply.

"DeArmado, you and Ward put her in the cell with those four." Thorne pointed. "No use wasting an entire cell on one prisoner."

"'Ey, we don't wanner in here!"

"Leave 'er where she be!"

The deputies bent down to gather the old woman under the arms.

A metallic squeal, followed by a distinct clang, echoed off the stones.

All four men spun around. The cell door was shut.

One of the women began to scream. "Her eyes! Her eyes!"

The four men turned back to the prisoner.

Lucritia Barker stared straight ahead. The whites of her eyes had become solid black, her pupils colorless circles that overtook her irises. A jade mist poured from her gaping mouth as if she were vomiting smoke.

The women in the adjacent cell shrieked and flung themselves away from the bars. Cries of shock and surprise arose from the other prisoners.

Thorne spun toward the cell door, grabbing Ward's shoulder and pulling him along. Royse and DeArmado stood motionless, their eyes bulging.

"Get that door open!" Thorne yelled as Ward fumbled for the keys on his belt.

The mist had nearly covered the floor of the cell but did not spread between the bars. It continued to spill from the old woman's mouth.

Royse stumbled to the side and collided with DeArmado. The deputy fell over, head ricocheting off the bars. He slid to the floor, groaning.

Ward's hands trembled as he found the key.

Royse gibbered something, but Thorne couldn't make out what it was.

All the women in the holding area screamed.

"Th-Th-Thorne!" Royse stammered hysterically. "L-Look!"

The Witchfinder glanced over his shoulder. The bulk of the lawyer blocked his view, but he saw enough.

The jade mist piled up into a thick, wide column between Lucritia Barker and the men. DeArmado moaned and began to stir.

"Hurry up, man!" Thorne shouted. His pulse quickened as the hair on his arms stood up. Prickly heat raced through his body. "What in the Church's name…?"

"Oh shit, oh shit, oh shit!" Ward rammed his arm through the bars and attempted to find the keyhole on the outside of the door. The key scraped and clattered against the metal but refused to land in the opening.

The mist coalesced in front of the old woman, becoming a mossy-colored hulk. Its body was twice as wide as a horse's flank, its arms elongated and ending in hands that possessed four multi-jointed fingers. The thing's head—or the place where the head should be—was a misshapen mass of gray-veined flesh. There were no eyes, only a broad mouth set with rows of narrow fangs. A pair of twitching mandibles sprouted from either side of the mouth. Along the spine, two rows of tentacles undulated as if to some unheard and unholy rhythm.

Royse shrieked and quivered like a sheep before the slaughter.

A diseased and guttural voice erupted from the old woman's throat. "Mal–a–chi Th–orne."

Ward's key hit the lock.

"Now–is–the–time–of–judgment. For–our–sisters–in–the–Communion—"

DeArmado got to his feet and crashed into Ward's back, furiously pushing on the door. The key jostled loose and dropped outside the bars.

Royse recovered enough to join the efforts to push the cell door. Between the lawyer's bulk and DeArmado's panic, Ward was jammed against the cell door. He snatched at the key ring.

"—whom–you–have–burned–we–consign–you—"

"Open it! Open it!" Royse blubbered.

"—to–the–Tenth–Plane–where–your–suffering—"

The creature lashed out and grabbed Royse, the most obvious target. Its hand encircled his waist, the nails nearly touching around his girth. It bellowed and lifted him off his feet.

"—will–never–cease. The–blood–of–our–sisters–will–be–avenged."

The lawyer squealed, hands flailing the air.

With a swift jab, the creature thrust the talons of its other claw into Royse's chest. His sternum shattered, bones piercing his lungs and heart. His scream broke into a gurgling hiss, and blood and spittle flew from his lips. The creature pulled its fingers from the ruined chest cavity, bits of bone and wet gristle trailing behind them.

The old woman cackled through lips that were still frozen wide open.

One of the creature's tentacles slid around DeArmado's chest. Another found his leg. His screams intensified.

The abomination stepped forward on three bloated, dwarfish legs. It flung Royse's corpse against the door. Ward's breath whooshed from his lungs as the dead weight of the lawyer landed on him. Pinned to the floor and against the bars, he gasped for air.

The old woman's head turned toward Thorne with a brittle crack. The creature did likewise. Another tentacle found DeArmado's head.

Fighting his terror, Thorne reached through the bars and grabbed the keys. The first one he tried went into the lock smoothly but wouldn't turn. Behind him, DeArmado's screams rose to a hysterical shrillness, then abruptly stopped—replaced by a moist tearing and snapping.

Thorne tried a second key. No luck. Unable to help himself, he glanced behind him. He immediately regretted it. Tentacles crammed DeArmado's severed head into the creature's mandibles.

Bile climbed his throat as he shoved a third key, then a fourth at the lock with no success. Fear threatened to overwhelm his senses. His fingers were slick with sweat. He fumbled with a fifth key. It, too, fit snugly in the keyhole. He twisted it. The tumbler clicked.

The creature's icy hand grabbed him around the waist and pulled.

The old woman's cackling laughter blended with the prisoner's screams. DeArmado's skull crunched between rows of savage teeth.

Thorne clung to the bars as the drooling obscenity pulled at him. He looked at the cell door. Unlocked, but still closed. Within reach, yet a hundred leagues away. If he let go of the bars to open it, he'd never make it out the door. The pressure around his waist intensified. He clung to the bars like a drowning man to a chunk of driftwood.

What had the abomination said? *"We consign you to the Tenth Plane…"* It was a demon from Tenth Plane—

The mandibles clacked behind him. The thing emitted an eager keening. It yanked him, and he nearly lost his grip on the bars.

Demon. Tenth Plane. What had he learned in his studies!?

A tentacle slithered around his calf, another around his ankle. The stench of meat rotting in the sun filled the holding area.

Thorne's panic surged as his fingers slipped a fraction on the bars. An instant of clarity washed through his brain. The bars! That was it!

Mustering his strength, he pulled himself forward as hard as he could. He slammed into the metal, pinning the demon's fingers against the bars.

The *iron* bars.

It bellowed again but not like before. Thorne knew a cry of pain when he heard one. He gripped the bars as hard as he could, pressing his face against their cool surface, trying to anchor his feet between them. He wiggled to keep the fingers trapped. Curls of acrid smoke sizzled from them. He forced every ounce of his strength forward, as if trying to squeeze his body between the bars. The smoke thickened.

The demon wailed again. Lucritia Barker twitched every time the fingers did. Tentacles flailed like headless snakes.

The claw and tentacles jerked away, releasing Thorne. Scrambling to the door, he drove his shoulder into it, and it sprang open. As the thing yowled, he dove through before it could slam shut again. He crawled away and pressed his back against the opposite wall. His breath came in great ragged gasps. Ward crawled out from under the lawyer's corpse and slammed the door.

The demon plodded around the enclosed space, tentacles probing between the bars. Whenever they touched the metal, it roared in pain. They snapped back inside, streamers of smoke trailing behind.

"Boss!"

The pounding of feet sounded somewhere in the distance. He watched the creature, unsure if the blurriness was the creature dissolving or his own vision clouding. The stench of blood and putrefaction choked the air. The demon reverted to its gaseous state.

Thorne heard more shouts, the scuffle of more feet. Voices surrounded him. Hands helped him to stand. He shook his head.

The creature melted away. The jade mist rose and reentered the old woman's ghastly, twisted mouth. In seconds, it was gone. All that remained was the old woman sitting in the middle of her cell. Her mouth closed slowly, as if someone cranked it shut. Her eyes closed. A shudder passed through her body, and she crumpled over.

Thorne's vision expanded. Deputies gathered around him, including familiar faces.

"—you okay? Talk to me!"

Eyes wild and glassy, Thorne looked from Cabbott to Warner.

"C'mon, Boss…"

He heard his own voice, broken and tremulous. "Is it—is it gone?"

"It's gone. Though what in the name of hells it was, I have no idea," Cabbott said.

"Name of hells…" Thorne repeated. "Exactly. A demon of some kind. Remembered Merrick's training… Iron bars. Demons despise iron."

Cabbott and Warner held Thorne up against the wall. Around them, deputies shouted orders; prisoners yelled and cried.

Hawkes raced in and skidded to a halt. "Malachi, you okay? What happened? Damn, you don't look so good…"

As the adrenaline drained from Thorne, tremors racked his body.

Cabbott motioned to his two deputies. "Get him out of here. Take him to the inn and send for a physician."

Warner and Hawkes put his arms over their shoulders. As they started down the hall, he took one last look at the cell.

The body of Deputy DeArmado lay sprawled against the back wall of the cell, the head missing. Blood had pooled underneath the stump of the neck, and flies zipped over the corpse. The lawyer's body lay in a heap, the chest nothing but a gory cave. Shards of broken bone protruded from the wound. Men helped Ward to stand. His eyes were glazed and unmoving.

Lucritia Barker's body lay bent over in the middle of the cell. Her corpse looked even frailer next to the remains of the lean young deputy and bloated lawyer. Despite the blood splattered throughout the cell, there wasn't a drop on her.

Thorne turned away, and his eyes drifted downward. Across his midsection, the fabric of his surcoat hung in tatters.

Neris Ahlienor, Kiya Mehrit and Sar Maramé looked at one another across the scrying pool as the ripples dissipated. They stood in the coolness of a cave a few miles from Neris's home. Their only light came from candles around the edge of the pool and the morning sun that slanted through the forest outside.

"Rythok-An'hea has failed," Sar Maramé, the tallest and least beautiful of the three, said. The whites of her eyes stood out against her dark skin and the surrounding gloom of the cavern.

Neris bit her lower lip and remained silent, toying with the sleeve of her gown and staring into the pool at her feet. She was the priestess; it was her responsibility to decide what to do next.

"What do you think?" Sar asked, her voice husky and loud.

Neris shook her head and continued to look at the water, as if the answer would float to the surface any moment.

"We—we could try again," Kiya ventured. She was the youngest and one of the newest in the Communion.

"No. It would take several weeks to prepare all of it again," Neris said. "And we'd have to find another volunteer to serve as the conduit. Lucritia Barker was dying and wanted to serve the Communion one final time."

Neris was not as tall as Kiya but came close. Kiya's light green eyes sat a bit too wide on her face, giving her an aspect of wisdom. She wore a light blue gown with strands of ultramarine and silver woven throughout. The strands caught the light like mirrored filaments when she moved.

"*Report.*"

The voice arose from the depths of the cave. It sounded like teeth scraping across stone. Sar and Kiya flinched. The air around them chilled. Flecks of ice began to form around the edges of the pool.

All three women dropped to their knees. The cave floor felt like ice through the thin material of their gowns. They extended their arms, palms up, and bowed their heads. The candles guttered in the chilling air, the flames becoming a coruscating blue.

"Moon of a Thousand Faces," Neris said, her breath visible on the air. "You honor us with your presence."

Outside, not a dozen feet from where she knelt, the sunlight played through the leaves, and birds chirped among the branches. The incongruity was not lost on her as her fingertips began to tingle.

Neither of the other women spoke or looked up, but Neris could see them shivering.

"Tell me what happened," the grating voice demanded.

"Matriarch—" Sar began.

"You do not speak! Only the priestess may speak!"

Sar's mouth snapped shut. Beside her, Kiya trembled. It occurred to Neris that this was likely the first time Kiya had been in the physical presence of the Witch of Tears. She remembered her own first time and felt a pang of empathy, as well as protectiveness, for the young woman.

"Thrice-Blessed Madonna," Neris said in a small, hollow voice, "our quarry still lives. The Elder Demon has…failed to kill Thorne."

A preternatural silence—like being buried in a snowbank—pressed in upon them.

"Why?"

She cleared her throat. "Thorne wasn't alone. Other men entered the cell with him. When Rythok-An'hea materialized, the others—they were in front of Thorne. The demon attacked but didn't get Thorne. He escaped from the cell."

The silence felt like a living thing. The scrying pool was almost completely frozen over.

"M-Matriarch?" Neris risked looking around but saw only her companions. Was she imagining it or did the entrance to the cave grow smaller? It seemed as if it were being stretched away from them, the circle of daylight shrinking.

"Did she—did she leave?" Kiya asked in a mousy voice.

Neris put a finger to her lips.

Without turning their heads, Sar and Kiya scanned the cave. Kiya moved to stand, but Sar put a firm hand on her shoulder, keeping her in place.

The light dwindled to the size of an apple, then a thimble, before being swallowed by the darkness. The candle flames offered a pitiful blue substitute.

A voice, like the bitter wind that howls beneath a door, pressed close to Neris. It was the chill that lingered in the stones of a winter's morn.

"Why did it not pursue?"

The priestess shivered uncontrollably. She closed her eyes and bit her lip. Sar and Kiya stared at her but said nothing.

"R-R-Rythok-An'hea did n-not pursue because the b-b-bars of the cell were made of iron." Spidery legs crept down both sides of her neck and skittered across her throat.

"Iron?" The voice grated beside her ear.

"Yes, M-Matriarch. We d-did not know that. Barker did not t-tell us." She felt pressure around her throat.

Kiya gasped.

A gnarled, blackened hand materialized around Neris's neck. Feculent, pointed nails dug into her flesh. The hand attached to a wrinkled arm with patches of peeling skin, like dirt too long without water. It stretched into the shrouded blackness behind the priestess.

Another period of extended silence followed. Neris's pulse hammered against the frigid claw that held her. She was sure she felt the cracked, pungent skin squirming against her throat. Or maybe it was just her skin prickling and freezing over.

"He must die." The hand around her throat tightened.

Her head felt light, and the cold crept up her jaw and into her temples. Something brushed her shoulder. She felt tiny legs against the back of her neck. Neris gasped. "It shall b-b-be as the Witch of Tears has de-decreed."

Had it crept onto her scalp?

Despite the glacial feel of her skin, sweat broke out across her body.

"Send the Carnifex."

She tried to nod but couldn't. "Yes, M-M-Matriarch." Now she was certain something crept through her hair.

"Do not fail me again, or you will be…replaced."

The pressure around her throat vanished. She gasped and massaged her neck. The candle flames resumed their natural color. The darkness did not dissolve as much as it scuttled back into the depths of the cave.

Neris remained motionless, staring at the other witches. Sar held her position and posture as if she were a statue. Kiya trembled, her eyes wide with terror.

"M-Matriarch?" Neris asked. She could no longer see her breath.

There was silence, except for the woodland noises outside.

Confident that the Matriarch was gone, Neris slapped wildly at the back of her neck and head. When she felt comfortable enough that whatever it was had been dislodged, she said to her companions, "The Witch of Tears has spoken. Make preparations for the Carnifex."

They understood the significance of this command. Like Rythok-An'hea, the Carnifex required a human host. But unlike a demon from the Twelve Planes, the Carnifex was nearly indestructible. Man-made weapons could not harm it, and it would not rest until it had claimed its victim. But if its intended target died before the Carnifex carried out its assignment, it turned on those who summoned it.

The three witches made their way out of the cave and into the early summer heat. Neris found herself praying to the Three Witches that nothing happened to Malachi Thorne before the Carnifex could make contact.

10

MASTER

Thorne suffered only minor bruising from the attack in the holding cell. Having gotten all the information he could from Ravenwood, he hurried his men onto the road toward Rimlingham after an early breakfast.

They traveled in standard formation. Thorne rode in the center, with Cabbott a few feet to his right and Darien the same distance to his left. Hawkes rode point, while Warner brought up the rear. They walked down the middle of the road, causing farmers and laborers heading into Colobos to move aside.

They hadn't gotten far from the city when Warner spotted three riders in the distance behind them. Shortly thereafter, the trio turned north and disappeared.

The day grew excruciatingly hot and miserable, although the sky behind them showed signs of a gathering storm. On either side of the road, fields baked in the sun. Some were separated by thick stands of mimosa, oak and magnolia trees, others by wooden fences or collapsed stone walls. Tobacco, corn, beans and cotton grew in most of them. A few had surrendered to nature once more and were thickets of weeds and briars. Occasionally, a small cottage and barn sat back from the road, like shy girls at a dance. Wildflowers, scrub grass and kuzda vines languished along the shoulders that dipped away from the road.

Thorne kept a constant pace across the green-and-brown patchwork terrain. Cabbott and the deputies became more vigilant whenever they passed close to a deep stand of trees or fields heavy with corn or brambles. Back roads were prime targets for highwaymen, though only a foolish bandit would attempt to attack servants of the Church. But it had already happened in Talnat. And it happened in other places as well. Cabbott thought that anyone who tested Malachi Thorne today would have better luck juggling hornet nests without getting stung.

They made good time and stopped just before noon to water their horses and eat a simple lunch of bread, cheese and jerky. Thorne and Darien conversed while Warner dozed beneath a tree. Cabbott and Hawkes kept watch. A flock of noisome and persistent ducks sat at the pond's edge waiting for morsels.

When they resumed their journey, Thorne took the point.

"You know that's not standard forma—"

"I know," he told Cabbott. "Fall back." He trotted Gamaliel out in front and reestablished their steady pace.

Cabbott reined his horse onto the road. "Solomon—"

"Lemme guess: the rear."

Darien pulled a book from his saddlebag and started to read. Behind them, the clouds massed closer.

They hadn't gone more than a mile when Warner said, "Thurl, could you drop back for a minute?"

Cabbott slowed his horse. Hawkes glanced at him but kept moving. Darien didn't look up from his book. Warner came alongside the constable.

"What is it, Solomon?"

"I was just wonderin' about Malachi," he said, never taking his eyes off Thorne's back. A hot breeze, stirred by the pursuing storm, lifted the Witchfinder's black cape so that he looked like a raven preparing for flight. "Is he okay? He ain't said half a dozen words since yesterday, and he's ornery as a possum in a trap. Did that…*thing* yesterday hurt him and he ain't lettin' on?"

Cabbott's eyes swept the fields and lumpy grassland to his right. "Malachi's all right. Other than being knocked around and a bit of shock, he's fine."

"Come on, Thurl. I know I ain't been with you as long as you've been with him, but I can tell that somethin' ain't right."

Thunder rumbled behind them.

"Was that the first time he's ever been attacked like that?"

"Oh, no. He's had run-ins with the Communion before, though I don't recall any of them being so…unearthly. He had a bout of sickness a few years back that was caused by the Communion. And they set a couple of hellhounds on him once."

"Hellhounds? Damn… Still, somethin's wrong."

Cabbott sighed. Since the land to his right had turned flat and featureless as the bottom of a skillet, he looked down at the hard, cracked road. A faded dashed line ran down the middle. "It's Rimlingham," he said, as if that explained everything.

Warner wrinkled his nose. "Rimlingham? What about it?"

The constable sighed again. "You know how everyone has a master—a teacher they learn from?"

"Sure. Like me and you."

"Exactly. Master and apprentice, teacher and student. Right now, you're under my command. I'm responsible for training you. And one day, you'll have deputies under your command." He wasn't sure if the wind pressing into his back urged him on or cautioned him to be careful. "Well, Malachi's master was a man named Valerian Merrick." He emphasized the name like the missing piece of a puzzle.

"I've heard that name. Pretty decent Witchfinder, too, if I'm thinkin' of the right guy."

Cabbott nodded. "He was one of the best. Ever. Tough old bird. Malachi once told me that Merrick refused to travel with any deputies at all. He took Malachi and a clerk. That was it."

Warner raised his eyebrows and whistled. Hawkes looked behind him at the sound, but Cabbott gave him an all-clear sign.

"Yeah. He was tough as tree bark. But Malachi absolutely revered him. Merrick was a bit older than most when he asked to train Malachi, and he became more than just a mentor. He was like a father as well."

"So what's Merrick got to do with Rimlingham?"

Cabbott lowered his voice and motioned Warner to do the same so it wouldn't carry on the breeze. "Merrick died in Rimlingham."

Warner eyed Cabbott, waiting for more of the story. The old constable looked off to the right, uncertainty clouding his features.

"How'd he die? Was Malachi there?"

"In a manner of speaking. Merrick's death hit Malachi extremely hard, and I know for a fact that he…well, I guess he's never really gotten over it." Cabbott edged his horse closer to Warner. "It's not just that Merrick died," he added. "Not long after that, Malachi received his promotion to the rank of Witchfinder. He was twenty-six years old. He felt—and I think he still feels—that his promotion came at the cost of his mentor's life."

"But it didn't, right?"

"Of course not. Naturally, a vacancy opened up when Merrick died, and promotions came as they always do at times like that." He thought for a moment. "I guess it didn't help that Malachi was the first person named when the promotions were announced. Made it seem like a reward for Merrick's death as opposed to a consequence of it. At least I think that's how Malachi saw it. And so he vowed to become the best servant of the Church possible in order to honor Merrick's memory and the influence Merrick had on him."

"Thurl!" Thorne yelled from the front.

"Keep this to yourself," he said. "I tell you because of where we're going—and because of who you're working under." He spurred his horse forward.

Closer now, the thunder reminded them of its pursuit.

By midafternoon, they arrived in Dade Village. Eggplant-colored thunderheads piled up above them. Bolts of lightning jabbed behind the hills. A cooler breeze pressed against their backs with increased urgency.

Dade Village was little more than a crossroads around which a collection of buildings huddled. The streets were packed dirt, though the main road did have chunks of grayed stoned and the ghost of a double line painted down the center. The jail and chapel—Dade Village wasn't large enough to support a cathedral— occupied the nicest building in the hamlet.

Thorne and Darien dismounted, and after instructing Cabbott to secure lodgings for the night, disappeared inside. The three officers continued down the street until they found the inn. They had just stabled their mounts when the wind blew the first drops of rain into the village.

It happened every time, without exception. Even when he *knew* it was happening, he was powerless to stop it: the closer he got to Rimlingham, the more withdrawn and sullen Thorne became. Remorse washed over him like a sheet of rain, soaking his soul with his greatest failure. He sat on the edge of his flimsy bed in one of the inn's upstairs rooms. The eaves sloped on either side, affording him only the exact middle where he could stand upright. He had learned that the painful way.

But that wasn't what bothered him. The pain from a crack on the skull would disappear. The agony that haunted his soul, however, never had and never would. And that torment wasn't Kordell's escape, though it infuriated him.

It was Merrick.

Merrick had taught Thorne everything he knew and had embrace him as a son. And how had he repaid the man?

I killed him.

Thorne stood and paced the center of the room, but the repetitive movement did not silence his thoughts. Merrick had been there for him, had taken an interest in his well-being after he became a ward of the Church. Merrick sponsored him throughout school and fostered his ambitions to serve the Church. He welcomed Thorne as his apprentice. Growing up, Thorne had no greater goal than to make Merrick proud. But instead, Merrick's blood was on his hands.

He stopped and dropped to the bed again. He sat with his elbows on his knees, head hanging down, and imagined he could see his mentor's blood actually discoloring his hands. His throat tightened, and he squeezed his eyes to keep his tears in place.

Someone knocked on the door.

Thorne cleared his throat and blinked several times. "Enter," he said, glad for the distraction.

Darien stepped in. He glanced around the tiny room and raised his eyebrows. "I see you've got the master suite."

"Not much, is it?"

"No, but then again, you don't have to share a room with Thurl." He smiled. "You've been up here since dinner. Everything okay?"

Thorne managed a smile that he hoped was sufficient to fool the clerk. "Yes, I'm fine, Dario. I just…needed some time alone."

"You mean in addition to all the time you spent alone on the road today?"

He said nothing but wished the room had at least one window he could look through to avoid Darien's gaze.

"Malachi, I know this journey is a difficult one for you," Darien said in his soothing way. "It always is. But what happened to Valerian Merrick wasn't your fault. And Kordell's escape wasn't your fault, either."

Thorne only looked at his friend.

"Do you plan on taking a walk tonight?"

Over the years, Thorne had developed a routine in the towns and villages he visited. Every night he had the opportunity, he enjoyed walking through the streets. He did it to get a sense of the community and to have a basic idea of the lay of the land.

Thorne pondered the question longer than he wanted. It should be an easy decision. Although there wasn't an abundance of streets to explore, he could still use the exercise. He could enjoy the stars. He nodded, got up, and they walked downstairs.

Cabbott and the deputies followed them outside.

"Walk with me, Tycho," Thorne said.

Normally, he walked alone with his friends a discreet distance behind. But tonight, he welcomed the company of the gregarious young man who'd been raised in a traveling fair with his three sisters. Perhaps some of the stories from his youth would serve to distract Thorne's mind—although Hawkes had already started asking him about the demon in Colobos. They walked down the main street, with Darien, Cabbott and Warner following.

The evening was cool after the storm had barreled through. The thickness of the summer air had abated but would return tomorrow with a vengeance. Puddles spotted the road, and cats crouched in the shadows. The men passed a few homes set back from the road, a window or two faintly illuminated. There probably weren't a dozen streets in Dade Village, and they had already finished their third.

Behind them, Warner sidled close to Darien. Keeping his voice low, he asked "Do you know about Valerian Merrick?"

"Yes. Why do you ask?"

"Well, I—earlier today, I was askin' Thurl why Malachi was so withdrawn. He told me about Rimlingham, about Merrick."

The clerk looked at Cabbott, who shrugged his shoulders. "I thought he should know since we're headed that way."

"Just as long as you don't talk to Malachi about it," Darien said. "And it doesn't go beyond our group."

"How did Merrick die?"

"Go ahead, Thurl." Darien sidestepped a puddle. "You started this."

Up ahead, Thorne and Hawkes turned a corner.

Cabbott cleared his throat. "The night Merrick died, the Church conducted a raid on a group of agitators outside Rimlingham. They were meeting in a village called Toadvine. The Church had the opportunity to arrest all of them at once. So they rode out to Toadvine late that night and raided an old farmhouse where their meeting was taking place."

The three men turned the corner, following Thorne and Hawkes across the street.

"Merrick led the raid. He had about twenty men with him—"

"Eighteen, according to official sources," Darien said.

"And Malachi was one of them," Warner said, more a statement than a question.

"Well, yes and no. He was *supposed* to be. Malachi was part of the detachment. However, he didn't ride out with them."

"He was backup?" Warner asked.

"No," Darien continued. "He should've been with them the whole time, but he was…delayed in getting to Toadvine, and the raid started without him."

"Those freethinkers put up more of a fight than expected," Cabbott said. "At some point, the old house caught fire. Thing was a damn tinderbox to hear them tell it. Merrick got trapped inside, and the roof collapsed."

Thorne and Hawkes turned another corner, back toward to the inn.

Darien took out his pipe, lit it and blew gray smoke into the darkness. "When Malachi arrived, the building was an inferno. No one could get in."

"Yeah, he believes that if he'd been there—like he was supposed to be— Merrick would still be alive. Merrick wouldn't have needed to go inside."

"What was he doin' that kept him away?" Warner asked.

There was a moment's pause.

"We don't know," Darien said. "To my knowledge, Malachi's never spoken of it to anyone."

"When the roof fell in, it took out the floor and foundation as well." Cabbott held his right hand over his left and brought them together with a hollow clap. "The whole thing went right into the ground."

"The land in that region is honeycombed with caves and sinkholes," Darien said. "The farmhouse was built on top of a cave, and when everything collapsed—"

"Merrick fell into the cave?"

"That's correct. The next day, when the fire died down, Church officials went down into the cave to retrieve Merrick's body. It was little more than a charred shell and buried deep under the debris."

"Took them the better part of a day to get all the bodies out."

Warner took a long stride over a puddle, his foot squelching in the mud as it came down. "Was Malachi there when the body was found?"

"He was." Darien exhaled smoke. "Malachi carried Merrick's body back to Rimlingham. From what I've heard, he grieved tremendously. Merrick got a Church burial with full honors in Rimlingham. Every time we pass through, Malachi becomes distant. It preys on his mind and soul. But he'll be fine once we're finished in the city."

The inn came into view. Thorne entered, but Hawkes waited outside for them.

"Join me for a drink, guys?" he said as he leaned against the doorframe.

"You buyin'?" Warner asked.

"No, I'm not buying. But you can sit at the same table as me."

Warner groaned.

"I'll join you," Darien said as they reached the door.

Cabbott nodded. "Me too."

"Oh, what the hells." Warner followed them inside.

They had their choice of tables, and the landlord hurried to the bar to pull their drinks. He distributed their cups and tidied up the room. They drank, talked and laughed until the landlord barred the front door for the night. He bade them good evening and lumbered upstairs. The soft glow from an oil lamp on their table, the only light in the room, cast their shadows across the walls like playful ghosts.

They were preparing to retire when a hard pounding on the door startled them. Cabbott signaled the deputies to readiness as he moved to the door. The knocking repeated, more rapid and urgent.

"Who's there?" Cabbott called through the door.

"My name's Jack Carrier. I'm a posel for the Church. I have an urgent message for Dario Darien."

The messenger was so loud and the room so quiet that they heard every word, even through the door. Cabbott withdrew the wooden bar. Footsteps sounded overhead, and the innkeeper descended the stairs, his hair sticking out like a hedgehog.

"What's goin' on? Who's there?" he demanded.

Hawkes quietly filled him in.

Cabbott opened the door enough to peer into the night. He stepped back, and a young man entered. He wore muddy breeches, a simple gray tunic and dark cloak. He smelled of rain and horse sweat. "Dario Darien?" he asked the room.

"Here," the clerk replied, raising his hand.

As Cabbott closed the door, the posel reached inside his cloak and withdrew a piece of parchment. "I've been sent from Colobos to deliver this message to you."

Darien took the parchment. It was sealed with two dollops of hardened red wax. One held the imprinted seal of Talnat, the other the seal of Witchfinder Tang Tien Qui.

"It came from Talnat early this morning," Carrier said as he looked longingly at the bar.

"Talnat?" Darien's eyebrows rose in surprise.

"Yes, sir." Carrier lowered himself into a chair and stretched his legs out. He asked the innkeeper for a cup of ale.

Darien cracked the seals, and broken chips of wax fell to the floor.

More footsteps sounded on the stairs.

Darien unfolded the parchment and moved closer to the oil lamp.

"What's going on?" Thorne asked as he reached the bottom of the stairs.

"Dario got some kind of message from Talnat," Warner told him.

In the jaundiced lamplight, Darien's eyes widened as they moved back and forth.

"What's it say, Dario?" Cabbott leaned in closer.

The innkeeper returned with Carrier's ale.

"Dario? What is it?" Thorne sat down beside his friend. "Have they found out who killed Jairus?"

The clerk laid the parchment on the table and looked at Thorne. "No…it's not about Jairus." With trembling hands, he slid the parchment toward Thorne: "It's Demerra. My sister's been accused of witchcraft."

11

FERRY

THURSDAY, JUNE 4, 999 AE

In the charcoal gray of predawn, Dario Darien packed his saddlebags outside the inn. He said nothing, his brow creased with worry and determined intensity. The velvety shroud of night receded from the east, and birds started their songs to welcome the new day. Across the road, a dog wandered by, nosing the ground.

Hawkes led his horse out of the stable. He yawned as he placed a blanket and saddle on its back. He checked each strap and buckle, fitted the bridle and made sure his weapons were ready. He tied his travel kit behind the saddle. After fitting spurs to his boots, he climbed into the saddle and waited.

Thorne walked over to his friend. He'd spent most of the night trying to persuade Dario from leaving immediately after receiving the message. It wasn't safe for one man to travel alone, especially after dark. The clerk finally relented, agreeing to wait until dawn to depart. Thorne had ordered Warner to accompany Dario, but Hawkes volunteered instead.

"This has to be some sort of mistake," Darien said. "Demerra would never... She needs me. Cassidy and Cassandra need me."

Thorne nodded. "You should make Talnat in two days. We'll keep on to Rimlingham and then Baymouth if need be. If our plans change, or we come across new information, I'll send a redvalk."

Darien nodded. "I'll keep you informed about what's happening."

The two men clasped arms.

"Tycho, look after him," Thorne said.

"Don't you worry. We'll be fine."

The sky was a hazy pink behind the trees as both riders spurred their mounts down the road.

Back in the common room, Thorne sipped his tea and watched the inn-keeper start the fire. They were the only guests; nevertheless, the owner prepared breakfast as if the Heiromonarch himself were present.

Thorne stared into his teacup and frowned. Why would the Church arrest Demerra? And who had named her as a witch?

The process for acquittal could be lengthy—a period when people some-times died from malnutrition, torture or disease before their cases were resolved. The Church usually viewed such consequences as fortuitous: it was God's will. It also saved the Church time and money. But for the first time, Thorne really knew the accused, and not just from court documents or interrogations. He'd taken dinner with Demerra Gray and her family several times. They'd become the closest thing to having a family of his own as he was likely to get.

And what about Cassidy and Cassandra? The message hadn't mentioned them. Were they in the holding cell with their mother?

It wasn't uncommon for the children of accused witches or traitors to re-main under guard. Although children received more leniency, they could still be kept from other family members. They could also be tortured, but only within certain limits. The Code established strict rules regarding the interrogation of children.

But the Code had been rescinded. Thorne's stomach turned cold, and he scowled.

If he didn't need to get his hands on Kordell and Traugott so badly, he would be riding with Dario right now. He could put an end to the baseless accusations against Demerra. He cursed his quarry for forcing him to choose between them and Dario, but Dario could handle himself. The clerk would figure out what was happening without Thorne. For now, it was vital that Thorne silence Kordell and Traugott soon; otherwise, they'd only become bolder. And more dangerous. Still, having to choose between them and his friend left him bitter.

The innkeeper appeared with a plate of scrambled eggs, thick strips of ba-con and a hunk of fresh buttered bread.

"Morning, Malachi," Cabbott said as he came down the stairs.

Warner trailed behind him. "Mornin', Boss."

He acknowledged their greetings but kept chewing and staring into the distance. The innkeeper brought them cups of tea and hustled away to fill their plates.

"Dario and Tycho get away okay?" Warner asked.

"Yes, they left about half an hour ago."

"What's that runt Qui up to, you think?"

Thorne sipped his tea. "It isn't Qui, you know that. Someone has falsely ac-cused her."

"But what for, Boss? I ain't never met the woman, but I can't imagine that Dario's sister could be a witch. Why lie about her?"

"Probably someone with a grudge. You know how easily a small rebuke or whispered rumor can lead to an accusation." He savored the fresh bacon and eggs; the bread was warm and springy to the touch.

"Boss?"

"Hmm?"

"I've been wonderin'... How many people have we—that is, the Church—how many have we put to death who were like Dario's sister? I mean, who were innocent?" Warner searched Thorne's face like a poor man hunting for a misplaced coin.

Well, go ahead—answer him. How many innocent people has the Church—have you—condemned to death?

The thought tasted foul in his mind. It wasn't the first time he'd considered it. He'd just gotten good at suppressing it in favor of his zealousness. Rules and procedures ensured that justice was served. It had worked for centuries. After all, the Church was right in its pronouncements and decisions. The Church didn't make mistakes.

The Church was God.

Except something wasn't right in Talnat. An innocent woman was going to be subjected to the Ordeal until she confessed. Or died. And Dario was convinced there was more to Jairus's death than simple thievery.

Warner's gaze never strayed from Thorne's face. The innkeeper returned with Cabbott and Warner's breakfast. Thorne welcomed the interruption. The morning sun eased through the small windows as constable and deputy worked over their plates.

"Boss, you didn't answer my question."

Thorne knew what thoughts darted around the young deputy's mind: Could my widowed mother be accused so easily? Would my younger sister receive proper justice if arrested? He looked at Warner again and knew he couldn't escape the question any longer. He sighed. "I don't know, Solomon. I truly don't know."

The Church doesn't make mistakes.

Does it?

By the time they finished breakfast, packed their gear and set out for Rimlingham, the sun was already cooking the land even though it was barely nine o'clock. The air was thick and heavy; it was like trying to breathe through mortar.

Deiparia had two seasons. People either suffered under bitter cold and incessant snow—even in the southern lands—or through the sweltering heat of the long summer months. There wasn't a spring or an autumn to speak of. One day, the trees had leaves; the next, they turned brittle and fell off. One day, their branches were bare; the next, they were budding.

Thorne, Cabbott and Warner rode across the gently sloping land of thick pine forests and open fields. Tall grasses, kuzda vines and brambles separated plots of beans, carrots and some of the worst-looking corn they had ever seen.

About an hour before lunch, they came to the Talpohsa River. The road descended to a small shack and a ferry waiting along the bank. Fat flies annoyed their horses as they passed the shack, where the greatest concentration of them buzzed in and out of the windows. Two passengers stood on the ferry.

The ferryman—a broad-shouldered fellow—tied a rag around his head to protect it from the relentless sun. As they drew near, Thorne could make out the man's patchy beard and mustache. His nose was flat and wide, as if someone had hit him across the face with a board.

"G'day, ya Grace," the ferryman said with a bow that seemed a little exaggerated. "Constable. Dep'ty." He nodded in each of their directions. "Ye've come just in time. I was a'setting to put out." His voice fluctuated between different accents, as if he couldn't decide which one he liked best.

"Our God, the Church, smiles upon us this morning, then," Thorne said, dismounting. He prepared to lead Gamaliel on board when the ferryman raised his hand.

"I'm sorry, ya Grace, but I'll have to come back for the hawses."

"Why? There is plenty of room. I have been this way many times before."

"Aye, yeah, there is. But the ol' damn thing ain't s'strong no more. Landowner's supposed ta get a new one, but ain't happened yet. So hawses have to wait."

Grumbling, they hitched their mounts to a nearby post and stepped onto the creaking ferry. The two passengers at the front turned to look. Both wore the simple traveling garments of pilgrims: thin blue tunics, breeches and sandals. One was female, shorter and quite attractive, with red hair plaited in a single braid. The other was a tall man, older than the woman by at least fifteen or twenty years. Father and daughter, most likely. A heavy oilcloth lay on the deck between them.

Thorne nodded in their direction. "Congregants."

"Your Lordship," the man replied. The girl remained silent but bowed. They turned back around and looked across the water.

The ferry was a rectangular platform lashed together with sun-bleached ropes. Two waist-high railings stuck up on the right and left sides. On the right railing, two ropes—one at the front, the other at the rear—attached to pulleys on a guideline overhead. The guideline stretched from a large tree behind them to one on the opposite bank. A second guideline ran through pulleys mounted horizontally atop the left railing and likewise anchored to the trees on either side.

Thorne stared at the weather-beaten boards beneath his feet. They fit together tightly, the cracks sealed with pitch. He stomped on them. They seemed sturdy enough.

The ferryman hopped on board. He pulled a pair of thick gloves from his wide belt and dug his hands into them before grasping the rope that ran across the top of the port railing. He hauled on the rope, and the ferry slipped away from the bank.

The Talpohsa River ran swift and swollen. Several miles upstream, the river descended through a series of rapids, where the water built momentum before it leveled out at the ferry crossing. Recent rains had muddied the water, giving it a turgid ochre color and littering it with broken tree limbs.

As the ferry left the shallow water, the current grabbed it and tried to push it downstream. The ropes creaked, pulled taut by the force of the river. The ferryman continued to haul them forward, muscles straining against the water pressure.

Thorne sat down on a bench that ran along the right side of the ferry. Warner stood in the middle of the deck with his arms folded. Cabbott walked over and sat beside Thorne.

"Looks like he's had some rough customers," he said low enough that no one else could hear.

Thorne glanced up at the ferryman. His face and arms were crisscrossed with scars. It looked as if he'd fought several gorah cats and hadn't fared well against any of them. Seen in profile, the bridge of his nose climbed straight up to his forehead without the slightest bit of indentation.

The female pilgrim kept glancing back at Warner.

The river sloshed against the side as the ferryman breathed heavily at his task. The air smelled of mud and fish. While the temperature on the river was somewhat cooler, the sun still simmered with unrelenting force.

When they reached the middle of the river, the ferryman halted to wipe sweat from his forehead. The river buffeted them up and down.

"Now!" the female pilgrim yelled.

The ferryman yanked a dagger from its sheath and turned toward Thorne. The two pilgrims spun around, steel flashing in the sun. The male pilgrim held two curved blades. The woman, a slim dagger gripped in her fist, screamed in rage and launched herself at Warner.

"Damn it!" Cabbott cursed, heaving himself upright.

"About bloody time," the male pilgrim said.

The ferryman remained silent as he went for Thorne. He held the knife waist high.

Cabbott ripped his saber from its sheath and stepped in front of Thorne. The ferryman snarled as he jabbed at Cabbott. The constable had the advantage since his saber gave him a longer reach. However, this did not deter the ferryman, who continued slashing the air.

Thorne jumped up and drew his rapier. He edged toward the rear of the ferry, careful of his footing. His eyes never left the burly, flat-faced attacker. The ferry rocked back and forth, churned by the river and the conflict.

"What the hells is this?" Warner shouted at the woman. Her blade had already opened a gash in his leather armor. He parried her next attack with his own dagger.

"This is for Marco!" she screamed. Her blade, a silver gleam in the sunlight, opened another gash, this time on his left arm.

The male pilgrim slipped past the woman and Warner, and moved along the left rail, joining the ferryman. Together, they formed a human shield that separated Warner and his assailant from Thorne and Cabbott. The pilgrim grinned beneath his braided mustache; the ferryman remained stern and silent.

"Who's Marco?" Warner shifted his dagger to his left hand and drew his saber with the right.

Thorne and Cabbott advanced. Their opponents rushed forward. If the woman, answered they didn't hear it.

Thorne's sword was a blur of motion as he probed for an opening. The ferryman's long dagger met his blade stroke for stroke. He was quicker than he looked.

Beside them, the pilgrim's twin blades slashed back and forth. They clanged against Cabbott's saber, seeking an opening. The air filled with grunts and the grating of metal on metal.

Warner, his saber free, crouched and braced himself. The woman scuttled back, dropped to one knee and reached under the oilcloth. Warner wiped sweat with the back of his hand.

He panted. "Who…are you? And who's…Marco?"

The woman pulled a falchion sword from under the cloth and stood up. The sun shone brilliantly on her fiery red hair. She snarled like a feral dog, brows knit in fury. "I'm going to kill you, you bastard!" She moved toward him, sweat covering her face, sword slicing the air.

"Why? Who the hells…are you, anyway?"

"You don't remember," she said. "I'm not surprised. You were too concerned with my boyfriend to pay attention to me. Bad mistake, Churchman." She lunged forward, the sword shimmering in the light. "For Marco!"

Warner dodged aside.

Thorne and Cabbott gasped the humid air in great gulps. Their opponents did not seem as winded. Aside from a small nick here and there, none of the four had yet to land a significant blow.

"Who sent you?" Thorne's black hair lay plastered against his head and face. The ferryman kept smiling. Saber and daggers struck, parried, struck again—a metallic dance accompanied by the grinding of blade against blade.

Cabbott made to charge, feinted, rushed forward. The pilgrim was caught off guard and stepped back. Cabbott hacked at him, pressing his advantage.

Warner sidestepped another attack. He countered with one of his own and pulled back. He stood in the right front corner of the ferry. The river splashed around his feet.

The woman kept coming. With a cry of exertion and rage, she swung her sword at his head. Warner barely ducked. The blade whistled past and sliced through the front rope that tethered the bow to the guideline overhead. The ferry bucked as the current slammed against the loosened bow. Warner lunged for the right railing and held on, crouching. The woman fell backward and gripped the opposite rail.

The lost mooring pitched Cabbott and the pilgrim toward the ferryman. All three men piled up against the left railing. The left guide rope that the ferryman had been using pulled taut. It creaked as it held the ferry like a slingshot ready to fire. Thorne stumbled against the left railing, and the ferry tilted down even more. The uneven weight and the water pressure lifted the right side of the ferry out of the river.

Cabbott punched with his free hand. He caught the pilgrim under the chin, and his teeth cracked together. The jolt caused him to drop one dagger, and it disappeared into the river.

"Solomon!" Thorne yelled.

The deputy looked at him, nodded and tightened his grip on the railing.

"Thurl!" Thorne stretched his arm toward the constable, who lunged and grabbed Thorne's wrist.

The pull rope behind them snapped. The loose ends zipped through the pulleys and into the river.

The ferry shot sideways, tethered now only by the stern rope that connected to the guideline overhead. The ferryman and pilgrim fell backward, tumbling down the river-washed deck, grasping for any handhold as they did. The woman grabbed the ferryman as he slid past. She strained to hold his soggy weight against gravity. The male pilgrim slid off the front and into the roiling water.

The guide rope overhead frayed under the strain.

"We've got to get off this thing!" Thorne yelled.

Warner pulled himself up. "Oh shit." He looked up the length of the ferry, past the others, past the stern, to the river.

Thorne and Cabbott turned around just in time to brace themselves.

A thick tree trunk slammed into the back of the ferry. The guide rope snapped. The ferry and its passengers plunged beneath the water.

Thorne awoke to bright light and the muffled drone of the river. He took in the leafy canopy above him—and realized he couldn't breathe. Panic seized his brain. He gulped for air, but his chest refused to cooperate. He clawed at his throat, tossing his head from side to side.

Two dark shapes appeared above him. Hands rolled him onto his stomach. Something hard pressed into his back repeatedly, rhythmically. He would've screamed that he couldn't breathe, but he still had no air. The repeated pressure on his back intensified. Then, a torrent of water geysered from his throat. He inhaled with ugly, ragged gasps before vomiting again, less water this time. His chest burned, and his throat was raw. But the air tasted deliciously sweet compared to the fishy murk of the river—

The river!

He flailed about and struggled to push himself off the ground. His arms were wet ropes; his legs trembled.

"Easy, Boss. Take it easy. You're safe. Just breathe easy." Warner's voice sounded wrapped in cotton.

Thorne shook his head, but it wasn't hard enough to dislodge the water that clogged his ears. The hollow sloshing inside his skull threatened to drive him mad.

He pushed himself onto his hands and knees and looked around. They were in the shade of several trees. The ground beneath him, soft with new grass, glistened with the water he'd thrown up. Wildflowers and thick bushes grew nearby.

"Think you can sit?" Cabbott's hands were on his shoulders.

He attempted to reply, but only a raspy squeak emerged, so he nodded his head.

"Just rest a few minutes, Malachi."

He nodded again and sat breathing in and out, head drooping. His friends talked amongst themselves, but he couldn't make out anything they said. He shook his head, more forcefully this time, but still couldn't dislodge the water. His chest blazed like a blacksmith's furnace.

At some point, he lay back and watched the sunlight through the leaves. The summer heat felt good and made him drowsy. He fell asleep, awoke and drifted off to sleep again. When next he awoke, he felt better. Even his throat didn't hurt as bad, and his clothes were nearly dry.

They sheltered in a grove of trees on the river's floodplain. Cabbott and Warner dressed, having laid their clothes out to dry. Thorne shook his head again, and this time, his ears popped. The sounds of birds, insects and the river rushed in, clear and precise. He stood and walked over to his friends.

Warner adjusted his eye patch. "How you feelin', Boss?"

"I'm okay, I think. What the hells happened?"

"You don't remember?" Concern filled Cabbott's voice. "You didn't crack your head on something, did you?"

"I remember the ferry, those three people—who were they, anyway? And where are we?" He didn't have his boots on, and the grass felt like spongy moss beneath his feet.

"Well, the good news is that we're all alive, and we're on the western bank of the river," Warner said. "I figure we're about three miles or so downriver from the crossin'."

"You two okay?"

"Yeah, we're fine. Thurl latched onto a plank from the ferry, and I've always been a pretty good swimmer. Other than being waterlogged, we're good."

"As for those people," Cabbott said, "from what Solomon's told me, the woman is—was—the crazy girlfriend of a criminal he helped catch. Guess she wanted revenge on him."

"And the men?" Thorne retrieved his boots and pulled them on. His cloak hung drying on a branch.

"We don't know. Maybe brothers or cousins."

"Where are they now?"

Warner shrugged. "Feedin' the fishes and eels is my guess."

Thorne looked toward the river. "Western bank, eh? Good." He studied the sky and the shadows on the ground. "We've still got the afternoon ahead of us. Let's head for Alexity. We can pick up some horses and gear there." With that, he started north, parallel to the river.

"Boss, you sure you don't wanna rest some more? You just about drowned."

"We're going to need pretty much everything," Cabbott said to no one in particular. "None of us have any weapons. All our stuff's still with the horses."

"I'm fine, Solomon. We've got a lot of ground to make up." Thorne set a quick pace, and they discussed the attack as they walked.

Cabbott picked up and discarded potential walking sticks as they went. "The ferryman's dead for sure. He floated past us not long after we fished you out."

"Solomon, tell me about the woman," Thorne said.

"Her name's Teska Vaun. You remember me tellin' you about the jester in the play and how I lost my eye? Well, the jester's name was Marco Bursey. And Teska Vaun was his girlfriend or fiancée or somethin'. Thinkin' back, I do remember seein' her around at the time."

"Marco Bursey," Thorne mused. "I've heard that name before."

"Well, she sure wasn't pissing around." Cabbott, having found a stick he liked better, slung the previous one into the bushes along the riverbank. "Those two bulls she had with her weren't pushovers. They were trained and experienced."

Thorne nodded. "Sellswords, most likely."

By midafternoon, they regained the ferry road. They gratefully accepted a ride from a farmer in a wagon, and as it rambled along the gray stone road, Thorne turned to Warner.

"I've been thinking about Vaun. If she's who I think she is, she's wanted for theft, robbery, prostitution and probably a few more things since last I heard of her. They call her the Ghost."

"With a list like that, I'm surprised she hasn't been caught already."

Thorne snapped his fingers. "That's it! Now I know why that name's familiar. She *has* been caught before. Her name's been on at least two different dockets." He paused a moment. "She's the one who caused all that trouble along the coast a few years back."

"So why ain't she dead? Or at least in custody somewhere?"

Thorne shook his head. "That's a good question. She wouldn't have been released… She must've escaped."

"*Twice?*" Cabbott said. "I doubt that."

The three men lapsed into silence. The driver hummed to himself as the wagon creaked and rattled over the uneven road. Farms appeared on the countryside as they neared Alexity.

Thorne stared at the passing scenery. How had she managed to escape twice? The thought was like a splinter in his mind. Was someone in the Church helping her? But for what possible gain? Had they gotten too relaxed?

Is this an example of why the Council wants me to strike fear into people?

Late afternoon shadows lengthened across the fields as the wagon lurched its way into Alexity. Like Dade Village, it wasn't big enough to support its own cathedral but did have a small chapel.

It would have to do until they could reprovision at Rimlingham. Thorne hopped off the wagon as it passed the white-stone chapel, leaving Cabbott and Warner to ride on to the inn.

The Cleric of Alexity, Will Gethen, was a humble young man serving his first assignment. He recognized Thorne and welcomed him graciously. Gethen was genuinely distraught when he heard about the events that had brought

Thorne to his village. He gave Thorne enough money to see them through to Rimlingham and assured him they would have new horses by morning.

One benefit of serving the Church was the availability of resources. Every chapel and cathedral kept spare weapons and clothing on hand for emergencies. They also kept funds for food, transportation, lodging or anything else a servant of the Church might need on the road but found himself without.

"I'll send some men to the river to retrieve your horses from the eastern bank," Gethen said. "Of course, that's assuming they haven't been stolen already."

It only took half an hour, and when Thorne left the chapel, he had a new capotain hat, tunic and breeches. He kept one of the daggers Gethen had given him; the other would go to Warner. Cabbott could have the short sword. They'd all have to make do and pray to the Church that nothing else happened before they could make it to Rimlingham.

12

FAMILIAR

With fresh horses under them, they'd set out on Friday morning and made good time, arriving in the hamlet of Buzzard's Roost just after nightfall. They'd gotten on their way again that morning before dawn.

As they traveled through the outskirts of Rimlingham, the road grew wider and the farms to either side sat closer together. Carts and wagons, merchants in guarded caravans, pilgrims and laborers passed with increasing frequency. In places where the road became congested, people obediently moved aside to let the Church officials pass.

The road ascended the gentle incline of Red Mountain, where veins of rust-colored rock stood out like the gigantic claw marks of some titanic beast. They crested the mountain, and moments later, the road dropped away into a valley, where the city hunched under the blistering sun. As they descended, a monumental statue along a flattened ridge caught their attention.

Atop a pitted and crumbling obelisk stood the figure of a man. The sun reflected off its iron surface. Its right arm, extended toward the sky, held a short arrow, as if challenging the heavens. The left arm and head were missing.

"How long has that thing been there?"

"Nobody knows for sure," Warner said. "It's called *The Warrior*. Been there since before the Great Cataclysm."

"That's right. You were born here, weren't you, Solomon?"

"Sure was, Boss. Lived here until I was fourteen, then moved to Attagon to finish my studies and join the Order."

They completed their descent and entered the shallow valley, joining heavier traffic on the winding road toward the city center. It wasn't long before obstinate herds and cursing wranglers slowed their progress. The pungent smells of beast and man intensified. Up ahead, a cart had overturned, spilling a load of vegetables and providing an unexpected snack for the herd of swine that clogged the road. The cart driver yelled at the herders, who cursed back and worked valiantly to get the pigs underway again.

Of all the cities in Deiparia, Rimlingham—once called Birmingham—was the only one where people did not shun the remains of its old identity. The gutted, twisted pre-Cataclysm buildings were used as much as their structural integrity allowed. Tales of specters and demons did not dissuade the people from adapting them for homes and businesses. The congregants of Rimlingham were a tough lot, fit to be watched over by a towering metallic sentinel.

"Solomon, since you know the area, why don't you lead us from here on in?"

"Sure thing, be glad to."

Thorne and Cabbott parted, allowing Warner to pass. As soon as he took the point, he rode between two forlorn and exhausted buildings. They hadn't gone far when the deputy reined to a halt. He watched a second-story window on his left.

Thorne's hand fell to the dagger at his side.

"What's wrong, Sol?" Cabbott asked. "Another ambush?" He had his sword halfway out of its scabbard when the shutters on the window flew open. "Shit!"

Warner pulled his horse back toward them.

A pair of arms emerged from the open window with something in hand. With a quick flip, the item was upended, and its contents were dumped into the alley. The shutters closed again as the smell of excrement reached them.

"Yep, you called it, Thurl." Warner chuckled and moved forward again, skirting the freshly spattered mess.

Five minutes later, Warner delivered them to the door of the Iron Pig Lodge. The three-story building was made of smooth, white stone and accentuated with dark, iron-bound timbers. The Pig was the fanciest and most expensive place to stay, its accommodations a welcomed relief after the last few inns the men had used. Warner stabled the horses while Thorne and Cabbott went inside.

As they settled into their rooms, someone knocked on Thorne's door. Without waiting for an invitation, Cabbott opened it and stepped inside.

"Got an old friend here to see you, Malachi. Your favorite familiar." He stepped aside, allowing the visitor to enter.

A bowlegged man shuffled in, grinning at Thorne, the majority of his teeth a distant memory. Dirty, threadbare clothes hung from his scarecrow-like frame. He wore a tonsure, the greasy brown hair dangling to his shoulders in matted strands. He carried a battered, brimless cap in his hands.

"G'day, Master Thorne," he said in a nasally voice as he bowed his head.

"Well, well, if it isn't Keegan Lang." Thorne walked to his bed and sat down. "You certainly did not waste any time."

"Oh, no, sir, Master Thorne, sir. When I heard you been seen in Rimlin'ham, I says to myself, 'Keegan, you best git on over there, an' fast.' An' I knows you always stay here. Yes, sir."

Thorne motioned to Cabbott. "Get Warner." He kept his distance and tried to avoid looking at Lang as much as possible. The man's bulbous, watery eyes never seemed to blink as his gaze darted from one thing to another in the room.

"Sit, Keegan," he said.

"Thank ye, Master Thorne, sir."

Footsteps sounded from the hallway; Cabbott and Warner entered.

"Solomon, I need a clerk since Dario isn't here. Go downstairs and get some parchment, quills and ink, please."

The deputy nodded, glanced at Lang and departed.

The three men passed the time discussing recent events in the area. Word of the missing ferry had reached the city, but stories were confused about what had happened. The body of a man had been found downriver, but no one had identified him.

The familiar told them about all the arrests that had been made since the Code was lifted, cheerily pointing out where one of his morsels of information had played a part. It pleased Thorne to hear about the number of new cases. It seemed the Council's plan to bear down and root out heresy and rebellion was working, at least in Rimlingham.

Warner returned, and Cabbott closed the door behind him. The deputy sat down at a polished oak table and opened a leather folio. He removed several pieces of parchment, a small vial of ink and a black quill. Thorne waited until Warner was ready.

"Take it slow, Boss. I don't write all that fast."

Thorne nodded and turned back to Lang. The familiar stared at him and twisted his raggedy cap with nervous hands.

Now I remember why everyone calls him Fish-Eyed Lang... "What news do you have for me?"

He licked his flabby lips. "Uh, is uh...my fee still the same, Master Thorne, sir?"

"Yes, yes. Now tell me what you know."

"Well, Master Thorne, sir, I know you been chasin' Barnabas Kordell, and I can tell ya that he *did* come through here."

"When?"

For some reason, the scratching of the quill annoyed Thorne. Warner pressed on the stylus like a leatherworker with an awl. Thorne missed the skill and sensitivity Dario approached his work with, how he knew the exact amount of pressure to use for different strokes. He also missed having his friend by his side. Lang rolled his eyes upward, as if trying to see his own forehead. They reminded Thorne of watery eggs.

"It was…lemme see…the twenty-seventh of May. Yes, sir! That's when it was."

Thorne's brows knit together. "You are sure of this?"

The little man backhanded his runny nose and wiped it on his trouser leg. Thorne preferred not to think about what the other stains there might be.

"Yes, sir, Master Thorne, sir." Lang paused, searched for his forehead again. "Yep, he came in, stayed for a few days, an' left…lemme see…a week ago yesterday."

Warner cursed under his breath. "Hey, Boss, come on. Give me a chance here." He went back to writing, the tip of his tongue peeking from the corner of his mouth.

"Sorry, Solomon."

"So that would've been—"

"May 29th!" Lang said a bit too loudly, as if he'd just given the right answer on a test.

Thorne sat back in his chair and stroked his mustache and goatee.

Damn. Kordell was still a full week ahead. He could've been just about anywhere by now. Thorne looked at Lang's slender, grimy face. "Did you report this to the Church?" *Maybe it's not the sound of the quill so much as that moist gaze…*

"Oh, yes, sir, Master Thorne, sir. Soon as I knowed the details, I went straight to the head Witchfinder hisself."

Warner cursed again, louder this time, and Thorne suppressed a smile.

"What happened when you told the Witchfinder Supreme?"

"Well, he sent out a bunch of search parties. But they didn't find nothin'."

Thorne remained silent for a moment, to give Warner a chance to catch up as much as to consider Lang's information. The familiar fidgeted with his cap as he smiled at Thorne.

Thorne sighed. "Nothing of what you have told me is of any help."

Lang's smile evaporated. "No?" He recovered his composure immediately—a skill learned in his profession as spy, snitch and barely tolerable human being. He sat up straighter. "No, sir, Master Thorne, sir. I didn't think it might. But…"

"Go on."

The familiar leaned forward. From this distance, Thorne smelled onions and fish on the man's breath.

"Well, I jus' learned—and I mean jus', as in the other day—that Kordell went to Meridian. From what I heard, he told folks he was goin' ta Baymouth. But I has it on good authority that ain't what he did. No, sir, Master Thorne, sir. Kordell went ta Meridian!" He leaned back and swiped his nose again. "Word is, he was meetin' someone down there."

"Traugott, I'll bet," Cabbott said.

Thorne nodded. "What else, Keegan?"

"Sir?"

"There is something else you need to tell me. I think you just remembered it."

Lang studied him, a mixture of shock and reverence in his unblinking gaze. "Aye, sir, that there is. An' you're right—I did just remember it." He paused before adding, "But I was goin' to tell you, honest, I swear. I wouldn't be keepin' nothing from you, Master Thorne, sir. No, sir."

"What is it?" Thorne demanded, leaning forward despite the familiar's rancid breath. "Tell me."

"It's a message."

"Who's it from?" Cabbott asked.

Lang fidgeted in his seat. "Okay, okay, gimme a second…" He wiped his forehead. "It's like this: last Saturday, a friend of a friend gave me a message ta give to you."

"For me?"

"Aye, said it was for Malachi Thorne hisself."

"What did this message say?"

"Well, Bobbo the Thick—he's always hangin' around at The Cock's Tail—said he saw Spider Dennis come in. An' Spider Dennis gets hisself a drink and goes to sit with the Wolf sisters. We call 'em that 'cause they're both ugly as dogs—"

"Do any of your friends have real names?" Cabbott deadpanned.

Lang ignored him. "—and Spider Dennis hears from one of them Wolf sisters—I think it was Liza; she's the ugliest of the two—that Alaister Roddy had been given a message for Malachi Thorne for when he came to town."

Thorne raised his hand to interrupt. "How did anyone know I was coming to Rimlingham?" Thorne and Cabbott exchanged troubled glances.

Lang shrugged. "Beats me, Master Thorne, sir. Anyways, Alaister Roddy met some man who wanted to be sure you got his message."

"What was the message?"

"Who was the man?" Cabbott asked at almost the same time.

Lang looked back and forth between them. "Alaister said the message went: 'Tell Malachi Thorne it won't be long now.'"

Thorne's eyes narrowed, and his brow creased. He repeated the message slowly, drawing it into a question.

"Yes, sir, Master Thorne, sir."

"And the man?"

Lang shrugged again. "No idea. Alaister didn't get no name."

"What did he look like?" Thorne demanded, his voice clipped and tense.

Once more, Lang's eyes roamed upward. "Liza told Spider Dennis that Alaister said it was just a scrawny black man—bald, missin' an eye and walked with a bad leg."

Thorne and Cabbott stared at each other in disbelief. Cabbott closed his eyes and shook his head.

Thorne leaned back and gritted his teeth. "You're free to go, Lang."

Although the afternoon grew long, Thorne rode straight to the offices of the Paracletian Order. He'd paid Keegan Lang his fee and sent the little man away with orders to inform him immediately if he heard anything else. He barreled through the streets, heedless of obstacles, his mind seething. Flocks of geese honked and flapped out of his way. Cats hissed and scampered back onto window ledges.

His pulse raced as he contemplated finally catching the cowardly Traugott and his fugitive follower. He grinned as he rode, hunched over the neck of his mount. Congregants could be forgiven for assuming he was the very specter of Death itself, his cloak billowing behind him, his face the image of hostility and determination.

At the offices, he leapt from the saddle and threw the reins at a stable hand. He took the crumbling stairs two at a time, then burst into the expansive lobby of one of the dark gray steel towers. People going about their business stopped and stared as his long strides carried him to the main desk.

"I will see Zadicus Rann," he declared.

The man behind the desk looked at him and the diamond rank insignia that held his cloak in place. "Yes, yes, of course, Your Grace. Just give me a moment." He signaled to another man and passed along the order. The second man hurried up the stairs at the back of the lobby.

The hum of conversation and routine business resumed. Thorne paced in front of the desk, his hat in hand. He was about to make his demand again when the man returned.

"Your Grace," he said in a polite, well-cultured tone, "I'm afraid that the Witchfinder Supreme isn't in right now."

"Where is he?"

"According to his office, he's in court."

"Send for him."

"Your Grace? But the Supreme is hearing cases and—"

"I don't give a damn if he's hearing a confession from the Heiromonarch himself! Get him here right now!"

The second man shrugged and called for a posel. He instructed the messenger, who paled upon hearing his assignment. His expression jumped from fear to uncertainty and back to fear again.

"Go on," the man urged. "The Imperator doesn't have all day."

Swallowing hard, the messenger dashed out of the building.

The man behind the desk smiled as if nothing had happened. "Something to drink while you wait, Your Grace?"

Thorne was nearly apoplectic by the time Zadicus Rann arrived. Nearly an hour had passed, and he had no desire for small talk. He followed Rann up to the third floor, to a suite of offices that overlooked several other pre-Cataclysm buildings. Through the wide, tinted windows, the light from the setting sun appeared dingy and feeble.

Closing the door, Rann folded his arms and glared at Thorne. "What the hells do you want, Thorne? I don't have time for this." His tenor voice was loud and dominating. A bullish man with broad shoulders and a disagreeable temper, it was said that he was even more adept at extracting confessions than Thorne. Rann wore the same uniform as Thorne but was one rank below him.

Thorne whirled around to face him. "Where are Barnabas Kordell and Traugott?"

"Who?"

"Do not play dumb with me, Rann. I know Kordell has been in Rimlingham recently—probably Traugott, too."

Rann offered a patronizing smile. "Still haven't found your fugitive, eh?" He did not try to hide his distaste for his superior.

"Where are they? Why have you not apprehended them?"

The Rimlingham Witchfinder strolled past Thorne as if he had all the time in the world. He ran his finger along the edge of his desk as he walked past and stood in front of the window, the sunlight forming a halo around his body. His face was a mask of shadows.

Thorne disliked Rann's very public ambitions, while Rann seethed over the fact that Thorne outranked him while being nearly ten years his junior. Being summoned in such a fashion must have infuriated him.

"Who says I haven't caught them?" Rann asked, narrowing eyes the color of polished steel. He slid a tabák from a gilded case on his desk and lit it.

"You have them in custody? I will see them immediately!"

Rann exhaled, the smoke swirling in the dying sunlight. Beneath a wide brown mustache that looked like a porcupine rolling downhill, he wore his patronizing smile with practiced ease. "I don't have them."

"You just said—"

"I didn't say I *do* have them in custody. You're jumping to conclusions, Thorne."

"Damn it, Rann! I do not have time to play games! Do you have Kordell and Traugott, or not?"

"And I don't have time for your pitiful crusades! You think you can just come in here and push me around?" Rann was accustomed to bellowing his way to what he wanted. "Let me tell you something, *boy*—"

Thorne jabbed a finger at Rann's chest. "No, *you* listen! I do not give a damn about your campaign to climb the ecclesiastical ladder. I know you covet my rank—and likely more beyond it. But you should be more concerned about defending the faith instead of lining your own pockets and entertaining expensive whores."

Rann seethed, his lip curling. The light around his flat-top haircut seemed less a halo and more a smoldering fire.

"I will ask you once more: do you have them?"

"No, I don't!" Rann snapped. He paused to relish the anger on Thorne's face. "Even if I did, I wouldn't turn them over to you. This is *my* jurisdiction." His tone now oozed smugness and confidence.

Thorne took two steps toward him. "You are under my command. When I am here, I am in charge."

Rann waved the tabák at him. "Yes, yes, how silly of me to forget." He narrowed one eye at Thorne. "But things are going to be changing very soon."

"What does that mean?"

Rann said nothing, but he wore a knowing smirk.

Thorne imagined himself vaulting over the desk and beating the living hells out of the man. He trembled as he worked to suppress his rage.

"I want to interrogate Alaister Roddy and someone called Spider Dennis." His tone was clipped, tight.

"Then interrogate them."

"Do you have them?"

Rann made a show of thinking carefully before looking at Thorne. He pulled on the tabák. "No"—he held in the smoke—"but I know where they tend to congregate." He released the smoke toward Thorne's face.

"Bring them in. Immediately."

"Oh, I can't do that, Thorne. I haven't got the manpower right now." His tone was condescending, as if addressing an errant child. "Everyone's busy. If you want them, you'll have to find them yourself. You *do* have the authority, after all." He crushed out the tabák in a round tray.

"You son of a—"

"Now, now—such temperament is unbecoming to someone of your exalted rank."

"I'll see your lack of cooperation is addressed by the Council," Thorne hissed. "By the Church, I'll have you busted down so fast you'll be thankful to sweep horse shit off the streets!"

"Oh, I doubt that very much. In fact, your own campaign for higher rank is likely to end before it begins."

"What? By all that is holy, I am not seeking higher—" He stopped himself and clenched his jaw. It wasn't worth it.

While he paused to collect himself, Rann made a show out of sitting down. He regarded Thorne with the sort of scrutiny reserved for a pool of vomit. "Good luck in your search, *Imperator*," he said, then picked up a parchment and pretended to look it over.

Thorne pivoted and stormed out before he did something he would regret.

13

UNBEATABLE

SATURDAY, JUNE 6, 999 AE

Cabbott and Warner followed Thorne through the benighted streets of Rimlingham. They'd scoured the worst district of the city but after two hours had nothing to show for their efforts. Thorne's anger raged, and the constable and deputy said little to him. He'd briefed them on the meeting, and they'd kept their questions to themselves.

They stopped congregants departing the taverns or closing up their shops. No one knew Alaister Roddy or Spider Dennis, or if they did, they knew enough to keep their mouths shut.

Thunder rumbled in the distance. Thorne turned back toward the center of town. "We'll start again first thing in the morning."

They walked in silence until Warner said, "Boss, what about that message? What's it mean?"

"I don't know, Solomon."

"It won't be long now." The deputy said it almost like a mantra.

Thorne snorted. "If I have my way, it won't be long until Traugott's dancing in the fire."

"Could be setting up some kind of ambush," Cabbott said. "Won't be long, maybe, until he springs it on us?"

"Or maybe he knows his time is just about up? Maybe he knows his little adventure won't last much longer," Warner said. "And speakin' of messages, have you heard anythin' from Dario or Tycho?"

"Not yet," Thorne replied.

Thunder rumbled again, closer now, and they lapsed into silence once more. A breeze heralded the approaching storm. They passed through the city's market square. Scraps of cabbage lay on the ground alongside onionskin and stubby, wrinkled potatoes. Rats scattered into the shadows as they approached. Thorne led them south out of the market square.

"Uh, Boss? This ain't the way to the Pig…"

He stopped. "I'm not going to the Pig. You go on back and get some rest."

"So where you headin' now?"

The Witchfinder didn't reply.

Cabbott edged closer to his deputy. "To the cemetery. Merrick's tomb."

Warner nodded but lingered.

"We'll be fine," Cabbott told him. "Go on, get back before this storm catches you. And be careful."

Warner nodded again and hurried away into the windy darkness.

Ten minutes later, the thunder settled over the city, delivering jagged forks of lighting. Thorne and Cabbott were on the southwestern edge of Rimlingham at Fairfield Cemetery.

"Wait here," Thorne instructed.

"You sure, Malachi?"

"Yes. You know how this works."

"I just thought that after what happened in Colobos, and on the river—"

Even the darkness couldn't hide the spark in Thorne's eyes. Cabbott surrendered with a placating gesture. "All right, all right."

Thorne sighed. "I know you're just doing your job. I appreciate that. And I'm sorry, my friend. This is…"

"I know: it's personal. I understand." Cabbott leaned against the crumbling stone archway that supported the main gate. "I'll just stay here. That okay?"

Thorne put a hand on Cabbott's shoulder. "That'll be fine. Thank you." He opened the rusty iron gate, and the gravel crunched under his boots as he walked a path that had become all too familiar. The wind swept his cape around his legs as he pondered the conflicted emotions within his heart. Since leaving Colobos, he'd been determined to get to Rimlingham—and away from it—as quickly as possible. Coming here was like sitting at the bottom of a dry well: there was light in the distance, but it wasn't enough to offer hope against the wall of guilt and shame that encircled him.

His mind returned to the events of a decade ago. Like a child's merry-go-round fitted with spiked saddles and demonic beasts, he'd ridden it around and around, unable to stop or get off. Despite so many years of whirling purgatory, the spikes still pierced him like icicles.

The thunder bellowed again, and the wind swirled past, as if racing him to his destination. Stone slabs the color of corpses jutted from the uneven ground.

The path branched, and he followed the left fork, turning deeper into the cemetery. It was bordered with flowers that swayed in the wind. Ahead of him stood a mausoleum inscribed with the symbols of the Four Orders. Two stone benches waited like sentinels just outside the metal fence that surrounded it. Beyond the single open gateway, a narrow gravel path led to a locked inner gate in front of the sealed main doors. Valerian Merrick's mausoleum was one of the largest in the cemetery, befitting a man of his rank and prestige.

Thorne's steps slowed as he approached, and he lowered himself onto a bench and faced the tomb. Lightning flashed, turning the crypt bone-white for an instant. Thunder boomed over the city.

He stared at the list of Merrick's accomplishments chiseled across the front walls. He knew them by heart. The last one taunted him with its soundless, granite voice:

SURRENDERED HIS LIFE
FOR THE GLORY OF THE CHURCH
WHILE BRINGING HERETICS TO JUSTICE
TOADVINE 988 AE

The emptiness that he'd grown adept at hiding yawned inside him. Every day, he kept it in check behind his tasks and responsibilities. Rarely did he allow himself to touch that emptiness. But in this place, he did. As much as he dreaded coming to Rimlingham, part of him also welcomed the opportunity to release his pain. It was his constant companion, as permanent as a freckle or a tattoo. The void left by Merrick's death had never been filled, and he had given up hope that it ever would. His shoulders slumped, and he hung his head, pulling one side of his cloak closer to his chest.

In this place, the memories returned, melancholy but embraced. He thought of their many adventures together. He remembered Merrick's teachings. He'd tried his best to emulate his mentor's bearing and confidence, his devotion and orderliness. But as Thorne sat in the circling wind, a morose awareness crept over him: he could no longer remember the sound of his mentor's voice. A stone sat in his chest and tears stung his eyes.

He remembered their travels and sitting in front of a fireplace together at the end of a long day's ride. He remembered Merrick taking him to the fair when he was a child. Those memories came smoothly and vividly. But in none of them could he recall the elderly man's tone or cadence.

He conjured up Merrick's face—robust and white-bearded, with inquisitive eyes the color of deep water, and narrow spectacles he always wore to read—but even that didn't provoke the voice to materialize. Some of his memories were fragmenting and drifting away, like rose petals upon the water. He yearned to grab them and pull them back together, to preserve every detail, yet was agonizingly aware that it could never happen. His heart ached, reminding him of why he could never forgive himself.

Speaking of rose petals…

He reached into a pocket inside his cloak and took out a single white rose he'd purchased from a vendor earlier that afternoon. He turned it slowly between thumb and forefinger. The seller had removed the thorns, and he slid his fingers along the tender stem. It felt peculiar doing so. The anticipation of a prick persisted even when there was nothing left to cause one.

Is a rose still a rose if it has no thorns? It's a pretty flower, yes, but is it truly a rose? Does the flower alone make it a rose, or must it have thorns?

He rubbed his eyes and pushed the thought from his mind. That was a question for the philosophers—though he had to admit that Merrick would have appreciated the metaphysical riddle. The old man had always loved a challenge.

Thorne stood, walked inside the gate and placed the flower in a small vase mounted on the bars of the inner fence. He stood motionless, staring at the crypt doors. The thunder rolled four times before he stepped away and knelt on one knee before the gate. With his head bowed, he signed himself, then stood up. He looked once more at the brooding mausoleum and turned back toward the front gate.

Cabbott stood a few feet away in the middle of the path.

"Damn it, Thurl!" he said with a start. "I thought I told you to wait by the gate!" He stomped toward his friend. Thunder cracked. "Let's get back to the inn before this storm—"

Cabbott's hands locked around Thorne's throat and squeezed. A bolt of lightning flashed across the clouds. It wasn't Cabbott. Eyes the color of butter gleamed from beneath a hood as thumbs ground into his windpipe.

Thorne instinctively clawed at the hands, but they were as cold and unyielding as the mausoleum. The yellow eyes displayed no emotion. They simply bore into his with merciless precision.

Training overrode instinct. There was no use wasting time with hands and arms as strong as these. Thorne kicked. The toe of his boot crunched into his assailant's groin. There wasn't so much as a grunt of discomfort.

Thorne tried to throw himself into his attacker, but he had no leverage. His feet dangled above the ground. Thunder boomed again, but this time, it was muffled by the ringing in his ears. Black spots began to pepper the edges of his vision.

He fumbled at his belt and yanked the dagger free. He cursed himself for not rearming as soon as he got to the city. No matter now—the dagger was all he had. He drove it as hard as he could into the bottom of his assailant's jaw.

One hand released his throat. Thorne sucked in a little of the storm-tossed air. But not enough.

The robed man clawed at the dagger with his free hand. His mouth opened and closed like a hooked fish. The blade had pierced through the tongue and into the roof of the mouth, leaving the handle buried beneath his chin.

The force of the thrust had turned Thorne's body. His momentum and weight pulled his feet back to the ground. He yanked down on the assailant's arm as he threw his weight back. The attacker lost his balance, staggered and released his grip.

Thorne fell back and collided with the fence around the mausoleum. Pain flared down his spine. He slid to the ground as the man regained his balance and stepped toward him. The assailant reached into his robe and pulled out a sickle-shaped blade. The malevolent yellow eyes fixed on him. The man came forward, tugging the dagger from his jaw and casting it aside.

With the fence at his back, Thorne scrambled into a squatting position. He shook his head in an attempt to clear it.

"Thurl!" He meant to yell, but what came out was merely a strangled groan that disappeared beneath a clap of thunder. The hooded figure raised the sickle.

Thorne leapt into his attacker. He hit the stomach as he threw his arms around his midsection. The body underneath the robe was rigid and smelled like a grave. His assailant flew backward, and both of them tumbled to the gravel. Thorne rolled sideways, out of range of the flailing sickle. He got to his knees and stood on shaking legs.

On the path, the attacker sat up with jerking, unsure movements. He did not seem to have full control over his body. He stood up like a marionette without strings that was still being manipulated all the same. The head turned, eyes fixed on Thorne, then he started to close the distance between them.

"Thurl!" This time his throat cooperated, and the shout reverberated off the mausoleum.

Fat drops of rain thunked against Thorne's hat.

Both men circled each other—mostly Thorne retreating from the other's advances. He stepped on something solid and glanced down. His dagger lay in the grass. He grabbed it. There wasn't a drop of blood on it.

"What the hells are you?" he said into the wind.

The hood fell back. A bald pate, covered with sallow, pulsating veins, rose above the baleful golden eyes that glared at him. The thing did not bleed at all. It rushed forward, sickle raised above its head. "You die, Malachi Thorne," it gargled.

Thorne gritted his teeth and leapt sideways. He was too slow. The sickle bit into his left shoulder. He grunted, then feinted left but twisted right. The sickle reversed course, and he heard the swish of air as it passed too close to his throat.

The sprinkle of rain became a shower.

Thorne rammed his dagger straight into his opponent's chest. The blade pierced cloth, flesh, then scraped against bone. He yanked it back and side-stepped again. The thing wheeled around. The sickle slit Thorne's right thigh. He sucked air through clenched teeth as fire raced along his leg.

"Your head goes with me!" the thing brayed.

Thorne barely dodged the sickle as it arced through the space his neck had occupied a second before.

"You cannot hurt me. I am the Carnifex. I cannot be killed."

"We'll see about that…"

Rain dripped from the brim of Thorne's hat. The ground grew slicker.

The Carnifex advanced.

Thorne hobbled back, putting a crumbling, spired gravestone between them. His left shoulder stung. Blood ran hot against his skin. His enemy pursued, and he continued to retreat. His heel hit a child's marker, and he nearly lost his balance.

The Carnifex was upon him in an instant. The sickle slashed back and forth, up and down. The blade sank into Thorne's left shoulder again, and he screamed in pain. He jabbed the Carnifex in the stomach, but the dagger came away unbloodied yet again.

"Malachi!" Cabbott's yell boomed through the rain.

"Thurl! Over…here!"

Thorne staggered, regained his balance and found himself back on the path. The Carnifex stepped between him and the mausoleum. Thorne turned and ran for the front gate. Cabbott raced toward him, short sword drawn.

"Get…back!" Thorne gasped. "Dagger…didn't hurt it."

The creature loped toward them. It moved with surprising speed, although its movements remained jerky and uncoordinated.

"Shit!" Cabbott exclaimed. "Maybe we could both—"

"Run! Now!" Thorne shoved Cabbott's shoulder.

They fled down the gravel path as the rain intensified. At the front gate, they looked back. The Carnifex still pursued, eyes gleaming through the rain.

Thorne hissed as he pressed a hand against his bloody shoulder. His thigh ached like a rotten tooth.

"You're bleeding. Where've you been hit?"

"No time. We've got to keep moving. We've got to get away…from that thing." Footsteps crunched on the gravel behind them. "Come on, this way."

They ran through the gate and down the street, Thorne slowed by his pro-nounced limp. He knew the area relatively well thanks to his nocturnal strolls. He loped off the street into an alley. They reached the end and emerged into the next street. The Carnifex charged down the alley behind them.

Every street was empty. Even the prostitutes had surrendered to the storm and remained indoors. Thorne and Cabbott cut across streets and through alleys. At every turn, the Carnifex drew closer, never tiring, eyes fixed.

Thorne's breath came in erratic gasps. "Pig's...not much farther."

Cabbott didn't reply. His breathing was ragged, and he had fallen several paces behind Thorne.

"Once...we're through there," Thorne pointed to a dark opening, "it's only...two more streets." He cut down the alley, boots splashing through the mud, Cabbott trailing behind. Thorne limped out of the alley and stumbled to a halt.

Cabbott nearly ran him over.

For the second time that night, Thorne cursed himself.

They stood in the courtyard of a stable. To either side stood buildings, but neither had any visible windows or doors. The Carnifex skidded to a halt at the mouth of the alley, then walked toward them.

"Dead end," it growled.

14

ACCUSATIONS

"We're trapped…" Cabbott's voice trailed off in the rain. "This wasn't here the last time I came this way. Damn!"

"C'mon, Malachi. We can take this guy."

"It's from the Communion. Impervious to weapons. I hit it several times. It doesn't bleed."

Cabbott looked at him in surprise. "Then how in the Twelve Hells—"

"I don't know. Just stay away from it."

The Carnifex entered the stable yard. Both men backed up until they bumped into the stable doors. One door creaked and swung inward, revealing a sliver of blackness beyond.

"Inside!" Cabbott yelled as the Carnifex jerked toward them.

They slipped inside and slammed the door. Thorne threw his weight against it, careful not to use his left shoulder. There was a hard crash against the outside, and the door threatened to swing open.

"Find something to hold it!"

Cabbott looked around. It was impossible to see anything beyond a few feet.

"Look for a bar of some kind!" The door quaked again. Thorne grunted.

"Here, use this." Cabbott thrust a pitchfork through the handles.

"That won't hold—"

"It's all I could find. If there's a bar, I sure as hells don't see it."

The Carnifex continued its assault, and the doors vibrated under each blow.

Cabbott disappeared deeper into the interior.

Splinters of wood flew with the next hit, and the pitchfork handle bent under the pressure.

"Thurl!"

"Back here. Just looking for a way out."

"There better be one. This door's about to give way."

"Got something! It's a ladder—up to the hayloft."

"We'll be trapped—"

"No, I see a window up there. We can get out that way."

Horses stamped in their stalls, restless from the storm and the pounding on the door.

The pitchfork handle snapped, the two halves clattering to the floor. The doors burst open with the next hit. The Carnifex stepped inside.

"Caught you," it grated.

"Let's go, Malachi!"

Thorne scrambled up the ladder, his shoulder and thigh throbbing with each rung. Cabbott waited below until there was enough space for him to ascend.

Despite its uncoordinated motions, the Carnifex dashed across the hay-strewn floor. It slammed into Thurl before he could draw his weapon, knocking him halfway across the stable. He landed hard with a grunt and whoosh of breath. The Carnifex pivoted and snagged Thorne by the ankle.

He kicked at the hand but to no avail. The iron grip and dead weight stretched him down the ladder. His hand slipped from the top rung and snagged the one below it. The Carnifex grasped his ankle with both hands and pulled. Thorne clung to the ladder with all his strength. *Just like Colobos*, he thought as he twisted about, attempting to kick the viselike hands away. The ladder creaked, threatening pull loose from the top.

The horses stomped and reared.

Cabbott climbed to his feet, drew his sword and sprinted toward the creature. He roared in rage as he thrust the sword through the thing's back. It slammed into the ladder, the sword jutting from its chest, and released Thorne's leg. Growling in rage or annoyance, it turned and drove a fist into Cabbott's head. Once more, the constable left his feet and slammed into a stall door. The sudden crash spooked the horses even more. Cabbott crumpled like a poleaxed mule and lay still.

The Carnifex reached behind its back and struggled to withdraw the sword.

Thorne hurried into the hayloft and found the window. He hated to leave Cabbott, but he prayed this thing wasn't like the demon in Colobos, that it wouldn't waste time on anyone other than him.

"Will not stop, Witchfinder. Not until you are dead."

A metallic clang told him the creature had discarded the sword. The ladder creaked again.

Thorne limped across the hayloft to the window. Thank the Heiromonarch it was big enough.

He thrust the shutters open, and the roof of the building next door greeted him. A flat strip ran the entire length of the roof, broken only by a blackened chimney. On either side, the roof sloped precariously, rain cascading down the tiles and over the edges. He calculated a distance of two, maybe three feet at most. The hardest part would be maintaining his balance when he landed.

The Carnifex hissed as it reached the top of the ladder. Its eyes glowed like miniature suns in the darkness.

Thorne climbed onto the sill and jumped.

Rain lashed his face as the roof came up to meet him. He landed with a thud, crying out as pain blazed up his thigh. He crouched as low as he could to minimize his center of gravity but still slipped. His legs collapsed under him, and then he was sliding, falling. He flailed for any handhold he could find. His fingers locked on the edge of the center strip, and he stopped moving. Heart racing, he scrambled into a sitting position and crab-walked away from the window.

The Carnifex dropped effortlessly onto the roof in front of him.

Thorne retreated until he backed into the chimney. He couldn't navigate around it. He'd be exposed to attack, not to mention the treacherous footing.

Thunder rolled again as if the storm had settled directly over the stable. Yellow eyes gleamed through the downpour. The torn robe was bloodless where Cabbott's sword had skewered the body.

"End of the line. Now you die." Drawing the sickle from its soggy garment, the creature lurched forward. Its face twisted in gleeful anticipation as it towered over him.

Thorne kicked out, straight and hard. His foot cracked into the thing's knee.

In the lull between thunderclaps, a loud snap issued through the driving rain. The leg buckled outward and back. The Carnifex staggered, bellowing in surprise.

Thorne leapt up. He stepped forward and planted his foot in the thing's abdomen as hard as he could. The Carnifex spun sideways, arms pinwheeling, and raced the rain to the ground.

Thorne knelt on the roof, breathing heavily, shoulder and thigh inflamed, and watched the inert body for several moments. The bald head stared back over its shoulder; the eyes black, as if a candle had been snuffed out.

Thorne limped across the roof and climbed back into the stable.

❖   ❖   ❖

It was after midnight when both men staggered into the common room of the Iron Pig Lodge, supporting one another like drowned rats. Water and blood pooled in their wake. Despite the storm—or perhaps because of it—a few people still huddled around tables and the fireplace. The innkeeper raced upstairs to get Warner, who returned bleary-eyed and startled.

"Holy hells, Boss! What the—?"

With his good arm, Thorne motioned for the deputy to sit. The innkeeper sent for a physician. Most of the patrons helped shove two large tables together to serve as a makeshift medical bay. Thorne lay on one; Cabbott sat on the other, sipping a dark liqueur the innkeeper had thrust into his hand. Two men remained on the far side of the room, watching and whispering.

The elderly physician arrived quickly. He possessed a warm, reassuring manner. He assisted Thorne and Cabbott in disrobing, handing their soggy garments to the innkeeper to spread out before the fire. Spare quilts were draped around their shoulders. The doctor talked as he worked. He asked about their injuries, the weapon used and the circumstances of the attack.

Thorne and Cabbott explained everything that had happened. Warner's expression showed he wasn't happy about another attempt by the Communion.

After the story had been told, one of the men on the far side of the room got up and slipped out the door into the storm.

Thorne's two shoulder wounds ran deep but clean and required fifteen stitches between them. His thigh wound was also deep but had missed the major artery. It needed eight stitches to close. The physician finished by putting Thorne's arm in a sling. He washed his hands in a basin and checked Cabbott's head, his wrinkled but steady hands roaming across the lumps beneath the hair. Remarkably, Cabbott showed no signs of dizziness, nausea or blood loss. Splotchy bruises were already forming, however, on his back and arms from being tossed around like a bale of hay.

The physician told them he would return later to check on them. As he departed, Thorne instructed Warner to go to Rimlingham Cathedral and restock their weapons. Two patrons helped Thorne upstairs to his room while Cabbott walked slowly behind. The wounds, the days of travel and their fatigue outweighed the adrenaline left in their systems. As soon as they hit their beds, they were fast asleep.

"Your Grace? I beg your pardon, Lord Witchfinder… Your Grace…?"

Thorne eased his eyes open. Sharp, clear sunlight angled through the window. The innkeeper stood beside the bed, rubbing his hands together and looking decidedly uncomfortable.

"Yes, innkeeper…what is it?" he mumbled, grimacing. Fire danced across his shoulder and leg, as if the pain had been waiting for him to wake up.

"Ah, well, Your Grace, I—that is, your deputy—sent me to fetch you—I apologize, my Lord—sent me to *escort* you downstairs."

He sat up, wincing. Muscles all over his body rebelled against the movement. "For God's sake, why?"

Again, the innkeeper fumbled for the right words. Sweat stood out on his brow. If there had been bread dough in the man's hands, Thorne felt sure the innkeeper could've kneaded a pretzel by now. The man only shrugged, apologized again, then scampered from the room.

At the foot of Thorne's bed lay a fresh set of clothes, a dagger and a rapier. He tossed the sling aside, dressed as fast as his injuries allowed and limped from the room. He heard the commotion before he got to the stairs.

Cabbott, dark-eyed and furious, met him at the bottom of the stairs with Warner by his side. The common room buzzed with conversation. The two tables that had been pushed together last night remained. Congregants, bunched in rows four deep across the room, gawked at him as he hobbled to the two tables. The whispering and murmuring seemed directed at him. Several scowling Rimlingham constables and deputies stood around the room eyeing him with disdain. Zadicus Rann sat in a high-backed chair, smoking a tabák and watching him.

"What is going on?" Thorne demanded as he lowered himself into a chair. Cabbott and Warner took seats on either side.

Rann studied Thorne with sour contempt. He blew a column of smoke into the air and held the tabák between his index and middle fingers. He used it to gesture at Thorne, like a teacher correcting a wayward student. "What were you up to last night, Thorne?"

"What was I—?" He stared at Rann across the table, perplexed. "My constable and I were attacked in Fairfield Cemetery. I will ask once again: what is going on here?"

Cabbott shifted in his seat. "Malachi, he thinks—"

"Silence, Constable!" Rann's fist slammed against the tabletop. "This is my inquest."

"Inquest? What the—"

"You will speak only when I direct a question to you, Constable. Am I clear?"

Cabbott bit his tongue and glared daggers at Rann.

Thorne's face reddened. "You had better start giving me some answers, Rann. What is all this?" He gestured around the room at the expectant crowd, growing larger by the moment as more congregants streamed through the door.

"Malachi Thorne—" Rann declared, pulling a folded parchment from his surcoat. He flicked it the length of the table.

Thorne recognized it immediately. He'd issued plenty of them in his career. He looked from Rann to the parchment and back at Rann.

A smile crept onto Rann's face. Sadistic delight gleamed in his pewter-gray eyes.

"—according to the Laws of the Divine Church, and by the vows we of the Paracletian Order have taken, as Witchfinder Supreme of Rimlingham, I hereby charge you with practicing the forbidden art of necromancy."

The room fell deathly silent.

Thorne blinked as he took in Rann's smug expression. "What?!"

Cabbott leaned over. "That's what I was going to tell you. This son of a bitch claims to be arresting us."

"I am arresting you. All three of you. You're in violation of Church law— Thorne by engaging in necromancy, you two with complicity and grave robbing." Rann shook his head in mock sorrow. "So sad, coming from such well-regarded servants of the Church." He took another drag from the tabák.

Another few seconds of silence followed before the room exploded in confusion. People ran for the door; others jabbered in small groups. They'd never seen an Imperator arrested. Quite a few did not bother to hide their pleasure.

"What madness is this?" Thorne leaped to his feet. He slammed his hands on the table, sending a jolt of agony into his shoulder. He grimaced, picked up the parchment and waved it in the air. "A warrant?"

Rann smiled like a fox among hens.

"Have you lost your bloody mind? How dare you accuse *me* of witchcraft?"

More people crowded the door of the Pig, gawking on tiptoes.

Thorne started around the edge of the table. Rann once again held up the tabák and motioned for Thorne to stop.

"I'd be careful if I were you, Thorne. You don't want to add something like assault to the charges against you." He smirked.

Warner jumped up and grabbed Thorne by the shoulders. Thorne yelped in pain and nearly crumpled to the floor. Warner apologized and used the uninjured shoulder to guide him back to his chair.

Rann relaxed in his seat and blew smoke. "I suppose it's only fitting that your...*abomination* turned against you last night. Such is the price one pays for engaging with the Archfiend of the Twelfth Plane." He crushed the tabák on the tabletop. "I, however, am genuinely pleased that you didn't meet your demise last night. We wouldn't want to rob the good people of Rimlingham of a burning, would we?" He paused and smiled cruelly. "No, maybe not a burning... You know, I'm not sure what punishment would be fitting for a fallen Imperator."

Thorne glared through slitted eyes. "I am no necromancer, as you well know. You will not manufacture such baseless accusations merely to advance your own ambitions."

Rann faked woundedness. "My ambitions? Oh, you do me a disservice, Thorne. My only concern is for defending the faith, as you so eloquently pointed out yesterday. I seek to honor and protect the laws of our beloved Church, which you, through your infernal dealings, have corrupted." He leaned forward. "And as for baseless accusations…well, I have all the evidence I need to charge and convict you."

"You have no evidence," Thorne snarled. "There can be no evidence when there has been no crime."

Again, Rann raised his eyebrows in mock surprise. "But Thorne," he began, "how do you explain this?"

Standing, Rann gestured behind him. The crowd parted as if by some unheard command. On the other side of the common room, the body of a man lay stretched out on a table, covered from feet to waist with a white pall. Several knife cuts stood out against the pale skin. A long, narrow gash ran down the center of the chest. Thorne studied the bald head and the thin nose, the mouth closed in solemn repose.

Rann rubbed the stubble on his chin. "This body was discovered beside the same stables you claim to have been in last night. A milkmaid found it early this morning."

"Yeah, it's him, Malachi," Cabbott whispered. "It's who—or what—we fought last night."

Thorne shook his head. "That's not possible. The thing… The Carnifex… Its head was covered in veins. And its eyes…"

"I know. But I checked the body before you came down. That's where I ran my sword through the damn thing. The cut is the same width as my short sword. Rann already made me test it."

Warner's eyes were wide. "The cut under the jaw, the knee, the broken neck—it's all just like you said, Boss."

Thorne looked from the corpse to Rann. "That is the man—the *creature*—who attacked us last night. Some of the details are…different. But that is him."

"Impossible," Rann replied, cold and confident. He sat back down.

"What?"

"I said that's impossible. That poor congregant, Absalom Sutter"—he waved his hand behind him—"died over a week ago." He reached into his surcoat once more. "I have the death certificate here, if you'd like to see it."

Warner took the paper, unfolded it and scanned it. He nodded grimly at Thorne.

Thorne clenched his teeth. "Documents can be forged." His head had started throbbing nearly as bad as his thigh and shoulder.

"Well, of course they can," the imperious Rann agreed. "But the attending physician's signature is the same man who assisted you with your wounds last night. Perhaps you'd like to accuse him of perjury? Or malpractice? Forgery, maybe?"

"This means nothing. It is all a fantasy you have crafted—"

Rann snapped his fingers. Two shabbily dressed men edged forward, eyes downcast. They wrung their caps in calloused hands and tried to look invisible.

"I also have the sworn testimony of these perceptive and conscientious congregants. They saw you controlling the dead body of Absalom Sutter last night." Rann leaned back and watched in unmitigated delight.

Cabbott shot from his seat. "That's bullshit!" He stabbed a finger at Rann. "Nobody was on the streets last night in that storm, not even the whores!"

Thorne stood up less quickly but with no less determination. His eyes bore into Rann's. "Zadicus, I swear by the Church that I will have you hanged for this."

"Oh, I think not." Rann held up a fist and raised a finger. "First, I have the written statements of these two eyewitnesses who saw you working your foul magic." He dismissed them, and they wasted no time scuttling out the door. He raised a second finger. "I have the fresh corpse you—or one of your accomplices—"

"You son of a bitch," Cabbott spat.

"—disinterred and used for your necromancy. Third, I have one crime scene where the body was found this morning. Fourth, I just heard, as did all these witnesses here, your confession regarding the source of the wounds on the dead man. And fifth, I have the second crime scene: an opened grave in Fairfield Cemetery where you admit to being last evening. Very damning pieces of evidence, those." He paused. "Oh, and I think you even referred to your handiwork as 'the Carnifex,' so that's six. Quite a diabolical name. I didn't know you were so creative."

Thorne tried to jump around the table once again, but Cabbott and Warner restrained him. His breath came in short, ragged gasps between his teeth. He was sweating, but his skin felt clammy.

Rann walked to the door. The room emptied as he did so, leaving only Thorne, Cabbott, Warner and the innkeeper behind. Rann flashed his delighted grin once more. "I've already dispatched a redvalk to Attagon informing the Council of the charges and your case." He shook his head again in counterfeit disbelief. "I'm astonished and shocked to see a brother servant of the Church embracing such evil.

"You'll find that warrant confines you to this inn. I won't throw you in jail, as you deserve, because you *are* part of our common Order, and I extend to you this bit of dignity and comfort. If you attempt to leave the Pig however, I'll be forced to incarcerate you in less hospitable surroundings."

He donned his hat and smoothed his mustache. He was about to leave when he stopped, turned and walked back to Thorne. He leaned in close and whispered, "I told you things were going to change." He smirked, spun around and headed for the door. "You look terrible, Thorne. Better get some rest. And a lawyer. You'll need both."

15

MOTHER

SUNDAY, JUNE 7, 999 AE

The Great Appian Mountains began far beyond the city of Three Waters in the north. The massive spine ran down through Deiparia, dwindling to rolling foothills at Knox. Several trade routes climbed through the heights. Many needling peaks still remained unexplored even after centuries. The Storicos taught that before the Great Cataclysm, the mountains had been much smaller. The summits had been more rounded, easier to traverse and covered by dense forests of conifer and oak where game was plentiful.

The earth's upheaval had thrust the granite behemoths higher and had left them tipped with snow, even during summer. The range grew thicker and harsher as it made its way north, the peaks sometimes hiding their snowcaps in the clouds. Legends held that monsters descended from those peaks—abominable and unspeakable creatures with talons like butcher's blades—with a penchant for stealing children from their cradles and devouring travelers. Such tales, more than the geography, kept many of the remote peaks untouched.

Neris Ahlienor did not believe such tales, of course. She believed in something much worse. She knew that somewhere in the Great Appian Mountains, Matriarch Trahnen, the Witch of Tears, made her dwelling. Rumors abounded that it moved among the mountains, stalking the thick forests and shadow-haunted valleys on the legs of a great spider.

The priestess brushed a ringlet of golden hair from her cheek as both her companions spoke at once.

"How is that possible?" Kiya Mehrit asked.

"What in the name of the Three-Faced Moon just happened?" Sar Maramé's voice boomed in the predawn hush.

They stood once more in the cave, equidistant around the pool. Its surface had calmed and once again reflected the roof of the cave rather than the view through the Carnifex's eyes. Sar stared at the still water, eyes wide.

"I…I didn't think the Carnifex could be killed," Kiya said. She rubbed her upper arms, the bracelets around her wrists jingling. She stared at Neris as intently as Sar gazed into the pool.

Neris did her best to let the tension ebb from her body. Her shoulders were knotted, and her head felt trapped between warring armies. Every part of her body ached from exertion. Controlling the Carnifex from such a distance had been overwhelming, especially so soon after the summoning of Rythok-An'hea.

"It's not immortal. No weapon forged by the hands of men can cause it any pain or kill it." Neris sighed. "But it wasn't a weapon that caused its death, was it?" She walked to the edge of the scrying pool and sat down on the low rim of stones encircling it. She let her fingertips trail through the cool water.

"Thorne's a lucky bastard," Sar said. "Again."

"We were so close…" Fatigue crept into Kiya's voice. Even for the youngest of the triad, the spells necessary to command the Carnifex took immense physical and mental reserves. She, too, dropped onto the rim of the pool, her doe eyes on the priestess. "Neris, what happens now?"

Neris shook her head, her curls dancing, and felt a pang of guilt for lying to a fellow sister. *But it's not really lying—at least not completely*, she justified. She knew how the Matriarch would react to a second failure. But she didn't know what the Matriarch would *do*. That threat settled cold and heavy in her chest.

"We'll try again," Sar declared, as if the process were as simple as pouring a glass of wine. "And we need more brexia." She glanced pointedly at Neris. "I told you that before we started."

"And I told you," the priestess snapped, "the more brexia we use, the harder it is to control every movement of the Carnifex. You saw the difficulties the three of us had."

Sar stuck her hands on her hips and tilted her head. "We didn't need more help *controlling* it. We needed more power being channeled to the three of us."

Neris sighed. "There's only so much magic to go around. It's getting harder to find that kind of help. A lot of brexia don't want to lose what little power they still have."

Sar turned toward the mouth of the cave. "I'll go contact the others."

"No."

"What did you say?" Sar jammed her hands on her hips again.

"You're not going to contact the others. We don't have the energy or the resources for another try. At least not for a while—"

"The others can give us their energy, Neris!"

The priestess shook her head. "Didn't you hear what I just said? Besides, the Matriarch said it must be done before the summer solstice. That's next week. We don't have enough time to make all the preparations again."

Sar glanced from Neris to the cave entrance. Her mouth was a tight line, but she didn't move.

"Will we—will we be punished?" Kiya asked.

Sar cursed under her breath and folded her arms.

Neris laid a hand on Kiya's shoulder. It was warm beneath the straps of her gown, despite the coolness of the cave. Her eyes fell to Kiya's cleavage, and she felt a surge of excitement. She looked into Kiya's fern-colored eyes, at the face so unmarked by age. The young woman was full of potential.

Neris smiled weakly. "I don't know." *There you go lying to her again...* "But don't fret. If there's discipline to be meted out, I'll bear it for us all. The failure is mine alone."

Uncertainty and anxiety clouded the younger girl's face. Sar said nothing but appeared pleased.

"Return to my house and wait for me." When Kiya hesitated, Neris nudged her shoulder. "Go on."

At the cave mouth, Kiya paused and glanced back before following Sar into the gray forest. Neris listened as the rustle of garments and the soft pad of bare feet disappeared. She slipped from the edge of the pool and knelt on the cave floor, assuming the position of supplication and surrender. She bowed her head and waited.

After a while, she heard the tread of feet behind her.

"I told you to wait for me in the house," she said, unable to hide the anger in her voice. She would spare them—especially Kiya—the pain of discipline if she could. But she couldn't do that if they stayed here with her. She hoped that distance from her would mitigate the Matriarch's wrath.

She was about to turn and yell when something clamped down on her shoulder. She yelped in pain as her shoulder went numb with cold. It spread to her neck and up into her skull, like ice flowed through her veins. She couldn't feel her right arm any longer. Frost matted her lashes. The cave glistened with ice and hellish blue light. In front of her, the scrying pool became a miasma of pure blackness, an eddy of absolute nothingness. She trembled uncontrollably.

No—there *was* something inside the pool, something that gave her the sensation of being...studied. She tried to close her eyes, but her lids wouldn't move. She now stared into space, as if the water had been replaced, revealing a cosmos completely, maddeningly *wrong*.

Specks of scintillating light gleamed in the endless expanse, but she didn't recognize any of the constellations. Spinning, gaseous coronas surrounded some of the stars; others pulsated with colors she'd never seen before. A comet swept by, its tail sparkling with rock and crystalline gasses—and something on it stared back at her.

Her heart threatened to burst through her chest. Her mind tripped over itself, grasping for an explanation of what observed her with such malevolence. It was a glutinous mass of ropy, undulating tentacles, but she couldn't make out any head or limbs. Unblinking eyes and gnashing mouths formed and disappeared.

Neris felt herself falling, being sucked into the pool. She wanted to scream and flee, but her body wouldn't respond. In fact, she could no longer feel her body at all. She did feel her sanity fragmenting.

A sepulchral croak came from behind her: "Twice now, Priestess, you have failed me."

Neris trembled so violently she thought she might fall apart. She had never felt such brutal cold before, nor had she been scrutinized by such ancient, malignant eyes. Only the clawlike hand biting into her shoulder kept her upright. Glacial light seeped around her. The presence of the Matriarch was a frozen inferno against her back. Before her, the abyss yawned, pulsating with anticipation.

The tears she cried froze on her cheeks.

"You have proven yourself unworthy of my blessing and power. I have given you the freedom to draw upon my strength, yet you waste it again."

"M-M-Mer—"

"You ask for mercy, Daughter of the Moon?"

"Y-Y-Yes." Neris attempted to nod her head. She couldn't pull her eyes away from the pool. A spiral arm composed of chunks of rock, ice and gas formed and seemed to reach for her.

"Our enemy still lives. It is clear to me that you are unfit to be my priestess."

"I—I d-d-don't w-want to d-die."

A guttural, icy cackle filled the cave. The clawed hand bit deeper into her flesh. "Die? You think you will *die*? Oh, no. No, no, no." Again, the hateful cackle. The blue light quivered. "We are not like the Church. We do not kill brexia." The Matriarch leaned close, the brittle gray strands of her hair hanging at the edge of Neris's vision. The voice pressed into her ear while her mind threatened to surrender its sanity: "The Communion cannot afford to lose a single brexia. All are needed. But not all are needed the same way, Neris Ahlienor. It's time for you to *see*."

Neris had no feeling, no sensation, no hope. Her bulging eyes remained fixed on the portal that called to her in silent madness. She quivered and fell…

Darkness swallowed her.

The spatial void disappeared. The water of the pool reflected the cave roof once more.

The Matriarch stood motionless. The blue light receded and winked out, plunging everything into inky darkness, as if the cave mouth had been sealed over.

"Mother! Maiden!" the Witch of Tears snapped.

Across the pool, a shape formed, insubstantial, like a wraith seen through smoke. A voice tinged with softness and humility replied: "I am here."

"Welcome, Mother Depresja."

The matronly form grew more pronounced. The Witch of Sighs was short and plump with an oily sheen to her skin. She wore a stained gray smock that was belted at the waist, her belly hanging over it. Her breasts sagged on top of her stomach. Her eyes were dark and beady—like raisins pressed into the doughy face—and overflowed with decaying dreams. Wrinkles edged her lips and eyes. Her graying hair was tucked underneath an aged and crumpled turban. A single rusted key hung from a chain around her flabby neck.

"Our lovely sister remains busy," Matriarch Trahnen said.

"Oh, yes," Mother Depresja replied, wiping her hands on the sides of her smock. Something stirred at her feet in the wavering mist—a roiling, indefinable mass of claws, furry bodies and tails. "She fulfills our will in Last Chapel. But we shall soon have to join her. The Church has unleased its giant warriors—the Crusaders—against us."

The Matriarch nodded. "Then it's time…" She fingered a short key, one of dozens that hung from the belts that encircled her frail hips. Despite their great number, they made no sound when she moved.

"You're right, of course. We know we're…not what we used to be, eh? Our numbers, our power—it's all diminishing. Hecate curse that damn Church!"

Matriarch Trahnen shuffled around the pool, her steps filled with desolate dignity. She wore a shabby indigo dress that reached to the floor; the diadem that encircled her brow stood out against her blackened and cracked skin. She scratched at a hairy mole on her cheek. Mother Depresja lightly touched the same mole on her own face.

"You would have us join the Maiden?" the Witch of Tears asked.

The Mother's tone was soothing. "It's our best way now. If the Communion is to survive, we must find, raise up and train the Nahoru'brexia. Only then can we return to our place of prominence. We know this."

"It will mean going into hiding."

"Only temporarily. Only until the Nahoru'brexia are prepared. We have the time."

"*We* do. But what of the Communion? What about our rites and rituals? Who's going to keep our worship alive while we wait?"

"You fret over that which will not happen, Sister. Persecution forces its victims underground." The Mother crossed her arms over her ample bosom. "What the Church does not understand is that they cannot stamp us out any more than one can destroy a piece of glass by crushing it."

The Matriarch offered a wicked, toothless grin. "Each piece that is broken becomes even more pieces. We shall thrive. After all, we Three are the Chosen of the Moon, the Crossroads, the Way Beneath. We shall revive our power. Train our new sisters. And when we emerge—"

"When we emerge in the new millennium, the Communion will forever change the face of Deiparia."

"Let us depart then, to make our preparations."

"Until we meet again, Sister…"

A moment later, the light from the rising sun illuminated the cave mouth. Water bugs skated across the surface of the pool, beside which lay the inert form of Neris Ahlienor.

16
COLLUSION

TUESDAY, JUNE 9, 999 AE

O ther than his horse, only the unforgiving sun and sweltering humidity journeyed with Dario Darien as he made his way toward the village of Stockshire. The landscape of sunbaked, green hills and weedy fields passed unnoticed. He swiped his forehead with a handkerchief.

Last Thursday, he and Tycho Hawkes had ridden for Talnat as hard as they had dared push their mounts. They had traveled night and day, Darien only allowing them a few hours rest at a time. And thank the Church, they'd made it to Talnat in the early hours of Sunday.

He'd gone to the jail and spoken with Tang Tien Qui, demanding to see his sister and wanting every scrap of information regarding her arrest. The Witchfinder had been accommodating and had seemed as perplexed about the whole situation as anyone.

Demerra was being held with two other accused witches. When Darien was escorted in, Demerra had leapt up and clung to him, quaking in fear and anguish. She'd told him everything that had happened, asking more than once if he knew anything about Cassidy and Cassandra.

He'd instructed Hawkes to find out anything he could about Jairus's case while he investigated Demerra's. That way, they'd not only cover more ground, but would hopefully uncover the link between them. Darien was convinced that one existed.

He'd spent Sunday combing through the documents of Demerra's case. As often happened with charges of witchcraft, she'd been accused anonymously. However, the evidence against her was sketchy at best. Very little of it would stand up under the close scrutiny of a lawyer. *So why charge her?* he'd asked himself a dozen times. He felt confident that with his familiarity with the case, a lawyer's expertise and Qui's benevolent consideration, Demerra would be exonerated.

Late Sunday afternoon, Darien had questioned the congregants who lived near the Gray home. No one had anything bad to say about the family, nor was anyone aware of any feuds or debts that might've led to the accusation. As far as he could ascertain, their expressions of sympathy and concern had been genuine. None of them knew the whereabouts of the children. When pressed for the identity of the accuser, they had shaken their heads or shrugged their shoulders.

Monday had been spent in consultation with a lawyer, while Hawkes had sequestered himself with Jairus's case files.

Qui had said that Cassidy and Cassandra were in the care of the Church, but they weren't in Talnat. Darien could not determine why the children would not be there in town, nor why anyone would take them so far away.

While it was common practice to keep families separated—which ensured uncoached testimonies and provided useful psychological leverage—he'd never heard of children being removed so far from their home. He kept uncovering more questions than answers.

He'd lunched with Hawkes, and they compared information. Nothing new about Jairus's death had turned up. Local authorities considered it a closed case of attempted theft. The theory that the bandits had been interrupted during their attack and fled without taking anything of value still held.

The theory had merit, but Darien and Hawkes rejected it. Even the stupidest brigand would've grabbed Jairus's belt pouch—and anything else he could've tucked under his arms—even if someone had been coming to investigate. Jairus's horse, his tools and his wagon would've been obvious targets. But Qui wouldn't reopen a closed case without substantial new evidence, nor would he spare any manpower for a wild goose chase.

Darien and Hawkes were at a loss to explain the accusations against Demerra. Charges of witchcraft were often leveled at people on the margins of society: widows, scolds, the recalcitrant or downright odd. Accusations emerged from spite or jealousy. The lawyer or Witchfinder had to sift through such allegations and discover the truths, if any, that lay behind the claims.

Qui had handled the complaint against Demerra according to established procedure. He'd drawn up an arrest warrant and had dispatched two deputies to serve it. Everything had been by the book. No one would expect anything less from Tang Tien Qui.

Demerra had been brought in and processed. The children had been taken to the cathedral, again as protocol dictated. The thing that had troubled Qui, however, was the message he'd received later that day.

According to him, a posel had delivered a standard Church-issued document saying that the children were being escorted to Attagon. He hadn't been able to read the signature, and the seal bore only the regular sigil of the Paracletian Order. Qui had admitted the peculiarity of the situation but had no reason to challenge it. When Darien had asked to see the document, Qui had been unable to find it. The Witchfinder's confusion over its disappearance had been authentic, and when he'd questioned the clerks, none of them could remember filing it.

Late Monday afternoon, Darien and Hawkes had taken the Northern Road out of the city to Windsor Road. They'd located the crime scene where Jairus had been murdered, but after nearly four months, there had been nothing left to discover. Frustration, anger and a creeping sense of hopelessness had ridden back with them.

Now, as the sweat poured from him and his clothes stuck to his body, Darien spotted the village of Stockshire ahead. It was dusty and unremarkable, a collection of wood and stone buildings bordered by sparse forests and arable fields. He spurred his mount, eager to see this task completed, troubled over what he would—or would not—find.

He stopped in the town square, where his horse drank from the community trough. Congregants went about their business and paid him little attention, exactly as he'd hoped. What he needed to do demanded secrecy. He had to be seen as just another unremarkable traveler. He wore the faded, threadbare attire of a peasant and had his story prepared in the event that anyone questioned his presence in the area. He removed his hat and plunged his head into the trough. It felt like warm bath water.

He returned to the saddle and rode west out of Stockshire. He passed the occasional broken-down farmhouse with kuzda vines smothering the sides, and fields of defeated brown weeds bordered by overgrown hedges or aged trees. No birds stirred in the miserable heat. He felt exposed beneath the cloud-dotted sky, as if his plan were as visible as the wide nose on his face.

Yesterday, upon returning from the crime scene, he and Hawkes had wolfed down their dinner before resuming their investigations. This time, however, Darien had switched their pursuits. He focused on what he could turn up regarding Jairus, while Hawkes had brought a fresh set of eyes to Demerra's case. But by nightfall, neither had anything new to report.

Frustration and fatigue had led to a heated argument. Darien was surprised it hadn't happened sooner, considering how hard he'd been pushing himself and Hawkes, and how hopeless the situation had become. After a while, he'd gone to the deputy's room to apologize, but Hawkes hadn't been there.

This morning, when he'd returned to Hawkes's room, the deputy had been sleeping. Darien had penned a quick note apologizing for his behavior and asking Hawkes if he could try to stir up anything on either case one last time. He'd debated over whether to tell Hawkes about his plan, finally deciding it best if the deputy didn't know. If anything went wrong, at least Hawkes wouldn't be complicit. He'd finished by saying that he was going to look into a thin, probably worthless lead, and that he'd fill him in as soon as he returned this evening.

He'd put together a kit of food and water and made a map from the notes he'd copied from the case files. If Rebekkah Barlowe still lived—and by the Church, he prayed she did—she might be his only chance to find the missing pieces of this puzzle.

Checking the map again, Darien steered his horse off the rutted road and onto an overgrown, narrow path. It led into a stand of elm trees, and he welcomed the shade. He followed the path for ten minutes through slender, towering pines and hearty oaks before it vanished at a brook in a scattering of stones.

Darien dismounted with a curse. He stomped to the edge of the creek and stood with his hands on his hips. His heart sank, and an invisible weight settled on his shoulders. He stared at the water for several minutes, at a loss to know what to do next. There were no more options. His shoulders slumped, and he felt what little energy he had left seep from his body. He crumpled onto a rock, tears of impotence and failure flowing.

After a while, he turned back to his horse, and it was then that he saw the faintest suggestion of an opening a short distance up the creek. The persistent spark of hope rekindled as he hurried toward it. Although it was nearly invisible, the slim trail showed signs of recent use. Darien backtracked and tied off his horse, took a long drink of water and set off on the trail.

It followed a twisting course, gradually leading uphill. Twice, he thought he'd lost it and had to backtrack a short distance in order to reorient himself. The forest became thicker and wilder as he climbed. He hadn't planned on a hike, and his calves reminded him of that. He prayed to the Church yet again that this would be worth it.

Half an hour later, the trail leveled off and emptied into a clearing. In the middle sat a small house of hewn logs, surrounded on every side by gardens of flowers, herbs and vegetables. The stream he'd crossed several times coursed through the trees on the opposite side of the clearing. A dog barked and raced toward him. Darien froze.

From among the stalks of corn, an old woman appeared. She whistled, and the dog halted but continued snapping and growling. She carried her hoe like a halberd and wiped her free hand down the side of her patchwork dress, eyeing

Darien with aggravated suspicion. He raised his hands to show her—and the dog—that he meant no harm. The old woman spat in the dirt and frowned.

"Who are ye? What ye be doing here?" she demanded as she limped out of the corn—one leg bent inward, the foot twisted at an unnatural angle. Darien recognized the injury from her interrogation records. She leaned the hoe forward as a sentry might do guarding a gate.

"My name is Dario Darien. I mean you no harm. Please—I'm looking for Rebekkah Barlowe."

The dog continued to growl but approached no closer, for which Darien was grateful. It looked powerful—and hungry.

"Don't know nobody by that name. Begone!" She raised the hoe and brandished it back and forth.

"*Are you* Rebekkah Barlowe?"

She stabbed a gnarled finger at him. "That be none of yer business. Now git, I says! Or I snaps my fingers and Grizzel there tastes yer black hide!" She squinted one eye at him before turning back to the corn.

"Wait!"

The old woman looked around.

"Please…" He held out pleading hands. "My sister, her children—they're in trouble. I need your help."

She studied him for a long moment, after which she closed her eyes as if meditating. She stamped the handle of the hoe into the dirt three times, then knelt—a feat that surprised him given the condition of her leg—and placed her palm against the ground. She remained that way for another moment before looking up at him. With a curse that was half growl, she stood up and clapped her hands twice. Grizzel quieted, eyed Darien once more and trotted back to her. She said something to the dog that Darien couldn't hear, and it laid down at the corner of the house, dark eyes watching him.

"Dario Darien," she said. "Ye come to me for help. Ye come of yer own free will, do ye?"

"I do, yes."

"And ye come without malice or guile?"

Darien nodded. "I do."

"And ye be willing to bear the *price*?"

"Yes."

"Best be sure. Ain't no changing yer mind later on."

Darien lowered his hands. "I'm sure. There's too much at stake."

"All right, then…the risk be upon yer own head." She turned and limped toward the house. "Come on. I ain't got all day."

With Grizzel's eyes following his every move, Darien crossed the clearing and entered the old witch's home.

Darien wasn't sure what he'd expected: cobwebs, a rack of potion jars, spiders creeping over musty books? He'd never been in the home of a witch, and this one surprised him with its tidiness and order. The best word he had for it was "cozy."

They sat at a rough oak table in the main room in front of an unlit fireplace, yet the room was still warm, and that made him drowsy. Shelves lined one wall, holding a variety of knickknacks, geodes and a few plump clay jars. A table that appeared to serve as a shrine of some sort sat against the other wall. A sculpture of a three-faced female figure stood in the center, surrounded by hardened blobs of candle wax. Two windows, the shutters open, looked out on the gardens. The smell of lavender and basil mixed with the distinctive smell of old age in the room.

Out of the direct sun, he saw the woman more clearly. Extremely old and spindly, her gray hair fell long and clean across her bony shoulders. She had an egg-shaped face—a broad, wrinkled forehead dotted with skin tags that tapered down to a pronounced, narrow chin. Wrinkles covered her sagging beige skin like a thousand cobwebs. Her eyes burned with intelligence, scrutinizing him across the table. She said nothing, waiting for him to begin instead.

Darien cleared his voice. He never had difficulty speaking, but here, he felt unsure of himself. Lethargic.

"Thank you very much for seeing me. You don't know how much it means to find you—" He hesitated. "Well, to *find* you." He had no doubt she saw the embarrassment on his face.

"Find me alive, you mean?" Rebekkah Barlowe tilted her head and laughed. "It's all right, Dario Darien. Don't ye be ashamed. I be a lucky old woman, that's for sure. Accused twice, I was—and released twice, too." She chortled through her crooked mouth.

"That is, uh…most unique."

"The Mother watches out for her own. That Church"—she hocked a wad of phlegm into the fireplace—"ain't nearly as sharp or powerful as it lets on. But ye didn't come here to talk about my fortunes, did ye?"

Darien shook his head, tightening his mouth into a thin line.

"Why'd ye go to all this trouble?" Her eyes blinked wider. "How the hells did ye find me?" She studied him with the cool, beady gaze of a serpent eyeing a bird.

"My sister, Demerra, has been accused of witchcraft in Talnat. The Church"—it felt odd saying it as an entity separate from himself—"has taken her two children."

"And ye want old Rebekkah to scry for them, is that it? Or ye want something to give yer sister—something to dull the pain, mayhap?"

"No, it's not that." He leaned forward, resting his elbows on the table. "There's something I'm curious about..."

The old woman raised an eyebrow.

"Can you—I've heard that your kind can—" He hesitated, cleared his throat again. "Can you see into the past?" His voice was barely above a whisper now.

She likewise leaned forward and gripped the table with wizened hands that resembled bird claws. "Maybe," she whispered, then pushed herself back and yelled, "Why the hells ye be whispering? Old Rebekkah ain't half-deaf."

Darien smiled and nodded but continued to lean forward. "I apologize. I'm...new at this."

"Ain't never been to a witch before, has ye?" She didn't wait for his reply. "I knows it. Hells, you probably ain't never even seen a witch before."

He nodded. *If she only knew...*

"What is it ye be wanting to see in the past?"

Darien told her about the events surrounding Jairus's death and Demerra's incarceration. "I'm convinced there's a connection between the two. I've been... allowed access to certain files in Talnat, trying to figure out what happened to my brother-in-law. In the course of my...research...I stumbled across the files of your cases and saw that you'd been released. You're my last hope."

Rebekkah watched him as he talked. She seemed to gauge every word he said, every expression he made. It made him uncomfortable. He couldn't slip and divulge his connection to the Church—this interview would be terminated, perhaps in some *unnatural* manner. The awkwardness of the situation tightened around him.

"Ye be a lawyer?" she asked.

"No, uh, I have some...connections...to a lawyer or two back in Talnat. They helped me get access to the records."

She squinted at him again.

He squirmed under her stare. *Can she see into my heart and mind? Is that something witches do?*

It grew uncomfortably warm in the room. She folded her arms across her bony chest. "So ye be wanting to look into the past... Aye, I have the ways and means. But ye won't like the price." She shook her head for emphasis.

"What's your price?"

She cackled. "*My* price? Ye want to know my price?"

He rubbed his forehead as tension tugged at his muscles. "Yes, that's what I said. Is there some other price you were referring to?"

She grinned, and a wave of dread engulfed him. He suddenly felt very small in front of her. He imagined it was what the fly saw as the spider scuttled toward it. Despite the warmth, he shivered. This only seemed to make the old woman's grin more unsettling.

"My price, Dario Darien, is that ye will owe me a favor, to be called for when I needs it. But the spell ye seek has a price as well. Most spells cost the spellweaver something. But in this case, it costs him that receives."

"And that is?"

"The past takes its toll in the present, drawing the future back so that all three reshape the watcher. It be a permanent price. Once started, it can't be stopped. Ye'll see what ye desire to see in the past, but the future'll be changed." She paused. "Do ye wish to do this, then?"

Darien folded the old woman's explanation over upon itself, trying to unravel its cryptic meaning. *Leave it to a witch not to give a straight answer.*

Her eyes pierced him as she tapped a yellowed fingernail on the tabletop.

He was certain he could understand what she meant if he had time. But he didn't. Every moment he spent there took away from his hope of releasing Demerra and locating the children. Discovering what happened to Jairus was the first step in saving his family.

"I do," he said.

Again, Rebekkah offered the disquieting smile, and he couldn't help but think of the fly.

"Then let's get ready."

She led him into an adjoining room, where a single window overlooked the back of the cottage. The shutters stood open, revealing two gardens, and in between them, a cow munched on the rough grass. Bees droned among the flowers. Lavender and mint drifted in on the occasional breeze.

"Drag that over here," Rebekkah said, pointing at a chair, "and put it there." She indicated a bare spot in front of the window. "Sit."

Darien did as instructed. He could see the cow from this vantage point and beyond it, the edge of the clearing.

She walked to a door opposite the one they'd entered. "I've got to get ready. Ye sit there and don't ye get up fer nothing."

She closed the door behind her. Darien looked around. The small room contained a simple wooden bed frame along one wall. A table held a washbasin, some pungent soap and two clay jars with matching lids. The wide rafters overhead reminded him of a rib cage. Staring out the window, he watched the cow for several moments, listening to her bell clank when she moved. The buzzing of the bees, the warmth of the house and the smell of lavender relaxed him, and he dozed off.

17
RELIVING

T he sound of the door closing snapped Darien awake. He looked around, disoriented, and saw Rebekkah Barlowe limping toward him.

"Rest good, did ye?"

"I—yes, I suppose I did." He yawned. "My apologies."

"Ye ain't got to apologize none to me. It's rest ye be needing. This spell will weaken ye." She stepped behind the chair and placed her palms, slick with an oily substance, against his temples.

"What's that?"

"It's an ointment—helps make ye see."

He wrinkled his nose. It reeked of mud, burnt fat and wet dog, and felt like cool lard against his skin. As she massaged his temples, trickles of it oozed down the sides of his face.

Rebekkah walked to the window and closed the shutters. A few slivers of sunlight peeked between the cracks in the wood. She began to mumble under her breath. Darien listened, but the words were unknown to him. She reached into a worn fabric satchel dangling from her belt and drew out a child-sized, mummified hand.

"What's that? What's it for?" he asked, the words coming too fast.

"Quiet now! Pit'cher in your mind where ye wants to go."

Darien thought back to the road he and Hawkes had visited—the scene of Jairus's murder.

She circled the chair three times, chanting, and with each pass, she pulled the leathery appendage gently across his eyes. It had an ancient, noxious odor, like a tomb opened after centuries. He couldn't suppress a shudder each time she did it.

She stopped in front of him and lifted his left hand, then drew a curved knife from her belt and nicked his thumb. He winced as she squeezed the drops of blood onto the floor. Still chanting, she wiped up some of the blood and smeared it on his eyelids. She tottered behind the chair, and her invocation took on a stranger, forced quality.

He felt drowsy again. Then the room tilted. Darien gripped the arms of the chair in panic. He felt himself falling—or did he? No, it had to be the concoction on his head, an ingredient that caused light-headedness. His eyelids were heavy as steel, and he could not keep them open. A cushion of comforting darkness welcomed him.

Rebekkah Barlowe stopped chanting and walked to the shutters.

"Remember, Dario Darien—"

Her voice sounded leagues away.

"—this be what ye asked for, of yer own free will. Look now."

His opened his eyes, the lids gummy from the blood, as the old woman opened the shutters.

No sunlight flooded the room. There was no cowbell, no bees, no gardens, no witch.

It was night. Before him, a road crossed the countryside, its edges flanked by dark trees, weeds and fields. He blinked several times, but the image remained. Looking around for Barlowe, he found himself standing alone at the side of the road. Behind him, a lumpy, overgrown field lay smothered in shadows. He turned around twice, taking it all in. He was standing on Windsor Road.

The scrub and weeds along the roadside swayed, but his ears registered only silence. Nor did he feel any breeze against his skin. He took several steps, but his feet made no sound. Kneeling, he reached for a stone, but his hand passed through it. He recoiled as if burned but realized there was no physical sensation.

He looked around again with more care and attention and saw shapes in the dim starlight. A group of men scurried around a coach and supply wagon. They wore the symbols of the Four Orders. The doors on both sides of the coach and at the back of the supply wagon hung open. Pieces of clothing, open trunks, weapons and the bodies of constables and deputies littered the road. The brazen fellows rooted for valuables like hogs in a barnyard. Darien moved closer, using trees for cover, even though he didn't need to hide.

The highwaymen all stopped at the same time and looked down the road behind them. One of them waved his arms and said something. The others rushed to gather up what they could, mounted their horses and disappeared toward the distant tree line. Darien squinted and made out the shape of someone on a buckboard wagon approaching along the road. The rider halted at the scene of the attack.

Darien edged closer, growing more confident of his spectral nature. He stepped onto the road, in full view of the rider, who had hopped down from the seat and was checking the bodies.

The man's head jerked up, and he stared straight at Darien.

Darien held his breath before remembering that the man couldn't see him. The new arrival surveyed the area, no doubt trying to determine if the culprits were still around. As Darien moved closer, the man stood up.

It was Jairus Gray.

In a rush of excitement, Darien called out to him, but his voice made no sound. He jogged toward him, waving his arms. Jairus didn't respond. Darien's heart sank as he remembered this had already happened months ago. He could do nothing to change what he saw before him, only watch as the events ran their course.

Jairus poked his wooly head into the coach and supply wagon. After a few moments, the broad-shouldered, muscular man pulled a nondescript bundle of cloth from the depths of the supply wagon. He knelt on one knee, sat it down on the road and removed the cloth.

Darien gasped.

The item was the size of a hatbox, and the gilded ornamentation appeared dull in the gloom. Jairus turned the box and studied it before standing up. Darien stepped closer, already knowing what he saw. Through the glass panes of the reliquary, a cracked, gray skull stared out with empty sockets. It was the Skull of Cain Broadstreet, seventeenth Heiromonarch of the realm—one of the Church's most important relics.

Jairus looked around the way a small child does when lost in a crowd. He rifled through the remaining contents of the supply wagon but found nothing else. He bundled up the reliquary and stowed it underneath the seat of his buckboard before driving off toward Talnat.

So Jairus had stumbled across the robbers, frightened them off and then discovered the Skull, which the Church had been transporting from one cathedral to another...

Darien looked at the mess of ransacked vehicles and bodies.

But if Jairus went to Talnat, how had his body ended up back here? And why didn't Qui and his men find all these bodies?

Darien glanced along the deserted road, and in the blink of an eye, the light changed. Dawn approached. He estimated it had been about half an hour since Jairus left.

He now saw more shapes along the road, moving south toward Talnat. As they came closer, he made out two more supply wagons, a single driver seated on each. A mounted rider in a helmet rode a warhorse in front of them. One of the drivers raised an arm and waved at Darien—no, not at him. They couldn't see him. Somebody behind him. He turned.

Another rider approached from the south, leading a horse and wagon. Like the other rider, he wore a helmet and towered over the head of his horse. As the tall man galloped closer, a queasy feeling settled in Darien's stomach.

He glanced at the others approaching the ransacked wagons. The two wagon drivers wore dark robes with deep hoods hiding their faces. The giant riding with them was outfitted in chain mail, a plum-colored cloak flowing from his shoulders. Something that resembled a rank pin was affixed to the left side of his armor.

Darien turned back to watch the lone rider—and his stomach turned to ice.

In tow was Jairus's horse and buckboard.

He put a hand over his mouth when he saw Jairus's body draped across the rider's saddle horn. Bent backward, the spine snapped, it flopped side to side as the horse slowed to a trot. Blood dripped from the arms. Ribs jutted through his ripped tunic. Darien cringed as they passed. Tears sprang to his eyes, but he couldn't look away from the busted figure dangling against the sides of the horse like a shattered doll.

The group gathered in the middle of the road. The robed figures climbed down and discussed something. The giants dismounted their warhorses. Using the horse for comparison, Darien estimated them to be at least seven feet tall. The robed figures seemed like children beside them.

One giant checked the horses harnessed to the coach and supply wagon and turned everything around so it faced north. The other giant lifted Jairus's body from the saddle. He raised it above his head like a sack of wheat before hurling it to the side of the road. Darien looked away as the body landed, limbs flopping like eels, and rolled into a ditch.

The behemoth turned and gathered up the bodies lying in the road, pitching them effortlessly into one of the supply wagons. The first robed figure led Jairus's horse and wagon to the side of the road and left them there. The second gathered up every item scattered along the road. He threw it all into a supply wagon.

Finally, with the road clean and clear, the first robed shape removed the reliquary from beneath the buckboard's seat. He carried it reverently and placed it inside his wagon, then motioned for the giants. They remounted, and the group trundled north just as the eastern sky was creased by a pale pinkish orange.

Once more, Darien was alone, except for Jairus's mangled body and the horse. With tears in his eyes, he understood why the Talnat authorities had written it off as a bandit attack.

So somewhere on the way to Talnat, that giant had killed Jairus—presumably to recover the reliquary. The body had been planted back here while the relic was secreted away by—

Never in his service to the Church had he seen robes such as the smaller men wore. And the rank pin worn by the giants…he was completely unfamiliar with the design. They had worn them on the left side, not the right as the Orders required. While they retained the overall diamond shape of the standard rank pin, theirs had been made of two smaller triangles—the apexes pointing up and down—separated by a wide red line. The color, as best he could tell, had been similar to the inset of his own pin that contained the bone sliver.

Who—or what—the hells were they?

Darien felt physically sick and mentally numb. It wasn't until he noticed a group of farmers on the road that he realized he had no idea how to stop seeing what he was seeing.

He needed to get back. He needed to find a way to signal Rebekkah Barlowe.

With that thought, his eyes opened as if from a deep sleep. He squinted. Sunlight filled the room through the open window he faced. The cow mooed somewhere out of sight. His head felt fuzzy, and his fingers and joints ached. Rebekkah stood nearby. What he'd seen came rushing back like an enraged bull, and he couldn't stop the tears that spilled onto his cheeks.

"I've…I've got to get back…to my sister." His voice sounded thinner, weaker in his own ears. He went to stand, but his body responded lethargically.

He pushed himself out of the chair and stood on unsteady legs. Rebekkah Barlowe watched him from beneath narrow gray eyebrows.

"W-Why am I…?"

"I told ye." She crossed her arms.

Darien shook his head. "What did you tell me? What's going on?"

"Ye paid the price for yer knowledge, that's what it be." She hobbled over to the washbasin on the table.

He held his hands in front of him, staring. They looked as if they belonged to someone else. "What in the Church's name?"

"Here." She picked up a turtle shell mirror, the glass cracked and dingy with age. She held it up to him. "The price, Dario Darien."

He looked at himself, dumbfounded. He touched his face with palsied fingers, as if it might break and fall off his skull. Beneath overgrown gray eyebrows, his eyes filled with horror and disbelief. Pronounced creases edged his eyes and mouth, the skin far looser than it should be. His hair was a bluish gray. His hands trembled, and he couldn't get them to stop.

"What did you do to me?" he demanded, his voice thin and watery. He stared at the mirror, repulsed and transfixed.

"I didn't do nothing, Dario Darien. Ye did this. Ye got what ye asked for, and the spell's done took what it does."

He shook his head, unwilling to accept what he saw. "No...no, it's a trick. It's one of your damned tricks!"

Rebekkah Barlowe threw her head back and cackled at the rafters. "That be no trick o' mine! I told ye there'd be a price to pay."

"But you didn't say it would be *this*!"

"I said that the past takes its toll in the present. It draws the future back so that all three reshape the watcher. Ye see what ye want in the past—and the future be changed." She hacked another wad of phlegm up her throat and spat it out the window. "I says yer future's changed, right enough."

He looked from the mirror to her face, back and forth, trembling with shock. His knees ached, and he had to grip the back of the chair to steady himself.

"How...how long?" he croaked.

"Ye age three year for every week ye go back. What be the date you seen?"

He chewed his lip. "March... It was March 11th."

The old woman closed one eye. When she scowled, her face multiplied its wrinkles. "Fourteen weeks back, that be! Hoooo! That be forty-two year ye be adding."

"Forty-two?" His voice was little more than a whisper. "You mean I'm *eighty-two* years old now?"

"It's a good thing ye didn't need to go back to last year. Ye'd be dead!" She cackled again. "Or ye'd have needed to be a sight younger than ye are—I mean, *was*."

"I could've died! What if I had to go back farther?" He wheezed, and his chest started to burn. "Damn you! Damn you to all the Twelve Planes!" He followed her out of the room on unsteady legs. "It's no wonder the Church burns the likes of you!"

She walked out the front door. He had to hurry to keep up.

The sunlight hurt his eyes as he stepped outside. He shielded them with an age-spotted hand and glared at her.

"Ye best be getting on now." Rebekkah jabbed an arthritic finger toward the edge of the clearing. "And ye best do so quick-like. Wouldn't do no good for ye to be stuck in these woods after dark." She giggled. "And don't ye be falling and breaking a damn hip! I'll not waste me time looking for ye!"

Fury burned in his chest—*or is that my heart exploding?*

He cursed her again as she lumbered back to her corn patch. Grizzel eyed Darien before huffing and laying his head between his paws.

With tears of rage and shock running down his face, Darien began the long, uncomfortable trek back to his horse. As he reached the clearing's edge and found the rabbit trail he'd followed, Rebekkah Barlowe hooted after him:

"Don't be forgettin' our pact, Dario Darien! You owe me a favor when I needs it."

He stumbled into the forest as fast as his as elderly body would allow.

18

PURSUIT

Malachi Thorne stopped eating and looked up from his lunch. His gaze pinned Stuttering Tomas against the chair. "Say that again."

The boy, no more than fifteen, sat like a chunk of stone across the table. His dirty blond hair hung over his forehead and reminded Thorne of straw left out in the rain.

"I-I only said, Your Grace, that the t-t-two men you s-s-seek left the city this morning."

"How do you know, boy?" Cabbott bent over the young man. The lad trembled like a trapped deer. "Just take it slow. You're in no danger."

The boy's caramel-brown eyes searched Cabbott's before returning to Thorne. "Early this morning, I was unloading some bales for M-Master Valer-ri—he's a sh-sh-shopkeeper near the Market District. I overhead two men talking a few doors down. One of them said something about T-T-Traugott and K-K-Kordell."

"What did they say?" Thorne pressed.

"I only heard bits and pieces 'cause I was going in and out of the sh-shop."

Thorne sat up straighter. Cabbott laid a hand on the boy's shoulder.

"The t-t-two men had been with Traugott and Kordell last night. They attended s-s-some sort of meeting with th-th-them."

Thorne's heart beat faster.

"Where was this meeting held?" Cabbott asked.

Thorne motioned for the constable to wait. "Before we ask that"— he looked back at the boy—"tell me what you know of their departure. You said they left the city. When? In what direction?"

The boy nodded, his hair flopping as he did. "One of the men s-s-said that Traugott and Kordell rode out at dawn. They're going to B-B—"

"Baymouth?"

The boy nodded again.

Thorne looked at Cabbott. The constable rubbed his beard, evaluating the information. Thorne noticed more gray in Cabbott's beard than he could remember seeing before. The lines on his forehead seemed deeper, too. "Did they say anything about a route?"

The lad pondered for a moment while Thorne ate another mouthful of stew.

"Yes, Your Grace. I remember one said s-s-something about the N-N-Niapel Road…"

"Makes sense," Cabbott said. "Too much risk of being recognized or discovered on the 22 Road."

"Did the men say anything else—anything at all—about Traugott or Kordell? Think hard, son."

After a moment, he shook his head. "No, Your Grace. As I s-s-said, I was in and out of the sh-sh-shop. But I thought it was something you'd want t-t-to know."

Thorne smiled and nodded. "It is. Thank you, my son. You have done the Church a great service today. May the favor of the Heiromonarch be upon you." He made the sign of the Church over the boy, who brightened with pleasure. "Thurl, show him our appreciation."

Cabbott pulled two silver coins from his belt pouch and handed them to the young man.

His grin broadened. "Oh wow! Th-Thank you, Your Grace!"

Thorne dismissed the lad, and Cabbott sat down in his place.

"What do you think?" Cabbott asked.

"I think he's telling the truth."

Cabbott nodded. "So do I."

"Keegan Lang and the other familiars we have on retainer speak well of Tomas."

"Could be a trap, though. Those two men could've been put there intentionally to drop this information so it *would* get to us. Traugott and Kordell have to know we're in town."

Thorne swirled the wine inside his cup before taking a drink. He stared over the rim at Cabbott. "I'm sure they do. And if they know that, they also know that Rann's confined us here to await trial."

"So a trap would be a waste of time since we're stuck here."

Warner descended the stairs and crossed to the table. He sat down between them, and they told him what Stuttering Tomas had said.

"What do we do, Boss?"

Thorne looked at both men. They were not only his assistants; they were his friends. Friends he didn't want to risk. He finished off his wine and stood up. "I'll tell you what *I'm* going to do. What they least expect. I'm going after them."

The constable and deputy stared at him.

"And you two are staying here."

Will Gethen had proven true to his word. The day after Rann had placed them all under house arrest, a group of men had arrived from Alexity with their horses. Thankfully, all of their weapons and possessions were accounted for.

Now, Thorne urged Gamaliel harder. His quarry had at least a five-hour head start. By maintaining a hard pace, he hoped to cut into that lead.

It was nearing two in the afternoon. The scorching eye of the sun watched as he rode northwest along the Niapel Road. The thick humidity made it difficult to breathe, and he knew that he taxed Gamaliel to the extremes of even his formidable strength.

They came upon a small stream that cut across the road. The horse slowed, drawn by the water. Thorne dismounted and let Gamaliel drink his fill while he refilled his waterskin. He splashed water on his face, welcoming the refreshing tingle against his skin. When he heard horses behind him, he sprung up and whipped his rapier from its scabbard.

Cabbott and Warner looked down at him from their saddles. Both dismounted and let their horses join Gamaliel at the stream.

"What in the Twelve Planes are you doing?" Thorne demanded, sheathing his weapon. "I ordered you to stay at the Pig!"

Cabbott nodded. "You did. But I'll be damned if I'm going to let you do this by yourself."

"You need us, Boss." Warner offered a lopsided grin.

Thorne clenched his fists. "I explained this to you. By leaving Rimlingham, I'm a fugitive. I'm willing to accept that and deal with it, but I don't want either of you charged. I'm going to catch Traugott and Kordell, one way or another."

"Even if you have to break Church law to do it?" Cabbott asked.

"I'll do what I must to see them brought to justice."

Warner uncorked his waterskin and put it to his mouth. "Well, Boss, that's how we feel about followin' you." He took a long drink.

Thorne sighed. He put his capotain hat back on and wiped water from his goatee. "You don't understand. I'm trying to protect you. If you're not with me when I do this, you can't be held responsible." He took the reins and pulled Gamaliel from the stream.

"We get it, Malachi, but we're not just going to sit on our asses while you do this. You can get mad as all hells if you want. But we're still with you."

"Whether you like it or not," Warner added. "Hey, I don't think I've ever said anythin' like that to a Witchfinder before." His infectious grin caused Thorne to smile in return.

"So what you're telling me, Jester"— he swung into the saddle—"is that you're disobeying my direct orders."

Warner wiped sweat from the end of his nose. "That's about it."

"Very well. So be it." Thorne sighed. "Remind me to have you written up when we get to the next city."

They fell in beside him as he started off again.

"Sure thing, Malachi," Cabbott said. "We'll put that at the top of our to-do list."

"Yeah—right after we arrest you for runnin'," Warner added.

Thorne's smile was genuine, relaxed. It was an honor to have the kind of friendship and loyalty that transcended mere vocation. As they galloped toward Niapel, Thorne hoped that Dario and Tycho had been successful in securing Demerra's release. Something stank in Talnat. If he got through this with his hide intact, Thorne was going to see that she was fully exonerated—and remunerated for all her pain and suffering.

He stared at the road ahead, straight and flat, sandwiched between ancient trees. *But first, that mealy-mouthed Traugott... And I'm going to see Zadicus Rann excommunicated for what he's done.*

What had begun as a simple mission to recapture a heretic and traitor had grown into a full-blown mess. Weeks of pursuit and this was the closest he'd been. Plus, Rann's hatred of him had twisted into some kind of perverse power grab. When all this ended, there'd be plenty of tribunals with the Council. He was an Imperator, with a spotless—or nearly spotless—record. And as Gemmas Earl had said, others saw the potential for even greater leadership in him. While the idea of ecclesiastical politics was distasteful, he now had to consider whether such advancement might prove beneficial.

No! That was the kind of thinking that motivated someone like Rann. Using rank or power for his own ends would make him no better than him. Thorne would continue to serve the Church as he always had. He would find Traugott and Kordell, and then he would confront Rann and his ridiculous allegations.

They slowed when they came to several tree trunks lying across the road, victims of one of the recent storms. Limbs, bark and sticks lay everywhere. Other travelers had created a narrow path around the exposed roots. Thorne led them to the side of the road, where Gamaliel picked his steps carefully down the soft shoulder. He was almost back on the road—Cabbott midway around the roots—when they heard a grunt and a curse behind them.

Thorne urged Gamaliel onto the road and turned. Cabbott stopped and looked back. A mounted figure erupted from the woods on both sides of the road. They converged on Warner, who sat grimacing with an arrow protruding from his upper arm. Helpless, Thorne looked for a way past the fallen trunks.

The red-haired woman roared as she tossed the bow aside. She drew an arming sword and was beside Warner in an instant. She slashed at his head. He threw himself sideways, and the blade glanced off his armor. He toppled from the saddle with another curse.

Cabbott turned his horse and regained the road just in time to intercept Rennick Glave. Their swords met with a clang; horses collided side against-to-side. Glave released the reins, and then his fist crunchinged into Cabbott's jaw. The constable pulled back and swung has saber again, but Glave moved out of range.

Teska Vaun leapt from her horse. She lunged at Warner, who stood with the aid of one of the tree trunks. Her sword cleaved down. Warner twisted aside. The blade bit into the wood, bark flying. He lowered his uninjured shoulder and drove it into her midsection, knocking her back. The separation allowed him to draw his saber, but not with his sword arm. He clenched that to his side, the shaft still protruding from his right arm. Blood crept to his elbow.

Warner swung and parried as Vaun pressed her advantage. She pinned him against the tree trunks so he couldn't retreat. She grinned around gritted teeth.

"Lady...what's wrong with you?" he demanded between gulps of air. His dark skin glistened with perspiration. Sweat stung his eye, but he couldn't take time to wipe it away.

"You!" she screamed, grasping the arming sword in both hands and hacking viciously. "You! Killed! Marco!"

In an instant, his sword felt lighter. He shouted back at her as he parried each of her swings and began returning them, pushing her back. "I'm sick of this shit! I didn't...kill Marco! I...just recognized him through his disguise! There were other deputies...who actually arrested him." He continued to advance against her.

"That's the same...as killing him!"

Warner fought like a man possessed, saber whirling and twisting as the woman continued to retreat. She jumped behind her horse, seeking a moment's reprieve. The animal pranced and nipped the air.

Warner grasped his saber with both hands; agony flared along his injured arm. He ignored it, his vision reddening. With a scream of fury and pain, he swung with all his strength. The horse screamed as half of its back leg spiraled to the ground, blood gushing onto the hot road. It tried to rear, but its other back leg crumpled beneath it. Vaun cursed. The horse fell sideways, carrying her to the ground.

Cabbott turned his horse and regained the road just in time to intercept the male rider. He recognized him as the pilgrim from the ferry. Their swords met with a clang; horses collided side against side. The mercenary released the reins, and then his fist crunched into Cabbott's jaw. The constable pulled back and swung has saber again, but his opponent moved out of range.

The pilgrim turned his horse to face Cabbott, his sword a shimmering blur in the sunlight. Teeth clenched, sweat flying, the constable countered blow for blow. All at once, the sellsword yanked the reins, forcing his horse to rear. Its hooves flailed the air. Cabbott did his best to pull away but wasn't quick enough. One hoof smashed down on his arm just above the wrist. He yowled in pain, saber flying from his hand. Another hoof grazed his forehead and cheek, drawing blood to mix with the dirty streak it left behind. Breathing hard, the assailant reined the horse aside and prepared to attack again.

"Thurl!" Thorne yelled, pulling Gamaliel back, preparing to charge.

Cabbott swayed like a drunkard before sliding out of the saddle. He landed hard. When he moved, it was as if he were stuck in molasses.

The mercenary rode toward Cabbott, leaned down and swung his sword in a low, curving arc. Blood spurted upward as the blade completed its swing.

"No!" Thorne shouted. He spurred Gamaliel as hard as he could. The horse snorted and shot forward. The tree trunks raced toward them, and Thorne gritted his teeth.

Thorne rose in the stirrups and pushed the reins forward. Gamaliel jumped.

Time seemed to stand still. He saw everything as the horse sailed through the air: the tree trunks slipping beneath him, Warner's sword slicing through the air, the woman falling beneath her horse, the pilgrim from the ferry looking down at Cabbott. He realized that he'd been holding his breath from the moment Gamaliel left the road. As the horse hit the ground, Thorne gripped the reins, hunched over and tightened his knees to keep from being thrown. He gasped air as the horse's momentum carried him past the mounted sellsword.

Cabbott stood swaying, his dagger slick with blood halfway along its length.

The mercenary's face twisted with fury as he looked from his bleeding thigh to Cabbott.

"Gotcha, you bastard," Cabbott spat.

Thorne drew his rapier and spurred Gamaliel again.

The man cursed and raised his sword to parry—but missed. As Gamaliel thundered past, Thorne's rapier sank into the sellsword's neck. The momentum of the charge carried the blade through flesh and bone as smoothly as a hot knife through butter. The hand guard cracked into the throat, and the bloody blade wavered in the air on the other side of his head.

The impact ripped the fighter from his saddle. He flopped across the road like a speared fish, rapier jutting from his neck like some massive hook. He gagged and coughed, clawing at the hilt with sticky, spasming hands.

Thorne wheeled Gamaliel around.

Cabbott stood on shaky legs and swiped blood from his face. He looked from Thorne to the sellsword and back again. "I'm…getting too old…for this shit." His hand relaxed, and the dagger clattered to the road. He dropped to his knees and collapsed.

"Solomon! You all right?" Thorne called.

"Yeah. I'm okay, Boss. How's Thurl?"

Thorne wasn't sure. He leaped from his saddle.

"Damn you, Solomon Warner! *Damn you!*" Vaun screamed as she wriggled beneath the shrieking horse's weight. Its movements slowed as blood continued to pool from its severed leg. Its eyes were black holes of fear.

Thorne knelt beside the constable. "I think he's okay," he called to Warner. "Looks like he took another shot to the head, though…" The flesh around the half a hoof print was already darkening beneath the blood and dirt. "We need to get him out of the sun. What about her?"

Warner swiped perspiration from his forehead and grinned. "She ain't goin' nowhere."

Vaun cursed and twisted, her hands beating against the horse's back. "You're dead, Warner! Damn it all to hells, I'll kill you!"

Cabbott moaned as they lifted him and moved him into the shade.

"We need to get that arrow out of you. Sit down by Thurl," Thorne told the deputy. "I'll see to her."

He pulled his rapier from the mercenary's neck and walked toward the dying horse and the cursing Teska Vaun.

Zadicus Rann hurled the clay figurine at the head of the familiar, who barely dodged out of the way. It shattered against the wall. He immediately regretted doing it, not because he cared about Harwith Tanner, but because it had been his favorite piece. Knuckles against the tabletop, he leaned his weight forward on them. They cracked, and Tanner flinched.

"When did you find this out?"

The familiar scratched behind his ear. "I jus' found out, Master Rann. Honest to the Church. I came here straightaways." He peered across the room through small, droopy eyes that sat too close together.

"Damn it all to hells," Rann growled under his breath. "Tanner, I want you to—"

Someone knocked on the door.

"What!"

Tanner flinched again and curled his lip. The prickly blond mustache that struggled for purchase beneath his bulbous nose twitched like a cat's whiskers.

The door opened just enough to admit the head of Deputy Sabian Vincent. He looked whitewashed beneath his mop of unruly dark hair, as if he'd rather defang a cargellha snake with his bare hands than face Zadicus Rann right now. He opened the door a little wider.

"Master Rann, sir. We have a—"

"Don't you dare say problem, Vincent, or I swear I'll throw you out this fucking window."

"Uh, no, sir… It's a… Well, I guess you'd call it—"

Rann slammed his fist onto the table. "Out with it!"

Tanner edged toward the door.

The deputy exhaled. "It's Malachi Thorne, sir. He's…not at the Pig."

Rann seethed. His eyes searched the desktop for something else to throw. The familiar cringed and tried to make himself as small as possible. Later, rumors would circulate among the taverns that in the moment, the Witchfinder's eyes had glowed white.

"Get the hells in here, Vincent," Rann snapped.

The deputy looked like a dying man who'd forgotten to make out a will. He slipped into the room but left the door cracked behind him. Shattered bits of clay crunched underfoot.

Rann sat down and placed his chin in the palm of his hand, two fingers resting against his cheek. "Tanner tells me the same thing, but he doesn't know anything beyond the obvious. I hope for your sake, Vincent, you have something more to share." If Rann's eyes had been fire, both men would've been piles of ash.

Vincent cleared his throat. "Yes, sir, that I do. Shortly after lunch, Thorne and his men took their horses and left the city. They must've done it in disguise, as part of that trade convoy that left about the same time."

"How did they get their horses? We confiscated them."

"That's still being looked into, Master Rann. But it seems like they had some inside help."

Rann shook his head in disbelief. "Of course they did, Vincent! They didn't just walk in and check their horses out for an afternoon jaunt in the damned countryside!" He drummed his fingers on the table. "Where was the convoy bound for?"

"Baymouth, Master Rann," Tanner interjected. The late afternoon sun winked off the ancient metal towers outside the window. Tanner glanced at Vincent.

Rann pushed himself out of his chair. "Tanner, go downstairs and find a clerk—I don't give a damn who—and bring him up here. I need a formal declaration prepared."

The familiar nodded and dashed out the door.

"Vincent, I need the 'valkmaster alerted. I have two messages that are to go out immediately."

The deputy turned to leave.

"Oh, Vincent, one other thing…"

The deputy swallowed hard.

"Tell Witchfinders Ravengrave and Daiyasu I want to see them."

"Sir." Vincent rushed out, the back of his neck damp with sweat.

Tanner returned with a harried-looking clerk in half the time it should have taken. Rann dismissed the familiar with instructions to find out who had aided Thorne's departure. By the time he'd finished with Tanner, the clerk had prepared his materials. Rann walked to the window, crossed his arms and looked at the sun through the cracked, tinted glass.

"The first message is to Torcull Democh, Witchfinder Supreme of Baymouth." He dictated the brief message, pausing to let the clerk keep up. When he finished, the clerk signed the document. Rann countersigned it and ground his seal into the bottom of the parchment. The clerk rolled it up and slipped it into a finger-sized metal cylinder that would go on the redvalk's leg.

"The second message," he said, his voice cold and domineering, "is to the Paracletian Council in Attagon." He collected his thoughts as the clerk scribbled. "As Witchfinder Supreme of Rimlingham, it is my duty to inform you of a rogue action taken by one of our own.

"As you know from my previous message, I had to arrest and detain Witchfinder Imperator Malachi Thorne, along with his companions, Constable Thurl Cabbott and Deputy Solomon Warner, on charges of necromancy. However, as of today, Wednesday, June 10th, I must inform the Council that Thorne and his men are in violation of their warrant. All three fled Rimlingham earlier today. I think you will agree that their flight casts suspicion on their claims of innocence. It is therefore my decision, as ranking servant in this jurisdiction, that Malachi Thorne, Thurl Cabbott and Solomon Warner be identified as wanted fugitives. It is my professional recommendation that you consider stripping all three men of their titles and tasks, until such a time as this disreputable situation can be resolved."

The clerk signaled to Rann by flopping his writing hand in the air. Rann nodded and sat down at his desk as the clerk massaged his wrist and hand. After a moment, the clerk noted his readiness, and Rann continued.

"I have dispatched men to pursue them and return them unharmed so that we may get to the bottom of Thorne's peculiar behavior. I will keep the Council informed of future developments and will ask my colleagues in the surrounding region to apprehend the fugitives with the greatest care and deference."

The two men signed and sealed the document. Rann ordered the clerk to deliver both messages to the 'valkmaster immediately. As he left the office, two Witchfinders stepped inside.

The shorter of the pair had black hair that hung in long braids down the front of his tunic, reaching to the top of his belt. Half of his face was covered in a black mask that resembled a contorted, grinning demon. His right hand was hooked in his belt, but the left hand terminated in a wood-and-metal prosthesis that sported a three-pronged claw.

The taller man was Ahzin. His eyes peered from beneath thin, perfectly black eyebrows; a small black goatee balanced his angular but handsome features.

"You sent for us, Master Rann," the masked Witchfinder, Ravengrave, said with a deep southern drawl.

"Close the door. You've heard what happened?"

Both men nodded.

"I want that son of a bitch Thorne," he spat. "Take a team of eight men. They're on the Niapel Road, probably chasing after his phantom heretics. Find them. Bring them to me."

"Ah there any…conditions…ta be observed in their apprehension?" Ravengrave asked.

"No, none. Let me make that perfectly clear, gentlemen. I don't care how you bring them back here. Alive would be fine"—he pulled a tabák from the box on his desk, lit it and inhaled—"but 'killed while trying to evade capture'?" He exhaled a cloud of smoke. "Well, that would take care of any needless Church trials, don't you think?"

Ravengrave nodded; Daiyasu grinned.

"I'm sending a message to Torcull Democh, asking him to dispatch some men as well. He owes me a favor or two." He stood, blowing smoke into the air. "You're the hammer; Democh's men are the anvil. You know what to do." He waved the tabák toward the door. "The Church is God."

"The Church is God," they replied before striding from the room.

Rann sat back down and turned to face the weakening sun. He drew the hearty tobacco into his lungs, held it, then exhaled. He watched the smoke spiral and dissipate, and smiled. His promotion to the rank of Imperator was all but assured.

19

HILLTOP

"Boss, you heard anythin' back from Dario? No wait, never mind… How would he know where to find us?" Warner scanned the landscape around them. For three of the past five days, all they had seen were heavy forests encroaching on the road, their heights sometimes entwining to form emerald and brown tunnels. Otherwise, it had been broad expanses of rolling fields that went nowhere and everywhere. "Hells, I don't even think I know where we are…"

"We're about five hours outside the town of Corinthia," Cabbott said. "And I'd guess a little over a day and a half from Baymouth."

"We've got to pick up the pace," Thorne said.

"If they hit Baymouth, you'll lose them." Teska Vaun smirked. She rode behind Cabbott, her horse roped to his. Her hands were bound behind her, and her feet were tied together beneath the horse's stomach. They'd had no choice but to resort to such measures after her two escape attempts.

The first time she almost got away. One moment she was there around the campfire, the next she vanished into thin air. The men had sat dumfounded for several heartbeats, staring at the place she had just been sitting. Then Hawkes noticed one of the horses being removed from its picket line. The next instant, Vaun had been standing beside it, picket rope in hand.

She'd sucked in a deep breath of air—and vanished again. They heard a slap, and the horse bolted into the night.

Shouting and cursing, the three men had fanned out when they realized she was not with the horse. It had taken them half an hour to locate her—which wouldn't have happened if she hadn't blundered into a small pond in the darkness.

The second attempt came two nights later. She had managed to wiggle out of her bonds while everyone slept, except for Cabbott, who stood watch. When he wasn't looking, she held her breath escaped into the nearby trees. It took them much less time to recapture her, because Thorne had ordered Warner to pretend to be asleep in order to keep her under additional surveillance.

Now that best she could do was spook them by holding her breath when they least expected it. That, and needling comments had become her only way of retaliating. "You sure you want to go to Baymouth, Witchfinder? From what we've heard so far—"

"Shut up, Vaun," Cabbott snapped.

"—you and your sanctimonious lapdogs are wanted men." She laughed at the irony.

"Vaun, I swear to the Church…" Warner said.

"It's all right, Solomon," Thorne said. "Whatever lies Rann has spread, we'll put them right when we deliver her to the Baymouth authorities. She can sit in their dungeon and pretend to be a ghost there."

She glowered at his back and jerked her head in defiance. Her red hair shimmered in the sunlight. "I hope you die. I wish your whole damned Church would die in misery."

Thorne looked behind him. Cabbott rode next with Vaun in tow, and Warner brought up the rear.

By the Church, just look at us.

Gone were the capes and uniforms of the Paracletian Order. In their place, they wore frayed, thin shirts, vests and breeches like ordinary peasants. Rank pins had been tucked away in saddlebags and large weapons buried in bedrolls. At a glance, they formed a simple band of travelers.

Two days ago, they'd been attacked by a group of bandits who had recognized Thorne. In the ensuing fight, they'd discovered that they were wanted fugitives; the Church promised compensation to whoever brought them in. So they couldn't keep traveling as members of the Order. Until Thorne could get to Baymouth and refute Rann's accusations, they had to keep a low profile. "If it's open season on us," Cabbott had said, "there won't be any shortage of hunters."

In the nondescript hamlets they'd passed through, Cabbott had purchased ordinary clothing for them so they wouldn't stand out. They'd waited in the nearby forests, like bandits themselves, while Cabbott had picked up supplies. Thorne detested such waiting. He was accustomed to striding through obstacles, getting or taking what was needed. Instead, he'd been reduced to skulking in the bushes while others handled the simplest tasks for him.

Following their encounter with the bandits, on Saturday, they'd lucked upon a caravan and had ridden with them for some distance. The discovery of a 'valkmaster in the caravan, along with two massive redvalks, had lifted Thorne's spirits. He had paid to send one of the birds to Attagon with a message for

Darien: he wanted him and Hawkes to meet them in Nashton on the twenty-second for the Feast of David the Guardian.

"Boss, you okay?"

Thorne blinked and realized that he'd been staring at Teska Vaun all this time. She hadn't noticed—at least he didn't think so. She was preoccupied with scowling at the unremarkable fields and distant hillocks. "Yes. Yes, I'm fine, Solomon. Just checking behind us." He turned to face the road ahead, as empty and dull as any of the others they'd been on.

An hour later, they stopped to water their horses. Thorne didn't give them time for a meal, so they ate jerky and cheese back on the road, passing a slab of bread between them.

They had to be getting close to Kordell and Traugott. Whenever they encountered other travelers, they carefully inquired about their quarry. They were still on the right trail. The anticipation of the capture fueled Thorne, and he pushed them harder every day.

Their pace had been mitigated, however, by Vaun's presence. They had to be careful with her. She was an important part of clearing their names. When he rode into Baymouth with Kordell, Traugott *and* the Ghost as his prisoners, Rann's little game would be finished. He smiled, picturing the look on Rann's face when he handed down the bastard's excommunication.

"Give me a bite of that bread," Vaun demanded.

Thorne glanced back, then slowed Gamaliel to let Cabbott pass.

"You could've just given it to me to give to her," he said as he rode by.

Thorne fell in beside Vaun's horse and held the bread to her mouth. She bit off a piece, chewed, then swallowed.

"I'm done," she said.

Thorne still held the bread out as he studied her.

"I said *I'm done*," she repeated, loud and hateful.

He returned the bread to his saddlebag. "When did you learn about your… About what you can do?" His tongue seemed to trip over his teeth. He cleared his throat.

"What the Hell's wrong with you?" She spat in his general direction. "Why're you so nervous?"

"I'm not nervous. How long have you had it?" he asked, this time with more firmness and authority.

She looked at the road ahead and said nothing. He studied her profile for a moment. The slope of her nose, the sensuous lips, put him in mind of another woman he'd once known. He spurred Gamaliel and rode to the front.

Vaun had been trouble ever since they'd taken her into custody. Defiance and rage made for a volatile combination, and she had plenty of both. In addition to the escape attempts, she'd cursed them, spit on them, tried to pit them against one another, fought and scratched at every opportunity—but her outbursts toward Warner had lessened over the last day or two. It seemed as if she'd turned her pent-up fury on Malachi instead. She never missed a chance to gloat over his failure with Kordell. She seemed almost compelled to goad him.

In the midafternoon, they stopped again. Thorne led them off the road and to a small stream that meandered across the uneven ground. They untied Vaun and lifted her off the horse, accompanied by a chorus of her curses and jabs. With one hand tied behind her and another rope around her waist, Cabbott let her into the bushes to relieve herself. Thorne rode farther away from the road, toward a tree-capped hill. This would be their last stop before he pushed them into Corinthia, where he prayed he could apprehend Kordell and Traugott at last.

His plan fell apart when he reached the top of the hill.

"Shit!" He turned Gamaliel and raced back down. "We've got company!"

"Who?" Warner asked.

"Not sure from this distance, but there are several of them headed this way."

"Pilgrims? Another caravan?" Cabbott asked as Vaun stepped out of the bushes.

"Maybe..." Concern lined Thorne's face. "Let's get up that hill. We can hide in those trees until they go by."

The hillock rose about fifty yards above the surrounding terrain and leveled out to a distance about twice that length. They galloped up through a patchwork quilt of colorful wildflowers. Bees weaved through the heavy air.

They crested the hill into the stand of trees.

"Best gag her, Boss," Warner said. "Or else she's liable to give us away."

He nodded and signaled for Cabbott to follow him. Warner rode up beside Vaun, tugging a handkerchief from a pouch on his saddlebag.

"Get away from me!" She tried to kick his horse but couldn't. She cursed and struggled until he pulled her over and got the gag tied. An inferno blazed in her hazel eyes.

Thorne and Cabbott found a clump of bushes large enough to hide behind but short enough that they could see over while mounted. Both horses nibbled the leaves but found them not to their liking.

"Can you believe that?" Thorne spat in disbelief. "Those are Rann's men."

"I count eight. How about you?"

"Yeah, same."

"And I'll be damned...he's got two Witchfinders out in front."

The posse halted not far from where they'd left the road. Two hounds sniffed and padded toward the field.

"What do you want to do?"

Thorne studied the men and the surrounding terrain. "I'd like to avoid them completely. But with those dogs…"

"I know. They've got our scent good now. You think you can reason with them?"

Thorne shrugged. "With what we've encountered so far? No. I'd bet my rank pin that Rann's given them strict orders to kill us on sight."

The dogs tugged on their leashes at the edge of the field and began to bay. The men guided their horses behind them.

"Come on. Let's go," Thorne said.

They returned to the middle of the copse. Vaun glared in his direction, but Thorne didn't know if it was meant for him or for being gagged. Probably both.

"Solomon, ride that way"—he pointed north—"and see what the terrain ahead of us looks like. We could really use a river right about now to scatter our scent."

"Yes, sir." Warner turned his horse between the trees.

"So we fight?" Cabbott asked.

"We probably won't have any choice." Thorne and Cabbott dismounted and took their sabers out of hiding, then tied all their horses loosely to the trees.

The dogs' baying grew louder. From below, a voice rose to them: "Malachi Thorne! We know you're up there!" The voice had a pronounced drawl. "Surrendah peacefully."

Thorne had chosen a spot where the trunks grew close together so that anyone approaching from the rear couldn't do so on horseback. He hoped Rann's men would stay mounted since riders would be at a disadvantage among the trees.

"Malachi Thorne! This is Pierce Ravengrave, Witchfindah of Rimlingham. With me is Witchfinder Kitani Daiyasu. You ah undah arrest, by ordah of Zadicus Rann. Come out, and no one gets hurt."

The hounds reached the summit, still baying and pulling the man on horseback behind them. The two Witchfinders also appeared. Behind them rode three other men.

"Didn't we count eight?"

"They'll be maneuvering around behind us."

"Boss!" Warner barreled through the trees and dismounted before his horse had stopped. "We got big trouble!"

"Thorne! This is your last chance to surrendah. You ah fugitives from—"

Ravengrave stopped speaking as another rider crested the hill and pulled up beside him. They exchanged words, but Thorne and Cabbott heard nothing except Warner's bad news.

"We got another group of riders comin' in from the northwest. And unless I miss my mark, they're from Baymouth. They're ridin' hard."

"Did you see how many?"

"Ten."

"Thorne!" Ravengrave yelled again, gesturing with a prosthetic claw. "What's it gonna be?"

"Solomon, how long until those reinforcements arrive?" Thorne asked.

"At the rate they're going, I'd say ten minutes. Fifteen, tops."

Thorne motioned for Cabbott and Warner to look around. Several of Ravengrave's men had dismounted and spread out across the hilltop. They edged toward them.

"This is not going to end well." Thorne gripped his saber tighter. The thunder of hooves grew louder.

Thorne slashed his attacker's neck. Blood sprayed against the trees, and the man collapsed. His cries dissolved into a foam-flecked gurgle. Thorne leapt back, trying to keep a tree between himself and his other opponent—a wide-eyed deputy who looked extremely out of place. Flanking the deputy was a tall Witchfinder he didn't recognize, whose delicate features and almond-shaped eyes reminded him of Tang Tien Qui.

Cabbott held his own against the one-handed Ravengrave. However, two other men crept closer, looking for an opening. Warner was losing ground to a constable and the eighth man—a deputy who assaulted him relentlessly.

The trio were slowly pressed back toward their horses. The clang of steel filled the air.

"I am Witchfinder Kitani Daiyasu," Thorne's opponent said. "Drop your weapon and order your men to stand down."

Thorne maneuvered so Daiyasu and the wide-eyed deputy remained in front of him. He had no trouble keeping the deputy at bay, but the Witchfinder was another matter. He fought with grace and controlled power, and like someone with twice his years' worth of combat experience. Every step, thrust and parry seemed at least one step ahead of Thorne's. Like a serpent striking, Daiyasu's blade tore through Thorne's clothing and sliced his side.

Rann's men herded them back to Vaun, who struggled against her bonds and screamed into her gag.

Cabbott yelped as Ravengrave's sword drew blood.

Warner's movements became more defensive, his attacks sloppy and less purposeful.

"This is the final time I will say it: lay down your sword. You are under arrest, Malachi Thorne." Daiyasu's voice was sharp and clear.

Thorne shook his head. "You don't know what you are doing." He turned and sprinted toward the horses. An idea—a stupid and dangerous one—had just entered his mind. It was insane, but their options were running out.

Warner slipped, fell, rolled to his feet—but couldn't parry a downward swing. The blade caught him across the back, slicing through his light tunic. He screamed and collapsed in the trampled grass.

Cabbott stood only a few feet from Warner but could do nothing to help his deputy. Ravengrave and the two men slashed at him from different angles. His arms were slick with blood—some of it theirs, most of it his.

Thorne ran straight to Vaun's horse, rapier ready to strike. He saw the stunned surprise in her eyes as he swung the sword at her. His sword sliced through the ropes that held her feet. Two more cuts and her hands were free.

"Find a weapon!" he screamed. "If you don't, we're all going to die! I need your help."

Bewildered, Vaun pulled the gag down and stared at him from the saddle.

Thorne glanced around, saw Daiyasu and deputy closing fast. He looked at Vaun and read the intention on her face as easily as his own name.

"Don't do it," he told her.

She looked around for an escape route.

"Damn it, don't run! They'll cut you down!" Thorne yelled as he parried the Witchfinder's strike—and felt the deputy's sword slice down his chest. Fire raced through his body; his vision blurred. He knew he had to raise his sword, that another blow was imminent, but his arm moved too slowly. Blood oozed down his chest like warm snails. He staggered back.

Out of the corner of his eye, something moved.

He held the saber across his body in a feeble attempt to protect his torso. There was a scream, followed by the sound of a body hitting the ground. He shook his head to clear his vision. In front of him, Teska Vaun leapt to her feet. Daiyasu lay flat on his back, legs kicking. The deputy stared after her, dropping his guard.

Thorne swung as hard as he could with his injuries. His blade caught the deputy in the side of the head. The young man fell sideways with a groan. Blood trickled from beneath the dent in his helmet.

Vaun grabbed the fallen deputy's sword. Her eyes flitted between Thorne and Warner, Warner and Thorne…

She screamed again, then charged toward Warner—and disappeared in the blink of an eye.

Thorne moved quickly, pinning Daiyasu to the ground. The point of his sword quivered at the Witchfinder's throat. "Call it off!" he demanded. Daiyasu looked up, his face sweaty and disgusted.

Thorne risked a glance at Warner. His deputy knelt on one knee, feebly trying to defend himself. Then the assailant who towered over Warner dropped his sword, eyes bulging. He clutched his throat. Blood fountained between his fingers.

Vaun materialized behind the falling constable, her sword dripping red. The deputy closest to her stopped, mouth hanging open in shock and surprise. She spun around, swung. He was dead before he hit the ground.

Warner also stared at her, the truth settling on him with dreadful finality. If she wanted to kill him now, there was nothing he could do to stop her.

Cabbott fell. Ravengrave and the two men descended on him.

Thorne sprinted toward Ravengrave, screaming to get his attention.

The Witchfinder turned, his half-mask spattered with blood. The leering demonic image, meant to intimidate witches and heretics, only enraged Thorne. Despite the searing agony in his chest, he felt a surge of strength. He slashed Ravengrave away from Cabbott.

Now there was someone to his left; he sensed them more than saw them. He turned to swing—and stopped himself.

Teska Vaun, also spattered with blood, stood beside him. She shot him a brief glance and vanished again. A hard ripping sound followed, and another of Rann's men collapsed, his intestines spilling onto the ground.

Vaun now stood between the gutted man and the other attacker, who gaped at her as if she were a ghost. One swing and she severed his arm just below the elbow.

Pierce Ravengrave surveyed the area in astonishment. Thorne did likewise.

The grass was slick with blood. Three men lay dead at Warner's feet. One man lay in a pile of his own guts, while the other paled and screamed as his arm spurted blood. Witchfinder Daiyasu was nowhere to be seen. The deputy Thorne had struck down lay on his back, moaning and holding his head.

Vaun's sword dripped gore down to the hilt. Her face and clothing were splattered with blood. Standing over the two bodies, she looked like a primordial goddess of death. She pushed a strand of hair behind her ear.

"So Rann's right," Ravengrave said to Thorne. "You ah a sorcerah!"

"I'm no sorcerer, Ravengrave." He wiped his forehead, smearing blood.

"Then explain *that*!" He pointed at Vaun with his metal claw. "She disappeahs and reappeahs, surely at your command!" He looked around the area again, as if searching for something.

"You're a fool. Rann has filled your head with lies. He's after my rank and title. He's willing to go to great lengths"—he gestured at the bodies—"as you can see for yourself, to get what he wants. He cares nothing for you."

Vaun wiped her sword on the back of the gutted man.

"Solomon! Thurl! You okay? Talk to me!" Thorne yelled, turning from Ravengrave.

"I'll live, Boss. I think. But I need to…sit down." Warner crumpled to the ground, his breathing ragged and shallow.

"I've been better." Cabbott gave him a weak smile. He looked at Vaun, and his expression changed from confusion to surprise. "What's she—"

"Teska saved us," Thorne said before thinking. "She helped us. I had to do something…"

The man with the severed arm groaned and writhed on the ground. Vaun drove her sword through his throat and into the earth. She left it there like a tombstone and walked back to her horse. She didn't look at Warner as she passed.

Hooves and voices pulled Thorne's attention from his friends. Ravengrave smiled, the line of his mouth almost perfectly symmetrical with the carved grin of the demon mask. Behind him, Torcull Democh's men from Baymouth crested the hill on horseback. Face flushed but stoic, Witchfinder Daiyasu accompanied them.

Thorne's heart sank. *So this is how it ends—on some hill in the middle of nowhere?* He could add Thurl and Solomon to the list of those he'd gotten killed. At least he wouldn't be around to feel the guilt.

He didn't recognize any of the men in front of him, but they were members of his Order. With a heavy spirit, he realized that every one of them probably believed they were doing the right thing by killing the fugitives. In their minds, they were simply fulfilling the will of the Church. *And the Church is God. The Church doesn't make mistakes.* He wasn't sure if the nausea sweeping over him was from his wounds or from the realization that he'd felt the same way throughout his career.

Daiyasu walked over to Ravengrave and whispered something in his ear. The masked Witchfinder nodded, whispered something back and smiled at Thorne.

Daiyasu drew his rapier; the men behind him did the same with their sabers.

"Make peace with God, Thorne," Ravengrave said, stepping forward. "You and your men."

"You'll kill us where we stand? You're filth."

"The official report says, 'killed while trying to escape.'" The Rimlingham Witchfinder smirked. "I'm afraid I'll have to let Master Rann know that our efforts to bring you back alive failed."

"What about the woman?" Daiyasu asked.

"Ah, yes. That sweet little peach." Ravengrave licked his lips in appraisal. "She'll go back with us—when we're done with her. I'm sure her capture will be an added bonus when it comes time for our promotions."

For the first time that day, Kitani Daiyasu smiled.

Cabbott knelt over Warner. Vaun caught Thorne's eye and looked away. As the adrenalin leeched from his body, Thorne's limbs felt like stone. He took a deep breath. Agony engulfed his chest.

"Kill them," Ravengrave said.

20
TRAUGOTT

MONDAY, JUNE 15, 999 AE

The six mounted men nocked arrows in their longbows and leveled them at Thorne, Cabbott and Warner. Four others dismounted and drew their swords.

Thorne gripped his rapier tighter and gritted his teeth. If this was to be his end, he would not go easily. Cabbott raised his sword and stepped in front of Warner. Vaun stood beside her horse, watching.

The twang of bowstrings filled the air.

Two men choked and pitched forward into the grass.

Thorne stared wide-eyed at the bodies of Ravengrave and Daiyasu, three arrows protruding from each of their backs. He looked up at the riders in disbelief.

"Devane—you, William and Elijah give me eyes on the road—north, east and south," the lead rider said. Ruggedly handsome with blond hair that swept down over one eye, his face was bare of mustache or beard, which accentuated the hard line of his jaw.

"Well, well," he purred, his blue eyes taking in Vaun. He winked at her and smiled. He had excellent teeth. And dimples.

Thorne finally found his voice. "You are not Torcull Democh's men. Who in the Divine name of the Church are you? You've murdered two members of the Paracletian Order!"

"Would you prefer I let those two members of the Paracletian Order kill *you?*" the man asked. "Besides, how many innocent people have *they* killed?" His voice became frosty. "They got what they deserved." He looked at the remaining riders. "Old Gattus, you and Martin see to their injuries."

The older man dismounted and rummaged through his saddlebag.

"That is not for you to decide," Thorne told him. "You are no arbiter of justice and righteousness. Only God decides who lives and who dies. And the Church is God." After days of pretending to be someone he wasn't, it felt good to say that again.

"The Church is no more God than I am a fish."

Thorne went rigid. His chest burned, but he grimaced through the pain. "You speak blasphemy!"

"Malachi, what's going on?" Cabbott still held his sword ready as the man called Old Gattus and a rakish youth approached them with bundles in their hands.

Thorne brandished his rapier at them. "Hold!"

Both men stopped and glanced back at their leader. He ran a dirty hand through his hair and sighed. "They're just going to tend to your wounds. That one"—he pointed to Warner—"looks like he's lost a lot of blood."

Thorne studied the leader and the two men who stood motionless half-way between them. He glanced at Warner, who sat propped against a tree trunk. Thorne waved Old Gattus and Martin forward but stepped closer to keep his sword trained on them.

"Blasphemy is a language I'm still learning," the leader said with an easy smile. "But I think I'm getting better at it."

"You will be hanged—for all of this!" Thorne gestured around the area with his free hand. "I will see to it personally." He grimaced as the movement tore at his chest and side.

The rider continued smiling.

The four men on foot had spread out among the trees, picking up weapons and forming a loose perimeter around Thorne's group. Old Gattus and the youth set to work cleaning and dressing Warner's injuries. They worked quickly and efficiently, talking softly to each other as they did.

"You're correct, Witchfinder. We're not from Baymouth. We, uh, intercepted those men on their way here."

"You mean you killed them." His voice was stone-cold.

"Yes. You didn't think they gave us these garments, horses and weapons from the great storehouse of charity in their hearts, did you?"

"What is your name?"

"Richard DuBose. Most people just call me Rich."

"Except you ain't wealthy, eh!" One of the men picking up weapons guffawed. "Hey, this one's still alive!" he said, standing over the deputy Thorne had struck in the head.

"Check him out, too," Rich said reluctantly.

Old Gattus didn't look up but mumbled an acknowledgement.

Thorne tried to manage his impatience. "I ask you again: who are you?"

"I just told you, Witchfinder. My name's Rich. That's Gattus and Martin tending to your friend. Over there's—" He paused. "Do you really want the name of every man here?"

Thorne moved the point of his rapier closer to Gattus, who ignored him and continued to wrap strips of cloth around Warner's torso. "I want the truth. And by my authority as Witchfinder Imperator, you are all under arrest."

Everyone stopped and looked at him. The authority in his tone and bearing was unmistakable.

The men broke out in boisterous laughter as they went back to their tasks.

Rich's grin brightened, which accented his dimples. He threw his head back and laughed. Thorne stared at him in stunned silence.

"You're funny, Malachi Thorne. I didn't know you had a sense of humor. I'd heard you were far too serious." His grin faded. "But you're in no position to arrest anyone. I think you can see that you're surrounded. And besides, you're no longer an Imperator."

"He's not even a Witchfinder anymore," a muscular, dark-skinned man with a single braid of hair at the base of his mohawk said. His voice rumbled like a waterfall.

Rich nodded. "Carden's right, you know. You've been stripped of your rank and title. Church's orders."

"That son of a bitch Rann," Cabbott snarled as Martin cleaned the cuts on his arms.

"So you work for Rann?" Thorne didn't bother to hide his scowl.

"Zadicus Rann? Hells no, we don't work for him. Or for anyone associated with the Church. We're what you might call—"

"Bandits," Thorne said. "Highwaymen."

Rich smiled. Thorne grimaced at the sight of those dimples again.

"Oh, no, nothing so common. We're fighters of freedom." He sat up straighter and squared his shoulders.

Old Gattus looked up. "It's *freedom fighters*—for the umpteenth time."

"Freedom fighters?" Thorne asked. "Is that some new term for cutthroats and blasphemers?"

"You'll find out soon enough," Rich replied. "Carden, get them tied up and on their horses as soon as they're ready."

Old Gattus and Martin moved over to Thorne. He still held his weapon toward them.

"You're bleeding," Old Gattus said, nodding at Thorne's chest.

He hesitated, uncertainty and doubt etched across his face.

"Sit down, Thorne. They're only trying to help you. If we wanted to kill you, we wouldn't waste supplies by giving you medical attention first."

Thorne sat but kept his rapier close. Old Gattus eased him onto his back. Martin cut away the front of the tunic, and the old man swabbed away blood with unpleasant-looking rags. Fatigue washed over him, and he had trouble keeping his eyes open. His chest felt the way a limb does when it falls asleep. The stench of a poultice roused him to wakefulness. It reeked like vinegar in a tanner's shop. He fought the urge to gag.

"Yeah, it's nasty," the old man said in his soft but resonant voice. "But it's good for clotting and helps against infection. Them stitches in your shoulder'll come loose, too. I'll need to fix them when I got more time." He helped Thorne sit up. Martin gathered up the ointments, poultices and cloth, and moved to the helmeted deputy who slumped against a tree.

Three men on the perimeter moved forward at Carden's signal. A fourth handed them coils of rope. They helped Thorne, Cabbott and Warner stand and bound them more gently than any of them expected.

"How is he?" Rich asked Martin.

The young man dabbed crusted blood from the deputy's hairline. Neither of them looked more than twenty-four years old. Martin wrapped a bandage around the deputy's head. "Cut ain't too bad. Helmet took most of it. Head'll be sore for a few days. Nothing serious." Martin bundled up his things and stood. "What you want done with him?"

Thorne glared at Rich. "Don't touch him." His voice was like ice.

Rich sighed. "I can't let him live. He can identify us."

Thorne's eyes narrowed. "I said leave him alone. He's barely conscious. He hasn't seen your faces." He glared at the handsome man on horseback, fuming over his own helplessness.

"All right, leave him," Rich said after a moment. "We need to go."

Thorne, Cabbott, Warner and Vaun were manhandled onto their horses. Warner slipped in and out of consciousness and slumped forward in the saddle. Cabbott glared. Vaun looked at Rich as if appraising him. From Thorne's perspective, it seemed she liked what she saw.

He felt a twinge in his chest. He tried to convince himself that it was just the foul-smelling poultice or the aching wound, but when he looked at her again, he knew it was neither of those. It was jealousy, pure and simple, and he didn't like how it felt.

Rich turned his horse. The men on foot walked beside the prisoners' horses. They picked up the three watchmen at the edge of the hill, and the healer and his assistant brought up the rear. At the bottom, those on foot mounted their own horses.

"Rich, what're we gonna do with these hounds?" a man with small ears asked. The two dogs lay in the grass, their leashes tied to a log. They panted and looked around with droopy faces. "Can't just leave 'em like that."

"Let 'em go."

Cabbott perked up. "No, don't do that. They're hunting dogs. Trained to sniff out game—"

"So they'll be fine," Rich said, his tone shorter now.

"No," Cabbott continued, "they're domestic hounds. They've been raised and cared for by the Church. They wouldn't last long. Too many predators."

"I'll keep an eye on 'em," a man with a beard but no mustache said. He dismounted, removed the leashes from the log and remounted. The hounds stood, shook themselves and waited.

"We ready now?" Rich asked. Without another word, he led them behind the hill and farther from the road.

"Where are we going?" Thorne demanded.

"Nowhere you'd know, probably. It's off the beaten path, if you know what I mean."

"And what do you intend to do with us once we are there?" He tried to maintain a level of authority in his voice, but Rich didn't seem to care. He chafed inwardly.

"There's someone who's been waiting to meet you. Someone you know— well, not exactly *know*… It's someone you're familiar with. Let's put it that way."

"What the hells is he talking about, Malachi?" the constable asked.

"I don't know. He sounds just like—" He went rigid in the saddle, his mind racing. *He sounds just like Jarmarra Ravenwood did before he died…* "Who is this person? Is he in charge?" He feared he already knew.

Rich halted and looked at Thorne. "His name is Traugott."

Thorne's insides froze, and he trembled in anger. The coldness erupted into a consuming rage. "Traugott!" he barked in disgust. "That son of a bitch!"

"It seems that the hunter has become the hunted." Vaun chuckled. "Or should I say, 'the captured'?"

He remembered the way she had looked at Rich and wished he could knock her off her horse, then felt guilty for thinking it. "Why is Traugott waiting for me? Surely he knows that I intend to arrest him and see him brought to trial."

"Well, that's for the two of you to hash out." Rich swatted a scorpion fly away from his head. "As for arresting him—you're not a Witchfinder any longer, remember? You're just an ordinary congregant, like so many you've condemned to death." He said the last words with a viciousness that Thorne hadn't heard from him until then.

Rich turned back around and said no more as he hurried them through fields and culverts. After several miles, they plunged into a thickening forest. Once inside the trees, they stopped.

"Blindfold them," he instructed.

Thorne lost his sense of time after a while. He couldn't remember how long they'd been riding. They stopped once to water their horses, but Rich wouldn't answer any of his questions.

He also had no idea where they were. They'd spent considerable time in the forest before returning to a road. They'd left the road shortly thereafter and traveled across low hills and stretches of flatland. He hadn't heard anything distinctive to mark their location. Once, they crossed a stream or creek. They went through a smaller forest, and the group rode on into the late afternoon. With the rhythmic swaying of Gamaliel beneath him, he might've even drifted off to sleep.

His chest had gone from a piercing throb to a dull ache. The poultice had lost some of its pungency but none of its efficaciousness. Gauging from how he felt, the damage wasn't as bad as he'd first thought, but it still burned and hurt when he breathed deeply. The cut in his side also nagged him from beneath its bandage.

And then Gamaliel stopped.

Thorne heard movement and voices around them; someone said something about Warner. Vaun lashed out at someone on his right, who laughed in reply. Hands pulled him from the saddle and left him standing.

"Thurl, can you hear me?" he asked.

"Yeah, right here, Malachi."

"Solomon?"

"They took him off someplace," Vaun said, quite close to him. "Good riddance. I hope he dies."

Perhaps because he couldn't use his eyes, his hearing seemed sharper, but her tone held less threat than before. Still, he fired back, "Shut up, Teska."

Movement continued around them. Someone led their horses away. Thorne smelled rabbit cooking. He slid first one foot, then the other, around the ground. He took a tentative step forward and repeated the movements. He encountered no resistance or obstacles. He heard the sound of a spoon against a cooking pot, the scraping of a blade against a whetstone, the creaking of wooden wheels amid murmured voices and plenty of laughter. The smell of rabbit made his mouth water. Bits of conversation caught his ear:

"...killed two...ten others from Baymouth..."

"...have they eaten or..."

"…turning point…"

"…medical help…

"…see Traugott…"

Thorne's blood boiled at the name. With his eyes covered, he had no problem conjuring up his mental image of the frail, arrogant Traugott.

Footsteps approached.

"…ahead and take them all in. He's waiting." It was Rich's voice.

"Where's Deputy Warner?" Thorne demanded.

Someone pulled on the rope that bound his wrists. "Come on. Let's go," a different voice said. It sounded like Carden. "Your deputy's being tended to by our physician again. He lost more blood on the way. Once he's stable, Old Gattus will tend to you all."

Thorne heard Cabbott and Vaun shuffling beside him.

"Four steps coming up," Carden said.

They navigated the stairs, guided by the hands on their arms and shoulders. They were herded through a doorway, where the air felt slightly cooler and their footsteps had a thin, echoing quality. They walked a short distance, turned left, walked a little farther, stopped. A door opened and closed in front of them.

"I can't believe it's happening like this," Cabbott said under his breath.

"What's that?" Thorne asked.

"We're finally going to meet Traugott. I just never pictured it this way."

"It doesn't matter. One way or another, I'll have him in irons and hauled into Attagon by the hair of his head."

The door opened again. "Bring them in," Carden said.

Inside the room, they were instructed to sit. The chairs felt unsteady and creaked under their weight. A familiar odor permeated the air, ancient and comforting, and reminded Thorne of his childhood.

"Untie them," a voice in front of them said.

Thorne stiffened. *There's something…*

"You sure?" From the tone of his voice, Carden wasn't.

Someone pulled Thorne's hands out in front of him; fingers deftly released the rope and dropped it on the floor. The same sound was repeated to his right and left.

Footsteps retreated. The door closed.

"Please, take off your blindfolds," the voice said. "They should've already done that for you."

Again, Thorne's mind grasped at something he couldn't identify but pierced his brain like a needle. He yanked the blindfold off and blinked several times, his eyes adjusting to the light. Vaun sat to his left, Cabbott to the right. Both removed their blindfolds.

The room was spacious but cluttered with piles of school desks. One corner held a mound of broken and rotted wooden chairs. To Thorne's left stood row after row of empty bookcases, most missing shelves and some reduced to little more than scraps and splinters. The ceiling was a peculiar series of empty rectangles through which the upper reaches of the roof could be seen. On his right, rows of large, empty windowpanes looked out onto scrubby grassland, trees and a few ruined buildings. Directly in front of their chairs was a U-shaped wooden counter, its wormy and cracked surface seemingly insufficient for the piles of brittle, musty books stacked haphazardly across its surface. The familiar smell was that of a library, but with a greater sense of antiquity than Thorne had ever experienced.

His mind raced. It wasn't the words the man had said as much as the voice with which he'd said them. That voice struck a chord of memory deep within him. He knew he should be focused on the chance to finally arrest Traugott instead of dwelling on the voice, but it was so familiar…

Thorne glanced at Teska. He wanted to be sure she was all right. He couldn't help himself. Her presence distracted him yet filled him with a sense of warmth and anxious possibility.

"Uh, Malachi…" Cabbott stared straight ahead.

Behind the counter and the books, the man who'd spoken stood up.

Thorne glared at the figure as he leapt from his chair. His chest burned at the sudden movement. He threw his blindfold aside. "*Traugott!* Face me, heretic! Now I've got you—"

His voice died in his throat as the man turned around.

Thorne couldn't breathe. He wasn't even sure his heart still beat. The needle in his brain stabbed into awareness. He gaped like the village idiot.

"It would seem, my student, that it is I who have you."

Valerian Merrick smiled at him.

21
REVELATIONS

MONDAY, JUNE 15, 999 AE

The dying sun slanted through the empty windowpanes, drawing elongated shadows across the room. Dust motes floated in the light.

Malachi Thorne floated with them. The next whisper could sweep him away. The floor didn't exist. His body belonged to someone else while he watched, dumbfounded, from somewhere near the ceiling. His eyes never left the man behind the counter. The face was older, more weathered, but familiar. At least he wanted it to be familiar...

There's no way...

Traugott stepped around the side of the counter. His thinning silver hair was cut short; his beard and mustache matched. He moved carefully but not slowly, despite the cane he leaned on. His attire was that of an ordinary merchant, and he carried no weapon. His smile lifted the edges of his mustache, and the narrow rectangular spectacles that framed his blue eyes.

"You—you're—you're not him," Thorne stammered, a dust mote that finally found its voice.

"Not Traugott or not Merrick?" the older man asked as he stopped in front of Thorne. "It's good to see you again, Malachi. Please, sit. I know this is a tremendous shock for you." His manner was relaxed and easy. He might've been at a fancy dinner or conducting business over spiced wine instead of facing the man who intended to arrest him.

"You're not... You *can't* be..." Thorne's thoughts refused to cooperate; his voice had nothing to work with.

"Malachi, please, sit down." Traugott reached for Thorne's shoulder.

The touch jolted him, yanking him back into the moment. His legs trembled. His chest burned with every shallow gasp. He couldn't tear his eyes from the face that unleashed a torrent of memories.

"You're not the man I knew!" he yelled, jerking away from the hand. His head swam with confusion and shock. "I doubt you're even Traugott!"

"I am, Malachi. Both of them."

He wanted to deny it, needed to deny it, but the voice—it was the puzzle piece that completed the memory he'd believed gone forever. But it had to be a trick, a deception of some sort.

"Who the hells are you?" Thorne snarled. "You look like him, but you're not him. You can't be. Are you a cousin? His brother, perhaps?" It was the only explanation his mind found plausible.

"My cousins are all dead. And as you know, I never had a brother. Only sisters."

The room threatened to turn upside down. Or did he float once more? "There's no other explanation. You can't be him…"

Traugott slid a stack of books aside and leaned against the counter. "And why is that, Malachi?" The question held no malice or taunt. The teacher simply sought to help the student grasp a difficult concept.

"Because… Because I carried your body—that is, Merrick's body—back to Rimlingham myself. I helped put it in the crypt. I watched it be sealed." Shock bled into anger. "So stop these childish games! You are under arrest for heresy and treason." This time, he reached for Traugott.

"Wasn't her name Elaine?" the old man asked with genuine curiosity, glancing between Thorne and Vaun.

Thorne froze, his hand halfway to Traugott's arm. Those blue eyes gleamed so familiar, yet they couldn't be what he thought—what he yearned for them to be.

"Yes. Yes, that was her name," Traugott said. "I do remember."

"Shut up," Thorne snapped.

"Malachi, what's he talking about?" Cabbott and Vaun had dropped their blindfolds and sat enthralled, as if watching a morality play by traveling thespians in a town square.

"Thurl Cabbott, I believe," Traugott said, smiling and nodding. "I've heard much about you." He looked at Vaun. "And who might you be?"

"I might be the fucking Heiromonarch's mother," she snapped. "What's it to you?"

Traugott raised his eyebrows and pursed his lips. He turned back to Thorne. "Elaine had red hair too, didn't she?" He nodded to himself. "But as I recall, her temper wasn't quite as…pronounced." He winked and smiled at her like a grandfather with a shared secret.

"That is enough!" Thorne shouted. "I have heard enough of your deceptions! You are not Valerian Merrick. You are an imposter." He ground the words between his teeth. "You must be some family relation. And…and before he died…Merrick told you these things. To try and confuse me."

"Why would I want to confuse you?"

"I…I don't know." He fumbled but recovered his authority. "Perhaps you have used sorcery to appear different."

Traugott's eyebrows rose again. "Sorcery? There's no magic that can change how a man looks."

Cabbott stood up. "Actually, you'd be surprised on that point."

Vaun also stood up and stretched. She eyed the door. A brown-haired woman sat close to it, watching them, a short sword across her lap.

Thorne squared his shoulders. "Traugott, according to the Laws of the Divine Church, and as Witchfinder Imperator of the Church of the Deiparous, I hereby charge you with heresy and treason."

The elderly man laughed, and the sound rooted Thorne to the spot.

"I can see that you do recognize me," Traugott said. "I understand your confusion, Malachi, but trust me. I *am* Valerian Merrick."

"No. No, that's just not possible." His confidence leeched away. His legs belonged to somebody else, somebody unfamiliar with them.

Merrick smiled at the woman by the door. "Margaret, would you get our friends something to eat and drink? I imagine they're quite hungry. I'll just have a cup with them."

She sheathed the sword and left the room.

"Malachi, let me try to help you understand. You were promoted to the rank of Constable in 885 AE and assigned to protect me. For three years, I supervised you, honed your fighting skills and taught you how to serve the Church. And you were an excellent student—the best I ever trained. Before that, I sponsored your application into the Paracletian Order." He searched Thorne's face for a spark of recognition.

"Okay, let's go back a little further: I visited you in the orphanage after your parents died. I still remember the first book I ever gave you—and my goodness, how you used to love books! It was…" Merrick squinted, deepening the wrinkles on his forehead. His prickly white eyebrows bunched together over the bridge of his nose.

By the Church, he looks so much like him. And sounds so much like him… Thorne's heart battled his will, a clash of titans that was pulling him apart.

"Yes, yes, it was *Malachi the Strong and the Keeper of the Gate*," he said, pleased with his recollection. "You used to love Malachi the Strong because I told you that you had been named after him."

Weightlessness enveloped Thorne once more.

"Th-Those are things that—that anyone could find out." Thorne struggled to regain mastery of his voice and the situation. "A besotted, one-eyed clerk could discover such things."

Merrick nodded. "Perhaps. But would he know that when you were eight, we made plans to go on pilgrimage to visit the shrine of Malachi the Strong? And we didn't get to because I was called away. Would someone else know that when I returned, you wouldn't speak to me for three months because I'd broken my promise to you?"

Thorne stood silent and motionless, only his eyes flitted over Traugott's face—*or Merrick's face.* Memories and possibilities raced, collided, reshaped, dissolved. But his heart refused to surrender the faint glimmer of hope that this man might indeed be his mentor.

Cabbott folded his arms. Vaun poked around the room, edging closer to the door.

"You said—that is, Merrick told me that day—"

Merrick raised a hand. "I told you that promises are easily made, but only the actions that follow the promises—"

"—are to be trusted."

The old man nodded. His smile was light breaking from the darkness, a spark erupting into a bonfire. "Malachi, it really is me. I'm not trying to fool you. There's no magic involved here. I survived Toadvine."

Thorne's throat tightened, and tears threatened to spill over his eyelids. Nothing could coax his gaze from the old man's leathered skin, the kind eyes, the inviting smile. He still couldn't believe he wasn't a ghost...

A ghost!

He spun around. "Thurl, where's Teska?"

"Oh, you've got to be kidding me..." The constable moved toward the door. "I swear to the Church she was just here. No way she could've left this room."

"I didn't." She stood up from behind a shoulder-high bookshelf, a coverless book in her hands. "What? You thought I snuck out?"

"The thought did cross my mind," Thorne replied. "It wouldn't be the first time you've tried to escape."

She tossed the book onto a shelf, folded her arms and stared at him.

"And I know that if you got a clean shot at Solomon—especially considering...your gift—you'd take it," Cabbott said.

"Maybe I'm not interested in killing him anymore."

"Right," Thorne deadpanned. "Thurl, keep an eye on her." He turned to Merrick. It was like stepping back in time.

"Who is she?" the old man asked.

"A thief named Teska Vaun. She has a grudge against my deputy and has tried to kill him twice. She's going back to stand trial." He paused awkwardly as he looked at Merrick.

"And so am I. Is that it?"

Thorne sighed. "You have promoted heretical ideas that have led people away from the Church. By doing so, you have endangered their immortal souls. You're the leader of a group of rebels and traitors. Your people killed two deputies in Talnat when Kordell escaped, and they killed the men from Baymouth out there." He pointed toward the windows.

"God only knows how many more bodies can be laid at your feet," Cabbott said. "Speaking of Kordell, where is he?"

"And you…you have turned against everything you believed in." Thorne searched Merrick's eyes. "*Why?* Why didn't you return to the Church? Why adopt this disguise as Traugott? Why leave that message in Rimlingham? Where have you been all these years?" He paused to catch his breath. He needed to bend all this chaos into order, to find a meaning and purpose that made sense.

The old man's smile faded as Thorne spoke. For the first time, Thorne didn't see Traugott or even Merrick. Before him, stooped and frail, stood an ordinary old man staring through the empty windows at the gathering darkness outside. This chaos wouldn't be tamed easily.

"Barnabas is around here somewhere," Merrick told Cabbott. "I'll explain everything to you. And I hope that in doing so, you'll be able to accept things as I have."

"What do you mean by that?"

The library door opened. Margaret and a young boy of about nine carried in wooden trays with bowls and cups. The aroma of rabbit stew and fresh bread swept in with them.

"Just put them here," Merrick said, moving aside another stack of crumbling books.

"Where's my deputy?" Cabbott demanded.

The boy stared at the new faces as he followed Margaret out the door.

Merrick handed Vaun a bowl of stew and offered one to Thorne. Cabbott grabbed Thorne's arm.

"It's all right, Mr. Cabbott," Merrick said. "It's not poisoned, if that's what you're thinking. Please believe me: no one here is going to hurt you." He distributed cups of ale, keeping one for himself. "Your deputy is just down the hall, being tended to by Old Gattus, our physician. If you wish, you can see him after you eat."

Vaun tipped her bowl and sipped from the rim. Merrick gave them wooden spoons. They stood around the counter and ate.

"Where are we?" Thorne asked after swallowing a mouthful of vegetables and warm broth.

"This"—Merrick waved his arm across the room—"is one of the many places we use for stopovers. It's out of the way enough that it doesn't attract attention, but close enough so that people can join us if they want."

"Like Toadvine?" Thorne said.

Merrick nodded. "Like Toadvine. This particular building used to be a high school. Do you know what a high school was, Malachi?"

Thorne tore off a piece of bread. He plunged it into the stew and savored the combination. "With the word *school*, I'd imagine it was a place of learning?" He wanted to sound sure, but it came out as a question.

"It was, before the Great Cataclysm. There were many of them back in those days. Students came to these places to learn."

"Like the Catechisms," Vaun said.

"Yes and no. They paralleled what we use as Primary, Secondary and Advanced Catechism, so in that respect, they were similar. But on the other hand, no—they were quite different from what we have." He paused. "Back then, students took courses that helped prepare them for their next educational step."

"What do you mean? Like our two levels of seminary?" Thorne asked.

"In a way, yes. Once they completed high school, they progressed to a higher level of study wherein they applied themselves directly to skills they wanted to acquire. For example, if they wanted to become a sculptor, they studied art. If they wanted to become a farmer, they studied agriculture. If they wanted to become a teacher, they studied education. Men *and* women chose what they studied and what sort of vocations they pursued. Naturally, there were some things, such as language and mathematics and writing, that everyone had to know, just like in our system. But after that, they had the freedom to choose for themselves what to become."

Cabbott shoveled as fast as he could chew. The food warmed their bellies and relaxed them.

Vaun slurped the last of her stew. "Men *and women*? Everyone knows the Church doesn't allow women to be educated beyond Advanced Catechism."

Merrick nodded. "Yes, but remember—this was in the days before the Great Cataclysm."

"But...what if the students chose wrong?" Thorne's eyebrows knit together in confusion.

"If they learned something they didn't like or couldn't use, they simply learned something else." Merrick paused again. "There was no limit on knowledge. Whereas under the Church's system, you learn one thing—something related to your apprenticeship or vocation—and that's what the Church tells you to do with your life. Or more accurately, the Church tells you what to do with your life and you learn the skills necessary to do it."

"So, is this why you brought us here?" Vaun raised a brow. "To talk history?"

Merrick smiled across the top of his cup. "Oh, no. Not at all, Miss Vaun. Our cause needs you." His eyes shifted to Thorne. "I need you."

Thorne chewed slower, digesting words as much as stew. "What cause do you speak of? Jarmarra Ravenwood babbled of such a thing."

Merrick frowned. "You didn't have to kill him, you know." The disapproval and criticism pricked Thorne.

"He was a traitor." Thorne studied the old man like a merchant eyeing a fine gem. "How did you survive?" he asked, changing the subject. "I was there. Your body…"

Merrick pulled up a chair. "Please forgive me. My leg doesn't allow me to stand for very long." He sat down, leaned forward on his cane and looked at Thorne. "You didn't find my body. I wasn't in the cave under that farmhouse."

Thorne and Cabbott exchanged perplexed glances.

"The foundation of the house collapsed; all of us fell into that cave. That part you know. What you don't know is that *another* cavern sat beneath that one. The floor of the upper cave broke open in places. I fell down one of the chasms, into an underground river in the lower cave. I was barely conscious. Pitch-black and freezing cold, it was. I hit rocks as the river swept me along. I thought I was going to die.

"But somehow, I survived. Eventually, the river emptied out of the hills into another river. By that time, I didn't have any strength and couldn't fight the current. Somewhere along the way, I found a log and stayed afloat, but the river was wide and strong, and just kept sweeping me farther south."

Vaun was the only one still eating. Merrick took another drink.

"I honestly have no idea how long I was in that river. I'd been washed over falls, battered against rocks, tumbled through rapids—probably sucked down enough water to fill a small lake. I broke this arm," he said, raising his left hand, "and my right leg. The leg got the worst of it. It broke in three places. It wasn't set well and didn't heal properly. I also broke several ribs."

"Then who did the Church bury? Whose body is in your tomb in Rimlingham?" Thorne asked.

"Well, I suspect it was probably one of the freethinkers. The fire consumed everything. The Church had no way to identify the bodies that were recovered, so it's only natural they'd assume one of them was mine."

Thorne nodded. He rubbed his forearm, remembering the charred, peeling corpse against his skin.

Vaun laughed. "So the mighty Church buried a heretic, thinking it was one of their great Witchfinders? Oh hells, how I'd love to see their faces when they find out!"

"You won't have to worry about it, Vaun. You'll be hanged long before then," Cabbott reminded her.

Thorne felt a momentary flash of dismay at the thought, followed by a sense of confusion as to why he felt that way. He glanced at Cabbott but couldn't keep his eyes from drifting to the perfect symmetry of Vaun's face.

"Let's go outside," Merrick said. "It's getting dark in here, and we don't keep any torches in this room. We can go sit by the fire if you like."

"Thurl, get that rope"—Thorne pointed to their former bonds on the floor—"and tie her up."

Merrick limped to the door. "Is that really necessary, Malachi?"

"It absolutely is. She's got a long list of crimes to answer for. We have to keep our eye on her all the time because she's—well, let's just say she's a flight risk."

Merrick shrugged and led them into the dark hallway. Cabbott kept a firm grip on the rope that held Vaun's hands behind her. Malachi closed the door after them.

The sun had completed its descent. Merrick took them to a nearby fire with several logs and a few flat stones encircling it. "Sit down," he said, then lowered himself onto a log and massaged his leg. A few smaller fires flickered around the building, surrounded by people who talked quietly in their glow. The humidity had lessened, and the wind caressed their skin. Thousands of stars glimmered above like ice chips on velvet.

"So where'd you end up?" Vaun asked. She sat on a log between Cabbott and Thorne and watched Merrick over the flames.

"As I said, I don't know how long I was in that river, but I eventually ended up in the Arkan Sea and got washed farther south. Days passed, maybe even weeks, I don't know." A faraway look settled over his face. "I kept passing out from lack of food and water, and from the pain. Then I remember hands pulling me out of the water, voices I didn't recognize. I drifted in and out of consciousness for a long time…"

He refocused on their faces. "Anyway, when I finally regained my senses, I discovered I'd been rescued by a tribe of people who live in the west. They're along the coast—well, south of the Devouring Lands."

Cabbott's forehead furrowed in disbelief. "That's bullshit. There are no other tribes, especially not in the west."

"That's what we've always been led to believe, isn't it?" Merrick said. "But I assure you, there are. They saved my life."

"Malachi, do you seriously believe that?" Cabbott even looked to Vaun for support.

"Who are these people, this tribe?" Thorne asked.

"They call themselves Tex'ahns. They say there are more of them farther west, but I never found any evidence of that. Their language is the same as ours."

"Surely they're part of the Church?" Though a sliver of doubt nestled in Thorne's mind.

"No." Once again, Merrick paused, his eyes searching the faces across from him. "They'd never heard of the Church, at least not until I told them."

The sentence hung in the air like the smoke from the fire.

Cabbott chuckled. "Then who do they worship? Who provides the order and structure in their lives?"

"God does."

Thorne raised a finger. "But you just said they've never heard of the Church."

Merrick nodded.

"I don't understand."

"The people who saved my life worship a being they simply call 'God.' But it's not the same as the Church. Their God can't be seen. As for order and structure, they do that on their own. They have their own laws." He hesitated and poked the fire. The wood snapped and cracked. Tiny embers floated up with the smoke and vanished. "They don't need our Church."

Vaun peered at him with curious intrigue.

Thorne jumped up as if snakebit. "You're blaspheming! Everyone needs the Church!" He paced a few steps, pivoted and studied Merrick. How could he say something like that? It was madness. "Now I know you're not Valerian Merrick! The man I knew would never descend to such base heresy. Who are you?"

"And what the hells do you mean by their God can't be seen?" Cabbott scratched his beard and leaned forward.

Merrick shook his head. "I once thought that such ideas were heretical, too, Malachi. In fact, I'm the one who taught that to you. But I've seen all this with my own eyes. I lived among the Tex'ahns for years." He shifted his gaze to Cabbott. "The God they worship is invisible. They say he lives somewhere up there." He pointed toward the stars. "He's supposed to be a very powerful being."

"The Church is God," Thorne said, his voice like granite, as if he could compel Merrick to acquiesce by sheer force of will.

"I'm sorry, Malachi. I truly am. But the Church…well, the Church is not God. The Church isn't what you think at all."

Thorne paced like a caged animal, hands clasped behind him. He mumbled to himself and kept glancing at Merrick as if the man were the source of some deadly disease.

"Malachi, I know this is all very hard to accept," Merrick said. "It was for me as well. It went against everything I'd ever believed in and taught. But my recuperation took a long time, and I learned a lot about their culture. They're good people. Different in their beliefs and practices, but good people."

Thorne stopped and put his foot on a rock, his features as firm as the ground. "They're pagans. They're outside the salvation of the Church."

"No, Malachi, they're not." Merrick's tone grew as unyielding as Thorne's, and his gaze burned.

Thorne looked at Merrick—and found himself staring back. He had always wanted to be just like his mentor, and in that instant, he realized that's just who he had become. He was a mirror image, a younger version of Valerian Merrick's determination, fortitude and purpose.

"Your mind is twisted, like Ravenwood's," Thorne said. "Is this the 'goodness' these people have to share—dissidence and schism? This is exactly why the Church must eradicate heresy." He refused to back down. Merrick's story had redoubled his zealousness. "Whatever your cause, it is an affront to the Church."

Merrick watched him but said nothing.

Cabbott sneered. "So you've come back to do what? Teach everyone these new ways? Turn us all into pagans?"

"Might not be a bad idea," Vaun added with a smirk.

Thorne crossed his arms. Merrick turned to face Cabbott.

"Constable, I don't advocate any sort of pagan or atheist agenda. I want people to be free to live their lives according to their own choices and consequences—not have the Church do it for them. Despite what you might think," he glanced at Thorne, "you are slaves to the Church."

Thorne threw his hands in the air. "More blasphemy!"

"I offer people an alternative, a new perspective."

"By the Church, Thurl! He's barking mad!"

Merrick said nothing else and let Thorne vent his frustration and disbelief.

Vaun brushed a strand of hair behind her ear and said to Merrick, "What do you mean we're slaves?"

"Let me wait until tomorrow to answer that, Miss Vaun. Right now, I think you all desperately need some rest." He stood, massaging his leg again. "There are plenty of empty rooms in the school building. I'm sorry we can't offer better accommodations."

Thorne stepped close to Merrick. "We are *not* finished," he whispered. "I still don't know who you are—"

"Yes, you do, Malachi."

"I do not believe you are Valerian Merrick."

"Then who am I?"

Thorne clamped his lips together as if to keep his words hostage. Their eyes flicked back and forth, sizing each other up.

"You're Traugott, a heretic and—"

"That's the name I go by now, but you know the truth. Deep down, where you keep everything buried away, you know. You don't want to admit it, and I understand that. I truly do."

The old man's voice was the one he'd heard growing up. It tugged at his memories, pleading for acceptance. Merrick laid an age-spotted hand on Thorne's shoulder. It weighed little more than a bird.

"This isn't something you can resolve in one night. It took me years, and it'll take you just as long." He left the fire and limped toward the school. Thorne followed. "All I ask is that you listen and consider what I'm saying. It will be the most challenging thing you've ever done. And it'll likely be the most courageous thing you've ever done."

Cabbott and Vaun walked past and disappeared into the school.

"But why me? Why do you want to drag me into your heresies?"

"First off, they're not heresies. You'll understand that later. But I need a strong leader, someone who can help our cause. I've heard some in the Church see higher levels of leadership for you. I would ask your assistance in something far more precious."

"Like what?"

"Setting people free."

Thorne glanced sideways at the old man. "There you go again."

Merrick stopped on the porch outside the front doors. A few crumbling columns remained that had once supported a roof. He turned to Thorne once more. "I understand your suspicions. I know you don't trust me yet. But I hope that after you hear about our cause, you may see things differently. All I ask is that you listen."

Thorne didn't reply. He stared into the shadows around the building. His head ached. Shock and the overload of information formed a vise that squeezed his temples. He rubbed his side where his tunic was torn and bloody.

"Go inside and see Old Gattus," Merrick said. "Please, my boy. It's obvious those injuries are troubling you."

Thorne didn't know what to say—or if he should say anything at all. His mind felt as thick as buttermilk. He nodded absently and started into the school. Merrick's hand landed on him once more.

"It's good to see you again, Malachi."

22

FREEDOM

TUESDAY, JUNE 16, 999 AE

Thorne dreamed about the end of the world, but it wasn't the Great Cataclysm. Before him lay a devastated vista of smoking city ruins and forests of charred timber. The jaundiced sky hung low, tendrils of—mist or flesh?—touching the ground like vaporous legs holding up the swollen clouds. The sun cast ominous shadows across the land. Before it disappeared, the suggestion of a face in the clouds—that reshaped itself without aid from any wind—observed him with foul delight.

The woman snuggled closer to him. He put his arm around her shoulders as they sat amid the debris of a collapsed building, watching the stars come out. Despite the smoky stench of annihilation, her red hair remained fragrant and silky to his touch. He knew nothing about her except that she was alone and needed protection. She dropped off to sleep, her head easing onto his shoulder.

He smiled down at her. No matter what happened, he would keep her safe.

Her eyelids fluttered. He placed his hand on hers. The skin remained soft despite the rigors of the unforgiving world. How long they'd been together, and how they'd found each other, remained a mystery. And no urgency compelled him to solve it. He pulled her closer, awed and humbled that she entrusted her vulnerability to him.

Where they went tomorrow, or even if they would survive another day, didn't matter. Not right now. Only the calmness and peace of the moment mattered as he held her tight.

He awoke to a tray on the floor beside him. He ate the day-old bread, wedge of cheese and raw carrots as he gathered up his bedroll. The dream vanished like fog in sunlight.

Nibbling the cheese, he walked to the windows and studied the sky. The morning was overcast and heavy with humidity. A storm would hit by midafternoon, if not lunchtime.

Now he could see the library in full light. Sections of disintegrated plaster revealed the naked construction beneath. A few picture frames still clung to the walls, the images within them obliterated by time. A faded placard above them read:

PRESIDENTS O T E UN TE AT S

Thorne considered what a president might be as he finished the cheese. Blank spaces on the wall testified that there had been a great many of them.

A different frame drew his attention to the wall behind the counter. The image was completely ruined, but the script across the bottom remained: *All for the people and all by the people. Nothing about the people without the people. That is Democracy, and that is the ruling tendency of the spirit of our age,* attributed to Lajos Kossuth. He didn't know what it meant, yet something stirred in his spirit. The door opened.

"Solomon!" he exclaimed. "How are you?"

The deputy's smile brightened the room. "Better than I should be. Feel like I've been run over by a horse stampede, but I'll live. Thanks to you."

Thorne placed his hand on Warner's shoulder. "You don't need to thank me. You know I wouldn't let you die out there. The thanks goes to Old Gattus. He fixed me up pretty good last night, too."

Both laughed and compared injuries, like grizzled fisherman displaying their catches.

"Boss, are we still gonna be able to meet up with Dario and Tycho in Nashton for the Feast of David the Guardian seein' as we're prisoners? What if they've tried to get a message back to us?"

"They don't have any idea where we are. We'll figure a way out of here," Thorne replied. "Stay sharp. Where's Thurl? And Teska?"

Warner hooked a thumb over his shoulder. "Up front. We've been talkin' with that guy and a couple of his men." His eyes widened, and his tone became reverent. "Boss, is he *really* Valerian Merrick?"

The Witchfinder looked at the floor. "I don't know, Solomon."

"If it's really him, that's gotta be rough on you—him bein' your mentor and all."

Warner showed him a small room where he could clean up. Afterward, they continued through the school and arrived at a set of offices near the front doors.

Merrick, Cabbott, Vaun and Rich DuBose sat in a room that had a long, broken counter on one side. A hallway with more rooms continued on the other side, with one marked for the 'Principal.'

Carden leaned against the sturdiest section of the counter. Close up and in the light, the man was a wall of muscle and as tall as Thorne. A single T—the Church's marking for a thief—had been branded into the back of one of his hands. Multiple earrings studded both ears.

"Ah, good morning, Malachi," Merrick said. "I trust you slept well?"

"Yes, I did, thank you. And thank you for breakfast."

"How you feeling, Malachi?" Cabbott asked.

"Like you: sore and aching."

Cabbott nodded, smiled.

Vaun and DuBose sat close to one another, their chairs almost touching. They smiled at him, but he got the bitter impression he'd interrupted something.

"Mornin', mate!" DuBose said. The dimples only enhanced his youthful appearance. But they faded away, along with his smile. "What's wrong?"

"Malachi?" Vaun asked.

DuBose raised his hands as if to ward off Thorne. "Who pissed in your boot this morning?"

Thorne averted his gaze. The slow burn of resentment in his stomach had obviously made it to his face. He took a chair between Vaun and Cabbott that kept him from direct eye contact with DuBose.

"Thank you for the medical aid, food and place to stay," he told Merrick.

The old man nodded.

"However," his tone grew firm, "I'm still obligated to arrest you and take you in for trial. You and your men."

Carden chuckled. DuBose shook his head.

"Why?" Vaun asked. Her hair was neatly parted, and the side closest to DuBose lay behind her shoulder. The side closest to Thorne hung like a curtain between them. She looked at him around it.

"Same reason we're taking you in. And after some of the shit Merrick's told us this morning, can you doubt his guilt?" Cabbott said.

"Go ahead, Merrick. Tell him," Warner said as he stood beside Carden.

The old man sighed and searched the room for support.

Cabbott raised his eyebrows in exaggerated fashion and scoffed. "Did you know our rank pins are possessed, Malachi?"

"No, not possessed," Merrick said.

Thorne fixed his former mentor with an unwavering stare. "Enough games and riddles. Tell me everything."

"Well, I told you how I survived Toadvine and about my discovery of the Tex'ahns—or rather I should say their discovery of me. I told you that I wanted you to listen and consider what I've been teaching."

"Your heresies," Thorne said.

Merrick raised a hand. "Patience, Malachi. I said that I needed your help. Nothing I've told you has been a lie."

"You mean your version of the truth?"

"No, I mean the *actual* truth—truth that's not been buried or reshaped to fit the Church's agenda." He paused. "It took me over a year to fully recuperate from my injuries. I had a lot of time to talk with the Tex'ahns. I learned about them as a people and about what they believe. I weighed what they said against my own beliefs and those of Deiparia. And I discovered something that shook me to my core."

He sighed again, the sound of a man edging into treacherous waters. "The Church has enslaved everyone. People are not free to make their own choices." DuBose and Carden nodded as he hesitated, licked his lips and fixed his gaze on Thorne. "The Church is not God," he told him.

Cabbott scoffed. "See what I mean?"

"Shut up and let him talk," Vaun insisted. "I don't think he's wrong."

"Yesterday, you asked me why I didn't return to the Church. I could have. But I chose to stay out west. Like you, I had so many questions, as well as confusion and doubt." Merrick's voice and gaze lowered. "And guilt."

Another pause followed while he sorted his thoughts.

"For weeks, I could barely function as I tried to process what those people believed and how it challenged my own beliefs. I spent six years out there. And the longer I stayed, the more truth I saw in their beliefs and practices. The more I compared them with ours, the more I realized something is desperately wrong here.

"The Church controls too much of peoples' lives. The Church has a say in who you marry and what kind of work you can do. Education and knowledge, as I explained yesterday, are restricted. The Church perpetuates a culture of fear and oppression in order to maintain its authority. And that's not how human beings are supposed to live. We can make our own choices. Or at least we're supposed to." He paused to catch his breath.

Words and ideas swept over Thorne like a brutal winter wind, and he couldn't form a coherent reply.

"I believe," Merrick continued, "that people must be free. No group or person should dictate so many of our decisions. I want people to realize that they don't have to be subservient to the demands of the Church. We're more than capable"—he spread both arms to encompass the room—"of deciding and living as we see fit."

Thorne's words erupted like an avalanche. "This—this is blasphemy! It's madness! How did those Tex'ahns brainwash you? How did they convert you to their heathen ways?" He shook his head. "The Church is God. The *Church* is *God*. How can you suggest otherwise?"

Thorne's hostility and frustration slipped into a softer, heartfelt plea: "You must recant these theories and seek forgiveness from the Church. I have influence now. I know people. Add to that your years of impeccable service, and I can arrange a more lenient sentence than what you—"

"Malachi…" Merrick interrupted, his tone patient. "Slow down. It's okay. I told you this wasn't easy."

The avalanche became a flurry, and Thorne sat once more in stunned silence.

"It's actually all right there in the Testament of the Deiparous. Think about it. The first book of the Testament is what?" Merrick sounded like a Catechism instructor.

"The Genesis," Thorne replied.

"What does The Genesis tell us?"

"The history of the world. What happened when the moon exploded and fell to Earth. How the Deiparian tribe was formed. How the Church formed."

Merrick nodded. "And what's the second book?"

"The Divine."

"What does it tell us?"

"That the Church is God. All our doctrines are derived from it."

"So what?" The constable huffed. "Any Primary Catechism student knows this."

Merrick continued to nod. "Patience, Mr. Cabbott. What comes next, Malachi?"

"The Ordinances."

"Yes, yes. And after that?"

"The Concordat."

"And what is The Concordat, exactly?"

"It's the historical covenant between the survivors of the Great Cataclysm and the Church when it was first formed."

Merrick leaned forward, his blue eyes bright and eager behind his glasses. "What's in that covenant?"

"The survivors pledged their loyalty, service and obedience to the Church in exchange for the necessities they needed: food, shelter, protection. They worked together in order to survive—"

"And in the process," Merrick said, "congregants gave up some of their rights." He sat back, steepled his fingers and stared over them. "But over time, Malachi, as the Church grew, it took more and more rights from the people. Yes, it did create order and maintain stability. But those things came at a great cost. Our ancestors signed away their freedom so they could survive—and no one faults them for that. We all do what we must in harsh times.

"But we don't fear the Devouring Sickness as our ancestors did. We don't face starvation. People can work. We have built beautiful new cities. The things that the people originally needed from the Church are now readily available. But because of The Concordat, the Church is absolute ruler and master of everyone." He paused. "I believe that it's time the people of Deiparia exercise their rights to choose for themselves what sort of lives they want. I hope that the new millennium will begin an age of freedom for all people."

Confusion, shock and disbelief warred across Thorne's face.

"And you're trying to tell people to make their own choices?" Vaun asked. "You want us released from the old covenant?"

"I do. And I'd like the people of Deiparia to have a new covenant. But that's a discussion for another time. This is all very overwhelming for you right now."

For a moment, the room pulled away from Thorne, growing longer, the people receding into the distance. His world—*perhaps even my mind?*—teetered on the brink of collapse. *Overwhelming* wasn't the word for it. He exhaled and ran his hand through his long hair in an effort to anchor himself to reality.

He was not accustomed to juggling so many different emotions. His normally staid veneer was being chipped away, which left him feeling vulnerable out of control. Part of him—the part that loved and served the Church—wanted to consign these heretics to the stake. Another part still found it almost impossible to reconcile the Merrick he knew before with the man before him now. Teska's presence added another quandary. She had to face justice, which would mean her death. That troubled him the more he thought about it. And the fact that it troubled him, that he felt hesitant about fulfilling his duty, added even more turmoil. He wasn't ready to let her go, any more than he was ready to surrender Merrick.

Who was he if not a Churchman, a Witchfinder Imperator? His duty toward Traugott and Teska was clear: they were blasphemers, traitors, heretics, and they *had* to be held accountable. But could he do it? Obligation and emotion collided; friendship and love complicated what should've been a simple decision.

Nothing made sense anymore. Nothing fit together. He'd have been less surprised if the floor of that ancient high school collapsed and plunged him—*into what? A cave like Merrick found, an underground river that could sweep me away from this insanity?*

Something touched his hand, and he flinched. Teska's hand had brushed against his. She studied him with a hint of concern, her eyes darting back and forth, assessing him.

By the Church, she's beautiful. Had she touched his hand by accident…or on purpose?

Cabbott's voice penetrated his chaotic thoughts.

"So Merrick, you say the Church is not God. Assuming for a second that you're right—and I sure as hells don't think you are—if the Church isn't God—"

"Then who or what is?" Merrick said.

"Yeah."

Merrick pursed his lips. "I don't know. That's the truth. But I do wonder if there's something, or someone, out there who is a god."

Cabbott looked unconvinced. "Like the invisible god of the Tex'ahns?"

"Quite possibly. Or maybe there isn't any god at all. Maybe there never was. Or maybe there's one god or possibly hundreds…" He left the thought unfinished, waving his hand as if dispersing smoke. "But I do know that the Church is not divine. It's a human creation, an institution that's become too powerful. And there's something dark within the Church…"

Thorne needed reassurance that his mind still had control over his body. It didn't seem to have control over anything else at the moment. He stood and walked to the counter.

"What did Thurl mean about our rank pins?" he asked, grasping for something he could understand.

Merrick reached into the pocket of his merchant's vest. He pulled out a piece of cloth, unfolded it and held out his hand. A rank pin attached to a leather thong nestled in the cloth, its edges worn smooth by time, the metal lusterless. The four red triangle insets at each point of the diamond were dull and cloudy.

Thorne stepped closer; Cabbott and Vaun leaned in for a better look. DuBose got up and sauntered out the door. After a moment, Carden followed.

Merrick's pin was missing the small red diamond inset in the middle. Scratches in the metal indicated it had been pried out.

"The rank pins aren't possessed, contrary to what Mr. Cabbott said earlier. However, the Church does use them to control people."

Thorne screwed up his face. "Control people? Whatever in the hells for?"

"To ensure obedience. To ensure conformity and compliance of belief and practice. Through these, people are always subject to the Church's influence."

Cabbott shook his head. "I think this guy's mad as a rabid wolf—but far more dangerous."

"Shut up," Vaun said. "He's not mad. He's telling the truth."

Warner rolled his eyes. "Yeah, and we're goin' to believe *you*? Damn, girl. You're as flaky as he is."

"Why would the Church need to control people?" Thorne demanded.

"Because without some form of control, people *will* make their own decisions. And those decisions may not be what the Church wants. So we're given the illusion of freedom. But in reality, we're just puppets." He continued holding the pin out to the room. "In the center of every pin is a sliver of bone taken from the Church's greatest relic: the Ossaturan of Michael the First. I believe that something has been done to those slivers of bone. I don't know what, exactly, but they have some sort of…power. They cause people to be more susceptible."

Thorne laughed. "You can't be serious?"

"More susceptible to what?" Vaun searched the old man's face.

"To whatever the Church wants us to think or do or believe. These"—he brandished the pin around—"weaken our will. Think about it: how many rank pins exist?

"Hundreds. Maybe thousands…"

"Yes, thousands," Merrick said. "And what if every sliver of bone in every rank pin influences the people around it? Wouldn't everyone respond the way the Church wanted? Wouldn't people acquiesce to any demands or instructions that came from those wearing the pins?"

The room was silent. The idea was surely madness.

"This is just another of your fancies." Thorne turned back to the counter. "It's some fever dream you've convinced yourself is true."

"How I wish it were a fiction, Malachi. Honestly. But I've seen the effect they have." Merrick folded the cloth over the pin and slipped it back in his pocket. "When I was rescued, I didn't have my pin. I lost it somewhere along the way.

"It took me a long time to notice anything was different, mainly because I wasn't looking for anything. But after a while, I discovered that my words weren't met with the same compliance I'd received here. The Tex'ahns listened or obeyed because they wanted to. Or because they didn't want to."

"That doesn't prove anything," Cabbott said.

"No, it doesn't. And I didn't give it much thought. I just assumed it was because their culture was different from ours. I got used to their customs and never thought about it again. Then one day—I guess I'd been there about four years—a fisherman brought me my pin." He patted his vest. "He'd pulled it up in his net and didn't know what it was. I was glad to have it back since it was a link to my old life. One of them fashioned it into a necklace for me. And that's when I began to notice the difference."

"How they acted with you?" Vaun asked.

"Absolutely. After I had the pin around my neck, I discovered that if I gave an instruction or asked for something, it was obeyed"—he snapped his fingers—"just like that. It's like my word was law, and the people responded however I wanted.

"So I tried an experiment. I buried my pin outside one of their villages and waited. It wasn't long before it seemed a veil had been lifted from the people. Their eyes became brighter once again, their thoughts clearer. I asked for something outrageous, you know, to see what would happen."

"And?" Warner drew out the word.

Merrick laughed. "They looked at me as if I'd lost my mind!"

"I think you have," Thorne said under his breath.

"I tried the experiment a few more times over the course of several weeks. Each time, it was the same. I also tried letting other people wear the necklace. I was susceptible just like everyone else, so I know it has nothing to do with the wearer. The power—or influence—is in the pin itself. In that bone shard. That's why I removed mine. Wherever there's a pin, the Church has influence over what people believe and do."

"So the more pins in one place," Vaun said, "the greater the influence…"

For a moment, no one spoke. They thought about all the feast days and holy days, when Church officials gathered in great numbers. How much control did all those pins exert then? And in a place like Attagon, where so many pins were concentrated all the time—did anyone have a thought that *wasn't* manipulated by the Church? To what degree were anyone's actions truly their own?

"No matter where you go, there are pins…" Warner said.

"But what about all the freethinkers? What about the witches and heretics?" Cabbott narrowed his eyes. "We've got dungeons full of criminals who disobey the Church's teachings."

"Yes, I considered the same things myself." Merrick's eyes flashed. He leaned forward and tapped his fingers on the top of his cane. "I believe that some people are—shall we say, immune—to the effects. I don't know why. But it would explain why some people continually balk at the Church's teachings. The pins don't affect them."

Vaun's brows knit together. She stared off into the corner of the room. "Maybe I'm immune?" she said quietly.

"You might very well be," Merrick said. "How long have you rejected the Church's teachings? When did you first realize you thought differently than those around you?"

"I guess for as long as I can remember. I questioned everything. I wasn't satisfied with the things the Church did or said."

Merrick nodded so hard and fast his head seemed in danger of tumbling off his shoulders. His grin lifted his glasses and the edges of his mustache. "Yes, yes… You, Miss Vaun, are very likely immune to the pins' influence!"

She grinned. For the first time in as long as she could remember, she didn't feel like an outcast or a freak. Warmth spread through her body.

It was the first time Thorne had seen an expression of such pleasure and validation on her face, and he was captivated like a moth before a flame. He became aware that he was staring at her and awkwardly shifted his attention to Merrick. "Your speculations are quite imaginative, but they are only that: speculations. You must still stand trial for the crimes you've committed."

Vaun shot him a defiant glance.

"First thing tomorrow, we start for Nashton. Dario and Tycho are going to meet us there for the Feast. We'll turn the two of you over to Church authorities. Then I'll straighten out this mess with Rann."

Warner scratched behind his ear. "Uh, Boss, I don't think the people around here are just goin' to let us walk out with him."

"There's no one else here," Merrick said. "Aside from those you've already seen this morning, everyone else has gone back to their homes and vocations. They were only here last night to meet with me and Kordell."

"Kordell? Where is he?" Thorne snapped.

Merrick eyed him for a moment before looking away. "He left in the early hours with two of our people."

"What?" Thorne's hands balled into fists. "Damn it to all the Twelve Planes!" He stomped across the floor and towered over Merrick. "Where did he go?"

"I wanted him gone because I knew you'd be difficult to persuade. Barnabas has suffered too much already."

Thorne's eyes bore into Merrick's, his hands clenching and unclenching at his sides. "Then that is another charge against you: aiding an escaped criminal."

Merrick chuckled. "I rather think that's been on my charge sheet for a while now, don't you?"

"Why are you so flippant? Do you not care that you will be burned for your heresies? Your soul is in jeopardy."

Cabbott pointed at the old man. "Jarmarra Ravenwood died for your cause, Merrick. Doesn't that innocent blood bother you?"

Merrick ran his fingers through his hair, and his shoulders slumped. "Of course it bothers me, Mr. Cabbott. Just as it bothers me that good men of the Church have been killed while hunting me. But I have come to accept one thing: this cause is worth fighting and dying for. If it will help people think for themselves and live without oppression, then it's worth any cost. Freedom is the simplest and greatest of all human ideals."

"Jarmarra Ravenwood said the same thing," Thorne noted.

"We must be willing to sacrifice our lives for something greater than ourselves—for something that will benefit all of humanity."

Silence filled the room.

"Help me, Malachi. I need someone with your connections and your stature within the Church. I need someone who can find others who share the same ideals. Together, we can spread the word inside and outside the Church."

"By God, Boss! He wants you to become a traitor!"

Thorne walked to the door. To one side, the hallway stretched into the recesses of the building; on the other side, the front doors opened to the graying light outside. The air, oppressive and still, teased a storm's arrival.

Behind him, the four people in the room talked back and forth, sometimes over top of one another. Merrick's calm voice responded to every challenge, offered guidance with every question.

Zadicus Rann still had men looking for them, and it wouldn't be long before word reached Baymouth about what had happened to Torcull Democh's men. Not to mention the deputy who'd survived yesterday—he'd be sure to report to Rann. Thorne didn't have a lot of time to decide on his next course of action.

I'll die as a heretic and warlock if Rann has his way.

It would take everything Thorne had to convince the Council—assuming he could get as far as the Council—that he was innocent. He'd also have to ensure that nothing happened to Darien and Hawkes. Even though they weren't by his side at the moment, Thorne knew it wasn't out of the question for Rann to make them complicit in the allegations, too.

Thorne longed to see Darien again. He needed his friend's cool, analytical perspective. *I hope he secured Demerra's release. We could use some good news.*

His mind shifted from strategy and tactics to figuring a way out of their current predicament. They needed to get to Nashton to meet up with Darien and Hawkes, and he needed a way out of the mess that Rann had put him in. He weighed the options of turning himself in—*no!*—of running—*no more!*—or of getting to the Council. Other possibilities and plans took shape, were evaluated, rejected.

After several minutes an idea formed and solidified into a plan.

He didn't know when he started smiling, but one now stretched across his face. He could make this work. It would take care of Rann and his lies. And it would solve the problem of Merrick—though Thorne felt a twinge of uncertainty about losing the man who did seem like his old mentor. He turned around.

"Oh hells," Warner said, "now *that's* a look I ain't seen in a while."

Cabbott nodded. "You look like the cat that's just caught the mouse. What's up?"

The confusion and disbelief of the past few days began to evaporate. Thorne could almost feel Merrick's ramblings being flushed from his mind. Order had been imposed on chaos. Faith and truth triumphed over lies. The winds of heresy no longer buffeted him. Once again, he was the Hammer of the Heiromonarch, the rock of stability and certainty that the Church needed in such dark, divisive times.

Merrick stared at him, sadness and disappointment lining his features. "I see you've reached a decision."

"I have. We leave for Nashton tomorrow at first light."

"Aren't you forgetting something?" Merrick asked.

"Not at all, Traugott." He emphasized the name as if it were a dagger he wielded. "You and Tes—that is, Vaun here—will be handed over to the Church in Nashton, where I will inform the Council that our undercover work is completed."

"Undercover work?" Warner repeated.

A smile crept across Cabbott's face.

"That's right. I intend to tell the Council that everything we've been accused of—necromancy, heresy, being traitors—was the result of an undercover plan to flush out Traugott and Kordell. Rann's accusations won't mean anything when he learns that we've been on a secret mission to infiltrate and expose *him*," he said, pointing at Merrick.

"'Cept we weren't sent on no secret mission. Were we?" Warner asked.

"Of course not. But Rann and Democh won't know that. It'll buy me time to get to the Council, where it'll be my word against Rann's. And after I show how he abused his position for his own gain, no one will believe anything he says."

Warner smiled. "That's a good plan, Boss."

Merrick nodded his agreement. "You get to clear your name and take down your accuser in the process, while Miss Vaun and I are remanded into the custody of the Church for our trials and executions. Neat and clean." He nodded again before hanging his head in discouragement.

Vaun glared at Thorne, her large hazel eyes smoldering.

23

TRUST

"Move!" Thorne shouted. "They're almost on top of us!"

Rain lashed them as if the heavens sought to stop their flight. Clouds like ashen fungi massed just above the treetops.

Thorne hunkered over Gamaliel's mane. The forest to either side flashed by as steel-colored smears. Behind him rode Merrick and Vaun. Warner followed, and Cabbott held the rear.

"Where are we, Malachi?" Merrick shouted through the rain. His hands were tied loosely to the saddle horn, his feet beneath the horse; Vaun was similarly restrained. It gave them limited control of their horses with just enough complexity to deter escape.

"There's a sign up ahead," Vaun said.

Thorne read the name *HONVALE* through the downpour. Something white moved at the corner of his eye. He prayed it wasn't any more of Merrick's men.

They'd left Rich DuBose and Murnau Carden tied up in Kossuth when they departed with Merrick. Thorne had known it wouldn't take them long to escape. What he hadn't anticipated was the two men forming a posse to track them down. By his count, a dozen men closed in on them. He'd hoped to make it to Nashton, but that looked less likely with every passing moment.

Merrick had done his best to slow their progress. Thorne couldn't blame him. He'd have done the same thing if the situation was reversed. Regardless, with two prisoners to contend with, more horses tied together and their need to move cautiously, they simply couldn't maintain a steady pace. Twenty minutes ago, DuBose and his men had streamed over a hill behind them.

Thorne glimpsed more white to either side, like gossamer draped among the branches. He couldn't tell if it stretched across the road ahead or if it was just the rain and clouds. He spurred Gamaliel again.

"Shit!" Cabbott's yell echoed through the rain.

Thorne glanced around. The constable yanked an arrow from the bedroll behind his saddle and threw it aside.

Another arrow landed in the mud where Warner's horse had just been. A third sailed wide and left. One zipped high above Thorne's head.

They raced along a road labeled *S PARK*. As they neared the center of town, the lacy strands became thicker. It draped over the sides of buildings. In some places, it formed a ceiling above them that even the storm failed to penetrate.

Thorne looked back again and cursed. The posse closed fast. He hit the main intersection and turned right onto a road identified as 412. Now, the only rain that made it to the ground came through rips in the blanket of cottony webs crisscrossing overhead. Derelict, boarded-over buildings lined the street. Doors hung off hinges; windows had been shuttered or busted inward. The stench of death lingered.

"Boss, what is this place?" Warner glanced nervously from side to side.

"I don't know." He eased toward the side of the street.

Cabbott wiped a smear of mud off his cheek. "Why're we slowing down? They'll be on us any minute."

"We need to get out of here," Vaun said, her voice constricted. The color had dropped from her face—or maybe it was just the ivory light beneath the webs.

"What the hells is this?" Warner tapped his saber against a finger-thick strand that anchored to the base of a building. The vibration quivered into the massive canopy overhead.

"No, don't do that!" Vaun yelled.

"What's wrong?" Thorne asked.

Wild, unrelenting fear shone in her eyes. She looked back and forth, wet hair slinging from side to side. This was another expression Thorne had never seen on her before. It made him uneasy.

"Malachi, my boy," Merrick said in an urgent whisper. "I think we need to move. *Now.*"

Horses approached.

Gamaliel whinnied, flattened his ears and backed up. The other horses stomped and snorted.

"That's far enough, mate!" Rich DuBose yelled. The posse rode into the intersection behind them. "Give us Traugott and you can leave. My word on it." Half the riders held bows at the ready.

Vaun rode up beside Thorne. "We can't stay here." She didn't look at him but kept scanning the street. Her horse shook its head and laid its ears back.

Thorne stared at the men in the intersection. "I don't know that we have any choice now. Damn it. We're outnumbered, and our horses need rest." He hated indecisiveness as much as he did heretics. "We may have to fight," he added, though without confidence. Gamaliel's nervousness didn't help.

"It's no good, Malachi. We're outnumbered four to one," the constable reported.

"What'll it be, mate?" DuBose yelled again.

Carden led half the riders toward Thorne's group. Their mounts seemed equally reluctant and needed prompting every few steps.

The webbing darkened.

"Just kill 'em for fuck's sake!" one of the riders exclaimed. "And then let's get out of here!"

"Malachi, *please*!" Vaun pleaded.

The air vibrated. The hair on Thorne's arms prickled. His eyes widened as the daylight grew darker. "What in God's name?"

The webs across the street undulated. Horses screamed and reared, throwing two of DuBose's men into the muddy intersection before bolting out of sight. Everyone looked around, yelling and cursing and trying to control the frenzied mounts.

The buildings *squirmed*.

The two loose horses raced back into the intersection. They turned and galloped toward Merrick, Cabbott and Warner. Screaming, eyes mad with fear, both animals collapsed into the mud as if shot.

Dozens of large spiders scuttled over their haunches.

Spiders scurried down the ropy strands toward the ground. They crept out of vacant windows. They poured from the webbing between the buildings. The clicking of their segmented legs filled the air. Eight bulbous black eyes surmounted each of the heads that bore too much resemblance to human faces.

"Go! Go!" Thorne bellowed. As he turned Gamaliel, another sight froze his blood.

Flying spiders swarmed into the intersection. Legs curled under their plump bodies, they moved like bees, darting and zipping through the air. A writhing clump of legs, bodies and humanlike faces already buried the two fallen horses. A carpet of scuttling bodies spread out from the buildings toward the center of the street.

"Move!" Thorne barked. He grabbed the bridle of Vaun's horse and buried his spurs in Gamaliel's flanks. The horse lunged forward, the momentum almost dislocating Thorne's arm. Merrick, Cabbott and Warner charged after them.

The fear-crazed horses galloped down the street, unmindful of bridle or rein. Everyone swatted the air with swords or arms, trying to keep the flying terrors at bay. More spiders joined the chase from the webs overhead.

"There!" Thorne pointed toward a two-story building on the corner made of crumbling red stone, every window in which had been boarded up. What had once been the front door was now a gaping hole with blackness beyond. A large square of wood leaned against the building beside the door.

Thorne raced toward and through the doorway, leaning to the side to avoid slamming his head against the lintel. The interior was dusty and vacant except for scattered piles of stone and rotting timber. Gamaliel clattered to a halt; Thorne vaulted from the saddle.

"Solomon, let's get that piece of wood over the door! Thurl, get a fire going!" Thorne helped Warner maneuver the wood into place—something the former occupants must also have done. Judging by the lack of human life they'd encountered so far, Thorne wondered where all the congregants were now.

"What about us?" Vaun shouted, her horse sidestepping smaller spiders that had emerged from the debris.

"You got it?" Thorne shouted to Warner. The deputy nodded as he stomped the smaller spiders that scuttled between the wood and the doorframe.

Thorne unsheathed his dagger as he sprinted for Merrick's horse. He slashed his ropes as he ground spiders under his boot heel. He repeated the process with Vaun. For several moments, all they heard were grunts and curses, panicked horses, crunching spider bodies, then finally, the welcome crackle of fire.

"Man, the farmer's caught us with his daughter now," Warner said as he huddled close to the fire and fed it scraps of decayed boards from a pile they'd cleared of spiders. Outside, prickly legs clattered against the wooden barrier. "Whoever heard of flyin' spiders? I mean, for God's sake, *flyin' spiders!*" He scanned the room, never relaxing, sweat running down his face.

The building's second floor had collapsed in all but a few places. Rotted beams littered the interior, which they used to build smaller fires near the front windows and door. The ceiling of the second floor appeared intact, a miracle for which Thorne breathed a prayer of thanks.

Vaun and Cabbott kicked rubble aside; Merrick speared anything with more than two legs with Cabbott's saber. They flung the arachnids into the fire, where they snapped and hissed, their legs curling in over their bodies. The bitter stench of sizzling viscera replaced the mustiness.

"You've never seen these before?" Vaun asked Warner.

"Hells no!"

206 • J. TODD KINGREA

Thorne finished feeding the fires near the windows. Pallid smoke plumed toward the ceiling. He led their skittish horses to the rear of the room, away from the fires. The faint sound of scuttling tapped on the outside wall. "I'm with Solomon on this one. I've never seen anything like this."

Vaun squatted by the main fire. She hung her head and raked her fingers through her hair, attempting to dry it with the heat. "They're called Vulanti'nacha. 'Sky devils' is the rough translation." She shook her hair. "It's said they're a consequence of the Devouring Sickness."

"What's the Devouring Sickness go to do with those nasty bastards?"

Merrick limped over to Cabbott. "It wasn't the Devouring Sickness so much as the cause of the sickness. Something called *radiation*. During and after the Great Cataclysm, there was a lot of it around. That's why the Devouring Lands are so dangerous. They're covered with this radiation."

"What's radiation?" Thorne asked. "And how do you know that?" He glanced between Merrick and Vaun. "How do either of you know any of this?"

"You first, my dear," Merrick said with his grandfatherly grin.

Vaun nodded toward the door. "I've seen sky devils before—but none *that* size. And not this far north. Normally, they're only found along the coast south of Skonmesto and in much smaller groups." She worked on another length of hair.

"She's right about their location," Merrick jumped in. "The Tex'ahns have had to contend with them as well, but as Miss Vaun said, not in such numbers. Or size."

"What about the radiation?" Warner stood but remained close to the fire.

"Ah, yes, that... During my time among the Tex'ahns, I discovered some ancient writings: books, documents, things of that nature. They dated from the early years of the Apocalypse Era. I also came across a few scraps of pre-Cataclysmic writing. Fascinating stuff! Some of the things I read talked about this radiation.

"It was a byproduct of something called nuclear energy. Before the Cataclysm, humanity had massive keeps that housed this nuclear energy, but it was extremely volatile. So much so that when the moon fell, the impact of some of the fragments caused the nuclear energy to—please bear in mind I don't understand a great deal about it—erupt. The energy released the radiation, and the radiation in turn led to the Devouring Sickness. It also turned ordinary creatures into... Well, the Vulanti'nacha are one example. Hellhounds are another, by the way."

"We've got to get out of here," Thorne said. "That board won't hold forever." As if on cue, the wood vibrated louder with the impact of crawling bodies.

"Do you think Rich and his men got away?" Concern and frailty mixed in Merrick's voice.

Thorne, Cabbott and Warner said nothing but avoided looking at Merrick.

Vaun stood and tore a strip of cloth from her sleeve. She pulled a piece of wood from a pile, wrapped the cloth around the end, and thrust the makeshift torch into the fire. The flames caught the fabric and brightened. "If they had any sense, they rode like the wind." She walked toward the sole interior doorway. "But I wouldn't count on it. I saw a couple of them go down when we ran."

"Where do you think you're going?" Thorne demanded.

"To look for another way out." She edged into the open doorway and the dingy hall beyond, her torch smoking up the air.

"Solomon, go with her," he said. "Keep an eye on her."

"Uh-uh, no way, Boss! I ain't goin' back there."

"Shit. I'll go." Cabbott shook his head. "Sol, keep an eye on these fires. Don't let them go out. They're all we've got to hold those spiders back." Sword ready, he followed Vaun into the hallway.

"I can't deal with this, man..." Warner mumbled as he hopped nervously between the fires, feeding them desiccated wood and glancing at the windows.

Merrick recovered his cane from his horse and limped over to Thorne. "Are you okay, Malachi?"

"I'm fine." He scanned the upper reaches of the building.

"You don't sound fine. Did you get bit?"

"No, I don't think so." He folded and unfolded his arms, shuffled his feet, looked in every direction but at Merrick.

Merrick reached up and laid a hand on his shoulder. Thorne flinched.

"It's okay, my boy, just take it easy. We'll figure this out."

"I *said* I'm *fine*."

Merrick sighed and removed his hand. "It's okay to be scared, especially at a time like this. We all are."

Thorne spun around, emerald eyes blazing down at his mentor. "This is all your fault!" He poked Merrick in the chest with his finger. "If I didn't have to waste my time tracking you down, we wouldn't be in this mess!"

"You didn't *have* to track me down."

"Yes, I did!" His face flushed, and he clenched his fists. "You and your damned heresies and causes. You've broken God knows how many laws, and it's my job to see that you pay for every one of them. That used to be *your* job, too, until you turned into a traitor.

"You've had us running all over half of Deiparia looking for you. You've poisoned people's minds. Then you show up out of nowhere, with a story only a madman would believe, saying we're all slaves." Thorne jammed his hand into his belt pouch and pulled out his rank pin. "On top of all that, you've got some twisted notion that these"—he shoved it in front of Merrick—"are somehow dangerous and evil."

He clenched the pin in his fist and drummed it against his thigh in rhythm with his words. "You talk about freedom. You say the Church isn't God." His voice cracked. "Everything that comes from your mouth now is the complete opposite of what you taught me. You—you turn up alive after all these years, but you're not *you*..." He twisted away, his back to Merrick.

One of the horses stomped and neighed. The cheery crackle of the fires now almost drowned out the constant scratching at the wood outside.

"You don't know how long I've—how long it's taken me," Thorne said to the windows, "to get over what happened...back then." His shoulders slumped.

"But you've never gotten over it. Have you?" Merrick's tone was gentle, compassionate, soft as a downy pillow. "You still bear it."

Thorne said nothing, so Merrick continued. "Malachi, what happened at Toadvine wasn't your fault. You could've done nothing to prevent it." Like a dry leaf, his hand fell lightly on Thorne's shoulder again. It broke the moment.

Thorne turned, eyes angry and red, tears sliding down his cheeks. "I—I should've been there, so you wouldn't have had to go—go in alone. I should've been there..."

Merrick shook his head, his white hair still dripping rain. He removed his spectacles and cleaned them on his sleeve. "It wouldn't have made any difference, Malachi. I could've had a hundred men at the house that night, and none of them could've done anything to stop it from happening. I went in to do my duty. The house caught fire and went up like kindling." He paused and slipped his glasses back on. "It's not your fault. Let it go, son. I don't blame you. I never did."

Years of agony erupted from Thorne's soul. He could no longer keep it buried, even if he'd wanted to. It roared out of him like the inferno of a blacksmith's forge. His chest felt as if it would burst. He buried his face in his hand, and the tears came unhindered. Merrick tightened his grip on Thorne's shoulder, steadying his trembling form.

A wave of shame and guilt slammed Thorne against the sides of his consciousness, threatening to pull him under. He gasped between sobs and imagined the world coming unglued. Only the firmness of Merrick's grip kept him anchored—just as it had done all his life.

And then the old man embraced him. Thorne fell against Merrick as if he'd been shot from behind. He buried his face in Merrick's shoulder, inhaling the smoke, sweat and rain from his garment. Merrick's arms enfolded him, comforting and secure. He became the same frightened little boy who had once clung to this man's neck after his parents had perished in flames.

The room was a blur as he broke the embrace and stepped back. The tears on Merrick's cheeks glistened in the flickering light. Thorne rubbed his eyes, sniffed and dragged his dirty sleeve under his nose. He slumped, his body shaking from the long-delayed release.

"It's…it's really you, isn't it?" Thorne asked. The acceptance felt liberating. *Is this what freedom feels like?*

Merrick nodded and smiled. "Yes, Malachi, it's really me. As I said, I haven't been lying to you."

Thorne sniffed again, then nodded. "I'm…I'm sorry for not believing you, Master. It's just all been"—he sighed and shook his head—"it's all been so much to take in."

"Yes, yes, my boy. I know that. And you're not finished yet. You still have much to wrestle with—if you intend to help me."

A knot formed in Thorne's stomach, and he looked away. Accepting the truth of his mentor's existence didn't resolve the conflict over his heresies. Thorne couldn't imagine becoming a co-conspirator espousing such profane ideas. It flew in the face of everything he'd ever supported or loved. And yet, how could he continue to serve and believe in the Church if Merrick was right? One path required him to abandon everything—his livelihood, his faith, his purpose, his identity. The other allowed him to remain an Imperator but within an environment that might be built on a foundation of lies and manipulation.

"But we'll do it together," Merrick said tenderly. "I'll help you through it if you'll trust me."

"I do. At least, I *want* to," Thorne whispered. "I just don't know what to do or what to believe anymore. Please help me. Forgive me." Without thinking, he knelt before Merrick, just as he had done when assigned to be his constable. His heart hammered in his chest as he remembered the final words of Jarmarra Ravenwood: *"He will not lift a finger against you, and yet you will fall before him."* He choked back another sob.

"There's nothing to forgive, my boy. Stand up. You don't need to kneel before anyone any longer." Merrick grabbed his shoulders and helped him rise and continued to grip his shoulders as he stared up into Thorne's eyes. "I'll help you. But everything you've ever known is going to change. Your world will never again be the same. But that's a *good* thing." He brightened and clapped Thorne's shoulders. "Only by exercising our freedom to choose can change and transformation happen."

"I don't understand," Thorne said. He rubbed his temple. "How can what I'm feeling be a good thing? And doesn't too much freedom lead to chaos? How do I reconcile all of this?" His throat was raw with emotion. He wanted to say more but started coughing. He waved his hand to disperse the gathering smoke.

"Yes, I noticed that, too," Merrick said. "We'll talk more about your questions later. Right now, we need a way out. We can't stay here much longer."

Footsteps drew their attention to the inner doorway as Vaun and Cabbott returned. Vaun's torch was more smoke than flame now, and she tossed it into the large fire. Cabbott coughed. Warner emerged from among the horses that grew edgier in the polluted air.

"We may not have to," Vaun said, dusting her hands on her pants.

"What've you got?" Thorne asked. He didn't look at her. For some reason, he didn't want her to see him like this.

"It may be a way out," Cabbott told him.

Vaun offered a sly smile. "Or it may get us all killed."

24

VULNERABLE

THURSDAY, JUNE 18, 999 AE

Cabbott and Vaun led everyone through the hall and into a back room. It was as unremarkable as the others they'd passed, except for the black rectangle on the floor in the corner and a barred door on the back wall. They crowded around as Vaun knelt and lowered her relit torch into the rectangle. A short set of crude wooden steps and an earthy smell greeted them.

"How's that supposed to help?" Warner held a smoking torch above his head. Protection, he claimed, against anything dropping from the ceiling. "It's a hole in the ground."

"There's a tunnel down there," Vaun said into the cellar. The darkness ate her voice.

"Where's it go?" Thorne asked.

Vaun shrugged. "No idea."

"Tell me again how this helps us," Warner said.

"It may lead out of the building—maybe away from the spiders," Merrick thought aloud.

"*Maybe?* And what if it goes nowhere? I'll bet there's a big ass mama spider down there right now. Man, ain't no fuckin' way…"

"It has to go somewhere," Thorne said. "Tunnels aren't dug without a purpose." He looked at Cabbott. "Did you check it out?"

"Only a few feet. Looks like it was dug out in a hurry. Lots of footprints. And there's definitely airflow."

"What about this door?"

"Opens into a small courtyard with some alleys that lead back to the streets," Vaun said over her shoulder. Her hair was the color of dried blood in the wavering torchlight.

"Then let's get the hells out of here!" Warner exclaimed. He started toward the barred door.

Thorne put a hand on his chest. "Wait, Solomon." Thorne looked at Vaun. "More spiders?"

She nodded.

A crash echoed through the hallway.

"Damn me for a fool! One of us should've stayed behind!" Thorne sprinted down the hall. Cabbott and Warner followed, torches guttering, weapons ready.

Hazy gray smoke filled the room. Two of the smaller fires were nothing more than glowing embers. The others burned lower as they rapidly consumed the dried wood. Even the large fire showed signs of weakening.

A window board had broken and fallen into the room. Hairy arachnids poured through the opening. The majority of them, even with their wings, were no larger than a human forearm. Others, however, had eaten well. Their wing-spans measured twice that. They squirmed between the boards, spreading out across the wall; others hit the floor with soft plops, their humanlike faces fixed on the warm flesh in the room.

"Solomon! Get those fires back up!" Thorne shouted. He thrust his torch into the window gap and raked it back and forth. Spiders chittered and leapt away. He stomped those scurrying over the floor. Cabbott crushed bodies and legs beneath his boots and speared those on the wall with his sword. Sticky, greenish-black ichor dripped from the blade.

"We can't keep this up!" Cabbott yelled. "They're going to get in here."

Vaun ran in. She grabbed a board off the floor and slammed it against the opening just as Thorne withdrew the torch.

The thick sheet of wood over the front door rattled. Tips of legs clawed around the edges.

"Options!" Thorne bellowed over his shoulder. He helped Vaun hold the board in place, his arms above her head.

"Wish we had a hammer and some nails," she said through her teeth.

Cabbott crushed the last spider roaming across the floor. "Not many Malachi. We can take that damn tunnel, wherever it goes—" He broke off coughing.

Merrick entered the room and leaned against the wall. "We could try riding out."

"And go where?" Warner shouted. "You seen what it's like out there!" The smoke thickened as he fed the fires. "That's it, man—wood's all gone!"

"But if we rushed through them—scattered them—it could be just enough surprise and momentum that we could break away," Merrick continued. "We're on a corner. There are more roads than the one we came in on." He bent over coughing.

"I think at least one of those roads was webbed off." Thorne panted. "Besides, we don't know how many of those damned things are out there. Or how fast they can fly."

"I vote for the tunnel." Vaun leaned her shoulder into the board. "It's got to come out somewhere."

"And what if it don't, flaky lady?" Warner asked, his voice rising. "What if we get boxed in down there? These things would be all over us. And what about our horses? What do we do with them?"

"We use them." Thorne made sure Vaun had a firm grip on the board before he turned around. "I've got an idea. Solomon, can you get our horses into that back room?"

"Yeah, I guess so."

"Good, do it. Val, you help him. Let me know when you're done." Thorne coughed.

It didn't take long to move all five horses down the hall; they were anxious to get away from the fires. The two men returned to the main room.

"Here's what we're going to do," Thorne told them. "All of you grab as many torches as you can carry and get to the back room."

"What about you?" Vaun asked.

"I'll hold this board until you're all back there. Then I'll join you."

"Okay, so we all go to the back room." Cabbott's brow creased. "And then?"

"The door to that room is still on its hinges. We get in there, shut it, keep the spiders in the hallway—" He coughed, harder this time, and his eyes watered. "Our horses are already panicked, so we use that to our advantage. We line the horses up, unbar the back door and throw it open. As soon as the horses are out, we close and bar the door again. That should buy us enough time to get into the tunnel. Hopefully, the spiders will pursue the horses and forget about trying to get through the door at us."

"*Hopefully?*" Vaun asked.

He smiled at her. "I said I've got an idea. Didn't say it was necessarily a good one. Anyone got anything better?" He looked from face to face. "No? Then get ready."

He pinned the board to the window while everyone gathered up armloads of burning sticks and boards. Their coughing echoed from the hallway.

"Ready!" someone yelled.

He dropped the board and sprinted for the hall. Hundreds of Vulanti'nacha surged into the room.

❖　　❖　　❖

Cabbott removed the bar from the back door, careful to make sure it didn't swing open by itself. Merrick made his way down the steps into the cellar as quickly as his bad leg allowed. Thorne, Warner and Vaun held the horses' bridles. The animals jerked and stomped, whinnying in fear.

A wave of thumping and scratching came from the hallway door. Legs poked through rotted holes, digging into and enlarging them by the second.

"Now!" Thorne yelled.

Cabbott threw open the back door. Thorne slapped Gamaliel's haunches, and the massive horse bolted into the courtyard. Warner and Vaun smacked the other horses and shouted, "Hee'yah!" Their mounts surged forward after Gamaliel.

Spiders scurried everywhere and swarmed through the air. A few Vulanti'nacha attempted to scuttle through the doorway. The light reflected off their glassy black eyes as Cabbott yanked it closed. Legs and bodies squished between door and frame. Cabbott replaced the bar.

Vaun hurried down the steps. Warner threw a few torches down in the cellar and followed her. Cabbott insisted that Thorne go next.

The pressure on the hallway door intensified; more flecks of rotted wood flew into the room. They could no longer hear the horses.

Vaun entered the tunnel, Warner close behind. Thorne and Cabbott waited for Merrick to go next.

The tunnel had been dug from the soft earth by hand, and it narrowed or widened in places. They stumbled through piles of dirt, torches flickering, smoke stinging their eyes. The floor had been trampled smooth by the passage of many feet. The air was cooler, and the narrow confines filled with coughing and heavy breathing.

Thorne thought he heard something fall in the distance behind them. He quickened his pace, his hand on Merrick's back, urging him forward.

More than once, Cabbott wheeled around, sweeping his dying torch in arcs across the tunnel. If the Vulanti'nacha followed, they weren't close enough to see yet.

"Got some light up ahead!" Vaun's voice sounded small and dull within the earth. The tunnel floor sloped upward.

Merrick bent double, coughing, then used the sides of the tunnel to stay upright.

"Just a little farther, Val." Thorne gasped. "We're almost out."

Cabbott twisted around again. The sickly orange light glinted off hundreds of beady, unblinking eyes. "Move, move, move!" he screamed. "They're right behind us!"

Sheer horror propelled them up the gentle incline. The tunnel emerged through the floor of another vacant building. They shot out like rabbits flushed from a warren.

Warner gasped. "C'mon, Thurl." He stuck his arm into the tunnel to help his mentor out.

"As soon as he's up, Solomon, get out of the way," Thorne said. "There's a sheet of metal here—looks big enough to cover that hole."

Seconds later, Thorne, Merrick and Vaun slid the metal barrier over the hole and stepped back. Muted thumping and scratching came from underneath, but the metal didn't budge. They relaxed, gasping for air and coughing smoke from their lungs.

"Where are we now?" Thorne edged toward the front of the structure. He peered through a boarded-up window. "Looks like we're about seven or eight buildings from where we were. But there's a road, and it's clear. We're going to have to make a run for it and hope we aren't seen."

"Merrick can't run," Vaun reminded him.

Thorne thought for a moment. "Thurl and I will support him. It's our only chance. Unless you want to wait here for a rescue party?" He offered a lopsided grin to let her know he was joking. The one she returned flashed her dimples. Despite the smoke and dirt that streaked her face, her beauty seemed limitless.

With torches all but extinguished—Warner carried two that sputtered as he ran—they hurried down the muddy road, staying close to the buildings. Behind them, dark clouds of Vulanti'nacha circled the rooftops. Black spots crawled through the webbing above.

Warner led the way with Vaun just behind him. If she still harbored the intent to kill him, there would be no better time. His focus was elsewhere, his broad back a fetching target.

But her hands were empty.

Thorne and Cabbott held Merrick under his arms as he hopped between them. Distances between the buildings increased, with more foliage to use for cover. They didn't stop to rest until they crested a hill leading into the forest, the village of Honvale a shrouded mausoleum in the distance behind them.

They moved east as quickly as they could. Merrick found a twisted stick that made a serviceable cane, and despite the danger of patrols, they stayed on the 412 road. Little was said as they reserved their energy for vigilance and walking, until night settled, forcing them to stop. They found a secluded place away from the road and risked a fire.

"What weapons do we have?" Thorne asked as he walked the perimeter of their makeshift camp. "I've got a dagger."

"I've got my saber and a dagger," Cabbott said.

"Same here," Warner added.

"I've got a stick." Merrick offered a playful smile.

"Teska, what about you?"

She looked at him. It wasn't the first time he'd used her given name. "Nothing. I'll get by."

"Anybody got any idea where we are?" Warner asked.

"We're headed toward Nashton," Thorne said. "One day, maybe two, and we're there."

Merrick leaned against a tree and rubbed his bad leg. "What about food and water?"

"Nope." Warner shook his head. "Everythin' we had was on the horses."

The camp lapsed into silence.

"We'll find water tomorrow. Shouldn't be hard around here," Thorne said. "Try to get some sleep. I'll take first watch." He drew his dagger and held it in his hand, settling against a tree trunk a dozen feet from the fire. Everyone stretched out and quickly fell asleep.

Something snapped in the darkness.

Thorne jerked awake. His heart pounded, and he gripped the dagger tight. Someone stood near him. He jumped to his feet, dagger extended, furious at himself for his carelessness.

"It's just me." Vaun's voice, gossamer soft, floated through the darkness.

"Are you trying to escape?" he demanded.

"If I wanted to escape, I would've done so on our way out of Honvale." She sighed. "Or I could've gotten away anytime over the last few hours." The pride in her voice was unmistakable, and he silently cursed himself again.

"Then why didn't you?" he snapped. "Why're you still here?"

She hesitated, searching for a lie. "Safety in numbers—especially after what we just went through."

Thorne narrowed his eyes. "You're 'the Ghost.' With that little gift of yours, I don't imagine being on your own is a problem. You strike me as the type who enjoys going it alone."

"That's true," she acknowledged. "But I also know when to play things safe."

"You think you're safe around me?" Thorne chuckled. "I'm the one who's planning to turn you over to the Church, remember?"

She didn't say anything, but Thorne could feel her watching him.

"Just get back to the fire where I can keep an eye on you."

Another moment of silence followed. She stepped closer. "I—I feel safe around you."

"Huh? What're you—" His tongue turned thick in his mouth. He wanted to respond, but his thoughts jumbled together. His training screamed at him that this was a trick. She was baiting him, trapping him.

But why would she do that here, and why now? She was right: she could've escaped any number of times over the last few days. His attention had certainly been compromised often enough by her, by Merrick, by Darien and Hawkes, by Rann... No, she wasn't trying to trap him. Could she—could she be...feeling something for him?

"You asked why I haven't taken off," she said. "Truthfully, I should be leagues away from here by now."

"So what's stopping you?" His emotions surged like molten steel. He didn't know if he was excited or angry, hopeful or distrustful.

Vaun closed the distance between them with a single step. She seemed even tinier amid the forest shadows. The dying firelight painted part of her face in flickering orange, turning her eyes into black puddles and making her hair seem like mahogany. He could barely make out her lips and surprised himself with the desire to do so.

"I don't think you want me to," she said with quiet confidence.

"Well, of course I don't want you to. You've—you've got to pay. For your crimes. The Church's laws—"

She laid her hand on his arm. His skin tingled at her touch.

"I know too much about the Church's laws," she said. "That's not what I'm talking about."

He studied her face through the shadows, felt the molten steel course through his veins. This was ludicrous! He couldn't give in to feelings of lust, much less love. She was a traitor and heretic, probably a witch as well. Yet ever since he'd laid eyes on her, he hadn't been able to get her out of his mind. The thunder in his ears, the shallowness of his breath, carried him like the swells of a raging river.

"Malachi?"

Her voice scattered his thoughts like a flock of birds erupting from the tree-tops. She squeezed his arm.

"Then what're you..." His voice sounded weak in his own ears. He did his best to control his tone and said firmly, "What do you mean?"

Vaun giggled; the sound mesmerized him. "I think you know."

His head swam as all of his thoughts collided at once, none of them complete or useful. Her hand still rested on his arm, and he couldn't decide if he should try to pull away or stay where he was for as long as possible. He opened his mouth, but words eluded him. "I… That is…"

The shadows weakened as dawn approached. He could make out the smooth line of her jaw, her petite nose, dark lashes and dimples. His mind told him to run and to stay at the same time.

"You're trembling," she whispered and withdrew her hand.

In that moment, he wondered if he would ever feel her touch again and hated the sudden loss. With sweaty palms, he fumbled the dagger into its sheath in order to give himself something to do.

Beside the dwindling fire, Cabbott moved and stretched. Merrick rolled over.

Vaun lowered her gaze. "I'm sorry. I shouldn't have…" She turned, confusion and embarrassment lining her face, and hurried back to the fire.

He watched her go, his tongue a wad of cotton, his heart pounding.

When they needed a stroke of luck, they found it. Later that morning, they came across Gamaliel milling around in a field. Cabbott's and Merrick's horses pulled up the tender summer grass a short distance away. There was no sign of the other two.

Cabbott took point. Merrick and Warner squeezed onto Merrick's horse. Vaun rode on Gamaliel behind Thorne, one hand on his shoulder. Despite his efforts to stay focused, his thoughts kept returning to the lithe form behind him. He could feel her breasts against his back.

They shared the remaining food in their saddlebags as they headed for Nashton. The heat made them listless, and sweat dripped from their faces. The horses switched their tails nonstop, keeping the scorpion flies away, which now seemed inconsequential after the horror of the Vulanti'nacha. They found a small stream, watered the horses and refilled their waterskins.

By midafternoon, traffic picked up as congregants made their way to Nashton for the Feast of David the Guardian. Thorne's grimy and battered group halted several times while Cabbott talked with other travelers, gathering information about what lay ahead. Thorne wrapped a filmy strip of cloth around his head and face—just another traveler protecting himself from the sun and dirt. He also hoped it might suggest that he carried some sort of disease, a sure way to avoid closer inspection. He coughed occasionally to sell the illusion.

This'll work for the present, but it won't pass a close inspection.

If he were the one out there looking for a group of rebels, even if they *did* bring in two wanted criminals, he'd have them all locked away as soon as they showed their faces. Incarceration first, questions later.

Cabbott led them a little farther before easing off the road. He took them behind the ruins of a pre-Cataclysm building that bore the letters *CONV N E C STOR*.

"What's happening?" Thorne asked, removing the cloth once everyone had slipped behind the vine-covered building.

"Nashton's crawling with guards looking for us. Every road and gate is being patrolled. They're stopping everyone going into the city, searching anything we might hide in. Damn that son of a bitch Rann," he spat.

"What about the Umberla River?" Thorne asked. "Can we take that?"

"Yeah, I suppose. We'd have to travel farther north to get to it. And there's no guarantee the docks won't be patrolled."

"Any way we might sneak past the patrols?" Merrick asked as Warner helped him dismount.

"Again, I suppose it's possible. We'd need a big diversion, though." He shook his head. "Vaun might be able to get through with her special gift. But not the rest of us"

"Oh, yes. You told me about this—*thing*—she can do," Merrick noted. "Very handy, that."

"I could be the diversion," Vaun said.

"Like we're going to let you just take off and run away from us."

"No, wait." Thorne gestured for Cabbott to stop. The look of surprise on the constable's face suggested he'd said it too harshly—or that Cabbott suspected something. He offered a conciliatory smile. "She's had chances to run before now and hasn't done so."

Cabbott scowled. "That was out in the country. You know how fast we could lose her in a city of thousands? With what she can do, we'd never find her again."

"I'll take the risk," Thorne replied. "Besides, maybe she's right. If she could get close enough to start a disruption of some kind, in the confusion, we might sneak in. Especially if she could somehow draw the guards away from the gate."

Warner wiped sweat from the top of his head. "I dunno, Boss. I can't imagine all of them leavin' their posts. And if even one of us gets caught…"

"Right now, it's our only option," Thorne said with a tone of finality.

They were working out the details of Vaun's diversion when Merrick—who Thorne hadn't even noticed was missing—stepped up to the group with two men right behind him. Everyone jumped, and weapons were raked from scabbards. Cabbott and Warner assumed defensive positions in front of Thorne.

"It's okay!" Merrick said. "Stand down. It's all right."

Rich DuBose and Murnau Carden, looking worn and weary, stood behind Merrick.

"Please, it's okay. They're not going to hurt you."

"They sure as hells ain't takin' you, either," Warner said.

"I think we're a bit beyond all that, don't you?"

"You're still a wanted traitor." Cabbott pointed his sword at Merrick.

Thorne sighed so loudly that everyone looked at him. He helped Vaun off Gamaliel and dismounted as well. "Val's right," he said. "I've been thinking about all of this. Things have changed. Even if we stroll in with Traugott and the Ghost in custody"—he offered her an apologetic look—"we're all going to be arrested and thrown in the dungeon."

"But I thought you said we were goin' to be undercover?" Warner lowered his saber but didn't sheath it.

"I thought so, too," Thorne said, defeat creeping into his voice. "But if what we've heard today is any indication, I don't think we're going to get a chance to use that story. Rann's men have orders to kill. I'm sure everyone else does too by now."

Silence descended as each considered the implications. The horses flicked their tails. An occasional voice or laugh drifted up from the road.

Vaun broke the silence. "I still say a diversion is our best chance."

"Not necessarily, my dear," Merrick said. "In fact, Rich and Murnau have what I consider to be a significantly better option."

"Everyone's heading in for the Feast of David the Guardian," DuBose said.

"We know that."

"No, no, think, Mr. Cabbott. What do we celebrate at the Feast of David the Guardian?" Merrick became excited, wrinkled hands gesturing in the air.

"The life and achievements of Stephen Bryce, who took the name David the Guardian when he became Heiromonarch in 660 AE," Thorne recited like a catechism student. "So?"

"And what's the one thing that's done every year at the Feast?"

"The Benedictium Morturas," Warner said.

"That's it, mate." DuBose flashed a dimpled smile.

"Exactly!" Merrick almost hopped up and down. "The Blessing of the Dead!"

Vaun looked up at Thorne. "I don't get it."

"Don't you see?" Merrick spread his hands. "People bring something that belonged to a loved one who died in the past year—a handkerchief or tool or bit of jewelry—so they can receive the Church's blessing. The Benedictium. Some even bring the bodies of the recently deceased—in *coffins!*"

Cabbott stared at Merrick. "What's that got to do with us getting into the…" His brows lifted.

"Yes, Mr. Cabbott! And what's one thing a guard would *never* disturb during a search?"

"By the Church," Thorne said. "You're not suggesting that we…? We'd be desecrating the bodies of the deceased." He shook his head.

Carden spoke for the first time: "Not exactly."

DuBose leaned against the wall. "After we got out of Honvale, we knew you'd be headed this way. We hooked up with some other travelers. Found a mate or two that we knew." His dimples appeared again.

Thorne glanced at Vaun and noticed that she watched DuBose with the delight of a child observing a puppet show. Something hot and ugly surged inside him.

"Turns out one of them is part of a caravan taking some goods in for the celebration."

"Empty coffins," Merrick said.

"What? Wait a second…" Vaun's eyes widened.

"It's perfect," Merrick continued. "Our friends say they're bringing deceased relatives for the Benedictium Morturas. The guards won't bother the coffins. We can ride in without being detected."

Thorne looked around. Cabbott and Warner wore expressions of bemusement as if waiting for the punch line. Vaun looked like a trapped deer. DuBose and Carden remained stoic. Only Merrick rejoiced at the idea.

"Come on. They're waiting for us," Merrick said, tottering around the side of the building. DuBose and Carden followed.

"Malachi, you aren't seriously considering this," Vaun pleaded. "Are you?"

It was the first time he'd heard her use his first name. The sound lingered in his ear, sweet as honey. He smiled in spite of himself. "Val's right. It's the best and easiest way into the city for us."

"You're going to trust those two guys?" Cabbott demanded incredulously, sword still in hand. "They were trying to kill us two days ago!"

Thorne walked to the edge of the building, then turned and looked at Cabbott. "No, I don't trust them. But I do trust Val." He disappeared around the corner. "Bring the horses and let's go."

"Seriously, I can be the diversion." Vaun trailed behind them. "I'd be a great diversion!"

25

SECRECY

Even though yesterday wasn't the first Worship Day Thorne had ever missed, it still felt odd not being in a cathedral, taking part in the rituals of the holy day. He felt ashamed for neglecting his duties even though circumstances had taken the opportunity to fulfill them out of his hands. Until he could clear his name and see Zadicus Rann excommunicated, he had to lay low. The problem was *how* to clear his name without making his presence known.

In addition, his emotions remained conflicted over Teska Vaun. She needed to pay for her crimes…and yet he didn't want to let her go. Whenever he thought of not being around her, his heart constricted. He'd chastised himself repeatedly for feeling this way about her. How would it look for a high-ranking Church official to be in love with a wanted thief? The very idea seemed preposterous—yet here he was, reluctant to see her face justice. Reluctant to be apart from her.

But I can't have it both ways. I can't keep her and turn her in.

It was the same decision he'd faced with Merrick. Either surrender all he'd ever known and accept his mentor's new beliefs, or remain faithful to the Church and bring the old man to justice. In that case, he'd put his trust in Merrick's honesty, in what he'd known all his life about his friend and surrogate father.

But if he'd already decided to stay with Merrick and pursue his freedom crusade, then he was automatically outside the Church. What did it matter if he loved a thief and wanted to be with her? Thoughts raced through his brain like wildfire. Merrick's ideas about freedom and choice had rubbed off on him. So that meant he was heading down the same path.

"What did that nutty message that you left in Rimlingham mean?" Warner asked Merrick.

Thorne had forgotten all about Keegan Lang's cryptic message.

Merrick had chuckled when Warner brought it up. "I wanted to let you know that I was waiting for you," he'd explained. "'It won't be long now' was just my way of acknowledging that, one way or another, we'd see each other again. And I suppose I had hoped that it wouldn't be long before Malachi joined our cause."

"You could've just told us where to find you," Warner had grumbled.

With some negotiating by DuBose and Merrick, they'd been fitted for coffins—something strange to think about, much less experience—though they didn't have to use them immediately. It was Saturday morning when they'd climbed in and the lids had been nailed shut—a twist to which Vaun had vociferously objected. It was necessary for the ruse, the coffin merchant had explained, since guards might search those with loose lids. In the end, Vaun had relented but only because Thorne had talked her into it.

Their jostling, claustrophobic ride had ended at the Vanderbilt Market. After being released from their premature burials, they had no problem blending in with the massive crowd. Cabbott had secured lodging some distance away at the Red Dog Saloon off the Broad Way Road. Other than drifting out once or twice to observe and eavesdrop among the market crowd, they'd spent the remainder of the day cleaning up, eating a decent meal, grooming the horses and finally, sleeping in real beds.

Yesterday, Merrick had sent DuBose to their local contacts to arrange a place for Thorne's group to meet up with Darien and Hawkes. Cabbott found an urchin willing to deliver a message for a silver coin. Warner had penned the note, and the tousled-haired lad ran off to deliver it to Dario at the inn where the group normally stayed. Thorne couldn't meet his clerk and deputy at their previously arranged location. Other eyes had undoubtedly seen the message he'd sent to Dario from Attagon.

Today, north of their present location, the tower bells of Nashton Cathedral bonged to life, their peals carrying through the muggy air. The service of worship for the Feast of David the Guardian was beginning. Everyone would pack shoulder to shoulder inside the grand edifice. Once more, Thorne tried to shrug off the awkwardness he felt at not being there and looked across the tangled ground for Dario and Tycho.

They all sat inside a strange box in the ground that Merrick called a dugout, from a time when this stadium had been used for some sort of sporting game. Rows of busted, ruined seats ascended behind them. In front lay a field covered with shaggy grass, bushes and trees. Thorne had no idea what sort of sport could be played among so much foliage or why a box in the ground would've been necessary.

"Got someone, Boss," Warner said from the top of the dugout. He lay flat on his stomach, watching the far side of the field. "Rich just flashed the signal."

Thorne stood up. With him were Vaun, Merrick and Cabbott. DuBose and Carden served as lookouts along the concourse. Thorne didn't expect any interference due to the worship service, but deputies still pulled street duty. He had no intention of being the reason one of them received a promotion.

The four of them climbed out of the dugout. Birds chirped while cruising among the treetops. Insects buzzed around wildflowers. The sun was a stark ball of blinding yellow against the viridian-streaked sky.

Warner stood and waved.

Through the bushes and tree trunks, two riders appeared. Hawkes waved back. As they approached, Thorne frowned. Warner jumped down and joined him. There was no mistaking Tycho Hawkes, but the man who rode with him wasn't Dario. He appeared to be as old as Merrick. Maybe even older.

Merrick and Vaun stood at the top of the dugout steps, both shielding their eyes from the sun. Warner stepped closer to Thorne. "Who's that?"

"I don't know."

"Malachi! Sol!" Hawkes yelled. He waved again. The elderly black man also waved this time.

"Hells, man, why don't you tell the whole damn city we're here?" Warner smiled as the two horses stopped. "It's good to see you again!"

"Same here," Hawkes replied, slipping from the saddle and bear-hugging Warner. "I actually missed your sorry one-eyed face." He returned Warner's playful grin with his own, then turned to Thorne. They clasped forearms. He did the same with Cabbott. "Listen, there's something you need—"

"Who's that?" Thorne demanded in a low, urgent tone, never taking his eyes off the other rider.

"Yeah, okay… That's what I was starting to tell you."

"It's all right, Malachi," the aged black man said. His voice sounded glutinous, and he spat a wad of phlegm into the grass. "It's me."

Thorne frowned and gripped the handle of his dagger. His eyes searched the face in front of him like a climber seeking a handhold on a mountain. Something seemed…familiar about the shape of the face, the width of the nose. The eyes—he definitely knew them. But how?

"Hello, my friend," Darien said. Hawkes assisted him from the saddle. He was stooped and palsied. Apologetic eyes stared from beneath bushy white eyebrows.

"Is *that*…?" Cabbott gaped.

The old man tottered closer, aided by a slick ebony cane. Hawkes's wore an expression of pity and resignation.

"By the name of the Divine Church." Thorne gasped. "*Dario? Is that you?*"

"I'm afraid it is, Malachi."

"What's happened to you?" Even as he asked the question, his mind refused to process what his eyes showed him.

The five companions stared at each other, the excitement of their reunion savaged by shock and disbelief.

"Do you mind if I sit?" Darien asked. "I don't do as well as I used to…"

"Come down here." Thorne turned to the dugout steps. "Can you…? I mean, the stairs…"

Darien raised a hand. "It's fine. I'll manage."

Thorne stepped aside. He watched in alien bewilderment as Hawkes assisted Darien down into the coolness of the dugout and sat him on a rusted metal bench. He and Cabbott followed, Merrick and Vaun behind them. Warner sat on the dugout steps.

Beneath the dugout's low ceiling, Darien looked even older. Thorne sat down beside his friend. He smiled, not knowing what else to do, but it felt unnatural.

Hawkes leaned against the front wall and scanned the dugout, his gaze stopping on Thorne. "Well, there are a few things we need to tell you."

For over an hour, Hawkes and Darien explained their trip to Talnat, after which Thorne shared his group's experiences over the past three and a half weeks. It stunned him to discover that Darien's impossible aging was the result of witchcraft—that his friend had voluntarily sought out. Thorne's predicament, however, wasn't as much of a surprise to Darien and Hawkes.

"After Talnat, we went back and spent a few days in Attagon," Darien said. "That's when I got your message to meet here. But word had already spread through the Church that you'd gone rogue. That you'd become involved in sorcery." He paused to catch his breath. "And after what I've done, it won't surprise you to know that I've also fallen out of the Church's good graces."

"Though how in the hells the Church found out about it, I have no idea," Hawkes said.

"What do you mean?" Thorne couldn't stop looking at his clerk, who was now over eighty years old.

"On our way here—" Darien said, but started coughing.

"On our way here," Hawkes picked up, "we heard talk along the road that we're wanted for conspiracy. Can you believe that shit? What's going on, anyway?"

The cathedral bells tolled the end of the worship service. The streets would soon fill with hundreds of congregants enjoying the day free of labor. The festival grounds would be bustling. People would celebrate and eat, dance and play, until the Benedictium Morturas was pronounced, then everyone would celebrate the Feast of David the Guardian with a ceremonial meal. Thorne missed the orderliness and holiness of it all.

"So we're *all* wanted by the Church. How's that for a kick in the skull?" Warner said.

"What do we do?" Hawkes asked. "I mean, hells, we've got Traugott and the Ghost in custody"—he nodded toward them—"but we can't turn them in without turning ourselves in at the same time."

"There are still too many questions we don't have answers to," Cabbott said.

"Speaking of which: what about Demerra? And the children?" Thorne asked.

The weight of the world seemed to settle on Darien's shoulders. He looked even frailer than Thorne thought possible. The old clerk looked up with tears in his eyes.

"Demerra's still incarcerated. I couldn't—" His voiced cracked. "I wasn't able to get her released. The lawyer's still working on it, but you and I both know…" He left the thought unfinished. "We were told that Cassidy and Cassandra had been taken to Attagon, but when we got there, we couldn't find them. Then we were told they'd been transported to Last Chapel."

Cabbott's eyes widened. "*Last Chapel?* What for? I mean, we know that Last Chapel has been asking the Church for reinforcements against the Communion, but what would a couple of kids matter there?"

Darien shrugged, shook his head.

"Okay, let's go over everything from the start," Merrick said. Thorne recognized the gleam in his mentor's eye. He had always loved puzzles, and this was one he couldn't pass up, especially since they were at the center of it. "Jairus Gray accidentally found a relic the Church had been transporting. He was on his way to Talnat to turn it over to the Church, but before he got there was killed by an unknown person, who was part of a larger group."

"Wearing rank pins, the design of which I've never seen before," Darien said.

"They made the scene appear to be a routine bandit attack. Let me ask you something, Mr. Darien—"

"Please, call me Dario." He coughed again, harder this time.

"All right, Dario. Was your brother-in-law an outspoken man? Did he, perhaps, question things more than other people? Did he speak his mind frequently?"

The wrinkles on the old man's face deepened as he considered the questions. "I suppose so. He wasn't a freethinker, if that's what you mean. But...yes. Yes, he did often raise questions that others wouldn't. He had some...strong opinions about certain things."

"Ah-ha!" Merrick rose to his feet. "Dario, I believe your brother-in-law was immune to the effects of the rank pins!"

Hawkes scratched his head. "That's what you mentioned earlier. Our pins are...dangerous? Magic?" He glanced down at his as if it were a scorpion poised to strike.

Merrick continued as if he hadn't heard Hawkes. "And if your brother-in-law had an immunity to the effects, then it stands to reason that the Church is likely concerned that your niece and nephew might also share that immunity."

"But what about Demerra?" Thorne asked. "Is she immune as well?"

Merrick waved his hand dismissively. "Doubtful—though not impossible. No, my guess is that charging her with witchcraft was simply a convenient way to get the children away from her."

"Malachi, do you believe this?" Darien asked.

Thorne thought for a moment before nodding his head. "It makes sense. Too much sense, in fact..."

"But it still don't explain why the kids were taken to Last Chapel," Warner pointed out.

"It's a trap," Thorne said. "The Church is after you and Hawkes. But you got out of Attagon before they could arrest you. They know you'll follow the children."

"Look, we've been here going on three hours, and we still don't have a plan," Hawkes said. "We know the Church was involved in some shady business with Darien's brother-in-law, and with his wife and kids now. We've got a couple of giants with weird new rank pins. Malachi's wanted for sorcery—"

"Necromancy," Warner corrected.

Hawkes shot him a sour glance as he continued. "Thurl, you and Jester over there are wanted as accomplices. So am I. Dario's been charged with conspiracy and who knows what else. We've got two convicted criminals in our custody that we can't do anything with, and there's a couple of heretics in the seats above us keeping watch, *helping us*." He paused to catch his breath. "Dario's older than pre-Cataclysm wine now. We can't go home. Traugott is really Valerian Merrick, who didn't actually die all those years ago, but was rescued by a tribe of fairytale people who taught him that we should all be free." He paused again. "Did I miss anything?"

"You forgot the flyin' spiders," Warner said.

Hawkes rolled his eyes, and Warner clapped him on the shoulder, grinning.

"Jester?" Vaun said. "Why did he call you that?"

"Oh, that's because—"

Warner cut Hawkes off. "That's a story for some other time," he said to her through a pained smile. "We've got more pressing things to deal with right now. Right, Boss?" When everyone looked toward Thorne, Warner jabbed Hawkes in the ribs with his elbow. "Don't. Not around her. I'll explain later."

Before Thorne could say anything, Darien spoke up, his voice controlled and determined. "I'm going to Last Chapel." He leaned back against the crumbling stone wall of the dugout as if the conversation were over.

"I told you it's probably a trap," Thorne said.

"You did. And I'm going anyway."

"You'll do no such thing. I order you—"

Darien raised an age-spotted hand. "I'm not listening to any orders, Malachi. You're not a Witchfinder any longer—"

"Something everyone seems keen to keep reminding me."

"—and I'm no longer a clerk." He looked around the dugout. "None of us are who we were a month ago. Too much has changed." His voice weakened again. "I—I don't have a lot of time left. I can almost feel my body shutting down. Malachi, I'm going to find Cassidy and Cassandra. I owe it to Demerra. If that means being trapped—well, it's not like I have much of a future left anyway."

The dugout suddenly felt cold despite the suffocating summer heat. Thorne sat down beside his friend and put his hand on his shoulder. He was shocked once more by the frailty of the body beneath the clothes.

"I'm going with him," Hawkes said. "He's right. We're a bunch of straws in a whirlwind right now. Who knows how shit's going to turn out? If nothing else, I'm gonna see that his sister gets her kids back."

"What about you, Malachi?" Merrick asked, followed by a long pause. "Will you help me loosen the Church's stranglehold and show people what freedom is?"

Before he could reply a new voice, young and light, drifted down the steps: "I would speak with Teska Vaun."

Everyone looked up. A young woman with long blond hair that hung in ringlets over her shoulders stood in the grass. She wore a simple green-and-blue gown with a silver necklace. She clasped her hands in front of her as if she were about to recite poetry.

"Who the hells is that?" Thorne got to his feet, followed by everyone else.

"Oh, no. This won't do," the young woman said, as if speaking to someone who wasn't there. She raised her hands. A breeze stirred the hem and sleeves of her gown. She tucked her chin to her chest and stared at the dugout with milky, upturned eyes.

"Magage, isa tao; no hee somnistu tu," she said in a sepulchral tone.

The wind swirled harder, whipping her gown around her lithe form; however, no leaf or blade of grass so much as trembled. She threw her hands forward, and the spectral wind rushed into the dugout, pollen and dust following in its wake.

Vaun shielded her eyes with her arm. Several heavy thuds sounded around her. After lowering her arm, she eased her eyes open. Every man in the dugout had collapsed. Their chests rose and fell rhythmically; Thurl and Darien snored lightly.

"What the…?"

Vaun stared at the woman, who now leaned against a tree, pale and trembling. With a quick look around the dugout, she bounded up the steps and into the sunlight.

"I'm Teska Vaun. Who're you? And what just happened?"

The woman offered a pleasant but weak smile. She pushed away from the tree, steadied herself and with a graceful flourish, knelt in the grass.

"My name is Neris Ahlienor," she said, looking up at Vaun. "I have come for you." The woman's eyes were white and unseeing.

"Come for me? For what? I don't know you."

"No, of course you don't. I'm from the Enodia Communion. You, precious Sister, have been chosen. You are Nahoru'brexia, one of the Ascendant Ones. I have been sent to escort you to the Moon, the Crossroads, the Way Beneath. You'll be trained in our ways." She paused to take a breath, then said, "You will lead the Communion into the new millennium."

Teska and Neris sat in two seats with odd folding bottoms in the rows behind the dugout. A collapsed overhang provided partial shade from the midday sun.

Teska looked at the other woman. They were roughly the same age. Neris was taller, though not as tall as Malachi. The blond-haired woman had a thin face with wide-set eyes and full lips—attractive in a pleasingly peculiar sort of way, despite the blind eyes that stared straight ahead. Her silver necklace had three delicate chains of equal length hanging from it.

"What did you do to them down there?" Teska asked.

Neris smiled. "It is only a sleeping spell. They'll awaken unharmed and quite refreshed, I assure you."

"Why?"

"They're men. Our business does not concern them. I came seeking you." Neris folded her hands in her lap. "Teska, you have a special gift."

"How do you know?"

"The Enodia Communion knows a great many things. One of the most important right now is that you are Nahoru'brexia."

She squinted. "You said those words before. What do they mean?"

Neris sighed. "The Communion has been struggling for decades. The Church has weakened us by destroying our numbers. In fact, attempts have been made to kill Malachi Thorne as a way of striking a significant blow to the Church."

In the silence, Teska frowned, her mouth set in a tight line.

"You disapprove?" Neris asked.

Teska said nothing but looked out at the trees in the field. She could feel the other woman's blind eyes on her. She twisted around in her seat to face Neris. "What?" she snapped.

"You love him, don't you?"

With that, time seemed to stop. The question pierced her heart, a needle in an emotional balloon. Hearing it inside her head—even her heart—was one thing; but hearing someone else say it made it…real. She knew all too well what that unsettled feeling in her stomach was when he was around, that yearning to be close, even the wondrous thoughts that seemed to push aside common sense. It all coalesced around that one simple, four-letter word.

It wasn't the first time she'd known such feelings. Marco came to mind, and she smiled. There had been others before him as well. She couldn't help wondering if this time—if this time came to pass—would be different. Or would he express his love like all the others: through violence or exploitation?

Neris's voice was like sunshine through a rain cloud. "It's all right. I may be blind, but I can see that you do." She smiled.

"What's it matter to you?" Teska snarled. She didn't know if the frustration came from her thoughts being interrupted or because Neris was right.

"It matters a great deal, Teska. You're one of the Ascendant Ones. You and those like you are the future of the Communion. I don't know how you would reconcile your obligations to the sisterhood with your love for—"

"Listen." She pointed a finger at Neris, although the woman couldn't see it. At least Teska didn't think she could see it. "I don't know you or where you come from. I don't know what any of this is about. But I think you'd better leave before I kill you."

Neris didn't move. "The Communion has discovered that over the past few decades there's been a special breed of brexia— what you call witches—who've been born. Each one has a special talent or ability. Gifts, if you will. You aren't the only woman who can do…*unique* things. The Matriarch, the Mother and the Maiden believe the Nahoru'brexia are destined to lead the Communion. They see these special gifts as signs of a new age, in which we won't be relegated to shadows and dungeons. But you need to be trained. The Thousand-Faced Moon will instruct you in the use of your gifts and show you the pathway to true power."

Teska laughed. "I'm nobody. Just a thief, a prostitute. I've never been worth anything to anybody." Though Merrick had suggested she may be immune to the influence of the rank pins—as if there were more to her than just her special gift. *Could this be part of it?*

"You're of immense value to us."

"So if I became one of these Nahoru'brexia—"

"You're already one of them. We would simply train you to lead us."

"All right, suppose I said yes and got trained. Then what?"

Neris nodded. "Then, with the divine guidance of Matriarch, Mother and Maiden, the Nahoru'brexia would assume leadership of the Communion."

Teska scowled. "Just like that? Everybody's just going to fall in line?"

"The Three-Who-Are-One have foreseen…obstacles to this course of action. But they can be dealt with and are better than the alternative."

"Which is?"

Neris remained silent for a moment. The countryside beyond the field lay hazy in the late June heat. The sky was so translucent one could almost see the stars through it. Neris turned to Teska, her face filled with concern.

"The Communion faces extinction," she said. "If we don't take drastic steps now, our numbers will be extinguished altogether. It's imperative that we regain our rightful place."

Now Teska went silent. Neris honored the moment.

Teska Vaun had played—and been played by—the best. She knew the tricks and strategies of con men and bandits. She'd lived with murderers and slept with thieves. She'd even loved a few of them. She'd escaped the Church, had stolen and destroyed one of their precious relics. She'd lived by intuition and initiative. And her gift. She was no fool.

And something deep inside told her this wasn't a trick.

Her knowledge of the Enodia Communion was limited, although she'd shared a cell once with some the Church claimed were witches. What power could they give her? And what did it mean to lead the Communion? The only things she'd ever led were thieving raids or gullible fops to her bed. She couldn't see herself as any sort of leader.

But did she have any other options? She could stay with Malachi, but for how long? Even if he *did* admit his feelings for her, she couldn't possibly expect anything to come from it.

Could she?

The two of them being together was an absurd notion. He was a high-ranking Churchman, and one way or another, it wouldn't be long before the Church welcomed him back. And then what of her? That was easy: if the Church got their hands on her again, the Ghost would finally be laid to rest.

She couldn't imagine him abandoning his beliefs just to be with her. He was not a man to surrender anything so easily—especially his faith—although she could see he struggled with Merrick's ideas about freedom, the Church and God.

But even if she *didn't* get caught, was she just going to trail after him, hoping their relationship might develop into something more? She wasn't some lost puppy. She'd never done that for any man. Why start now?

Face it: It will never work. He's not the man for you.

She needed to forget the hopeful whisper of her feelings. They'd gotten her in hot water before, and this had the look of a boiling cauldron of problems. She was surrounded by Churchmen, and she could never fit in and be like them. Sooner or later, they'd turn on her. When her guard was down, when she least expected it, it would be a stake at a tekoya for her—especially if it would help get them back in the Church's good graces.

Hells, you should've been gone a long time ago.

She stood, walked down the aisle of seats and stood on the crumbling gray steps that led up to the concourse. Neris remained seated.

For some reason she couldn't pinpoint, Teska sensed that Neris was sincere. This strange, sightless woman wasn't crazy. Teska had just witnessed six men fall asleep after Neris said a few words. Teska weighed her options. Remain with Malachi—who, knowing men like she did, would probably never return her feelings, even if he felt the same way. Or look into what Neris had said. Maybe there was more to her unique gift—and to her—than she knew?

Besides, a little power couldn't hurt, right? She turned and faced Neris. "When do we leave?"

26
HISTORY

"C'mon, mate, rise and shine." DuBose's voice filtered through the wool of sleep that clogged Thorne's brain.

The Witchfinder blinked. "What happened?" He looked around to get his bearings. They were still inside the dugout, but night had fallen. Nocturnal insects chirped across the field. Slow movement and murmured voices filled the dugout.

Thorne walked past the groggy men and climbed the stairs. A soft breeze blew through the night. One by one, the other men emptied onto the field.

"What the hells happened?" Cabbott asked, stretching. "Were we asleep?"

"That we were, mate."

"How—"

Darien coughed. "It was magic."

"I remember a woman…" Thorne said.

"Yeah, who was that?"

"We saw her, too," Carden added. "At least for a moment."

Thorne scanned the group. "Where's Teska?"

Everyone looked around and shrugged. Cabbott and Warner cursed.

Hawkes studied the glittering stars overhead. "What time is it, anyway?"

"I'd say it's about three in the morning," Merrick replied.

"You mean we've been asleep for"—Thorne paused—"we've been here for *fourteen hours*?" He cursed and jammed his hands on his hips. He looked around at the dugout and among the silky blackness lurking beneath the trees, as if waiting for Teska to materialize any moment. She didn't.

"So that blond lady really was a witch?" Warner asked. Hawkes nodded. "I ain't never been hit with an honest-to-God spell before."

"Just be thankful it wasn't the one I got." Darien barked a dry, humorless chuckle.

"We need to get back to the Red Dog," Thorne declared. "Sol, Tycho—get our horses."

Both deputies disappeared into the darkness.

Merrick talked softly with DuBose and Carden. Cabbott stood beside Darien.

"Do you have any idea where Teska could be?" Thorne asked his constable. He couldn't hide the concern in his voice.

"No. Did she say anything to you?"

Thorne shook his head. "Nothing. We knew she'd take off the first chance she got."

"Yeah, expect she's had dozens of chances to do that. So why now? And what kept her with us all this time?"

After their conversation in the woods after escaping the Vulanti'nacha, Thorne thought he knew. She'd seemed almost eager to remain with him. She'd said he made her feel safe. Unless she'd just been playing him for her own twisted purposes. Now, in hindsight, he realized that's what it must have been. She'd been manipulating him, setting him up for—*this*. Confusion, loss and disappointment flowed through him, along with the bitter tang of rejection. He'd become accustomed to her presence despite the misgivings he had about her intentions. He enjoyed her laugh. And those moments when he searched her eyes had made him feel 15 years younger. She had brought out a hopefulness in him, that he might yet find a lasting relationship. But he'd never told her any of that, had he?

Maybe if I had...

A void opened inside him, not unlike the one that had held him prisoner to the events in Toadvine. He gritted his teeth and looked away.

The deputies returned, horses in tow. The two men laughed and joked as they handed the reins to each owner.

Thorne vaulted into the saddle and jerked Gamaliel's head around. "Let's move!"

As everyone mounted, Hawkes said something that caused Warner to laugh.

Thorne twisted in the saddle. "Enough!" he bellowed, his voice resounding through the night. "Just walk into the cathedral and announce yourselves, why don't you? Shut up!" He spun around and urged Gamaliel into the trees.

The men looked at each other, wide-eyed, and shook their heads. They said nothing else as they followed Thorne into the shadows.

Behind them, nearly hidden in the grass and weeds, lay a small scrap of cloth that had fallen from Thorne's saddle. Charcoal letters on it spelled out a message:

I'M SORRY
GOING TO LAST CHAPEL
THEY SAY I'M SPECIAL
I HAVE TO KNOW ABOUT MY GIFT
PLEASE DON'T HATE ME
–TESKA

They rode through Nashton's still, empty streets. Soon, the fishmongers and fishermen would begin negotiations. Milkmaids would make their rounds. For now, only the soft clop of hooves on dirt, the pinprick stars and the occasional dog or cat accompanied them.

Thorne wasn't tired. In fact, he felt extremely well rested. He had the strange feeling that he could tackle anything right now. But his heart ached with longing and anger; his mind seethed as he tried to find balance and order between his faith and the freedom Merrick spoke about. The Church offered structure, intentionality, a way of life that allowed everything to exist in its rightful place. Merrick's freedom sounded just the opposite.

Thorne could see the attractiveness and lure of unfettered freedom. But how could chaotic, undisciplined freedom replace the only way of life people had ever known? There seemed to be too much opportunity for anarchy.

Yet if the Church *was* hiding secrets—if the only way of life people had ever known was a lie—what would happen when word got out? Wouldn't such information lead to rebellion and chaos? It hadn't happened yet, but that was only because Merrick hadn't had a chance to tell others about the rank pins. And what of those giants that Dario had seen in his vision? What role did they play in the Church? Were they to be used to quell the freedom movement?

Merrick had devoted the remainder of his life to promoting that movement—a cause he was willing to die for. Poor Darien had sacrificed half of his years in order to aid his sister and uncover the truth about Jairus. Each had taken these paths willingly, not knowing the outcomes. They'd done so in order to aid those around them.

What about me? What have I done to help those around me? What have I sacrificed for? What am I willing to die for?

Once, it had been the Church. Raised and nurtured in its comforting arms, he knew nothing else. Its doctrines and rituals felt as much a part of him as his own thoughts. But now, the Church had turned its back on him.

Or had he turned his back on it when he listened to Merrick's heresies?

Had he sinned and fallen away from the Church's grace? Was all of this the consequence of some temptation he hadn't refused?

Darien and Merrick rode up, bookending him. Darien's voice cut through his musings. "—said, are you okay?"

He glanced at his friend. "I'm fine," he replied curtly, hoping to brush them away. It didn't work.

"Malachi," Merrick said with gentleness, "she means something to you, doesn't she?"

He didn't answer.

"I thought as much. I saw that look in your eyes."

"Doesn't matter now, does it?" he spat. "Just forget it."

"Malachi, I wanted you to know that I didn't mean to challenge you back there, when I said I was going to Last Chapel," Darien said. "I didn't intend to be belligerent. It's just that—"

Thorne stared at the shadowy road ahead of him. "I understand. You must do what you believe is right." That was obviously what Teska had done. She'd made the decision that this was the proper time to leave.

Why hadn't he said something to her sooner? Maybe that would've changed her decision.

Or had he been too wrapped up in fulfilling his role as an Imperator? As he thought back, he realized that he had given her no good reason to remain. All he ever talked about was taking her in and seeing that she faced justice. She had left in order to save her life.

"Yes," Darien said. "And so must you."

"What do you mean?" Thorne glanced at the aged clerk.

"Something's happening, my friend, to all of us. Even you. Fate or destiny or God is forcing us down paths we never would've chosen for ourselves. You have to follow your heart and do what your instincts tell you." Darien barely finished before a coughing spell overtook him.

"What do you want to do, my boy?" Merrick asked. "What do you believe is worth living—and dying—for?"

That was the problem. His head was an orderly collection of old habits and beliefs that were at war with Merrick's new untamable, perplexing ideology. Thorne didn't know what to believe anymore. "Stable's up ahead." He spurred Gamaliel out in front of them. It was too bad he couldn't get away from the voices in his head as easily.

The stable sat across from the Red Dog Saloon. They rode up to the back. Hawkes dismounted and rapped on the door. Faint voices drifted through the night, but they couldn't tell from where. A moment later, a groggy stable hand, lantern glowing, pushed open the door. As they plodded in, the young man lit two more lanterns and hung them around the stalls. Once the horses had been put away, he blew out his lamp and retired to a small bedroll near the back door.

Thorne crossed the hay-strewn planks to the front door. Just before he opened it, he heard the voices, louder now. He peered through a large crack between the double doors.

Several men with horses milled around in front of the Red Dog. Lights flickered behind the saloon windows. It reminded Thorne of a raid. DuBose and Warner joined him.

"What's up, mate?"

Thorne shushed him under his breath. "Something's going on."

Two robed figures exited the saloon, lanterns in hand. Their hoods and the predawn darkness hid their faces. One of them spoke to the three men standing around the horses. Then one of the robed figures and the trio of men mounted and rode off.

The remaining robed figure started to turn back to the saloon but stopped. He raised the lantern and looked directly at the stable. A chill skittered down Thorne's spine.

"The lights!" he whispered. "Douse the lights. Now!" They snuffed out the lamps, and darkness consumed the stable.

Thorne watched the saloon. A broad-shouldered man walked out and joined the shrouded form. Another man, equally tall, followed. Then a third. The smaller robed shape pointed toward the stable.

"Somebody's coming! Hide!" Thorne hurried Darien behind a stack of feedbags. "Carden—get the stable hand and keep him quiet!"

Darien pressed himself into the corner. Thorne crouched at his feet. Someone settled into the loft overhead. Stall doors creaked. From his vantage point, Thorne could see the double doors. Amber light glimmered underneath them, then spilled inside as one of the doors opened. One of the tall men stepped inside.

Thorne, not prone to exaggeration, made him out to be at least seven feet tall. He wore chain mail armor, and a purple cape flowed from epaulettes on his shoulders. A massive broad sword was sheathed across his back. When he lifted the lantern above his head, Thorne saw a clean-shaven face with cruel eyes beneath a metal helmet. The light flickered off his rank pin. Dario was right. It wasn't anything he'd seen before.

So this is who killed Jairus. What the hells are they?

The giant took several steps inside the stable, swinging the lantern back and forth, his boots thudding on the planks. He turned a complete circle before walking to the closest stall. The horse on the other side puffed as he drew near. He held the lantern over the top of the door and looked down inside.

Satisfied, he thumped back to the door and closed it behind him. Thorne crept back to look through the gap. Darien broke into a coughing fit that he stifled with his sleeve. Cabbott, Warner and Hawkes crept forward to join Thorne.

The giant returned to the two others, also dressed the same way. He said something, and the robed figure nodded. A brief discussion followed, then all three armored men turned and started toward the stable.

"Shit!" Hawkes hissed as he spun around.

Once again, they scattered like mice back into hiding.

One giant opened both doors. The others entered the stable and spent a few moments outfitting horses before leading them outside. As soon as the doors shut, Thorne edged back to watch.

"I thought we had them. They should've been up there," one of the giants said as he gestured to the top floor of the saloon. His voice sounded like rocks tumbling together.

The robed shape leaned forward, his voice a sibilant hiss from within the hood. "Thorne and his men are still in the city. We shall find them."

"What about the woman?" one of the giants asked. His voice sounded like rustling corn stalks.

"She is to be taken alive. The Crimson Fathers want her."

No one spoke for a moment, as if the name demanded reverence.

"Thorne will be caught," the small figure said. "Soon, a new era will dawn for the Church. You Crusaders are the vanguard of that era."

"Speaking of dawn..." the stone-voiced giant said.

With that, the group mounted and trotted off down the road. Thorne waited until he could hear nothing before turning to the men who crowded around him, their faces gray ovals in the darkness.

"Dario, did those men look familiar?"

The clerk nodded. "Yes, they're the same men."

"That short guy called them Crusaders." Warner frowned. "What's a damn Crusader, anyway?"

"You mean to tell me they snuck into the Dog to kill us in our sleep?" Cabbott asked.

"Sure sounded that way," Hawkes replied.

Merrick tottered away from the group and drop onto a hay bale. Carden released the bug-eyed stable hand, who scampered out the back door.

"Yeah, what's a Crusader?" Hawkes asked. "Some new rank the Church's come up with?"

"Warner, eyes front. Hawkes, back door." Thorne walked over and stood in front of Merrick. The old man's head tilted up, but he couldn't make out the features. "Val, are you okay?"

"We have serious trouble on our hands." Merrick's voice sounded cold as a grave, and it spooked Thorne. He'd never heard his mentor sound like this.

"You mean more than what we've already had?" Thorne meant it to come out funny, but instead, it sounded petulant and exhausted.

"Oh, my boy…much, much more. If what I think is true…"

The others drifted over and formed a semicircle in front of Merrick. "Dear God… What have they done?"

"Traugott, you okay?" Carden asked.

DuBose placed a hand on the old man's shoulder.

"Val…" Thorne took a knee before him.

"Did anyone else hear them say Crimson Fathers? Please tell me it's just old age playing tricks on me."

All of them acknowledged that they'd heard it.

"What is that?" DuBose asked.

Merrick sighed, his face ghostly pale. "A long time ago, as I was making my way through the ranks of the Order, I heard a few stories—old wives' tales, I assumed at the time—about something dark and sinister at the heart of the Church. I figured it came from deranged minds, so I didn't pay attention to the details. But there was a common denominator mentioned in hushed tones: something called the Crimson Fathers."

"Take it easy, mate—you're shaking like a leaf." DuBose still had his hand on Merrick's shoulder.

"The Crimson Fathers…" Darien repeated under his breath.

"It's a forbidden part of our history. The Church goes to great lengths to keep it hidden. Even among the few who may know about it, most wouldn't believe it actually happened," Merrick said. "Legend has it that the Crimson Fathers were a secret sect of Church warlocks. It's said that they were formed in the early 200s, presumably at the orders of, and under the control of, Heiromonarch Tethion the Third. Years later, the cult was supposedly given a special task to accomplish, something of great significance to the Church. Once they were done, every member of the Crimson Fathers was slaughtered on the orders of Heiromonarch Okafo the Dark."

"Church magicians? Are you serious?" Cabbott's tone indicated he wasn't.

"Yes, a secret cabal known only to a few."

"So how come *you* know about it?"

Merrick sighed again. "I told you. I heard stories; over time, I uncovered bits of information here and there. That's what it pointed to."

"But you don't have any proof?" Carden asked.

"No. I always assumed it was all fables and myths."

"I dunno, man," Warner said half-heartedly from the front doors. "The Church burns witches. Why would they keep them on retainer?"

"Because as I said, legend has it that the cult was ordered to do something that benefited the Church to an unbelievable degree."

"It must've been something the Church never wanted duplicated if they wiped out the whole sect," Thorne said.

Carden leaned forward. "So you think people are starting that old cult up again?"

"Possibly. But I think it's worse than that, Murnau. I think…" He shook his head. "I think it might be the original sect."

"Say what?" Warner gaped. "First, it's flyin' spiders, and now you're tellin' me the Church's got walking dead cultists? Man…" He shook his head.

Dawn approached. It wasn't enough to brighten the interior of the stable, but it provided enough visibility for everyone to see the horror that lined Merrick's face. Once again, it startled Thorne to see such abject terror in a man he'd known to be almost fearless.

"Mr. Warner, the Crimson Fathers were said to have had powers that rivaled the Three-Who-Are-One." He adjusted his spectacles. "Perhaps even Hecate herself. Nothing was beyond their cruel imaginations. Or so the legends say."

DuBose shook his head. "But if they're all dead, and have been for centuries—"

The old man finished the thought for him: "Then who or what might be resurrecting them? It freezes my blood to even consider it."

Darien placed a hand on Thorne's arm. "Could I speak with you privately?"

The two men walked to the middle of the stable.

"What is it, Dario?"

"Is there anything else we need to discuss or do here in Nashton?"

Thorne thought for a moment. "No, I don't suppose so." He moved a piece of straw around with the toe of his boot.

"Then as soon as I'm provisioned, I'm setting out for Last Chapel. It takes me a little longer to travel now, as you might imagine. I have to find Cassidy and Cassandra."

Thorne hated the idea of losing his friend so soon after reuniting with him. "I'm going with you."

"No, Malachi, you don't need to do that." But the relief on Darien's face said something different.

"Yes, I do, old friend. I wasn't able to go with you to Talnat." He smirked. "And it's not like I have a lot of Church business to attend to. Right now, I think the best thing for me is to stay on the move and try to learn as much as I can from Val."

"Thank you, Malachi."

Thorne gathered his men together to discuss their plans. Merrick did the same with DuBose and Carden. Ten minutes later, they regrouped. Merrick and Darien sat on feedbags. Carden crouched on the floor, twisting his knife in a knothole. DuBose leaned against a stall beside him. Cabbott found a stool, and Hawkes and Warner stood side by side.

"I'm not sure quite how to begin," Thorne said. "This is… I've never said anything like this before." He paused, searching for words. "On our way back here, Dario said that events had set us on paths we didn't choose, and that everything had changed." He paused again. "I'm…not an Imperator any longer. I'm not even a Witchfinder. So I guess that means I'm not in charge anymore." He tried to chuckle it off, but it didn't work. He looked at his constable and deputies.

"I've made the decision to go with Dario to Last Chapel, to help him find his family. You're all free to do…well, whatever you want, I guess. I don't know if you can reclaim your good standing in the Church—or if you even want to." He sighed. "I just want to give you the chance to choose your own path. You deserve that much, at least."

Merrick smiled. "That, my boy, is the essence of our cause!"

"So you're cutting us loose?" Hawkes asked, raising his eyebrows.

Thorne nodded. "I can't order you to do anything. You three have served me and the Church faithfully. I'm honored to call you my friends. No Witchfinder has ever had a more loyal and committed group. But we're at a point where our futures might…diverge. I don't know why this has happened. I certainly don't understand why the Church has listened to Zadicus Rann, or what these Crusaders are, or—" He took a deep breath.

"We still got too many questions and not enough answers," Warner said.

Thorne nodded again.

"Well, if you're going to Last Chapel, I am too," Cabbott said. "I'm in it just as much as you. The Church won't look too favorably on me, either. Besides," he winked at Thorne, "I'm getting too old for this constable shit anyway." He grinned.

"I already told you that I'm going with Dario," Hawkes said.

"Then I guess my decision's been made." Warner smirked at Hawkes. "Somebody's gotta keep you outta trouble. Just look what happened the last time you and Dario went off together."

Hawkes punched him in the shoulder.

"We've talked about it as well," Merrick said. "I'm sending Rich and Murnau back. I want them to carry on the work in that area." He smiled at both men. "They're more than capable of taking my place."

"No one can take your place," Carden said.

"What're you going to do, then?" Cabbott asked.

"Well, if it's all right with you all, I'd like to come along to Last Chapel. There are some people I'd like to visit on the way, if you don't mind. I'll do it in the evenings. It won't slow you down. I'd like to check on some of our groups and encourage them." Merrick smiled. "What we're doing right here—making our own decisions, being responsible for our own actions—that's what being free is all about. More people in Deiparia need to know this."

"Then it's decided," Thorne said. "It's getting light out. Let's get provisioned and be on our way." He started to turn away but stopped and looked at them. "And be careful out there."

27

CRUSADERS

SATURDAY, JUNE 27, 999 AE

Once more, Malachi Thorne found himself adrift between two worlds. He'd been cut off from the Church because of Rann and with Teska gone without so much as a goodbye, he felt more alone than ever. Even the presence of his friends did little to diminish his melancholy.

They'd departed Nashton on Wednesday. It had been easier getting out after the Feast. Patrols had been fewer, and checkpoints were limited to the primary roads. They'd joined a caravan heading for Baymouth but left at the first opportunity and struck a course for Last Chapel.

So far, they'd visited three small villages along the way. Merrick had used his contacts in each to arrange meetings with other sympathizers. Thorne and Hawkes had accompanied Merrick. All of the meeting places had been in abandoned houses or deep-wooded glades. They'd traveled separately to avoid arousing suspicion and had staggered their arrival times. Guards were posted, and for several hours each night, Merrick and his supporters had discussed what it meant to be free, and how such freedom might be achieved. Many advocated for it by blood and sword. Others preferred a more circumspect approach.

Every night, the reactions to Thorne had been identical. Most of them had accepted him and Hawkes when they arrived with Merrick. It was only when their identities as former members of the Paracletian Order had been revealed that trouble began. Merrick had to repeatedly stress that they no longer had any connection to the Church. But that had done little to assuage the fears and animosity.

The more Thorne listened to Merrick, the more he saw the possibilities in what he said. He looked back over his life and saw the times when the Church had made decisions for him. While those decisions had taken him in the direc-

244 • J. TODD KINGREA

tion he'd wanted to go, his life would be incredibly different now if he'd had more say. Ironically, just like it was now. What would he have become if he'd lived under the freedom that Merrick espoused? What would his life look like now? Of course, there were no answers, but it was interesting to contemplate. He wondered how many other congregants of Deiparia would ask the same things if they could.

What captivated Thorne the most were the documents that Merrick knew by heart. In the west, Merrick had discovered information unknown in Deiparia. Or perhaps it was known, but only to a chosen few. Thorne remembered the rumors of secret buildings and forbidden documents beneath Attagon. He even remembered the idea that had once crossed his mind—the fleeting temptation to pursue a higher rank so he might have access to such things.

Merrick quoted many old writings he had discovered in the West regarding freedom, but Thorne's favorite was what Merrick used to close each gathering: "When in the Course of human events, it becomes necessary for one people to dissolve the political bands which have connected them with another, and to assume among the powers of the earth, the separate and equal station to which the Laws of Nature and of Nature's God entitle them, a decent respect to the opinions of mankind requires that they should declare the causes which impel them to the separation. We hold these truths to be self-evident, that all men are created equal, that they are endowed by their Creator with certain unalienable Rights, that among these are Life, Liberty and the pursuit of Happiness."

According to Merrick, these words came from a once-revered document called the Declaration of Independence, which was old even in the days preceding the Great Cataclysm. Merrick had attempted to explain the words as best he could, but every question raised more. Who or what was "Nature's God? Was it the invisible god of the Tex'ahns or some other deity? What "political bands" had to be dissolved and why? Why where those "truths" so self-evident?

The questions intrigued Thorne, as did the possibilities of the answers. While their friends slept, he and Merrick had sat by the dying fire every night, talking and reflecting on the words.

Regardless of the hopefulness in Merrick's teachings, Thorne continued to struggle with the concept that the Church wasn't God. If the Church wasn't God, then who or what was he supposed to believe in? Merrick's knowledge and explanations intrigued him, and the more he learned, the more he wanted to know. But all the while, he couldn't just reject everything he'd ever believed— could he? The battle of the old and the new chewed him up inside.

And if the Church wasn't God, that it meant the Church wasn't infallible. And if that could be true, then the very foundation of Deiparian society was imperiled. When Thorne pondered these things for long, his stomach tied itself in knots. Choice and free will came with staggering responsibility, and he had difficulty imagining a society ordered not by the Church, but by freedom and liberty. It made his head hurt and caused him to tremble when he lay alone in the darkness.

Today, as they rode through backwoods to avoid detection, Thorne came to a decision. He called them to a halt as they crossed a bridge. Clutching his rank pin in his fist, Thorne dismounted and walked to the edge.

"Malachi? What're you doing?" Merrick asked.

For a long moment, Thorne stared down into the rolling water. Then he opened his hand and stared just as intently at his pin—something so innocuous, yet Merrick claimed they were dangerous. Days ago, he'd encouraged them to dispose of their pins. At the time, it had seemed like a preposterous idea. After all, they'd worked hard to earn their respective ranks, and the pins symbolized those efforts. They represented the authority of the Church.

And the final link to my former life, Thorne thought. If he walked away from this symbol, he was turning his back on everything. It was the last vestige not just of his role as Witchfinder Imperator, but as a servant of God. As a man with an identity.

"You gettin' rid of your pin?" Warner asked.

The question sounded foreign to Thorne's ears. A small twig, caught in the river's current, swirled out from under the bridge, and Thorne recognized his own condition in its bobbing uncertainty. By tossing away this small bit of metal, he was also casting his own future into turbulent waters that would carry him to an unknown fate. Or drown him.

Merrick insisted the pins were more than what they appeared. Thorne wanted to hold on to his, if for no other reason than to remind him of who and what he used to be, but if it was somehow influencing his decisions, making him some sort of slave, he couldn't keep it.

Before he could change his mind, he opened his hand and let the pin fall in the water.

He sighed and turned to face the others. "I can't make you get rid of your pins, but I believe you should consider doing so. If what Val says about them is right, maybe it's best if we don't have them around."

One by one, they fished out their pins, pitched them in and watched them disappear beneath the surface. For a moment, Thorne, Darien, Cabbott, Hawkes and Warner stood at the edge of the bridge and said nothing as they watched the current.

Thorne felt as if a limb had been amputated. His distance from the Church, which had been increasing with every passing day, was now final. There was no turning back. He'd cast his lot with Merrick—and prayed that it was the right choice.

They continued on for several miles in silence.

"Last night, you asked a good question, Malachi," Merrick said.

"Which one? I asked a lot of questions."

"You asked if we have the right to offer people freedom."

"It bothers me. To have the kind of freedom that you talk about implies that the stability of society would be compromised. If people could choose whatever they wanted, wouldn't that lead to anarchy, like The Concordat describes? By offering this freedom, aren't we turning everyone's life upside down? Where does the order and structure come from if everyone is free to choose?"

"As I said, a very good question." Merrick smiled. "Although I counted three in there."

"Under the Church's leadership, people have security. They're taken care of. Aside from the occasional malcontent, society functions efficiently. And even the criminal element receives punishment for disrupting society."

"That's all true," Merrick replied. "But what if society were structured not by a single monolithic entity, but by allowing every person to have a voice? What if each person contributed to creating, building and maintaining a system that benefited everyone?"

Thorne raised his eyebrows. Sometimes, Merrick came up with the oddest notions. "If everyone had a voice, how would anyone be heard? Who would make decisions? I don't know… It still sounds like anarchy. And last night, you suggested that freedom extends even to belief."

"I believe it does."

"So you're saying I could choose to believe that the Church is God, while you choose to believe…I don't know, that pond over there is God?"

"That's correct."

Thorne raised his eyebrows and shook his head. "Then who's right? Which God is the right one?"

Merrick rode quietly for a moment. "I don't know the answer to that, Malachi. But I do know that freedom must include every aspect of life. No one is truly free if even one part of their existence is oppressed or restricted."

As the forest began to thin, they came across an increasing amount of burnt fauna. It looked as though numerous forest fires had broken out but only in contained areas. Scorched trees stuck out of the ground like burnt matchsticks. Hard-packed soot covered the ground. Soon, the skeletal trees were gone altogether, leaving the group exposed on the flatlands leading to Last Chapel. No birds soared or sang. An oppressive aura lingered over everything.

"Cheery, ain't it?" Warner said. But the landscape consumed his attempt at levity, so he remained quiet like everyone else.

After a while, they found the first body. It had been a Churchman by the looks of what remained of the clothing. Cabbott dismounted to inspect it and covered his nose as he approached. Fang and claw marks had shredded the flesh, which was now grayish black and teeming with maggots.

The closer they came to the Black River, the more corpses they encountered. All of them had been peasants or Churchmen. They crossed a small creek and followed a trail up a gentle incline. The land here showed signs of having been recently scorched as well. The hill descended onto the river's floodplain. Across the Black River sat Last Chapel.

The city had a bloody and brutal past, and a long history of witchcraft. Legends were told around campfires of chthonic beings that once stalked through the green-misted streets. Last Chapel marked the western limits of Deiparia, and the Church's influence wasn't as dominant here. Consequently, the congregants were hard, fiercely self-sufficient and considered by most to be immoral rogues.

The Black River bordered Last Chapel to the east. To the west stood the Kingsway Wall, a nine-mile-long barrier of stone blocks rising thirty-seven feet in the air, surmounted at intervals by watchtowers. The wall held only two gates, since beyond it lay the Devouring Lands.

"By the Church," Darien said, staring across the river. "It looks like a war zone."

Fires burned in dozens of places, their smoke adding to the clouds that swelled like ashen boils overhead. The middle of the city appeared to have been reduced to rubble. It looked as if a giant wagon wheel had rolled across the city in a southeast-to-northwest diagonal, leaving a scar-like swath of destruction from river to wall. Two of the four original bridges into the city remained intact. Flocks of birds circled through the gritty-tasting air.

"Let's rest here," Thorne said. "We need to figure out our next move."

"What's been going on down there?" Hawkes knelt on one knee, staring across the blasted floodplain.

Thorne leaned against a tree, one foot propped on the trunk. "The Church has repeatedly requested reinforcements, but nothing's been done as far as I know."

Merrick peered over the top of his glasses. "I've never seen such devastation."

"Our options for getting in are pretty limited," Hawkes said after they'd watched the city for a few moments.

"Swimming the Black is out," Warner said. A mile wide in places, the river always flowed strong and deep.

"We'll have to take the bridges, unless any of you have hidden wings you want to let us know about," Hawkes said. "I suggest we split into two groups and each one take a bridge."

"Could we pass ourselves off as guards and prisoners?" Darien asked.

"I doubt it." Cabbott smoothed his thinning hair. "Based on what I see before me, there's a good chance that every Church official down there knows all the others on sight."

In the end, they agreed that the bridges were their only option. Thorne, Merrick and Warner would cross Eads Bridge, north of what had once been a gigantic arch. Cabbott would take Darien and Hawkes across the 55 Bridge that joined the city south of the crumbling arch. They planned to rendezvous at a tavern called The Landing in an ancient part of the city north of Eads Bridge.

Entering Last Chapel had proven easier than expected. Although men guarded each bridge, they paid little attention to passersby. Their faces were sallow and lined with exhaustion. It seemed they couldn't be bothered with any activity that required more than minimal effort. The only thing that kept them working were the Crusaders with the new rank insignia. Thorne's group had learned along the way that they were supposed to be the Church's newest agents in the fight against the Communion.

Thorne and his men sat at a rectangular table in the back of The Landing, a war-torn wreck with holes in the teetering walls. They washed the soot from their throats with ale and tried to appear as inconspicuous as possible.

"Did you notice the demeanor of the Crusaders compared to the other Church officials?" Darien asked. "All of the constables and deputies we passed looked dead on their feet." He shook his head. "But not those Crusaders."

"They looked fresh as daisies," Warner agreed.

"You think they're the reinforcements the Church sent?" Hawkes asked Thorne.

"That would be my guess."

Warner took a drink. "But where'd they come from?" He wiped his mouth. "None of us have ever heard of them before."

Darien shook his head. "I don't know, Solomon. But I don't like it."

Silence settled over the table while they drank. A serving girl with her black hair in two long braids came around to refill their tankards.

"Young lady," Merrick said with his best smile, "we've just arrived from the eastern coast. The talk along the highways about your fair city has been confusing. I wonder if you could enlighten us as to what has happened here?"

She glanced toward the bar, her brown doe eyes flitting back and forth. "There's just been...trouble, kind sir. Nothing for you and your companions to worry about." Her tone and expression suggested otherwise.

"Oh my goodness." Merrick feigned surprise. "What sort of trouble? Will it affect our stay here?"

Once more, she glanced around, then refilled a tankard and started a third before answering. "The Church is at war with the Enodia Communion," she whispered through a practiced smile. "The Church claims the north, the Communion the south."

"And the path between them?" Thorne asked.

"A no-man's-land, kind sir." She refilled another tankard, sat her pitcher down and pretended to wipe up something on the table.

Merrick placed a silver coin on the edge of the table. "You missed a spot, young lady." He nodded at the coin. She paused, looked at him and understood. She dropped her bar rag over the coin and swirled it around the edge of the table. When she returned the cloth to her apron, the coin was gone.

"What about those tall fellows?" he asked. "My goodness, but they appear fearsome!"

She refilled Hawkes's tankard and whispered, "Crusaders. They're evil, kind sir. Pure *evil*. Stay away from 'em." Someone called her name from across the room. She nodded to Merrick, curtsied and hurried away.

Warner eyed his tankard. "She didn't fill mine up."

"She knows a drunken sot who's reached his limit." Hawkes grinned over the top of his tankard.

"Why don't you put some rocks in your pockets and go play in the river?"

The group talked in low voices and drank their ale but stopped when Thorne tapped the table to get their attention. He tilted his head toward the front but said nothing. They surreptitiously followed his line of sight.

Two Crusaders stepped through the door and scanned the room. Their presence struck the tavern mute; everyone stared into their drinks.

"Shit..." Hawkes whispered.

The two giants moved among the tables, searching each face they passed. Those who didn't look up had a gauntleted hand dropped on their shoulder. Both Crusaders wore chain mail and helmets. Plum-colored capes flowed behind them. Each carried a dagger and a short sword on their hip and a broadsword sheathed across their back.

"They lookin' for us?" Warner asked the tabletop.

"What do you think?" Cabbott replied into his tankard.

"Maybe they're not after us," Merrick said with shaky confidence. "In times of war, there's no shortage of targets: spies, smugglers, defectors, resistance..."

The Crusaders approached their table.

"What's the call, Malachi?" Cabbott had the glint of action in his eyes and both hands under the table.

The Crusaders stopped, one standing at each end of the table, sizing up the group.

"Gerald Kingston?" one of them asked, his voice menacing and cold.

Thorne gave an almost imperceptible twitch of his finger in Cabbott's direction—an old signal between them that meant *wait*—before looking at the Crusader. When the man turned his blue eyes onto him, Thorne felt a momentary chill. "No, sir," he said in a cowed voice. "There be no one here by that name."

He waited.

Both Crusaders stared at the faces around the table as if comparing them to some unseen criteria. Almost simultaneously, both turned and left the tavern.

Hawkes exhaled. "That was close."

Warner moved to stand up. "Let's get out of here while we can."

Cabbott put a hand on Warner's shoulder, a gesture that looked like two friends enjoying themselves. "Not yet." He pressed Warner down in his chair. "We rabbit out of here right now and they'll know it's us. Stay still. Finish your drink."

Ten tense minutes crept by. The group made small talk to appear innocuous, but their eyes kept shifting to the front door.

Finally, Thorne took a final drink and stood up. "Come on. We need to get out of here."

The sun slipped lower, painting the buildings and streets with long shadows. It remained hot and muggy, and the scattered clouds offered no indication of respite. A vacant lot sat across the street, its surface buckled and cracked from time, heat and the shifting ground. Ruined steel buildings rose up around them. Empty windows like hundreds of sightless eyes followed them. Some of the buildings still had upper floors; most were nothing more than debris-filled shells.

Thorne turned left out of The Landing and headed toward an intersection but halted after a few steps. Two Crusaders stood on the opposite corner of the intersection, watching his group. A third appeared around the corner ahead of them. Thorne glanced behind them and saw a fourth stepping out of an alley on the other side of the tavern.

"This isn't good."

"I'm guessin' we didn't convince them," Warner said.

All four Crusaders started toward them.

Thorne cursed as he looked around. His gaze settled on a door up ahead. "In there!"

The Crusaders converged at a casual but determined pace.

Thorne kicked the door open. Dust plumed in the dark, musty air as everyone rushed in. Shafts of dying sunlight filtered through holes in the ceiling.

"They're still coming." Hawkes slammed the door shut behind them.

Warner gawked in bewilderment. "What *is* this place?"

Scattered throughout the interior, on pedestals and in dioramic displays, stood statues of people. Desiccated and flaking, most of them lacked appendages, giving the impression of a leper house. Each brittle effigy wore tattered, moth-eaten rags. Soldiers and monsters, men and women, all posed in various stages of ruination. Darien brushed up against something that might've been a jester at one time, tipping it over. It struck the floor and disintegrated in a cloud of dry flakes, leaving behind a rusty armature.

"I think it was called a wax museum," Merrick said, the teacher in him coming out. "Such places—"

"Later, Val! See if there's a back door out of here," Thorne ordered his deputies. "Darien, you and Val get behind that counter."

The door latch rattled.

"Freeze!" Cabbott snapped. "Don't make a move."

The Crusaders entered, looking in every direction as they did. Thorne stood rigid behind what remained of a woman in a dress. Cabbott knelt among other figures. One of the Crusaders unsheathed his broadsword over his shoulder with only one hand; Thorne's eyes widened at the display of strength. The other Crusader remained empty-handed. From his vantage point, Thorne spotted a third just outside the door, broadsword drawn.

The Crusaders eased farther into the room. "There." One of them pointed toward the figure where Thorne hid.

"It's a statue," the other said in a strangely disconnected voice.

Thorne tensed to make his move when a crash sounded from the rear of the building. Both Crusaders walked in the direction of the noise. Thorne waited until they went past before shouting, "Now, Thurl!"

Thorne lowered his good shoulder and drove it into the back of the Crusader on the left. With a grunt, the giant staggered forward. Cabbott leapt up and kicked the other just behind the knee. The giant careened sideways but balanced himself on a waxwork that disintegrated beneath his weight. Both Crusaders turned to face their assailants.

"Shit and hells," Cabbott hissed. "So much for that."

The first Crusader swung his broadsword as if it weighed no more than a sickle. The front of Thorne's tunic ripped away on the tip of the blade. He drew his dagger, although he knew it would do no good.

The second Crusader leapt toward Cabbott. His brawny arms encircled the constable's torso, pinning his arms to his side. Cabbott struggled and kicked, but his efforts were as ineffectual as those of a butterfly. The Crusader squeezed.

Thorne backed toward the door. He glanced around. The Crusader outside faced him, sword extended at gut level.

He also saw Merrick and Darien. Even through the dark, dusty interior, he could read his mentor's face. Thorne shook his head. *Don't do it, Val.* Merrick motioned for Darien to stay down.

Merrick found a stanchion with the remains of a moth-eaten cord attached to it. He edged around behind the Crusader who held Cabbott. Stepping out of the shadows, Merrick swung the stanchion. It slammed into the Crusader's back, causing him to stumble forward. His grip loosened enough for Cabbott to break the bear hug. The constable fell back, gasping.

Hawkes and Warner reemerged from the interior. Both had swords drawn and breathed heavily.

"There's a door back there," Hawkes yelled, "but one of them's coming this way. We couldn't hold him off."

"We're surrounded," Merrick said, adjusting his grip on the stanchion. Warner stepped beside him. Hawkes slipped around so he stood in front of the counter, closer to Cabbott.

The Crusader in the doorway moved inside. Thorne retreated into the center of the room. His group pressed together, with Crusaders on either side. The fourth arrived from the back of the building, short sword out. The third, broadsword still leveled at Thorne's midsection, completed the circle.

Hooves clattered outside.

"Throw down your weapons," the first Crusader said.

"You will not be told again," the third Crusader added.

More shadows filled the doorway.

The Crusader closest to the counter spotted Darien crouching behind it. He hauled him up by the neck like a kitten and pitched him into his companions.

Thorne's eyes swept the room and the Crusaders, his frenzied mind grasping for a plan. Even though they outnumbered the Crusaders, the Church's new agents were stronger—almost supernaturally so. Any sort of fight here would take the lives of several of his men. He cursed and dropped his dagger.

A fifth Crusader entered the building but remained by the door while the Witchfinder accompanying him strolled in casually, head lowered, removing his gloves. He wore the new rank pin on the left side, just like the Crusaders. The Witchfinder stopped in front of Thorne. With one finger, he tilted up the brim of his capotain hat as he raised his head.

Thorne growled low in his throat.

"It's about time." Zadicus Rann sneered. "I thought you'd never get here."

28

ANGUISH

Thorne tasted blood as the numbing embrace of darkness faded once again. He blinked several times, trying to remember where he was. The right side of his face throbbed, and pain flared across his body. He moaned.

"Water," a curt voice said from somewhere nearby.

He tried to move but couldn't. Metal pressed against his back, under his arms, against the backs of his legs. He was bound to a punishment chair.

Ice-cold water struck his face like a bolt of lightning.

Spitting and gasping, he shook his head, his hair flinging water down his bare chest. The wounds from Rimlingham and the hilltop still smarted. His vision cleared.

Darien, Cabbott, Hawkes, Warner and Merrick sat restrained as well. Their chairs formed a circle facing in toward a brazier of glowing coals. Everyone's chair had a metal bowl on the floor directly underneath the seat. Thorne clamped down the terror crawling up his gut, all too familiar with what they meant. Darien and Warner appeared to be unconscious.

The torture chamber felt stuffy and reeked of fear and hopelessness. The stone walls dripped slimy moisture; manacles and gibbets dangled from the ceiling like bloodstained metallic stalactites. An iron maiden, a rack and a Judas cradle completed the room.

"Need another bucket full?" a different voice asked.

"No, that's enough. Go."

"Yes, my Lord."

"One more thing: have them brought down here."

"Yes, my Lord." A door opened and shut.

"Malachi, you okay?" Cabbott's eyes were dark slits in a mass of bruised flesh.

"Oh, he's just fine, Constable Cabbott," the first voice responded.

Familiar, it clutched at Thorne's chest. The owner stepped into his field of vision. "Rann," he growled, realizing when he did that his lips were split. Scabs of dried blood clung to them. The right side of his face ached from hairline to jaw. "You son of a—"

Rann's fist slammed into the side of Thorne's head. Sparks exploded across his vision.

"I'm in charge now. Not you."

Thorne raised his head and met Rann's icy gaze. "You'll never be in charge of anything, you ignorant bastard."

Rann's fist shot forward again and smashed into Thorne's temple. This time, he had to fight to remain conscious.

"That's enough!" Cabbott yelled.

Rann stared at each man in the circle. His expressionless face couldn't mask the cruelty that danced in his eyes. Tugging on a pair of blacksmith's gloves, he removed a set of tongs from the wall and plunged them into the brazier. He removed a clump of blistering coals, then walked around the outside of the chairs, finally stopping behind Darien. He bent over and filled the bowl under the seat.

Thorne's throat constricted. "Damn you, Rann. What do you want?"

Darien's eyes fluttered. He fidgeted against his restraints. Smoke curled from the burning coals, along with the smell of metal heating.

"What do I want?" Rann chuckled. "Absolutely nothing, Thorne. Other than to see all of you suffer. And eventually die."

A sound that was part yelp, part groan escaped Darien's lips. The next instant, he went rigid against the restraints, pain ripping across his wrinkled face. He screamed and wiggled and screamed again, the sound hollow and forlorn in the stone-shrouded room.

"By the Church, he's just an old man!" Merrick shouted. "Stop this!"

Rann stepped behind Merrick's chair and stroked his head, like a protective mother soothing a frightened child. "There, there, Grandfather. I won't forget you."

Darien screamed again, his voice growing hoarse. The queasy stench of burning flesh intensified.

Rann turned to a small table littered with all manners of torture implements. "Let's see…" he said. "Thumbscrews? No, no—too common. Red-hot pinchers? No, best left for tearing off a woman's breast… Ah-ha!" He glanced over his shoulder at Thorne. "I do so like fire."

"You sick son of a bitch!" Thorne thrashed against his restraints.

Darien's screams drowned out any reply that Rann might've made. Thorne stared in helpless shock and horror at his friend. Darien bucked and twisted in the chair, every breath a ragged scream torn from deep inside his chest. Sweat rolled down his face and torso. His eyes bulged when not crunched tight.

Impotent rage crested in Thorne. He struggled against his bonds once more, desperate to save his friend, but could only scream.

Rann used the tongs and slid the burning bowl from underneath Darien. The old man tried to arch his body away from the broiling metal seat but had little luck. His screams tapered to pitiful moans; his head lolled forward, and he passed out.

"Talk to me, Rann," Thorne said when he'd regained his breath. "What's going on? Why all this? What do you want?" Rann walked to the far corner of the room. "I see you've been promoted," he added, looking for some way to distract Rann from his work. "That's an interesting rank pin you have."

Rann opened a wire cage, removed something and returned to his table. With his back to Thorne, he continued at his task. "Yes, I was promoted to Imperator after you abdicated your oath and responsibilities."

Thorne seethed but kept silent. Arguing with him wouldn't get them anywhere. He'd become fixated, almost single-minded. Thorne had to buy them some time. "What's been going on in Last Chapel? I haven't been here in a while."

Rann continued working. "Of course not. You're a traitor. You wouldn't know about the Church's glorious work here."

"So tell us," Cabbott said, picking up on Thorne's stratagem.

Warner and Darien remained unconscious. Hawkes tested the limits of his bonds as surreptitiously as he could. The smell of burnt flesh lingered.

"For too long, the Communion has used Last Chapel as their own blasphemous playground. For ages, they've laughed in our faces, taunting us." Rann paused, and in the silence, rats squeaked. "But now, the Church shall be supreme. We shall ensure that no witch, no freethinker, no rebel exists within the glorious realm."

"Is that what the Crusaders are for?" Thorne asked.

Rann spun around, maniacal glee on his face. "Aren't they wonderful? The perfect servants with which to usher in the new millennium! They're twice as strong as a normal man and tire less frequently. They can survive longer without food or water—"

"Where do they come from?"

A faraway look had settled over Rann's face. Now, he blinked it away and looked at Cabbott. "The Crusaders will remove all foreign thought from Deiparia. They'll destroy anyone who refuses to abide by the Church's teachings. The

Enodia Communion will be eradicated. The realm will know a thousand years of peace!"

Thorne caught Cabbott's look that said: *He's lost his mind.* Thorne nodded. "So the Church has been using the Crusaders against the Communion?"

Rann smiled as if he were the parent of every Crusader. "They've been magnificent. The witches have put up a fight, but we possess superior numbers. And superior men. They're the future of law and order in Deiparia. Did you know that I've overseen a dozen tekoyas since arriving here a few weeks ago?"

"Wow, that many?" Hawkes played along. "You've been busy."

Rann turned back to the table. "Yes. The Crusaders capture them. I kill them."

"Don't you mean you save their souls?" Thorne asked.

The Imperator stopped working and stood silently, staring at the wall. "Witches have no souls. There's nothing to save."

Rann turned around. He held a long wire cage, which was divided in half. On one side, two rats squeaked and skittered over each other, their end of the cage covered by a wire trapdoor. An enclosed metal box formed the other half of the apparatus. Rann carried it as if it were a holy relic. He looked around the circle. Eyes the color of angry clouds gleamed in the torchlight as they landed on Hawkes.

The deputy struggled against his bonds. "No, no way, man…"

Rann placed the trapdoor against his stomach and secured the cage with leather straps behind the chair. Hawkes cursed and wiggled but had no leverage. With a grunt of satisfaction, Rann stood up and patted Hawkes on the shoulder.

A quick knock sounded at the door before it swung open. A torturer stepped inside. Two small figures stood in the shadows behind him. "As you ordered," he said to Rann.

"Good, good! Wake him up." He pointed to Darien.

The torturer—a broad-shouldered man with a hairy back and cone-shaped head—flung a bucket of cold water in Darien's face. It sizzled against the cooling metal of the chair. Darien sputtered awake, shaking his head and moaning as the pain took hold.

"Bring them in," Rann ordered.

Two small figures crept into the chamber, sheer terror etched across their young faces. They clutched each other and stared wide-eyed at the scene before them.

"Ca…Cassidy? Cass…andra?" Darien whimpered as he tried to focus through his pain.

Neither child spoke. Cassidy, the older of the two, had fuzzy black hair that nearly matched his skin. He kept a fierce grip on his sister, his protective instincts clearly still intact despite their circumstances. Tears welled up in Cassandra's haunted brown eyes, and her lower lip trembled.

"And here they are!" Rann grinned, as if welcoming them to a surprise party. "This *is* who you came to see, isn't it?" he goaded Darien.

Thorne studied the children. Despite some malnutrition and fatigue, both looked okay. He didn't detect any signs of torture, though ligature marks covered their wrists. The boy looked at Thorne as if trying to recognize him. Cassandra toyed nervously with her fingers as tears edged down her dirty cheeks.

"Cassidy…Cassandra," Darien whispered. "It's me…" The children looked at him in confusion. Cassidy pulled his sister closer.

"Have they been harmed?" Thorne asked.

"Oh, no," Rann said. "They're doing well. Maybe a little worse for wear due to the trip…" He discarded this idea in favor of a more agreeable one and smiled again. "They're just fine."

"So it *was* a trap," Cabbott said.

"Of course."

"Please, Cassidy, it's me… It's your Uncle Dario."

"Aw, they don't recognize you, Uncle. Of course, you have become a bit more seasoned since the last time they saw you." Rann laughed—a peculiar and uneven sound, coated with madness.

"Please, let them go," Darien pleaded. "They're just children. *Please.* Don't hurt them."

"Oh, no. No, no, no. We won't hurt them. In fact, now that you're here, we're going to get them out of Last Chapel." He leaned in and whispered, "A war zone is no place for children."

"Where are you taking them?" Merrick asked, with trepidation in his voice.

"These little darlings are going on one more journey. They get to visit the majestic Citadel of the Crimson Fathers. They're always in need of fresh resources to work with there."

"By God, then it's true," Merrick whispered. "They *have* returned." He looked at Rann in desperation and despair. "What have you done?"

"Cassidy, it's me," Darien beseeched him. "Don't you recognize me? Please…"

The children kept glancing from one thing to another, overwhelmed by the threats and dread around them. Whenever their gaze returned to Darien, they seemed confused but also worried.

"So you know of the Crimson Fathers?" Rann took a new interest in Merrick. He squinted. "Just who are you, anyway?"

"He's nobody," Thorne said.

"My Lord," a guard outside the door said in a tremulous voice. "Do you require the children further?"

Rann looked at Cassidy and Cassandra as if he'd forgotten they were there. "No, prepare them for departure."

"No!" Darien screamed. "Don't take them!"

Both children cried as the guard hustled them out the door. It thudded shut to the accompaniment of Darien's agonized pleas.

Rann nodded, and the torturer lumbered over to Thorne's chair. He grabbed Thorne's left index finger and pulled it back.

"Now, Malachi, tell me about the nobody over there," Rann said.

"There's nothing to tell." Thorne gritted his teeth. "He's just an old man who rode with us on the road."

"You lie." Rann nodded again. With a sharp crack, the torturer dislocated the finger. Thorne grimaced and clenched his jaw. Tears filled his eyes.

"Tell me."

Thorne shook his head.

Crack!

This time, he screamed. Sweat poured down his face.

Rann paced back and forth, then stopped. "No, no. This won't work," he said, conversing with himself. "He's too stubborn. Too proud." Rann looked around the circle again. A repulsive smile crept across his face as he remembered Hawkes. "Coals," he instructed the torturer.

Pleas to stop went unheeded. Warner had awakened and stared, horrified, at the cage strapped to his friend's stomach. The rats fidgeted and squirmed.

The torturer, tongs in hand, opened the back half of the cage and thrust the coals from the brazier inside the metal box. He secured it and raised the trapdoor on the end against Hawkes's stomach. The deputy gulped and steeled himself for the pain. Sweat beaded his forehead.

As the metal heated up, the rats panicked and scampered away. They began to claw and nip at the bare abdomen in front of them.

Hawkes screamed.

"Now." Rann grinned at Thorne. "No more lies."

The look of horror etched on the deputy's face made Thorne sick. He couldn't let Tycho die, but he couldn't identify Merrick, either. The choices sat like tumors in his mind.

Hawkes screamed again as the frenzied rodents drew blood and gnawed quicker.

"I'll tell you…"

For a split second, Thorne wasn't sure if he'd heard it or if it had been his imagination. But everyone in the circle looked at Merrick. Thorne's heart sank.

Rann studied Merrick, judging his sincerity, and signaled the torturer to replace the trapdoor. The rats scratched frantically at the wire mesh as the heat intensified. "I'd better like what I hear."

"No," Thorne said to Merrick. "You can't!"

Their eyes met. Apologetic sadness and contented resignation stared back at Thorne. *Just like Jarmarra Ravenwood...* Merrick understood the consequences of the choice he was making. It was an inevitability, something he'd prepared himself for a long time ago.

The no-win decision and his volcanic hatred of Rann surged through Thorne. He struggled at his restraints, cursing and shaking the chair.

"It's all right, Malachi," Merrick said.

"No, it's not! He's going to—"

Merrick nodded. "I'm prepared. A great man named Jesus once said, 'No one takes my life away from me. I lay it down by myself.' The greatest expression of freedom is when we choose to lay down our life for the sake of others." With that, he turned his attention to Rann. "My name is... Well, my former name means little. Now I am called Traugott."

Rann narrowed one eye and looked Merrick over.

"Val, please...don't..." Thorne pleaded.

"It's okay, my boy. Trust me."

Tears of helplessness and rage stung Thorne's eyes.

Rann paced, turned and sized Merrick up again. "You're the man Thorne's been after." He paused, letting thoughts coalesce. "You're the traitor. You're the one who's been spreading heresies about rising up against the Church."

"Yes, that's me."

"No!" Thorne interjected. "No, he isn't! He's not well. He suffered a blow to the head. He—makes things up..."

"Silence!" Rann clopped Thorne in the side of the head with his hand.

Merrick looked straight into Rann's eyes, his voice measured and calm. "I am Traugott, and I confess, fully and freely, that I have done my best to draw people away from the Church's teachings. I have taught them that they should make their own choices, unhindered by Church interference or dictate."

Rann's grin threatened to split his face in half.

"Let these men go. They have no part with me. They've been falsely accused of collaborating with me, but that's not the case. I've been in their custody, and through my own deception and manipulation, I've misled them."

"No! That's...a lie!" Thorne shouted, his voice cracking with emotion.

Merrick ignored him, his eyes never leaving Rann's face. "These men are good servants of the Church. I will gladly give this testimony to your clerk and affix my name to it."

Once more, Rann considered this and after a moment, signaled the torturer to remove the device from Hawkes. "Take Traugott to the other chamber," Rann said. "I want to assure myself of his…truthfulness."

The torturer removed the restraints, tugged Merrick out of the chair by his neck and marched him out of the room.

"Where are you taking him?" Thorne demanded.

Rann ignored him.

"Rann! Answer me!"

But the Witchfinder Imperator closed the door behind him.

"He's mad as a shithouse rat," Warner said when they were alone. "Oh…" He looked at Hawkes. "Sorry, Tycho…"

"No problem." The deputy huffed as he tried to relax. Bloody teeth and claw marks hash-marked his abdomen.

"We've got to get out of here," Thorne said. He tried his restraints again. He thought the right one had loosened somewhat, but then again, that could have just been wishful thinking. His left hand had swelled, and he couldn't budge it inside the restraint cuff.

They all tugged and jerked at their chairs. Warner's left foot loosened enough to gain some leverage, and he succeeded in ripping the restraint away from the chair leg. With a loud curse and a final heave of exertion, Thorne yanked his right arm free. He undid his ankles before releasing his other arm; the hand tingled as the blood rushed into it. He stumbled to the table where Rann had been working. Grabbing a knife, he freed the others.

Cabbott armed himself with an iron bar. Hawkes had the knife. Thorne found a length of chain and wrapped it around his right hand.

Warner released Darien but had to support him. His look told Thorne that he didn't know if Dario would make it or not.

The chamber door opened, and the torturer walked in. An awkward silence followed as prisoners and torturer stared at each other in dumbfounded surprise.

In a blur of motion, Hawkes threw the dagger. The blade sank into the torturer's right eye. He stepped forward, staggered, then pitched over against the iron maiden. A high-pitched, pitiful mewing escaped from his gaping mouth, then silence.

Hawkes vaulted across the room and retrieved the bloody dagger.

"Get Merrick!" Thorne said in a forced whisper.

The old revolutionary's screams drifted up the hallway from the other chamber.

"Hard and fast," Cabbott instructed Hawkes as they crept down the hall toward a closed door. "Don't give them time to think or react. We've got one shot at this."

They burst into the torture chamber, nearly separating the door from its rusty hinges. Merrick lay strapped to a table inclined at a forty-five-degree angle. Rann stood near the top, tightening a head crusher around Merrick's skull. Two guards, shaken from their boredom, stumbled to their feet.

Thorne flew at Rann, brandishing the chain.

Hawkes leapt onto one of the guards, slashing him with the dagger.

Cabbott swung the metal bar at the other astonished guard, catching him in the side of the head. The guard collapsed without uttering a sound. Cabbott took his sword.

Warner helped Darien through the door and steadied him against the wall. "Wait here," he said. He grabbed the iron bar that Cabbott had dropped and followed Thorne.

Rann snarled, his eyes exquisite slivers of hate. He reached for the dagger at his side.

Lips pulled back, exposing clenched teeth, Thorne punched. The blow was meant for the middle of Rann's face, but he shifted and backed up. It caught him in the collarbone, and he hissed like a serpent.

Cabbott drove the sword through the first guard's stomach the moment Hawkes gave him a clear shot. The guard doubled over, howling in agony, and Hawkes helped himself to his sword.

"Watch the door!" Cabbott shouted. "I'll get Merrick!"

Rann backed far enough away to unsheathe his rapier, but before he could raise it to strike, Warner slammed his right arm with the iron bar. The rapier clattered to the floor. Rann yelled in pain, lashing out and punching Warner in the face.

Thorne struck. He pinned Rann to the wall with his left arm and punched him in the stomach. Rann did his best to protect himself, but Thorne was relentless. His arm pistoned back and forth. He connected with stomach, ribs, stomach again.

"We've got Merrick!" Hawkes yelled. Cabbott hauled the old man off the table, threw his arm around his shoulders and stumbled toward the main door. Hawkes did the same with Darien.

Warner swung the bar and barely missed crushing Rann's head against the wall. Thorne hit the ribs again and heard one crack. Rann attempted to double over, but Thorne held him upright. Wheezing, with bloody saliva dripping from his mouth, Rann raised his hands in surrender.

Thorne's face was a twisted mask of rage. Hatred burned in his soul as he watched Rann start to smile. The grin broadened, and Thorne cocked his arm to smash it off his face.

"Never…show your opponent…your weakness." Rann gasped through his blood-flecked smile. His hands dropped out of the air like stones. They caught Thorne's swollen left hand and squeezed.

Light exploded across Thorne's vision. He screamed and went limp. Rann squeezed harder and twisted. Thorne bellowed in pain and fell to his knees.

Warner hesitated, and Rann drove a hand into his throat. The deputy's eyes bulged. He dropped the bar and staggered back, gasping and choking.

Hawkes flung the dagger at Rann's head, but this time, it missed its mark, ricocheting off the wall.

Thorne writhed on the blood-spattered floor, groaning and cradling his left hand. He needed the table to help him get up. Ashen-faced, he blinked repeatedly, his hair hanging in loose, sweaty strands. Warner collapsed onto one knee, struggling for breath.

"Stand…down." Rann grunted. "Or you all die. Right here…right now."

Six guards spilled into the room, weapons drawn.

Thorne slumped against the table, heaving like a wounded bear. Warner stood up on shaking legs and massaged his throat.

"*You—*" Rann said, pointing at Thorne. It seemed like he wanted to say more but stopped himself. He waggled his finger at Thorne as if to say, *Close, but not good enough.* The smile crept back onto his face. He gestured to the guards. "Lock them up."

"My Lord, our cells are full," the lead guard replied.

Rann sighed in exasperation. "Well, can't you squeeze any more in?"

The guard had a half-moon scar from the corner of his eye to his jawline. His dark hair was shorn nearly to the skull. He squinted as he looked at the ceiling. "Three, maybe four, my Lord. That's it until we can clear some of them out."

Rann considered this before breaking into a wide grin. "We need to have another tekoya, then." His face fell as if he'd been presented with crushing news. "But we can't do it today, though… Not tomorrow, either." He pouted like a petulant child before brightening again. "Wednesday! We'll do it Wednesday!" He turned to Thorne and his men.

"I hereby decree," Rann said, "that on Wednesday, July 1st, as Witchfinder Imperator of Last Chapel and surrounding regions, there shall be a tekoya held in the city square for the execution of Malachi Thorne and his men." The smile evaporated. "Now, take them away."

"Your Grace, the cells…" the guard reminded him.

"Yes, yes, of course." Rann stepped between Merrick and Cabbott but looked at Thorne. "As you can imagine, our war with the Communion has kept our dungeon filled. We just have too many people." He leaned forward and lowered his voice. "Don't you just hate when there's too much work to do and you can't savor it all? Anyway, we just don't have room for all of you right now."

"Don't..." Thorne croaked.

"Yes, I'm afraid so," Rann replied, his tone nonchalant. He yanked his dagger from its sheath, spun around and buried the blade in Merrick's stomach. The old man gasped in surprise as much as pain.

"Noooo!" Thorne screamed. He tried to leap forward, but guards held him tight.

Rann put his hand on Merrick's shoulder as if greeting an old friend and jerked the dagger—once, twice—up through the abdomen. Blood cascaded over the knife handle and Rann's hand. He ripped the knife up once again, the blade striking breastbone.

Tears streamed down Thorne's pale cheeks, and he gasped in horror.

Rann released the dagger and Merrick's shoulder at the same time. The old man coughed blood; his bulging eyes glazed, and he crumpled into Warner's arms.

Thorne dropped his head, repeating, "No, no, no..."

Rann smiled at the guards. "Well, now we should have enough room." They stared at him in stunned silence. Once more, his smile was erased. He spat on Merrick's body. "Get these traitorous bastards out of my sight."

29

MAIDEN

This was the first time Teska Vaun had been inside the remnants of the Dome—a thick plot of foliage beneath arched metal ribs that were said to have once contained hundreds of glass panes. Inside the perimeter, the foliage grew denser, forming an organic canopy over its pathways, which allowed occasional shafts of sunlight filter through. The ceiling of verdant leaves offered cool shade. Hundreds of birds called and sang; the aromas of pine and loam, bahreggia nuts and mimosa intermingled.

Everything around the Dome grew wild and untended, like woodlands never touched by any human presence. Teska knew this wasn't the case; however, many members of the Communion found safety and respite here. So, too, did those who had been forced from their homes by the war.

She followed a wide path among the thick-boled trees and couldn't shake the feeling of being watched. She felt like a small fish in an emerald sea. She had no doubt that predators lurked in the depths. She squared her shoulders and tried to force the feeling away. This was the easy part compared to what she risked next.

She'd never been a religious person. Until her adolescent years, she'd attended to the rituals of the Church with her family. But her mother's death had left her at the mercy of her father and brothers. The Church never came to her aid. Her father and brothers received no punishment for what they did to her. There had been no justice. So, at the age of fourteen, she had poisoned them, gathered her belongings and never looked back.

A bitter but familiar taste settled in her mouth. Her flight to freedom had not gone as she'd imagined. Instead of hope and possibility, she'd found a succession of men no different than those she'd left behind. Liberation brought chances to make the same mistakes over and over again.

Her gift had manifested not long after she'd left home, days after her first sanguinelle. She'd first thought it a punishment from God for murdering her family. But over time, and with experimentation, she'd learned the limits of her newfound ability. For as long as she could hold her breath, she could remain unseen by the human eye. It hadn't taken long before her gift had become a way of surviving what her so-called lovers had put her through.

Her relationship with Marco Bursey had been pleasant and real. Many times, she'd imagined them striking out into the west, forging a new life together, facing whatever they discovered with fierce passion and relentless hope.

But Marco was dead.

The reminder pricked her heart, and the face of Solomon Warner coalesced in her mind. She'd been desperate to avenge Marco's death, even though she knew Warner himself hadn't executed him. Unable to strike the Church, the deputy had been her most obvious—and accessible—choice for revenge. But that burning hatred had dwindled like the dying glow of a single ember. At first, this had shocked her.

Her attraction to Malachi Thorne had been so sudden, the rush of emotions so unexpected, that she'd struggled to cling to her vendetta. The longer she'd been in their custody and the longer she'd spent around Malachi, the less Warner had occupied her thoughts. She'd tried to fight it. She'd kept Marco's image in her mind as motivation, but even that had slipped away in Malachi's presence.

She feared for him now. Word from the Communion's sources said he and his men were in grave danger. Talk of their impending executions had spread like wildfire.

The light beneath the leafy canopy dimmed. It was like walking into dusk. Heavy fronds overhung the path; creeping vines intertwined with roots and stems, pressing the foliage in upon her. The sensation of being watched intensified, and now she could make out the bodies of serpents draped among the branches. Their golden eyes never moved yet followed her every step. She suppressed a shudder and hurried along. Her destination lay ahead.

The path opened into a circular glade, the sky unseen through the foliage that domed overhead. It was darker here and felt more like a cave illuminated by torches.

Two women, one bald and the other wearing a long braid, guarded the entrance to the glade. They nodded and let her pass.

Teska walked into the center of the glade. Ahead of her, on a throne made of roots and leaves, sat a woman. Teska had been instructed to lower her eyes and show deference, but the woman's beauty captivated her. Teska found herself staring, enchanted, at the perfect vision before her, even though she couldn't see the face.

Four women stood in a curved line to the right of the throne; four more stood to the left. They were of varying sizes and heights but all wore the same sparkling green gown. A ninth woman stood in front of the throne. "What is it you wish, Child?"

"I—I seek an audience with the Maiden," Teska said without her usual courage. She tore her eyes from the figure on the throne and remembered to bow.

"You are Nahoru'brexia," one of the women on the left said flatly. "You may approach."

Teska walked several paces closer to the throne, eyes downcast.

"Speak, Child of the Moon," the Maiden said. Her silky, delectable voice shifted the three veils that covered her face. Her eyes—small but penetrating and laced with cruelty—burned through the veils. Hair the color of midnight fell thick and strong to the top of her breasts. No wrinkles or blemishes marred her flawless skin. An extravagant silver crown rested upon her head. She radiated youth and sexuality.

"Thank you, Maiden Mallumo." Teska summoned more courage than she felt. "I…" She hesitated, trying to shape the words that held such gravity.

The women beside the throne looked at her, but she had the chilly impression that they also looked at something within her.

"I seek a favor, although I know I'm not worthy to ask," she finally stated.

"Your training has progressed well, Teska Vaun," the Maiden purred. "But there is still much to learn. State your appeal"

Teska swallowed the stone in her throat. Her heart thudded inside her chest. "There's a man—"

The women beside the throne tilted their heads in unison. The motion distracted Teska and raised gooseflesh on her arms. She rubbed them.

"I would ask—that is—" She fumbled her words, confused and flustered.

"Be calm," the Maiden commanded in a honeyed tone. "You are among your own. Fear not."

Teska nodded, swallowed again and started over, more in control. "Zadicus Rann and the Church captured a group of men on Friday. They've been subjected to the Ordeal, not for confession or information's sake, but because of Rann's mad cruelty. I know these men. I've traveled with them. I believe they could aid us in the war."

The Maiden said nothing.

"I would ask, Great Maiden of the Three, that the Communion…rescue these men." Her voice wavered as it faded away. She lowered her gaze and stood deferentially.

"Who are these men?" the woman in front of the throne asked. She was plump, with a pinched face and double chin. She crossed her arms over her heavy bosom.

"Why do you deem them so important that you would risk our limited re-sources?" a woman to the left added.

A deep and reluctant sigh escaped Teska's chest. *All right, moment of truth…*

"The men are—*were*—servants of the Church. But no longer," she added hastily. "They're wanted by the Church the same as us."

The Maiden's eyes narrowed. "You ask me to aid our *enemies*?" Contempt dripped from her voice.

"Of course not, Most Blessed Maiden. They're considered traitors and her-etics. The Church will kill them as surely as they will kill us."

A woman on the right sneered at her. "What do we care?"

"There is something you are not saying, Child," the Maiden said. "Some-thing you hold back. Tell me."

Teska sighed again. "It's…Malachi Thorne and his men."

Not a single leaf moved anywhere within the glade. Teska felt every pair of eyes glaring at her. The temperature dropped, and her skin prickled once more. She wanted to turn and flee, but fear—or stubbornness—kept her in place.

"Malachi Thorne?" the Maiden exclaimed, her veils rippling as she leaned forward and clutched the arms of her throne. "Be careful, Child. You tread on dangerous ground."

"Please, it's not like that. The Malachi Thorne you knew has changed! He supports the cause of Traugott, the freethinker. I've been with them. Hells, I near-ly lost my life alongside them! I believe they can aid us against the Church."

"Do you expect us to believe that the Hammer of the Heiromonarch no longer serves the Church?" The plump woman sneered. "I am disappointed in you, Teska Vaun. You have been deceived."

"No, I haven't!" she yelled, pointing at the woman. "And I don't give two shits what *you* believe!" The others raised their eyebrows at the rebuke. "I've gone along with Neris and come here. I've listened to your history and teaching. I've learned a few things. But I'm not a pampered little flower playing with paper dolls! I'm not stupid, and I'm not deceived! I know what the fuck I'm talking about." She snapped her mouth shut, realizing what she'd just done.

Part of her screamed that she should look away, kneel down, ask forgive-ness. But another part—the part that had helped her survive all these years—continued to burn. She put her hands on her hips.

The women on either side of the throne gasped and murmured among themselves. The woman in front, her faced even more pinched than before, turned and whispered to the Maiden. Teska folded her arms and waited. If they were going to strike her down and turn her into a fucking frog or something, she hoped they'd just get on with it. Her courage and attitude rose up. She didn't care anymore.

The Maiden sat back and looked at her. "You know the situation we face. The Fifth Order has revealed itself with the Crusaders and threatens to exterminate us all. We are fewer now than ever before. We must act wisely and cautiously." She paused. "My sisters tell me that we shall move underground soon, to regroup and regain our power. This is why the Nahoru'brexia are so important. You must know how to lead the Communion when the time comes. We cannot spare the power to investigate your claims regarding Malachi Thorne. Everything we have is being used against the Fifth Order."

"But if we don't act now, he'll be executed!" Her hands curled into desperate fists. "Rann has scheduled another tekoya for tomorrow."

"Let the servants of the Church perish," a woman on the right said.

"It's only fitting," another added.

"The fucking tekoya also has brexia in it!" Teska fumed. "You're just going to let them be killed, too—like the others you've lost recently?"

Eyes widened; faces reddened. The Maiden stood up—impossibly tall compared to the throne. It seemed that her crown nearly brushed the lower leaves of the canopy overhead.

"I-I'm sorry," Teska whispered. "I spoke without thinking." What else was new? Her mouth was going to get her killed someday—or right now.

The Maiden's eyes seared her. Teska could almost feel their heat in the chill of the glade.

"If we planned a rescue," the woman in front said, "it would be for our own—not for any man."

"But he can help us!"

"So you claim."

"One such as Malachi Thorne would never willingly betray his beloved Church," a woman on the left said.

"That's just it!" Teska threw her hands in the air. "He *didn't* turn his back on them. They turned on him! Rann set him up." She started to pace.

"Then such a betrayal can only serve our purposes," the Maiden replied. "The enemy of my enemy is my friend."

"Look, I know it's a crazy idea. I know the Communion has never helped the Church. But this is different. We aren't helping the Church. We're making ourselves stronger."

"By bringing *men* into the fold?" The plump woman scoffed. "Ridiculous."

The Maiden raised a hand. "Teska Vaun, what do you believe Malachi Thorne and his men could offer us?"

"Well, his connections. His fervor. Obviously his knowledge of the Church—its inner workings."

"We already know that," a woman on the right said smugly.

"And you're full of shit." Teska whirled around and pointed at the speaker. "You just said you don't have the power to investigate my claims about Thorne. Don't try to tell me you know all the intimate details of the Church."

The woman glowered and fumed.

"If Thorne has been excommunicated, he'll have a grudge against the Church for not standing up for him. They've thrown him to the wolves, and from what I know of him, he'll be happy to help bring down whatever the Fifth Order is trying to do."

The plump woman crossed her arms. "And what do you know of him? What is your relationship to Malachi Thorne?"

Teska hesitated. "I told you: I was his prisoner. He caught me while I was trying to kill his deputy."

The Maiden's eyes pierced Teska's soul. "You love him, do you not?"

Once more, she felt every eye picking her apart. She wanted to shake it off but couldn't. Shame flushed her cheeks, and she lowered her gaze to the thick carpet of grass. She wanted to stomp over and punch every smug woman in a green gown.

The Maiden sat down and closed her eyes. She stroked the top of her leg with a long fingernail. The other women glared at Teska but said nothing. A green-and-white serpent slithered from among the roots and coiled around the Maiden's shin. It stared at Teska, too.

After several moments of tense silence, the Maiden opened her eyes. "You have made your request, Teska Vaun. This audience is concluded."

"That's it?"

The Maiden nodded, her hair perfectly black in the half-light. "The Three-Who-Are-One have decided. We cannot risk what resources remain to agree to your request. The safety and survival of the Communion comes first. Now is not the time."

"But they'll die!" Teska pleaded.

"Yes, they will." The Maiden paused, then added, "And for your loss, I am sorry, Teska Vaun. All of us"—she swept her hand across the glade—"know the bliss and agony of love. But we are too weak and too few at this moment. Your boon is denied."

"Please—"

"Go, Child of the Moon. Continue your studies."

With a curse and huff of frustration, Teska stormed from the glade, fists clenched, ponytail bouncing. Behind her, the Maiden watched her go, noting the sheer anger in her body language. Teska Vaun would lead them to salvation. Or to ruin.

30

HELLCAGE

WEDNESDAY, JULY 1, 999 AE

Thorne rode inside the first wooden cart that rattled along in the tekoya procession. Cabbott and Darien occupied the second cart, with Hawkes and Warner in the third. The last held several women accused of witchcraft. Instead of the bentanni, everyone remained dressed in their own ripped and soiled garments. Despite Rann's maniacal glee regarding tekoyas, he had turned them into a parody of their original intent.

Heavy clouds drifted in from the west. They offered the promise of less heat today—a fact Thorne found ironic considering their ultimate destination.

Zadicus Rann rode up beside Thorne's cart, a triumphant smirk on his face. "Things are going to get very…heated soon." He chuckled. "I wanted to see if you had any last words."

Thorne glared at him. "Go to hells."

"That's it?" Rann asked, feigning injury. "I expected more from you. I thought Valerian Merrick had taught you better than that." He shook his head. "Imagine my surprise when I discovered that Traugott was *really* Valerian Merrick! Would've never expected that in a hundred years."

Thorne frowned; the right side of his face flushed. The left side remained covered with yellowing bruises. "I'm going to kill you, Rann." His tone was clipped and cold as he stared straight ahead at the cart carrying Merrick's corpse.

Thorne stared at the body and felt as if a dull knife had sawed a hole out of him. His soul ached with the knowledge that he'd gotten Merrick back only to lose him again—and in such a brutal, hateful manner. Merrick had prepared himself to die when he assumed the role and identity of Traugott, but Thorne wasn't prepared. Just like in Toadvine.

The procession turned a corner onto a wider street heading east. Last Chapel's original town square had been obliterated in the war, so Rann had established a new one near the Black River. The proximity, he claimed, made it easier to dispose of a heretic's ashes.

"Seems congregants have grown tired of your performances," Thorne said. A smattering of people milled about the street. Judging by their expressions, none of them wanted to be there. Even the balconies sat unused.

Rann glanced around in disgust. "They'll come out. The Crusaders will see to it that they enjoy the tekoya."

Now Thorne laughed. "Yes, I'm sure they thrill to being forced to participate in your madness."

Rann smiled and ran his hand over his bristly hair. "Not only will they witness the execution of five heretics and traitors, along with several witches, I intend to tell them how Valerian Merrick was also a traitor and a liar. I'll show them that one of the Church's greatest Witchfinders was nothing more than a common criminal." He sniffed arrogantly. "Our new millennium will be free of such duplicity."

Constables and deputies shoved people out of buildings and into the streets. Conflicted emotions and half-hearted responses followed the Crusaders' commands. For the first time in his life, Thorne saw pity on the faces of those who looked at him. "What have you done to these congregants?" he asked in quiet sorrow.

"We've established something new in Last Chapel."

"Who's 'we'?"

Rann turned in the saddle, something mad and zealous dancing in his eyes. He tapped his new rank insignia. "We are the Fifth Order."

"There is no Fifth Order."

"Oh, but there is." Rann turned back to face the procession. "The Fifth Order has been around for much longer than you could imagine."

"Then why have I never heard of them?"

"No one has heard of them. Theirs has been the unseen guiding hand of the Church."

"And how long has this been going on?"

"Centuries."

Thorne laughed.

"I don't expect you to understand," Rann said. "You're the worst kind of heretic and traitor. You come from within the Church's own ranks."

"And what about you? You've turned your back on your oath, the Code and the Church. You torture and kill without law or order—"

"The Fifth Order is the law now."

"—and you insist on some half-baked idea of a secret society within the Church!"

But hadn't Merrick said the same thing about the Crimson Fathers? Yes—but they were just a legend. Rann actually believed in the existence of this Fifth Order, and worse, thought himself part of it.

"Can't you see, Rann? You're sick. You need help. Release us, and I'll see that you're treated well."

"Did you know there's no Heiromonarch?" Rann asked conversationally.

"There's no—? What? What're you—"

"Really. There's no Heiromonarch. Hasn't been for many years."

"That's ridiculous," Thorne said, steadying himself as the cart thudded over a hole in the road. "I saw the Heiromonarch last year at—"

"No, you didn't." Rann smiled. "You saw what the Fifth Order wanted you to see. They rule the Church. They make all the decisions. When they came to power, they disposed of the Heiromonarch."

Thorne stared at Rann, who waved at congregants like some benevolent lord. He was completely insane. He had convinced himself—or someone else had convinced him—that all of this was true. How could there be no Heiromonarch? Thorne had seen him! And how could some unknown cabal run the Church as Rann claimed?

"In the early 800s, the Fifth Order took control," Rann continued, raising a hand to halt Thorne's protest. "And before you say it, the Order uses a simulacrum of the Heiromonarch for public events. Haven't you noticed that he appears less frequently in public?"

"Simulacrum of the—? You've lost your mind!" The Heiromonarch only made one or two appearances a year, if Thorne's memory served. He'd thought it was because he was old or sickly… "What does this Fifth Order have to gain? What do they want?"

More people lined the street as they neared the square. Most looked down or away from the procession.

They were in mortal terror. There was no way Rann could've done this on his own. He was crafty and cruel, but even he didn't have the resources to dominate an entire city. Thorne watched the Crusaders. *And where the hells did they come from?* Rann certainly couldn't have recruited and trained them all. A deputy caught his eye, and his expression pleaded with Thorne. Even his Order was cowed. He suppressed a shiver in the morning sun.

Could Rann actually be telling the truth?

"Oh, that's simple." Rann smoothed his mustache. "The Fifth Order is going to establish and lead a perfect new society."

"A new society? We're already a society."

"Ah, but not a *perfect* one. The Fifth Order will remake Church and society." Rann smiled blissfully. "Just like we've done here in Last Chapel."

"Did this Fifth Order instruct you to arrest me in Rimlingham?"

"Oh, yes. You'd gained some popularity in the upper echelons, and the Order foresaw this could be a problem. They wanted to send a message to the Church that no one is beyond their reach."

"And what of congregants who're beyond their reach?" Thorne asked. "Surely this cabal can't expect absolute compliance."

"The Order's preparing for that as well. Those who resist will be reeducated in special compliance camps. They'll learn to obey the Fifth Order in all things." Rann's icy tone contained the finality of a deep grave.

Thorne thought of Merrick's discussions and lessons. His mentor's ideas no longer seemed so radical and incomprehensible. If what Rann claimed was true, then the Church that Thorne had honored and served his entire life had been nothing but a façade. All he thought was real—had it all just been some manifestation perpetuated by this Fifth Order? Had all his work been for nothing—or at least for the wrong reasons? Warner's question weaseled back into his mind: *"How many people have we put to death who were innocent?"*

Despite a lack of food and water, Thorne's stomach rolled. He fought the urge to throw up as the cart rattled and swayed beneath him. More looks of pity followed him down the street. The market square came into view. Thorne hung his head as Rann's madness and savagery threatened to pull him under.

Their conveyances rolled to a stop near the center of the square alongside a device that Thorne had never seen before.

"It's what I call the Hellcage," Rann said with a proud grin. "A fitting end for heretics."

The Hellcage sat on a round stone platform, similar to a millstone, in the middle of a pile of straw and timber. Beneath it, a short column descended into a smaller stone. Five wooden beams extended like spokes from the bottom stone. A Crusader stood at each. A circle of well-trod dirt showed where the Crusaders pushed the lower stone in a circle, rotating the Hellcage.

"Your idea?" Thorne asked.

"Oh, no. I can't take credit for it. The Fifth Order devised it and had the Crusaders build it before I came here. You've got to admit, it's genius." He smiled. "This way, everyone can have a good view during a tekoya!"

Thorne's stomach lurched once more as the trembling, frantic women were hauled from their wagon and herded up a short ramp into the Hellcage. Rann rode toward the Judgment Seat on the northern end of the square. Thorne's eyes followed him and studied the grandstand. Beneath its colorful awning sat a clerk, a Crusader and in the dark recesses of the back, two robed figures.

Thorne was the last prisoner marched onto the circular platform. Bonds cut, he was thrust inside the Hellcage. The door clanged shut. A Crusader secured it with a thick chain and padlock. The cage reeked of burnt flesh. The top and bottom were solid metal; the four walls were made of horizontal and vertical metal bands.

Four of the seven women were middle-aged or older; the others were quite young. Thorne couldn't remember ever seeing a girl put to death as young as the one who crouched in the corner. She couldn't be more than twelve or thirteen. She hugged her knees to her chest and stared at the floor.

Like everything else in Last Chapel, the tekoya had been perverted. Gone were the trumpeters and minstrel bands. Children clung fearfully to their parent's legs instead of running and playing. The two meager vendor carts did no business. The crowd was sparse and nervous as forced participation replaced the usually festive atmosphere. Instead of the colorful banners of the Four Orders, a single purple banner proclaimed *DOMINION*.

Rann took his place in the cathedra, and the Crusader stepped forward.

"Attention!" he bellowed. "Our glorious leader, Witchfinder Imperator of Last Chapel and surrounding regions, Zadicus Rann." The Crusader nodded, gave an officious bow and stepped aside.

With a magnanimous gesture of appreciation, Rann stood and walked to the railing.

"Congregants of Last Chapel, we're gathered here today because the laws of our land—and of the Divine Church—as defined by the sacred Testament, have been broken. Within the Hellcage are seven who have congressed with the Archfiend of the Twelfth Plane and the Enodia Communion. Their malefic works are legion, and they have been found guilty on every count.

"But we also have a special treat today. Among them are five men who have served as members of the Paracletian Order. They're apostates to our faith. They have abrogated their responsibilities, and they have damned the souls of innocents with their heresies. These men were seduced by the fanatical ideas of the man called Traugott."

Rann signaled to a Crusader standing at the edge of the crowd. He stepped forward, tugging a small cart behind him. Once out in the open, he tipped it backward. A body and bunch of straw tumbled to the ground.

Thorne clenched his jaw and closed his eyes to keep his tears from spilling over as Merrick's pallid, gutted form stared sightlessly at the sky.

"This," Rann exclaimed, "is what remains of the heretic Traugott."

Sparse, muted murmurs spread among the crowd.

"How did one such as he seduce these servants of the Church, you ask? It was simple: Traugott was not his real name. This man was Valerian Merrick, at one time a staunch defender of the Church, an Imperator of noble renown, who succumbed to evil. He despised the Church and spread heresies. Valerian Merrick denied his faith and even his own soul and has led many into the Twelve Planes of Hell with him, including these men before you today."

Thorne gripped the bands and stared out at the crowd. "He's lying! Valerian Merrick was no traitor or heretic!" Anger boiled in him, momentarily overcoming his grief and the looming cloud of death.

"You see!" Rann's voice climbed over Thorne's. "They've been corrupted, and even in the face of sure damnation, they spout falsehoods and wickedness! When the Church enters the glorious new millennium of faith and prosperity, there will be no room for heresy."

Rann raised his arms as if offering a benediction. "This tekoya is hereby carried out by the authority of the Fifth Order. Let all that transpires here today be recorded for the salvation of our souls, according to the grace of the Church. Amen."

"Amen," the crowd said in resigned defeat. Most half-heartedly signed themselves; few looked at the cage in the center of the square.

"Begin!" Rann exclaimed.

A middle-aged woman broke from the crowd, screaming and crying. "My baby! My baby! Please have mercy! She's only a little girl!"

Two Crusaders left their posts at the beams to intercept her, but she slipped between them. She dashed up the ramp and reached through the bands. The young girl in the corner leapt up and grasped her hands.

"Here, use it!" the woman whispered, patting the young girl's hand. She pleaded and wept as the Crusaders removed her from the platform. Inside the cage, the girl slumped in the corner again, her hands clenched together.

The Crusaders laid burning torches to the kindling. The straw snapped and crackled, catching quickly, feeding the pitch-covered wood. Oily smoke billowed into the air. The Crusaders grunted and pushed, and the Hellcage began to turn.

Cabbott, Hawkes and Warner searched furiously for any weakness in the bands but found nothing. Darien checked the floor, but other than some minor rippling from the heat, all was solid. The fire spread along the sides of the cage, forcing the terrified women to bunch in the middle.

The floor began to heat, and the women's hysteria grew. They clung to each other, hopping from one bare foot to another. The young girl had left the smoky corner and moved to the door. She had her back to everyone and seemed to be busy with something. Thorne stopped his frantic search for a way out and edged sideways to get a better look.

Her arms were stuck between the bands, and she dug into the padlock with a rusted key. She worked with calm determination, seemingly unaffected by the mounting heat.

Thorne spun around to his men. "Create a diversion!"

"A diversion?" Warner squinted his one good eye.

"Yes! Get everybody looking at us, not the door!" Thorne leapt to the side of the cage currently facing the Judgment Seat. "Rann! You son of a bitch!" he bellowed. "You're the traitor!"

"Bastard!" Hawkes showed his middle finger. "Your mother sucks off midgets!"

Cabbott moved to the side facing the crowd. "You're being lied to! You've got to stand up and take back your city!"

Warner hammered on the bands opposite the door. He cursed and screamed, waving his arms through them until the flames forced him back.

As the platform turned, Thorne addressed the crowd: "Zadicus Rann and the Fifth Order are evil! There's sinister magic afoot! That's how they've gained control over you!"

Darien doubled over coughing as the smoke thickened. The Hellcage heated up, accompanied by a faint sizzling.

The padlock snapped open with a quiet pop. The young girl flung it aside, ripped the chain loose and threw the door open.

"Malachi! *Now!*" Hawkes yelled as he dove through the door. He hit the stone just beyond the flames, tucked into a forward roll and shot to his feet. With a running leap, he cleared the ramp and kicked the nearest Crusader in the head. Both tumbled to the ground. Hawkes vaulted to his feet in an instant.

Panic propelled the women through the door, skipping and hopping over the flames. They tumbled off the platform like ants from a disturbed hill, running and swatting at their burning garments.

"Get them!" Rann bellowed, his face splotched with rage. "Kill them all!"

Cabbott and Warner dragged Darien from the Hellcage. There was space between the lower wheel and the ground, and Darien scuttled into it.

Thorne pushed the young girl out, amazed to see that she didn't flinch when crossing the flames. Intense heat washed over his body. He ran and jumped, singeing the hair on his arms and legs.

Hawkes kicked the Crusader as he stood up, but it had little effect.

Cabbott and Warner stood beside the platform.

The freed prisoners scattered across the square in every direction. Crusaders pursued them.

Thorne launched himself off the stone wheel. He buried his knee in the back of the Crusader facing Hawkes. They went down, and Thorne rolled over and off the body. Hawkes yanked a dagger off the Crusader's hip. He flipped it in the air, caught it by the handle and slammed the blade into the Crusader's neck. He pulled it free, and blood pumped into the air as the body convulsed.

Coughing the smoke from his lungs, Thorne stood and looked around. He estimated at least twenty Crusaders. A group of women, armed with swords, ran through the crowd in his direction. Cabbott looked at him, doubt clouding his face.

Hawkes panted. "Fight or run? We're fucked regardless."

The women converged on them—a small ripple ahead of the cresting wave of Crusaders. They tossed their swords to Cabbott, Hawkes and Warner, smiling grimly. All three men grabbed the weapons, perplexed, and looked at Thorne.

The women drew short swords and daggers from their sides.

The ring of Crusaders tightened around the Hellcage.

Something moved at the corner of Thorne's eye. Something tugged at his hand.

"I hope you haven't forgotten how to fight," a familiar voice said in his ear.

Teska Vaun grinned and pressed a saber into his hand. She winked at him, red hair flying, held her breath, and vanished.

Adrenaline surged through Thorne's body. His emotions careened from fury to numbness to surprise and around again. Teska had just materialized out of thin air. A bunch of women had just given his men weapons. What in the name of all that was holy was happening? Confounded but hard-pressed, he clenched his jaw.

"Kill them all!" Rann screamed again, pounding the railing with his fist.

Thorne pivoted to face the grandstand, his confusion giving way to rage. His vision turned red with hatred and fury. He gripped the saber so tightly his knuckles whitened.

"Did you miss me?" the familiar voice asked.

Movement again at the corner of his eye.

He turned. Teska smiled at him, dimples showing, her short sword ready.

He had so many things to say, but nothing made sense in his mind.

"What?" she asked. "You not happy to see me?"

"I…"

"Come on. We need to move. Bad shit's coming."

He found his voice. "Where the hells did you go?"

"What? When?"

"In Nashton." He glared at her through the smoke.

"Didn't you get my note?"

"What note? You just up and left."

Hawkes backed up to them. "Hate to break this up, but we've got trouble. Big, tall, ugly trouble…"

The Crusaders closed fast, less than twenty yards away.

"We've got to get going." Teska's tone struck him as the same she'd used just before the Vulanti'nacha attack. She pulled Thorne's arm. "I left you a note. On Gamaliel's saddle."

"I didn't get any note. Why did you leave? Why didn't you at least—"

The woman closest to Hawkes—who looked to be in her midtwenties with spiky blond hair—interrupted. "Teska, we're out of time."

"No shit," Hawkes deadpanned.

"She's not talking about the Crusaders," Teska snapped.

"How did you end up in Last Chapel?" Thorne asked, more confused and angry than before.

Teska grabbed his arm and spun him around to face her. He looked down into her wide hazel eyes, and his heart expanded. Her beauty shone through the dust and soot on her cheeks. He hadn't forgotten what she looked like—far from it—but now he realized just how incomplete and shallow his memories were compared to the real thing. "Malachi, please, I'll tell you everything later. Right now, we've got to go."

He stood transfixed but nodded.

The snarling Crusaders were within ten yards. Thorne, his constable and deputies squared their shoulders alongside blondes, brunettes and raven-haired women. The Hellcage, consumed by flames on every side, stood at their backs.

The Crusaders attacked.

Swords clanged, glinting off one another, parrying and slicing. Thorne, his men and the women stayed between the spokes, as close to the burning wheel as the heat allowed. While it restricted their movements, the Crusaders could only strike from one direction and only in limited numbers.

Hawkes and the woman with spiky hair filled the space between two beams, barely holding their own against two Crusaders. Cabbott and Warner did the same between their beams. The other women had spread out so that someone stood between every spoke. Grunts and curses mixed with the crackling flames, continually interspersed with the grating ring of metal on metal.

"What's…with the sky?" Warner yelled as he parried and reestablished his footing.

Cabbott puffed. "Just that…storm we've seen coming…all morning."

"No, it's not!" a woman with short braids yelled. "It's too late—"

The sky grew ashen. The clouds and sun remained visible but faint and tinted, as if viewed through a dark glass.

"Shit…" Teska said between heavy breaths. "We weren't supposed to be here when this happened."

Thorne stepped away from a gutting strike. The sky darkened; a strong wind blew against them.

The clouds disappeared, and the sun dwindled into little more than a guttering match head. Around the perimeter of the square, the buildings dimmed and disappeared from sight as the gray turned to black.

Everyone stopped fighting and looked around. The wind whipped cloaks, dust and hair in all directions. The light grew dusky and uneven, like a sandstorm of charcoal dust. Figures were hazy, indistinct. It was as if some giant had plopped a massive lid over them.

"What is this?" Thorne asked Teska.

"Uh, Boss… There's somethin' up there." Warner pointed upward.

Inky black shapes, vaguely human in form, twisted through the swirling air. They flew in descending, ever-tightening circles.

Teska edged closer to Thorne. "That's our backup. The Witch of Darkness has sent the Maldormo."

"Which is what?" he asked, his voice sinking.

"Servants, agents—nobody really knows for sure. Only *She* can command them. Name means 'Dark Forlorn' if you're curious. It's said that those who displease Her become one."

"And they're on your side?"

"More or less."

"What's that supposed to mean?"

She looked at him with consternation. "It means they'll attack anything and everything within the dome of darkness. They don't differentiate between friend or enemy. Everyone is a target to the Maldormo."

31

ONSLAUGHT

WEDNESDAY, JULY 1, 999 AE

I f the Twelve Planes of Hell did exist, Thorne felt sure this dome of shadows had to be one. He stood at the base of the Hellcage platform, shielding his eyes from the swirling dust and smoke.

Crusaders battled the Maldormo—ebony emaciated beings with leathery wings, long claws and whip-like barbed tails. Their hairless heads were topped with two long, curved horns set amid a ring of several smaller ones—a piercing crown befitting such horrors. A round, heavily fanged maw was their only facial feature. Other than the flapping of their wings, they made no sound at all. They dove out of the sky, twisting and turning. Talons raked across armor; tails lashed through cloth and cloak. Two worked to lift a Crusader off the ground.

"Stay down!" Teska shouted. "The more you move around, the more you'll attract their attention."

"I'm not staying here." Thorne's jaw was set. "I'm going after Rann."

"You can't! The Maldormo—"

"I'll take my chances. I'm not letting that bastard get away."

Hawkes swatted and hacked at the Maldormo that tormented him. Despite their human size, they moved swiftly, and Hawkes had trouble fending them off. One crouched on a fallen Crusader's back. Its claw dug furiously into the armor while the other wrapped around his screaming head, pulling it back.

Cabbott and Warner stood back-to-back. They had better luck keeping the creatures at bay. Around them, Crusaders hacked off black limbs that quivered and twitched after they hit the ground. Black blood coated their broadswords. A high-pitched scream tore through the wind. A Crusader plummeted out of the air and smashed into the dirt.

Darien crept out from underneath the stone platform. He crouched low and shuffled past Thorne and Vaun, shielding his face from the gritty wind.

"Dario!" Thorne yelled. "What're you doing?"

The old man looked in his direction. Despite his dark skin, he was pale and shaken. "I'm going to find the children," he yelled through the wind. "Rann's got them. He has to have them."

Thorne couldn't miss the desperation in his clerk's voice. He nodded. "Come on, then. I'm heading that way myself."

All the women took shelter beneath the platform, giving the Maldormo more targets among the Crusaders. A brunette yelled as Vaun stood up: "Teska! What're you doing?"

"I'm going with them. Don't wait for me. That's an order. As soon as you have an opening, get out of here."

The woman nodded.

Thorne held his sword aloft and tried to guide Darien with his left hand. It still hurt even though Cabbott had reset the fingers yesterday. Teska hurried beside them for a moment, then disappeared.

Three Maldormo now circled around Hawkes.

"We gotta help him!" Warner shouted over his shoulder.

Cabbott grunted. "Can we edge over that way?"

"Yeah, just follow me."

The Maldormo pulled back, flitting and hovering in the air. The wind fueled the flames; the entire platform had become an inferno. Smoke plumed up only to be ripped to shreds by the wind.

Cabbott and Warner made it to Hawkes. Claw marks crisscrossed his exposed arms. He panted, coated in sweat and dust, his body spattered with red and black blood.

"How many we got left?" Warner asked. He looked at the dead Crusader with the ripped-open back.

"Crusaders or demons?" Hawkes replied.

"Both!"

"Hard to tell." Hawkes looked up into the gray haze at the creatures. "I'd say at least two dozen or so."

"At least there are fewer Crusaders now—maybe eight or ten," Cabbott said as he slashed a creature away.

"Where's Boss goin'?"

Thorne and Darien hustled toward the dome wall. Vaun appeared out of nowhere, grabbed Thorne's arm, and the trio stepped through the swirling dark barrier and disappeared.

The Maldormo attacked again.

They swept down in waves, the first group a churning black battering ram. They collided into every man standing, knocking them off their feet. Several Maldormo suffered deep cuts in the attack, and they writhed on the ground, spurting blood but offering no cries of pain.

Before anyone could get to their feet, the second wave hit. Groups of Maldormo surrounded every fallen man, black talons slashing, lamprey-like mouths ripping away chunks of flesh.

Thorne, Darien and Vaun crossed into sunlight so bright it hurt their eyes. Squinting, Thorne spotted Rann staring solemnly at the dome. A malicious grin spread across his face when he saw Thorne.

"Help Dario," Thorne said, handing his friend off to Teska, never taking his eyes off Rann.

Hawkes managed to roll over and leap to his feet. He bent over to pick up his sword when something crashed into the side of his head. He fell over and tried to blink away the spots at the edge of his vision. A Crusader splattered with sticky ichor stood over him, his foot on Hawkes's sword.

Warner fought like a madman, barely keeping the Maldormo away. Cabbott climbed to his feet. He faced a Crusader in front of him and a Maldormo behind.

Two Crusaders pinned a wiggling Maldormo to the ground with a sword; elsewhere, another Crusader bent a creature over his knee, snapping its spine. Two Maldormo dropped a Crusader on top of the Hellcage.

Hawkes twisted away from the Crusader's swing and found himself between two poles. His back hit the hot stone platform. The Crusader swung again and missed; Hawkes slipped under a pole and into the adjacent space. He grabbed a burning log from the fire and swung it at the Crusader's head. The Crusader caught the log in midair and yanked it away.

Warner fell beneath three Maldormo. Taking a leg and both arms, they hauled him into the air.

Cabbott lunged at the Maldormo, his sword slicing through wing membrane. The creature shrank back. Cabbott started to turn when the Crusader drove his sword into his exposed side. The old constable screamed, dropped his sword and fell to his knees. The Crusader leveled his broadsword against the side of Cabbott's neck, but then had to fend off the Maldormo instead.

Hawkes dodged the Crusader's slashing blade. He scampered into the open and grabbed a sword from the ground. Immediately, two Maldormo zeroed in on him. He raked sweat from his eyes with the back of his hand. The Crusader charged him; the Maldormo closed in on them both. Hawkes spun around to avoid the Maldormo's claws—and bounced off the Crusader's chest. The giant head-butted him. Hawkes's vision blurred again as he collapsed into the dirt. He didn't know if the dome of darkness was getting lighter or if he was passing out.

He gasped, raising a feeble hand into the air. "Sol…"

Four Maldormo hovered overhead, each grasping one of Warner's limbs. He screamed as they began to pull in separate directions.

Thorne took the stairs at the back of the Judgment Seat two at a time. As he reached the top, a sword thrust through the canvas flap, nearly skewering him. He brought his sword down against it and stepped back.

A Crusader appeared, raising his sword.

"Hey!" Teska yelled from the ground.

The Crusader looked, and she disappeared. Confusion crossed his square, clean-shaven face.

Thorne grabbed the Crusader's arm and yanked him off balance. The armored giant tumbled down the steps in a raucous clatter of metal. As he sat up, snarling and spitting dirt, Teska appeared in front of him.

"You guys may be strong, but you're dumb as a bag of rocks." She sliced her dagger across his neck. More confusion, followed by shock, filled his eyes. He clutched his neck and fell backward.

Thorne went through the flap as Darien started up the steps.

A few mismatched chairs, the clerk's table and the cathedra were the only furnishings. Rann stood beside the cathedra, a wolfish grin on his face, rapier poised. The two robed figures cowered in the front corner.

Wiping his brow, Thorne advanced. Beyond Rann was the dome of blackness, and it appeared to be thinning or disappearing.

Thorne gripped his sword tighter. His left hand throbbed. He wished he had his own rapier, but right now, the saber would do. It could penetrate Rann's heart just as well. He heard Darien's labored wheezing behind him.

"Where are the children?" Thorne demanded.

"You've made a serious mistake coming up here," Rann said.

"The children. *Now.*"

"I shall enjoy sending your soul to the Archfiend."

Darien entered. "Where…are Cassidy…and Cassandra?"

"You can't beat me, Thorne. I'm part of the Fifth Order now. We cannot die!"

Thorne smirked. "Let me test that." He sprang forward. Their swords met, metallic thunder in the confines of the covered grandstand.

Rann struck, parried. Thorne returned stroke for stroke. Rann hopped around the cathedra, putting it between them. "You're trapped." He grinned. "You can't escape Last Chapel."

Thorne jabbed over the cathedra, but Rann deflected it easily. "Who says…I plan to escape? I'm walking out of here…across that bridge…with your head on a spear."

Rann laughed. "You still don't understand, do you? The Fifth Order, the Crimson Fathers—"

"Are all traitors and madmen! Every one of you will pay for the chaos and death you've caused." He kicked the cathedra as hard as he could. The heavy piece of furniture skidded sideways, forcing Rann to leap out of its way. He planted his feet and met Thorne's furious blows.

❖   ❖   ❖

The two robed figures edged toward the flap. Darien drew his dagger and intercepted them. He pressed the tip into the chest of the taller of the two. "Where are my niece and nephew?" he roared, eyes furious beneath his bushy white brows.

The taller figure showed Darien his open hands before easing the hood of his robe back. The face that appeared was surprisingly normal, with brown eyes, an average nose and a short beard. "The children are no longer here." His voice was low, evenly paced. "They left the city yesterday."

"Where'd you take them?" Darien moved the tip of the dagger into the robe until he met the resistance of flesh. The man winced.

His smaller companion pressed his fingertips together in front of him. "They're on their way to the Citadel of the Crimson Fathers." His voice was a sibilant hiss.

Darien had heard the name before, when he was hiding in the stable across from the Red Dog Saloon in Nashton. "Where is that?" he demanded. "Is that what you are—members of the Crimson Fathers?"

The smaller man started to cough. He raised his hand to the opening of his hood to cover his mouth.

"No, we are merely servants of the Undying Ones," the tall one said.

The smaller man stopped coughing, opened his clenched fist and blew. Dark purple dust blossomed in Darien's face.

Darien coughed. He staggered back, dropping the dagger and scrubbing at his eyes. The coughing subsided into small, wheezing gasps. Darien felt around and found the back of a chair for support, but his legs gave out, and he hit the floor like a sack of grain.

Hawkes knew he wasn't dying, at least not yet. Every part of his body hurt too much. That, plus the light… He felt warmth on his face and opened his eyes. The first thing he saw was the sun. The dome of darkness had vanished.

The second thing he saw was Warner falling. Hawkes didn't want to watch, but he couldn't stop himself.

Warner's screams followed his flailing body down.

The sickening thud made Hawkes close his eyes and look away.

He forced himself to sit up. Carnage littered the square. In addition to Warner's inert form, there were at least a dozen Crusader bodies in various stages of evisceration and dismemberment. The dead Maldormo disintegrated into black mist as the sunlight touched them, leaving only sooty stains behind. The bars of the Hellcage glowed reddish orange as the fire raged. Two Crusaders stood beside him. A third picked up Cabbott.

The sights and smells, the exertion and pain washed over Hawkes. He leaned over and vomited.

"Dario!" Thorne shouted as his friend fell.

The robed figures slipped through the back flap like wraiths on the wind.

Rann sneered and brought his sword up in a wide arc when Thorne glanced away. The stroke sent Thorne's saber spinning through the air. Rann swung again. Thorne leapt back, barely escaping what would've been a disemboweling strike.

Thorne brandished a chair to ward off Rann's advancing blows. The rickety thing felt like a collection of brittle sticks in his aching hands.

Rann swung again, and the chair exploded in pieces. His feral grin turned his countenance into a death's-head.

Darien lay where he had fallen.

"You…should've taken…one last lesson from your mentor," Rann said, winded. The sheen of perspiration on his face gleamed. "Dying…without putting up a fight."

Thorne screamed. Hatred flowed from him as freely as water through a sieve.

"Hey, who's this little turd?" Teska's voice cut through the grandstand. She stood just inside the flap, the smaller robed figure in front of her at daggerpoint.

"I caught him and his partner flying out of here like their asses were on fire." She prodded the man's back. "Right, Sneaky?"

The small man's hood had fallen back. His head was misshapen due to a scar that ran from his scalp down below his right ear. Someone had tried to slice off part of his face, leaving behind a deep cleft that looked so blackened it could have been burnt. Wispy strands of hair dangled in front of malevolent, bile-colored eyes. The man's skin was shriveled, although he couldn't be more than thirty years old.

Panic crossed Rann's face when he saw the man.

Thorne lunged. Wrapping his arms around Rann, he drove his enemy toward the front of the platform, slamming him against the railing. Rann yelped and struck Thorne's back with the pommel of his sword. Thorne fastened his good hand around Rann's neck, pressing him back and over the railing.

Rann clawed the air for a handhold but found nothing.

Thorne shoved with his right hand. With his left, he hoisted Rann's legs off the floor, ignoring the pain that raced from his hand into his shoulder. Thorne's cry of triumph was followed by Rann's dwindling scream, then a soft thud.

Thorne hung over the railing, panting, his hand swollen to the size of a melon. Through blurred vision, he saw Rann slowly getting to his knees. Crusaders and deputies converged to help him up.

"Keep those hands where I can see them," Teska said, "or I'll hack them off." She tapped the toe of her left boot against the heel of the right. With a soft click, a dagger shot out.

"You'll suffer for this," the short man hissed over his shoulder.

"Rann's…still moving…" Thorne turned from the railing.

"Where do you think you're going?"

"To finish this and send that bastard to whichever Hell will have him."

"I don't think so!" Teska shook her head. "There's still probably a dozen Crusaders out there, not to mention constables and deputies. And you're in no shape to peel an apple, much less use a sword."

"I'm going…to kill him," he said through clenched teeth.

"Fine. But not now." She put her hand on his chest, stopping him before he could stumble past her.

Their eyes met. His normally bright greens were weak and heavy-lidded; hers flashed with stubbornness. The day's events smothered him like a wet cloak. He didn't have the strength to tangle with her fierce determination. He sighed, shoulders slumping, and looked away.

"Let's hightail it out of this madhouse," she said.

"You'll never make it," the scarred man snapped.

"Shut up, Sneaky, before I hamstring you." Teska tapped the back of his leg with the dagger projecting from the sole of her boot.

"Dario!" Thorne spun around, knelt down and checked his friend's pulse. Faint but regular.

"Sneaky and his buddy used some sort of sleeping powder on him."

Thorne stood up and looked around. "Where's the other one?"

"He's outside. Out cold. I whacked him with the flat of my blade when he came down the steps." She grinned. "He never knew what hit him."

"Thorne! Surrender and come down!" Rann yelled from the ground. "I've got your men—at least what's left of them."

Thorne hurried to the front of the grandstand and leaned on the railing. The fire had thinned around the Hellcage. A few hardy spectators peered from doors and half-shuttered windows. Below him, Hawkes knelt on the ground in front of a Crusader. Beside Merrick's corpse lay the bodies of Cabbott and Warner, both facedown. The side of Cabbott's tunic was dark with blood. Warner's shredded clothing lay upon him like rags.

"Oh God…" Thorne whispered. His chest tightened; the blood seemed to slow in his veins.

Rann stood between two battle-scarred, blood-caked Crusaders. Several others surrounded the Judgment Seat. A half dozen constables and deputies watched with detached interest.

Thorne couldn't pull his eyes from the bodies. "Thurl… Solomon…" He said their names as if it would raise them up. An icy knot formed in his throat.

Rann smirked through his bloody nose and mouth. "It's over, heretic. Drop your weapons and come down."

Thorne gripped the railing as if it were the only solid thing in existence. He shook his head, willing the things he saw to be an illusion. But nothing changed. He hung his head.

"Get up there and bring him down!" Rann bawled at the Crusaders, motioning them away. Those nearest the grandstand moved to obey.

Thorne squeezed his eyes shut to hold the tears—or rage—inside. He heard movement behind him, then beside him, and felt a soft hand on his shoulder. It took extra effort to look up, but when he did, he saw Darien. Purple dust clung to the lines on his wrinkled face, making him look like a miserable bruise. Tears cut runnels through the dust and dirt on his cheeks as he stared down into the square.

More movement caught Thorne's attention to his left. Teska walked up and leaned over the railing.

"Rann, you dickless son of a diseased whore!"

Thorne raised his eyebrows. Rann looked up in surprise.

"Here's how this is going to go: you put those bodies into that wagon over there"—she gestured toward the one the women had ridden in—"then we're going to come down and ride that wagon out of here."

Rann put his hands on his hips and guffawed. "You're barking mad, woman!"

"Oh, I'm serious. You do what I say, or I bring back the Maldormo. I'll have them swarming you in less time than it takes"—she snapped her fingers—"to do *that*."

Thorne stared at her with a mixture of disbelief and worry.

The two Crusaders beside Rann glanced at each other. The others in the square began to fidget and look around.

"I don't believe you," Rann said.

"You wanna take the chance?"

Rann snorted and motioned to the Crusaders. "Kill the old man. Bring Thorne and the girl to me."

"He called your bluff," Thorne said, disappointment creeping into his voice. He narrowed his eyes. "You *were* bluffing, right?"

She flashed her dimples at him, reached behind her and flung the robed man against the railing. Her dagger was at his throat in an instant.

"Rann!" she yelled again. "Last chance!"

Rann's eyes fell on the small man pressed against the railing, and panic swept across his face. "Hold position!" he yelled at the Crusaders. *"Hold!"*

"Interesting…" Darien said, almost to himself.

"Yeah, that's what I thought." Teska smirked. "Sneaky here means something. You wanna risk him?" She pulled the blade tighter against his throat. The scarred man rose onto the balls of his feet as the edge bit into his flesh. Hatred seethed in his eyes.

"Wait, wait!" Rann shouted. He looked down at the ground, his chest rising and falling, before looking up again. "Let him go."

"Not until we're on the other side of the Black. All of us."

"I can't do that."

"Then I guess this little turd gets a second grin."

"Wait!" the man pleaded. "Stop! Stop!" He waved his arms in the air like a chicken flapping its wings. "Do what she says, Rann!" His voice rose higher with each word.

"Wagon," Thorne demanded, pointing at the bodies. "Then safe passage."

Rann paced several steps, then stopped. He looked up with a face contorted by helpless rage. "God damn you, Thorne." He paced back to the Crusaders and said something. One picked up Cabbott; the other did the same with Warner. They placed them in the straw-filled wagon.

"Let's move," Thorne said. "But stay alert. This isn't over."

He held the canvas flap open while Teska maneuvered their hostage down the steps. Darien limped after them. Thorne followed, his eyes darting between the four grim Crusaders who waited for them, their blue eyes venomous slivers of ice. They led them around the grandstand toward the wagon.

"Stay back," the scarred man ordered with menacing authority. Vaun kept her dagger tight against the crinkled flesh of his throat. "Do nothing," he added as several bowmen tracked their every movement with nocked arrows.

After Merrick's body was placed inside the wagon, Thorne waved the Crusaders away. He helped Darien into the back and closed the gate. Teska prodded her hostage up onto the driver's bench and joined him, dagger at his ribs. Finally, Thorne climbed up and took the reins.

Rann watched with cruel eyes, nose curled in impotent rage, fists clenched.

"Remember: safe passage to the other side of the river," Thorne said to him. "No tricks or your sorcerer dies."

"You'll pay for this, Thorne. You and that whore!" Red-faced, Rann ground out the words.

Teska flipped her middle finger at him. Thorne snapped the reins, and the horses clopped forward. He steered them south toward Eads Bridge and glanced back. The Crusaders followed as far as the perimeter of the square and stopped. He didn't see Rann.

"Dario, keep an eye out behind us." He swallowed hard, thinking of his friends. "How…how bad are they?"

The clerk's thin, exhausted voice drifted from the rear. "Not good, Malachi. Solomon's alive but unconscious. Thurl is…" His voice cracked. "He's lost too much blood. He's dying."

32

ENDGAME

WEDNESDAY, JULY 1, 999 AE

Thorne pulled the horse to a stop in an alley. "We can't leave," he said. "Thurl needs medical attention, and if we cross that bridge, I don't know when we might find a physician. He won't make it."

Teska squinted at him. "You know any physicians here?"

He shook his head and ran his hand through his hair.

"Your friend's going to die," the scarred man said with glee.

"What's going on up there?" Hawkes yelled from the rear.

"Just stopped for a minute," Teska hollered back. Her expression said she knew he was right. Thurl wouldn't survive long after they left the city. "I've got a suggestion," she said in a low voice, as if the walls of the surrounding buildings were listening. "I know a girl… She's Nahoru'brexia, same as me—"

"What's Nahoru'brexia?"

"No time right now, but I'll tell you later. She can…help people heal faster."

"Would she help Thurl?"

Teska shrugged. "I don't know. But it's worth a try."

"Where is she?" he asked, his jaw set.

"With the Communion, on their side of the city."

"You'll all die soon," the hostage between them said. He tugged his hood back over his head.

"Shut it, Sneaky."

Thorne snapped the reins.

Darien called out. "Where're we going? We're moving away from the bridge."

"Change of plans," he answered over his shoulder. "Thurl needs immediate help."

"We're not going after the children?" Panic climbed in his aged voice.

"We can't right now. But we will. How's Thurl holding up?"

There was no response. Thorne didn't know if Darien was angry with his decision or checking Cabbott's condition. Most likely both. After a moment, the clerk's voice drifted forward, tight and worried.

"His pulse is extremely weak. He likely won't make it much farther…"

"I told you: he's going to die," Sneaky chirped.

Teska dug the blade into his ribs and pointed Thorne toward an approaching corner.

He turned the horse and wagon at Teska's direction before yelling over his shoulder: "How about Solomon?"

"He's conscious but still dazed."

"Anybody following us?"

"Nope, all clear," Hawkes replied.

No-man's-land swung into view as they exited a side street—a burnt, rubble-strewn diagonal stripe that bisected Last Chapel. It reminded Thorne of how a child might pull a toe across an anthill. Buildings had collapsed into mounds of stone and timber. Small fires burned here and there.

Teska halted them by an abandoned building. After dismounting and looking in both directions, she returned to the wagon. "We can cross here. Crusaders are stationed each way, but I doubt they'll pursue us."

"They won't," Sneaky said. "They know better."

She climbed up to the wagon seat, took the sword from Thorne and returned it to the small man's side. "Scared of the Communion, huh?"

Sneaky shook his head. "Crusaders are afraid of *nothing*. They're just waiting for the signal."

"Signal for what?" Thorne snapped the reins hard, and the horse lurched forward. The wagon creaked and rocked with every stone and hole it encountered.

"They're watching us, Malachi," Darien yelled over the clatter of the wheels. "But they're not following."

"I told you."

"But you didn't answer my question. What signal?" Thorne said, digging his elbow into Sneaky's chest.

A dark, unpleasant chuckle rolled from the depths of the hood. "You'll find out soon enough."

Teska directed them into Communion territory, where they stopped at the border. She dismounted again, talked in hushed tones with four guards—two women and two men—before climbing back up and motioning them on.

Thorne urged the horse faster. The wagon rattled and jolted, and grumbles of discomfort sounded from the back. It relieved Thorne that Solomon felt well enough to complain.

It took twenty minutes to navigate the streets. Teska's presence allowed them instant passage through every guard post and checkpoint on their way to the natural green dome that had apparently once been part of a grand botanical garden.

"Wait here. Let me talk to her," she said when they arrived.

Thorne dismounted, hauled Sneaky off the seat and went to the side of the wagon. Thurl lay stretched out on the straw, face white as a fish's belly. His breathing was so shallow, Thorne first thought he'd already died. Warner rested in one corner, a makeshift bandage wrapped around his head. Hawkes opened the gate and hopped out.

"Get in there," Thorne said, shoving Sneaky toward the door. Once inside, the small man paced the confines, mumbling to himself.

Darien and Warner climbed out. As they waited on Teska, Thorne told his men what was happening. Their attempts to get information from Sneaky resulted in either callous laughter or stubborn silence.

After an interminably long time—during which Thorne grew increasingly worried about Cabbott—Teska emerged from the green sanctuary of foliage.

"Mallory's willing to try." She looked from Thorne to Cabbott. "But there are no guarantees. Take him over there." She pointed to a grove a hundred yards away. "Leave him with Mallory. Then come straight back here."

Thorne nodded. Hawkes helped him ease Cabbott from the wagon. It surprised Thorne how the body seemed to weigh so little yet be deadweight at the same time.

"You think this'll work?" Hawkes asked softly.

Thurl murmured something. Beads of sweat stood out on his waxy skin.

"I don't know," Thorne replied in the same hushed whisper. "But it's the only chance he's got."

Inside the grove, they found a low stone bench in the midst of a cultivated flower garden. Mallory, he presumed, stood as they entered and gestured to the bench. She appeared to be in her late twenties, about the same age as Teska. Freckles dotted her cheeks and nose, and she wore her blond hair parted down the middle and hanging straight on either side of her face. Blue eyes watched as they laid Cabbott down gently. Both men looked at Mallory with a mixture of anticipation and curiosity before returning to the wagon.

"How long's this gonna take?" Warner asked.

Teska shrugged. "No idea. I've seen Mallory heal once before, but that was just a burn. Took her about fifteen minutes, I think. She was exhausted afterward." The fiery redhead looked toward the grove. "With his injuries? I just don't know…"

The clouds that had been amassing all morning had gradually changed color—from stormy gray to blackish purple and now to sickly ochre. The air felt charged, as if a lightning storm raged nearby. Despite the number of trees, no birds flew or sung. Even the scavengers overhead went unseen. A pregnant silence blanketed everything.

The horse grew restless, and Warner held the reins to keep it from bolting away with the wagon.

The clouds roiled over Last Chapel like liquid.

"This isn't good," Teska said.

"What's happening?" Hawkes asked her.

"I'm not sure… But I'd guess some kind of magic. *Bad* magic."

Several women ran toward the Maiden's dome and disappeared into the inner darkness of the sanctum.

"Should we get in there?" Hawkes asked.

Teska shook her head. "No. Men aren't allowed inside."

"Well, we're sitting ducks when this storm breaks."

"We can use the wagon for cover if we have to," Thorne said.

Warner stared at the distant grove. "How long's Thurl been in there?"

"About an hour." Teska dropped her gaze to the ground. Her expression told them what that meant.

The hair on their arms prickled.

"Whoa, what was *that*?" Warner asked, staring at his arm. "Did you guys—"

Hawkes rubbed his arms as if trying to keep warm. "I did."

"It's most likely something to do with this storm." Darien studied the clouds. They covered the sky as far as they could see and looked like a cauldron of boiling clay soup.

"What's he doing?" Thorne gestured toward their prisoner.

Sneaky knelt in the middle of the wagon, his arms raised in supplication. He mouthed words that were too faint for anyone to hear.

"Praying?" Hawkes suggested.

"Hey!" Teska shouted at the wagon. "Knock it off!"

"What in the name of the Church is *that*?" Darien's voice held equal parts awe and fear. Everyone followed his gaze.

East-northeast of where they stood, a glowing dome of purple light grew taller by the moment. Black streaks shot across its surface like reversed lightning bolts. A dull, distant thrum came over the treetops.

Hair prickled again.

Sneaky's voice grew louder, but his words were gibberish. He waved his arms in the air, and his fingers wiggled like desiccated worms.

The purple dome rose higher, like a balloon being inflated.

"It's coming from the Church's side!" Teska yelled.

Warner had trouble keeping the horse under control. He lashed the reins around the nearest tree. The animal snorted and pawed the ground.

Darien pointed toward the grove. "Look!"

Mallory staggered toward them.

Teska raced to her, Thorne and Hawkes on her heels, Warner several yards behind. Darien remained by the wagon.

Mallory reached for Teska but collapsed before they met. Teska dropped to the ground and cradled Mallory's head. Her hair lay plastered to her scalp, and her complexion matched Cabbott's. Her eyelids fluttered.

Teska put her ear to Mallory's mouth. Her breath felt tremulous and thin.

"I did…" Mallory started but nearly passed out.

"Take your time. I'm right here."

The bloated purple dome with its black lightning continued to rise above the treetops. The thrumming increased. The sky boiled with jaundiced light and angry clouds.

"Is Thurl okay?" Thorne shouted, coming to a stop.

Mallory reached out and held Teska's hand. "I…I did my best," she whispered. "But his wounds… Too bad… Too much…" She sighed heavily. "I tried…my best…" She closed her eyes and went limp.

Warner arrived just as Thorne and Hawkes turned away from the two women. "Oh…"

Thorne pinched the bridge of his nose with thumb and forefinger as he hung his head. Hawkes walked toward Warner shaking his head, clenching and unclenching his fist. His frown quivered. Warner stood dumbfounded as they walked past him.

Deep rumbling emanated from the Church's side of the city. The purple light darkened; the forks of lightning were barely visible across its pulsating surface as the sound escalated.

Sneaky threw his hood back. Gossamer strands of hair floated on the wind. The black scar appeared to pulsate in the aberrant light. He stuck his arms straight into the air and looked at his captors with sadistic glee. "The time has come at last! Victory is ours!"

The purple dome erupted.

Shafts of purple-black light crackled up and over the Communion's half of the city. They arched like rainbows before coalescing into a single beam that stabbed down into the wagon.

Sneaky spread his arms wide. The purple-black light struck his body, outlining him in a luminescent glow. He shuddered beneath the impact. His body rose from the straw-covered floor and hung in midair as if he had been crucified on an invisible cross. He opened his mouth to scream but only purple-black light erupted. His body convulsed a final time, and the light exploded from him in every direction, like ripples after a stone breaks the water's surface. A shock wave of cold followed, ripping leaves from trees.

The wagon exploded in a thousand shards of wood; a concussive force flung everyone to the ground. Teska shielded Mallory as the wave of light and cold swept over them.

Sneaky's body dropped from the air and into the splintered remains of the wagon. His robe had completely vaporized, and he glowed an eerie yellowish purple. When it faded, his corpse was charred beyond recognition.

"Malachi. Malachi, *come on*! Get up!"

Thorne groaned and opened his eyes. He lay on his back staring at the sky. It looked like rain.

Teska shook him again. "We've got to get out of here. Rann's coming. He's got a Crusader army with him."

Thorne sat up, shaking his head to clear the cobwebs. "What?"

"The Crimson Fathers released some dark magical power," Darien said. "That's what Teska and I figure, anyway."

Teska helped Thorne to his feet.

"What did you say about Rann?" he asked, looking down at her.

"Our guards just returned. Rann and the Crusaders have crossed no-man's-land and invaded our territory. They're wiping out anyone who resists them, and they're headed this way."

Warner offered Thorne his shoulder for support, but he refused. He took several steps to regain his strength and bearing. Teska was by his side; Warner and Darien followed.

Thorne glanced around. "Where's Tycho? And the girl?"

"He carried Mallory over to the Maiden's dome. She pushed herself trying to help Cabbott…" Teska hesitated upon saying his name. "Mallory needs time to recover."

The mention of Thurl's name hit Thorne like a hammer blow to the forehead. He couldn't be gone... Not Thurl. *Oh, God. Why him?* He stopped, nearly causing Warner and Darien to run into him. "We've got to get Thurl's body."

"And Merrick's," Warner said gently. "It was in the..."

Thorne stared at the scattered bits of busted wood where the wagon had been. Somehow, the horse had managed to escape. A blackened body lay curled in the debris.

"Val..." First Merrick, then Thurl. Tears stung Thorne's eyes. His legs trembled. Warner held him by the shoulders. This time, he accepted the offer of support.

"Come on. You need to sit down," the deputy said.

"He can't sit down," Teska said. "We've got to get out of here."

"How we gonna do that?" Warner pointed. "Our wagon's blown to shit, and the horse ran off!"

Teska cursed. "I know, I know... But we can't stay here."

"How long until they get here?" Darien asked.

"Thirty minutes, maybe less. Depends on how much resistance they meet."

At the remains of the wagon, Thorne looked closely at the figure in the debris. "That's not Val. Is that our hostage?"

Warner nodded. "Yep. Whatever happened went through him, at least according to Dario."

Darien nodded. "He acted as a conduit of some sort."

Teska walked over and kicked the corpse in the side. Part of it crumbled like stale cake.

"Where's Merrick's body?"

They searched the area, and after a moment, Darien found it. The explosion had thrown it into the bushes a dozen yards away. Hawkes returned and helped him carry it back to the group.

"Mallory?" Teska asked Hawkes.

The deputy nodded. "The women there, at the path—they took her."

"Then let's move. We're almost out of time."

"Wait!" Thorne shouted. "We've got to get Thurl's body, too. I won't leave it back there."

"You don't have to," a familiar voice said.

Thorne spun around. His mouth dropped open.

Thurl Cabbott walked toward them, a weak but thankful smile on his face.

33
REFUGEES

WEDNESDAY, JULY 1, 999 AE

As Thorne, Hawkes and Warner took turns embracing Cabbott, a slender woman in a green gown approached Teska. They exchanged words before the woman returned to the Maiden's sanctuary. The men were slapping each other on the back when Teska approached.

"Welcome back," she said to Cabbott with a weak smile.

"It's good to be back. What the hells happened to me, anyway?"

"They can fill you in," she replied.

Thorne didn't care for the expression of uncertainty and dread on her face. It made her look vulnerable. "What was that all about?"

She bit her lower lip. "The Maiden's demanded to see me."

"Do you want me to—"

"No!" She softened her voice. "No, men aren't allowed, remember? Besides, that would only make things worse." She sighed. "I've got to go."

Thorne nodded. "I'll wait right here." He watched her until she disappeared into the green, noting the absence of her usual swagger.

Teska followed the familiar path. The feeling of being watched was almost palpable this time. She kept her head down until she reached the clearing. Six women guarded the entrance, all battle-ready. She greeted them, but her spirit sank when she saw the animosity and disgust on their faces. They said nothing, and she tried to ignore the hateful stares that followed her.

Everything remained the same as yesterday—except the Maiden's eyes. They blazed scarlet with fury through her three veils. Several serpents moved fitfully through the roots and branches of the throne.

"Teska Vaun." The Maiden stood. Once again, she seemed to tower over the clearing, her eyes like molten steel.

Teska knelt in the grass without looking up.

"Do you *know* what you've *done?*" Maiden Mallumo demanded, her tone a razor of hostility. All the women surrounding the throne stared silently at the ground and didn't move.

"What I've done? I-I don't understand…"

From every side of the clearing, serpents of different sizes and colors slithered out of the undergrowth. They undulated toward Teska.

"No, of course you don't. You're a fool, Teska Vaun." The Maiden hesitated. "But we are more foolish still."

Teska risked a glance up.

The Maiden sat down, her immense size reducing so she fit perfectly upon the throne. Her eyes still burned with fierce intensity. The serpents wriggled forward, and Teska wondered what she should do. She wanted to jump up, but something told her to remain still. She swallowed hard and obeyed her inner voice.

"Despite concerns among the Three, I changed my mind and aided you in rescuing Malachi Thorne and his men. This was unprecedented, and we must see what will come of it. But at issue now is what you've done to the Communion."

Teska raised her eyes to the throne. "What do you mean?"

The Maiden's veils rippled as though serpents moved behind them, and both her hands were clenched. "You brought the enemy into our midst."

"I've already said that Malachi is no longer our enemy—"

"Not him!" the Maiden roared from deep in her throat. "The Crimson Fathers, you vapid child! You brought their agent among us!"

"Our hostage? But Maiden, he's dead. His body's outside."

"You are doubly a fool, Teska Vaun. Not only do you bring their agent here. You have no idea the destruction you've caused."

"Wh-What destruction?"

The Maiden remained silent. The other women could've been statues.

The clearing felt…different. Colder, maybe? No, that wasn't it… Teska couldn't identify it, but something felt off. Empty, maybe?

"Leave us," the Maiden said, and without a word, the women threaded down two parallel paths behind the throne. As the last one disappeared among the foliage, Teska noticed the difference again, sharper now. A wave of fatigue washed over her.

"Can you feel it?" the Maiden asked.

She felt…*something*, as if the air in the clearing had thinned.

"Of course you can," the Maiden continued. "What you feel is the loss of our magic. The Crimson Fathers have nearly stripped us of our power."

Teska stared at the throne. "Sorry, I'm confused. I don't—"

The Maiden sighed loud enough to interrupt. "Your training hasn't progressed to this point of understanding yet. Magic, like food or gold, is a commodity. There is only so much of it available in the world. The servant of the Crimson Fathers you brought with you—when they realized they had someone close to our heart, they seized the opportunity and sacrificed him to hurt us. The light, the shock wave—they were manifestations of their attack."

"What did they do?"

"The mystical explosion dispersed our magic, just as the seeds of a dandelion sail away when the wind blows. That is why you're so weak. Our reserve of magical power has been scattered. The Crimson Fathers will attempt to gather it for themselves, to add to their own, and in our impaired condition, they may very well succeed."

Teska wondered if the ground had dropped away from her feet.

All of the serpents had come to a stop, forming a circle around her. They hissed and writhed. Some coiled up, while others lay languidly in the grass. Oddly enough, none of them bit at each other or showed any sort of territorialism.

"The more brexia who gather together, the stronger our power," the Maiden continued. "That's the way it has always been in the Communion. While my consuls and attendants were here with us, you didn't notice your weakness. Their power enhanced yours. But now that they're gone…"

"Can I—do I still have my gift?" she asked.

The Maiden nodded, the veils waving gently but never occluding her eyes. "Of course. That is part of you and can never be taken away. But you'll find it harder to use now. It'll take more energy, and you won't be able to use it as often."

Teska brushed a strand of hair out of her face. "I—"

The Maiden raised a hand to stop her. "We cannot undo what the Crimson Fathers have done. We're weaker now than we have been in centuries. The Church will wipe out all who remain, and we'll be all but powerless to stop them." Sorrow and simmering anger coated her words.

"I-I'm sorry. I didn't know… But we have Malachi and his men with us now. They can still help us, like we talked about before. They'll fight against this Fifth Order. I know Malachi's beliefs and feelings about the Church are changing. We had planned to leave the city once we escaped the tekoya and keep fighting the Fifth Order. But Cabbott—"

"Yes. And once again you asked the Communion to aid servants of the Church. Mallory is a compassionate young woman, and she thinks of you as a sister. She went against the judgment of my court to offer her gift. There is a... stubbornness in her that is not unlike yours."

Teska didn't know whether to take that as a compliment or complaint.

"Mallory's recovery will take a long time since our power is diminished. It's possible she may never fully recover." For several moments, the only sound came from the reptilian circle around her. The Maiden closed her eyes and seemed more like a stone statue atop her organic throne.

Now that Teska knew what had happened, she understood that her fatigue wasn't merely exhaustion. It wasn't a lack of sleep or aching muscles. This tiredness lay in the center of her gift, at the core of her being. Some of her inner strength was gone.

And it was all her fault.

A group of Last Chapel congregants ignored Thorne and ran past him before he found one who slowed down enough to answer his question.

"Zadicus Rann...the Crusaders..." The frightened man panted. "They've breached our defenses. They're spreading out...coming this way."

"How long?" Thorne asked, shaking the man's shoulders.

He broke free of Thorne's grip and fled. More people streamed by, shouting and crying, with bundles on their backs and under their arms. A man approached, helping his wife herd four children. Thorne stepped in front of them and raised his hand. The man stopped but instructed his family to keep moving. More terrified people hustled past them.

Thorne looked into the man's bulging eyes. "Congregant, where are you going?"

"Away from here! Them Crusaders on their way. You gotta clear out!"

"Where are they?" Thorne demanded. "How many are there?"

"Too many." The man gasped. "A hundred, maybe more..." He grabbed Thorne's arm. "They're wiping out everything in their path!" With that, he sprinted after his family.

"Any bright ideas?" Cabbott asked, still a little unsteady on his feet.

"No," he said. "If Rann's got that many..."

More congregants flowed toward them. They separated to either side of Thorne's group like water around a rock.

Thorne looked at Cabbott. "I've got to get Teska out of there..."

The Witch of Darkness opened her eyes. Their cold light seeped through the veils. "Teska Vaun, the Three-Who-Are-One have decided. The Communion can no longer maintain this fight. If we do not preserve what little power that remains, we shall cease to exist."

"You're withdrawing?"

"Silence!"

Teska flinched. Even though the Maiden claimed that her power had weakened, Teska felt a mental shock almost as forceful as a charging bull. She folded her arms across her chest to keep them from trembling. The serpents grew agitated again as if prodded with fire.

"It is not for you to question the wisdom of the Three! You are to obey! Is that clear?"

"Yes, yes Most Beautiful One!" Teska's words ran together.

"We do not have much time. The Communion must gather our strength. You are ordered to find more Nahoru'brexia. You will teach them of the Three-Who-Are-One. Through the Nahoru'brexia, we will once more rise to power."

Teska stared, open-mouthed and wide-eyed. "Find more? You can't be serious."

It was the wrong thing to say.

The Maiden gestured with a clawlike hand. Teska's arms locked to her sides; her legs became immobile. She couldn't even turn her head. Another gesture followed, and the serpents slithered across the grass toward her. She tried to cry out, but her throat and mouth wouldn't work. She moaned in terror as the serpents reached her legs and began coiling around her body, entrapping her within a scaly cocoon. They layered her body from the ankles, knees, hips, moving inexorably upward. Sweat sprung out on her brow, and her body tingled with the rush of heat and fear. The snakes slithered around her chest, her neck—

And then all light extinguished. She still felt the cold, sinuous bodies against her skin. The overpowering reptilian stench forced its way into her nostrils. She thought she was going to suffocate. The scaly bodies writhed and undulated against her, and she imagined herself trapped like this forever.

She didn't know if she trembled or if it was the snakes squirming around. She fought to control her panic. A forked tongue flicked across her cheek. The Maiden's voice penetrated her ears.

"Never dispute our orders. You *will* find Nahoru'brexia. You *will* add their power to our own." The tongue flicked against her earlobe. "This is your fault; therefore, you will make amends."

The cocoon tightened, as if every snake constricted simultaneously. Her heart thudded in her chest, and she struggled to pull enough musty air in through her nostrils. Panic clawed at her sanity.

"This can happen anytime," the Maiden promised, "when you're awake or when you're asleep. Imagine waking up to this…" Once more, the bodies tightened around her.

Flashes of light appeared inside her eyelids. Her lungs burned like a swimmer too far below the surface.

"Do not disappoint us."

And suddenly, her body was free.

Teska collapsed in the grass, dragging deep, painful breaths into her lungs. She brushed and slapped at her arms and legs, trying to dislodge the serpents——that weren't there.

She gasped and looked around. There were no snakes. The throne was empty. The guards were gone. She could almost feel her power ebbing away. Coated with sweat, she shivered at the remembrance of the snakes. Had they really been there at all? She wiped down her arms a final time and stood; her legs felt like kuzda jelly.

"Teska!" Thorne's voice sounded discordant and tiny in the empty clearing. "Come on." He grabbed her hand and dragged her down the path. "We're leaving Last Chapel."

They joined the swarm of refugees who fled the Crusader army. Thorne carried Merrick's body over his shoulder. Darien had his arms around Hawkes and Warner. The deputies carried the old man more than he walked. Cabbott moved with a freshness of a much younger man, outdistancing them all. Teska remained at Thorne's side. Word had it that the army was twenty minutes behind and closing fast.

"Where're we headed?" Cabbott yelled behind him. "Do we have a plan, or are we just following the crowd?"

"Kingsway Wall." Thorne huffed, shifting the weight of Merrick's body. "We follow it south…out the gate."

Cabbott nodded and took off again.

"Won't they be waiting there?" Hawkes asked.

"I'm hope not," Thorne replied. "It's in Communion territory."

"Should be fine." Teska matched Thorne stride for stride. "Unless Rann sent Crusaders outside the Wall…"

As they limped and trotted along, Thorne fumed over Rann. He wanted—he *needed*—to bring him down. But that seemed impossible now. Even if the two of them could have it out, there was no way he'd get out of Last Chapel alive.

Cabbott veered left to help two elderly women gather up items that had fallen from their baskets. He motioned for Thorne to keep going. Mallory had done an even better job healing Cabbott than they could've expected. His new-found vitality seemed to be the opposite of Dario's condition.

Kingsway Wall came into view over the treetops and the remains of pre-Cataclysm buildings. The flow of refugees turned south like water divert-ed in its course.

Congregants clogged the gate. Some had horses and carts; others tried in vain to keep herds of livestock together. A constant din of yelling, cries and curs-es beat against the Wall. Animals bellowed and bawled. Carts overturned. Chil-dren clung to their mothers to keep from being trampled. Congregants streamed across the Desperes, a dried-out tributary of the Black River.

Teska remained by Thorne's side, and he chanced a quick look at her. She was flushed, and her hair hung in sweaty strands, its color more a muddy orange than its usual vibrant red. She breathed heavily, and her forehead creased. The creases weren't from concentration. It's was the look he'd seen in Honvale. And with the Maldormo. A look that had become far too common on her.

They made it through the gate like cattle herded down a chute for slaugh-ter. Once outside, congregants spread out and fled south as fast as they could. A line of refugees, like ants following a sugar trail, stretched to a bridge several miles south of the city. People fled through dusty fields of pitiful crops, along hard, gray pre-Cataclysm roads, through tangles of foliage and around the des-iccated shells of ancient ruins. Technically, they were in the Devouring Lands now. From here down to the Arkan Sea was habitable, but only the hardy—and most said the foolhardy—choose to live there. But its horrors mattered little at the moment. Only survival and escape did.

The sun sank low as the remnants of Last Chapel trudged over the bridge. Thorne led his group across to the other side and down to the banks of the Black River. They collapsed on the remains of tree trunks and against the smooth rocks that covered the ground. No one spoke. They stayed there until the flow of refu-gees became a trickle, and then merely a few stragglers. The sun dropped below the horizon.

No Crusaders appeared. If they had wanted to slaughter everyone who fled, they could have done so with ease. Their intent, it seemed, had been to overrun the Communion's half of the city and claim it for the Church.

Frogs called to one another along the riverbank. Insects buzzed through the muggy evening air. For safety, Thorne roused them all and moved them back underneath where the bridge met the ground so they had some cover. Once set-tled, everyone fell asleep.

Thorne didn't dare risk a fire, but he had to stand guard since he was the only one still awake. He leaned against one of the warm, rusty beams that held up the bridge and watched the stars come out over the smoking remains of Last Chapel in the distance.

He was sound asleep in minutes.

34

EPOCH

SATURDAY, JULY 4, 999 AE

Nearly a day's ride south of Last Chapel, the village of Saintgen nestled along the western bank of the Black River. Malachi Thorne looked out over it from the top of a nearby hill. Thatched roofs and curls of smoke peeked through the distant trees. In the flatlands around the village lay acres of corn and wheat; herds of sheep, cattle and goats roamed the grassy fields, utterly oblivious to how the world had changed.

They're the lucky ones, he thought.

The sun bathed everything with intense heat, and the sky was its usual watercolor wash of striated blues, studded with cotton ball clouds. No breeze stirred the leaves of the trees under which everyone had gathered.

Thorne turned to face his friends. Cabbott, Darien, Hawkes, Warner and Vaun stood around a freshly dug grave. Everyone looked at him except Cabbott, who stared at the carefully wrapped body of Valerian Merrick on the ground.

Thorne cleared his throat. "It's time to say goodbye."

"What about the Final Comfort?" Vaun asked, glancing at the shrouded corpse.

Thorne shook his head. "It's only for those on their deathbed, not those who've already died." He paused. "Besides, we're no longer part of the Church. And somehow, I don't think Val would've wanted it anyway."

Everyone nodded.

"This is where I'm supposed to tell you about Val's life, about his achievements, and that he was a faithful servant of the Church. But you already know that. He deserves more than this hole in the ground. The tomb constructed for him in Rimlingham"—he paused again, collecting his thoughts—"that's his *real* tribute. Not this.

"But as I've thought about it, *where* he's buried really doesn't matter. It's just a plot of ground. Or a marker. Or a mausoleum. It serves only to spur our memories of him. What I believe will better honor his memory, and keep his spirit alive, is embracing his cause.

"Val told me that during his years among the Tex'ahns, he found scraps of old documents and books—ancient things that predated the Great Cataclysm. He formulated his ideas about freedom from some of them.

"He said that long before the end of the world, this land—what we call Deiparia—was known by a different name. It was the United States of America. And just as we have feast days and holy days, our ancestors had special days of observance, too. One of those days occurred annually on July 4th. Val called it Independence Day. He thought it represented some great struggle in which those United States Americans had claimed their freedom. From what, he didn't know. But he was convinced that freedom is the key to the future of Deiparia. Today is July 4th. Somehow, I think it's appropriate that Val should be laid to rest on this day that once celebrated freedom."

Warner shifted his weight and leaned on his shovel. Cabbott finally looked up with an unsettled expression.

Thorne smiled. "At first, I thought him mad. So did you." He glanced between Cabbott and Hawkes. They returned the smile and nodded, Cabbott somewhat slowly. "I think Teska was the only one who really believed him from the beginning.

"But the more I talked to him and the more I listened to what he said, the more it made sense. You all knew his passion for it. He always became so…animated when talking about it. Tycho, you remember some of those meetings we attended on our way to Last Chapel."

It wasn't a question, but Hawkes nodded anyway.

"His enthusiasm was contagious." Thorne smiled again. "And he had a way—I guess it was the teacher in him—of explaining things. I learned more from him in the past few weeks than in my last ten years in the Church."

He cleared his throat. "You all know that I've…struggled to reconcile my faith with Val's ideas. I'm not completely there yet. But I believe he was right. The Church is not God. I don't know who or what is," he added quickly, "because I'm still trying to figure that out, too.

"The Church has been corrupt for a long time. The presence of a group like the Crimson Fathers proves it, not to mention the arrival of this Fifth Order and the Crusaders. We know nothing about them or where they come from. Dario believes the Crimson Fathers control them in some way, and he may very well be right. They're just one example of how far the Church has fallen from its original purpose."

He searched the branches over their heads.

"I can no longer give my allegiance to the Church. I can no longer worship it as God." He looked back at them. "We've all been discussing what happens next—with all of us—and I've come to my decision. I'm—"

He stared at the ground.

"I'm going to take up his mantle." The words hung in air that tasted like honeysuckle. Sunlight dappled the midsummer grass through the leaves. "So tomorrow, I'm going to find out more, if I can, about what Val learned. About freedom. And see that his cause—and his name—are remembered. Teska's coming with me. She's been given a…task of her own to carry out."

"I'm coming with you," Cabbott said.

Thorne nodded.

"Your task has to do with—what did you call them—Nahoru'brexia?" Darien asked.

"Yeah," she replied. "The Communion is all but extinct, at least in terms of power. Those who remain believe the Nahoru'brexia, with our unique gifts, are the only hope for survival. I've got to find more of us and somehow help rebuild what I tore down."

"You know my plans," Darien said.

Hawkes put a hand on the old man's stooped shoulder. "Solomon and I will be with you. We'll find those kids."

Darien smiled, nodded and placed his aged hand over the deputy's.

"A new era has begun," Thorne said, staring at Merrick's body again. "There's no going back to what we used to be—not for any of us." He looked at Teska. He was glad to see her smiling at him, her dimples faint like the promise of dawn. "Who I was—everything I believed and did—I owe it all to this man." He nodded toward the grave. "Who I am now—what I believe and what I do from this moment on—I also owe to him."

Thorne stepped forward and knelt on one knee beside the body. *He will not lift a finger against you, and yet you will fall before him.* He smiled. "Thank you, my friend. May you find peace and freedom in the Heavenly Realms."

He stood, nodded at Cabbott and turned away. He heard Cabbott's quiet instructions to lower the body. Thorne closed his eyes as he listened to the crunch of shovels in dirt, followed by the soft thumps of it filling the hole.

While Hawkes and Warner worked, Teska walked over to Thorne. She put her arm through his and laid her head against him.

"You did fine," she said.

Thorne nodded and opened his eyes. He looked down into her face. It seemed like forever since he'd seen her without dirt or soot or blood on her. For a moment, he remembered the dream he'd once had—of looking down at a redhead resting against his arm. The only other thing he could remember about the dream was that it had something to do with the end of the world. Had it been about the new millennium?

This is certainly the end of our worlds—at least as we've all known them. "It won't be easy, you know?" he said at last.

"No."

"And neither of us knows what we're doing."

"No."

Cabbott walked over and handed Thorne a rapier. Thorne shoved it into the ground at the head of the grave and stepped back. He wasn't sure how long he stood there, but when he finally looked up, his friends were waiting for him.

They talked easily as they returned to the Saintgen tavern for a final meal together.

Far to the northeast, at the headlands of the Great Appian Mountains, Vaelok Strang stood on a stone balcony outside the central hall of the Citadel of the Crimson Fathers. He stroked his long beard with bony fingers and studied the gathering clouds for portents. He sensed someone had joined him.

"What is it?" he demanded in a querulous but imperial manner.

The newcomer, short and round, scuttled up beside Strang. A detailed tattoo covered his sweaty scalp above his tonsure. He wore the purple, long-sleeved robe of a servant of the Crimson Fathers. He bowed. "I bring news."

Strang looked down. His eyes glowed in the recesses of his sockets. His skeletal visage was made more horrific by the gruesome absence of a nose, leaving only the dark nasal cavity. A curtain of stringy black hair straggled over his shoulders. His silver beard was braided and lay upon his emaciated chest.

"Speak, Megas," he commanded.

"Thank you, Undying One. You asked to be notified: Last Chapel has fallen." The fat man had learned not to expect any expression of gratitude from any of the Crimson Fathers.

Strang turned his penetrating gaze back to the clouds. Away to the south, the city of Three Waters crouched like a turtle between the foreboding hills.

"Zadicus Rann has proven to be most reliable," Strang said to the clouds. His crimson robe, embroidered with peculiar sigils, smelled like dead earth.

"Yes, Undying One."

A moment passed. Strang turned and stared at the smaller man the way one might look at a maggot. "Why are you still here?"

"Your pardon, Supremacy, but there is something else…"

"What?"

"Malachi Thorne and his men—they—Rann reports—"

Strang sighed. "They are no longer in Last Chapel."

Megas suppressed a shudder at Strang's knowledge. "That's correct. They escaped with the congregants who fled the city. The woman, too." The servant cringed, making him appear even smaller in his bulky robe. He kept his eyes downcast.

Another silent moment elapsed before Strang said, "It matters not. We have other ways of keeping up with them. By the way, have the children arrived yet?"

"The ones Rann had?"

"Any of the children we're expecting."

"Some are waiting in the city of Three Waters. They will be here within a day. Most are still being gathered by the Fifth Order. Early reports indicate that parents are letting them go without resistance. They believe what they are told: that the children will receive special education and a blessing from the Church for the new millennium."

"They do not suspect what we are already using them for?"

"Not that we have heard, Undying One."

Strang folded his bony arms. "Excellent. When the children arrive, they will begin the compliance camp re-education. We shall select the strongest for our army. You may go."

Megas backed away, bowing. He turned as soon as he was off the balcony and fled the central hall.

AUTHOR'S NOTE

Storytelling always begins with "what if?"

What if the Nazis had won World War II? What if JFK hadn't been assassinated? What if Frodo had kept the One Ring? *The Witchfinder* found its genesis the same way. The question I asked: what if the Inquisition of the Middle Ages became the basis for a whole society?

In the summer of 2010, my oldest son, Brett, and I were on a trip in the Czech Republic. One day we visited the charming town of Český Krumlov. The two of us stumbled upon a small museum just off the market square and inside were displays of medieval torture implements. As I looked at the various tools and mechanisms—used by men of the church to intimidate, wound, and in some cases, kill, those who had been accused of activities against the faith—I couldn't help but wonder why. Why had men of faith seen fit to inflict such cruelty on others? How did they reconcile such actions with their Christian beliefs?

And what would the world be like if that particular moment in history had continued—indeed, what if it had become the dominant worldview?

Upon returning home, I started to look for answers. I researched the Roman Catholic and Spanish Inquisitions, as well as the social, cultural, historic, and religious background of the Middle Ages. While you may cringe at the tortures and tools described in this story, let me assure you that they are historically accurate (with the exception of the Hellcage).

My questions also fueled the idea of this book—a world where a monolithic church held supreme power over the lives of every person. Where torture, oppression, and control were commonly employed by church agents who viewed their work as holy, vital, and just. Just as it happened in real life.

I've always been a fan of post-apocalyptic stories, and knew I wanted to tell that kind of tale. I elected to use an unidentified time in the future, long after a calamity had reshaped the geography of the United States and the world—and in which humanity had rebuilt itself to a medieval level of social and technological achievement. I wanted to explore what might happen to someone born and raised in that kind of world, who suddenly had his entire existence upended—whose beliefs and identity were challenged to the core.

I hope that you have been able to become part of this story—to see yourself somewhere in the characters or in the realm of Deiparia. If so, then perhaps you have started to ask questions about who you are, what you believe, what freedom and faith mean, and what truths you are willing to live—or die—for.

Maybe you have started to ask "what if?" about your own hopes, dreams, and identity.

If so, here's to the new roads these questions open up for us. May we have the courage to walk them together.

J. Todd Kingrea

ACKNOWLEDGMENTS

I am grateful to Vern and Joni Firestone at BHC Press for receiving this book with such enthusiasm. Their support and encouragement has been wonderful, and I am honored to be part of their publishing house.

Thank you to Chelsea Cambeis: her editorial work, attention to detail, and suggestions for improving this story have literally taken the straw I raked together and spun it into gold. She is nothing short of magical!

To the band Queensrÿche for the song "The Lady Wore Black," which was played many times while writing this to set the mood.

To Dario Argento, whose Three Mothers film trilogy brought images to the screen that have left an indelible impression on me. I have tried, in my own simple way, to pay homage to Mater Suspiriorum, Mater Tenebrarum, and Mater Lachrymarum.

To my friend, Chris Kelly, who has provided feedback, encouragement, photography, and lots of good times over waffles.

To my wife, Felicia, who has been forever supportive and who remains my inspiration; thank you and I love you.

And to you, the reader: I appreciate you stepping into the world of Deiparia. I hope you have enjoyed your first visit and will return as our story continues to unfold.

ABOUT THE AUTHOR

J. Todd Kingrea is the author of the Deiparian Saga. *The Witchfinder* is his debut novel.

An ordained pastor, he lives with his wife in Tennessee with their dogs, plenty of 80s metal, and an ever-expanding movie collection.

CPSIA information can be obtained
at www.ICGtesting.com
Printed in the USA
BVHW071019150921
616751BV00005B/595